Shades of Eternity ❦ Book II

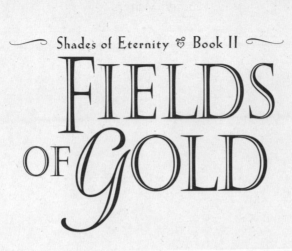

FIELDS OF GOLD

Shades of Eternity ❧ Book II

FIELDS OF GOLD

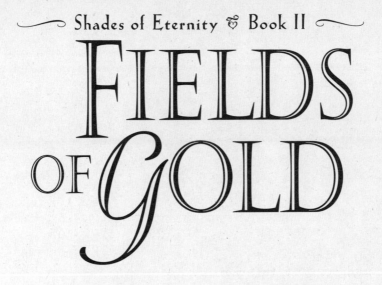

❖ LISA SAMSON ❖

ZondervanPublishingHouse

Grand Rapids, Michigan

A Division of HarperCollinsPublishers

Fields of Gold
Copyright © 2000 by Lisa Samson

Requests for information should be addressed to:

ZondervanPublishingHouse
Grand Rapids, Michigan 49530

Library of Congress Cataloging-in-Publication Data

Samson, Lisa, 1964–
    Fields of gold / Lisa Samson.
        p.   cm. — (Shades of eternity ; bk. 2)
     ISBN: 0-310-22369-5
       1. Title. 2. Series : Samson, Lisa, 1964- Shades of eternity ; bk. 2.
PS3569.A46673F54   1999
813'.54—dc21
                                                99-39343
                                                  CIP

Interior design by Melissa Elenbaas

Printed in the United States of America

00 01 02 03 04 05 /❖ DC/ 10 9 8 7 6 5 4 3 2

❖

For Elizabeth Tyler Samson
who gave me the gift of motherhood.
Eldest daughter, compatriot and friend.
My soul. Oh yeah, bay-bee! I love you.

ACKNOWLEDGMENTS

❖

Many thanks are due to many people, especially those in the Zondervan family, and it *is* a family. These people are: Lori VandenBosch, Dave Lambert, Joyce Ondersma, Sue Brower, and Amy Peterman. You all are first class, and your commitment to the cause of Christ is evident in every decision you make. What an honor it is to be among you. Lori, thank you for getting to know me better as a person so you could get to know me better as a writer. God bless the new chapter of your life just beginning.

Iain A. Fraser of Aboyne, Scotland, was most helpful in transforming my lackluster, American-tinged Scottish dialect into the real thing. "Many thanks to ye fae wifie, Samson. Lang may yer lum reek!"

Much gratitude goes to my wonderful husband, Will, my own computer specialist, who keeps things running and never gets upset when I call him at work in the middle of a meeting yelling, "This stupid computer just deleted chapter 5!" Thanks for giving me Tyler, Jake, and Gwynneth, who continually disrupt my writing time asking for water, snacks, or a new video, and have shown me what true love is all about.

Thanks to my family and friends who continue to encourage me: Joy Ebauer, Lori Chesser, Jennifer and Michael Hagerty, Bill and Arlene Samson, Gloria Danaher, Dawn Huth, and Karen Smith, the greatest room mother in all the world who never rode me too hard when I forgot to send in money for field trips or class projects while steeped in the writing of this book. *That* is something I'll *never* forget!

Most important are my thanks to my Lord and Savior Jesus Christ, author and finisher of my faith, King of Kings, Lord of Lords, and lover of my soul. My haven of peace.

PROLOGUE

❖

Scotland, late July, 1860

Blood drenched the back of his shirt, seeping through his waistcoat, black in the moonlight. His own footsteps hammered in his ears, synchronized with his pounding heart as he fled across the dark moor. What an unbelievable turn of events. What an extraordinary evening. Shot in the back, of all places!

If David Youngblood, Earl of Cannock, hadn't been so intent on escape, hadn't been so aware of the bullet lodged painfully somewhere near his left shoulder blade, he would have found the situation quite humorous. Two men had died tonight back at Greywalls, and ironically, he had killed neither. He wasn't sure whether he should be chagrined at the fact or thankful.

But he was lucky. He realized this. They'd probably send out a search party soon, for the truth would surface once the constable arrived. The murders he had committed in France at the behest of Claude Mirreault, a moneylender who must have made the Devil proud, would be dredged up like a rotting carcass from the muck of his recent past, before he had inherited his father's considerable estates.

A young lad, six years old, hopped on skinny legs beside him, his red hair whipped into a wild frenzy by the gathering, desolate winds. "It looks like the bleedin's slowin' doon a wheen, m'lord. Mind ye, yon storm isna." Angus MacDowell was easily keeping pace with the wounded nobleman. "Faraboots are we goin' ta, onyways, sir?"

"Do you know where the abbey ruins are, laddie?" He could feel himself weakening rapidly.

"Aye. Ma Grannie used ta take me there to pick the flooers. St. Ninian's."

Youngblood stopped, turned the lad to face him, and held onto his shoulders, willing himself to stay conscious. "I'll need you to come to me there tomorrow. But you must go back to the castle now and awaken Mrs. Wooten. Tell her I need medical attention right away. Tell her where I am and that she must find Dr. Sinclair. Tell her she must not breathe a word of this to anybody."

Angus's cherubic face was grave in the moonlight. Only the sweat glistening in his red hair kept him from looking like one of the angel statues in the graveyard not far from Greywalls. "Ah winna tell onybuddy m'sel' either, m'lord."

"I know, Angus. 'Tis why I brought you. But now I want you to go back and give Mrs. Wooten my message. And then, off to bed with you, or your mother will have my head."

Angus's eyes were dark and liquid and obviously comprehending the gravity of the situation. "Ye can trust me, m'lord."

"I know I can, lad. Go now. Hurry on your way, then." David turned him to face the right direction, and the boy ran off as fast as he could go. Youngblood resumed his flight. He knew he wouldn't be able to go on much longer in this state. The abbey was less than a mile away now. Thank God for that.

It seemed he had *someone* to thank for what had happened this evening. Positive he would have at least two more deaths charged to his already lengthy account, he emerged from the fiasco with no more blood on his hands than when the day had begun. Only God could do something as miraculous as that! But why would God have anything to do with him in the first place?

The sky was quickly filling with cloud as a thick front coasted in from the east. Lightning forked into the earth several miles behind him and thunder shook the hills. It had been a hot day, hotter than David had ever remembered as a boy. The heat pulled on him, weighed down his wound, clutched at his lungs. Perhaps the rain would do him well. Perhaps the storm would cover his tracks.

The ruins appeared as he crested the final hill. Three of the walls still stood strong, but the west wall was crumbled, and the roof was gone. The abbey hadn't been used as an easy source of stone as most abbeys had been after the dissolution of the monasteries hundreds of years before. The locals were even more superstitious than most Scots, and the tales of the ghosts of murdered monks had always been enough to keep them away. Even if he had believed in ghosts, David deemed it better to take his chances with the unknown than with the authorities.

He couldn't see much at present, for it was well past midnight and the moon was gone. But he remembered a stairway leading down to the crypt. It would be a good place for shelter from the coming storm. Or should he say storms? For certainly more than just this thunderstorm was rolling in from the horizon.

Finding the stairway in the floor of the north transept, where the altar of a chapel to St. Andrew had once stood, he made his way down amid leaves and bracken, feet slipping on the debris. Each jolt sent gales of pain through him. But he didn't cry out. David Youngblood never cried out. The darkness was dense and the air was close. But he was safe. He had left the chaos behind. For now.

He leaned against a squat stone pillar, sat down, and closed his eyes. Yes, he had left so much behind—his title, his lands, his beloved daughter, and the only woman he had ever loved. Sylvie de Courcey now knew all of his deeds, that he had killed her parents, and that the man for whom he worked, Claude Mirreault, had killed her brother, Guy. Almost all the de Courceys were now dead. Dead for the sake of the man she had called husband—Count Rene de Boyce—a man so consumed in debt, he had married her in hopes of gaining her family's fortune.

Now Rene was dead. A tragic death for a tragic man. A tragic night for all concerned. Death at the castle Greywalls.

He longed to comfort Sylvie, but knew he no longer possessed the right. Not that he ever really did. For Sylvie had never loved him as he had loved her. And she never would. He knew that now. But would Sylvie turn him in to the authorities? Another question to ponder in the heavy darkness.

David Youngblood longed for sleep, but two hours later, when Mrs. Wooten's lamplight soaked the stones in the stairwell, he was still charged by his thoughts. Following behind her was Dr. Sinclair, long retired, deaf, and almost blind. Unhindered by the darkness, with fingertips more sensitive than a lover's, he was the best man in all of Scotland at extracting a bullet. And there wasn't a better man in all of Scotland for keeping his mouth shut. Mrs. Wooten, the housekeeper, had followed orders without question. David had known she would.

The next hour was excruciating as Sinclair searched for the bullet. But when the sun came up, the wound was dressed in clean bandages, and Mrs. Wooten had helped him into clean clothes.

"There now." The older woman patted his forearm as she gathered her things in a patchwork bag David remembered from his childhood. Memories of going to market with her, holding her plump hand, and knowing she was glad he was there, made him yearn for the lad he once was. "There you are, m'lord. Good as new." Her crooked teeth shone in the dim lamplight.

Youngblood thanked her kindly, asked that food be brought regularly, and bade her and Sinclair goodnight.

Good as new.

Alone again, he shook his head. He could never be good as new again. It had all gone much too far this time. He had finally been found out.

The sun began to rise on a golden day. But David had fallen asleep, lost in the darkness behind his eyes.

CHAPTER ✦ ONE

The wind bore down from the east, across the moor, and straight into Miranda Wallace's face. She bit her teeth against the gust, running forward, eyes slits against the rushing air.

The echoes of gunshots still sounded in her mind, and she didn't blame Elspeth Youngblood one bit for the fact that she was now out on the moor, after midnight, on a moonless night.

She tripped over an unseen stone.

Down!

"Oh dear," she muttered, crawling to her feet via her hands and knees. She would be bruised most certainly tomorrow. And surely she wouldn't be able to remember how that bruise had begun no matter how hard she tried. But where were these mundane thoughts coming from, and why was she allowing them place right now?

It had been a terrible night. Two people were dead and a third had disappeared—Elspeth's father, the earl of Cannock. Upon learning that her father had fled the scene of a very messy ending to a very messy series of crimes, Elspeth had followed him. Or at least tried to, for Miranda suspected that the girl would have no luck in locating a fugitive as wily as David Youngblood.

Why did I have to go and volunteer? Miranda inwardly wailed. There were plenty of servants available at Greywalls to locate an errant child. But no, thinking that being found by someone almost as deformed as herself would help, Miranda had been out the door before an objection could be made.

And here I am, in the dark, while the authorities are investigating and more excitement than I've ever before experienced is taking place literally behind my back. She turned around and saw Greywalls, a beautifully preserved medieval castle, a pinprick of light in the darkness. It wasn't fair.

Dear Lord above, she began, knowing that someone needed to begin praying for all those involved in this hideous affair begun back in France over a year before. *Protect them all. Give them peace.*

The protection she knew would be answered posthaste. The peace . . . well, that was one of those things that sometimes took a while.

Miranda almost sighed.

Where is that girl?

The thought of the sweet eleven-year-old, who with her hare-lip and cleft palate was even more vulnerable, caused Miranda to hurry. Thoughts of Elspeth's birth defects made Miranda more acutely aware of her own. She absentmindedly rubbed a hand over the deep purple port-wine birthmark that eclipsed half her face.

Hopefully I won't scare the child in the darkness. The thunder blasts and the lightning flashes were almost simultaneous now.

And here I am in an open field!

Miranda shook her head, unafraid, but somewhat chagrined. If God calmed the storm on the Galilean sea, well, certainly he could take care of this little tuffle. But he didn't seem to be removing it, so she figured he was simply planning on protecting her through it. She would have preferred removal and told God so. *But protection is fine in the meantime*, she prayed, not wanting to sound as ungrateful as she felt.

Finally, the skies split beneath the weight of the rain, and down came the heavy droplets, soaking her in seconds. She picked up her skirts and her pace, crying, "Elspeth! Elspeth!"

A belt of trees was visible, a black mass against a sky lit only by flashes of storm. The girl would take cover there, Miranda decided, and ran even faster, wishing she knew the nuances of the landscape, praying she would find the distraught youngster.

Only thirty yards from the woods, the storm was upon her now, wild flashings, wind scouring her hair and clothing, thunder pulling at her eardrums with its deep reverberation. *Now* she was frightened. A loud crack, as though the entire world were being split like a walnut, sounded right beside her, and she jumped high into the air, watching in horror as a tree near the wood's edge was cloven by a giant sword of light. She averted her direction and began to run into the forest further down, and there just a few yards beneath the canopy of dripping leaves sat Elspeth, eyes covered by her hands as her shoulders heaved in frightened sobs.

Without hesitation, Miranda gathered the child into her arms. Elspeth screamed in alarm and began to fight, but Miranda held on tightly. "It's only me, Elspeth, Miss Wallace."

It took several seconds for the words to settle amidst the loud crashing of the storm, but they did, and Elspeth's muscles went limp, her head shaking from side to side, bowed low against her chest.

"Everything will be all right, Elspeth," Miranda soothed as the child's shoulders began to shake again with silent, pitiful sobs. But that was all she could say, or would say. The child was frightened, drowning in an ocean of difficulties into which she had been thrown the day she was illegitimately born and with such a hideous deformity. Words from a virtual stranger would mean nothing against such waves.

And so they sat, Elspeth apparently unable to cease the flow of tears that were supplied by an endless reservoir of misery. But she held on tightly, grasping at Miranda's wet gown, not pushing her away, but nestling into the wet warmth of the woolen fabric, her ear pressed to Miranda's heart.

Finally as the storm moved on to ravage some other hillside, the child stopped crying. The silence was complete, eerie almost, and neither knew quite what to do with it.

"I'm sorry," the girl apologized.

"You've nothing to apologize for."

"I shouldna be so scared. I shouldna have run off. Mrs. Wooten will be frightened to death."

"Mrs. Wooten is too busy right now to even realize you are gone. I will take care of you."

"My father? Has he been found?"

"I don't honestly know, child. But I doubt it."

Dawn was approaching, and Miranda could see the clouds had thinned and were marbled by a bluish light.

"I was tryin' to find him. He needs me ta take care o' him."

Miranda felt a seed of laughter begin to sprout, but she quickly stomped it back into the ground. David Youngblood needed no one. "He would be dreadfully upset if he knew you were out in the woods all night because of him. You know he wants you to be safe."

"Will he come back for me?" The child's face was now barely visible. The malformation was hideous indeed, far worse than her father's. And yet, her large gray eyes, and rounded, sweet forehead were beautiful. It was as if someone had placed a half-mask over an entirely ugly face, rendering at least part of it utterly lovely.

How do I answer that question? Miranda asked herself. But she knew the truth would be easier in the long run. "Elspeth, your father was wounded. I don't know if he will come back or not. But I can promise you this. I will not leave you until we know something for sure."

"Ye'll stay with me? But wha' aboot yer plans? Ye were leavin' Greywalls today onyway. Yer ain brother was seein' aboot tha' kirk in Huntly." More arguments rushed out, as if she were trying to save herself from yet another desertion.

"I promise, Elspeth." Miranda took the girl by the shoulders, leaned forward, and kissed her forehead. "I will stay with you."

Elspeth crossed her arms and nodded, already protecting herself.

The sky was lightening further, the grass of the moor dripping and soaked. "Let's go home," Miranda said. "Let's get you into a warm bath, some warm nightclothes, and we'll have a nice hot cup of tea."

It was funny the way her good sense seemed to take over at times, when things like hot water, warm clothes, and a cup of tea were the only things that would do. Small things, to be sure. Bandages over a yawning wound opened and reopened for years. But they would do for now, and they would do for later, and for the rest of their lives, because some wounds were never completely healed, they simply awaited the healing touch of heaven itself.

Later, when Elspeth was sleeping, Miranda made her way down to the kitchen where Mrs. Wooten was supervising the servants' noonday meal.

"Mrs. Wooten"—she pulled the round, happy-faced woman aside—"I want to volunteer my services to Elspeth until other arrangements are made. I'm not trained as a teacher, but I'm well-educated, and I've always been told I'm good with children."

"God bless you!" Mrs. Wooten threw her arms about Miranda's neck in a hug filled with more relief than a mother whose child's fever has finally broken. "If you aren't an angel sent straight from the bosom of the Lord, I don't know *what* you could possibly be!"

And so the arrangements were made. A servant would transport her belongings up to the room off the nursery. "It's a pleasant enough room, I'll warrant," Mrs. Wooten said as Miranda looked around the tiny chamber done in shades of green. A small fireplace stood ready and waiting for winter, and all in all, Miranda knew it would be quite cozy. Even a bookshelf awaited the volumes she would have Mother send from her childhood home in Leeds. Having her books with her once again was something she'd been wanting for years.

Miranda turned to Mrs. Wooten. "It's quite lovely, actually. I think I shall be most comfortable here." She was shown the cramped water closet containing a commode and a tub. "Yes, this is perfect."

After her things were brought and Miranda had put them away, she went to find her brother, Matthew Wallace. She didn't know how he would accept the fact that she was deserting his ministry after all these years. He was in the library, full of news about what had happened that morning and what had become of David Youngblood.

"According to the investigator, the trail of blood stopped about a mile south of here, and after that awful storm, any tracks there might have been were washed or blown away. It seems as if the earl virtually disappeared!" Matthew exclaimed.

"I thought he was dead when I first came upon him in the library. He couldn't have gone far."

Matthew shook his head. "I doubt that as well."

"I believe they'll find him eventually. But considering the wound he must have sustained, I fear they'll be finding a corpse." She thought of the daughter he had left behind. "Poor Elspeth."

"At least she has you," he said. "Mrs. Wooten has told me you have settled here at Greywalls to care for Elspeth indefinitely. Is that what you really wish to do?"

Miranda Wallace listened to the words of her brother, wondering if life could become any stranger. Two weeks ago she had been firmly rooted in a peaceful life at St. Jude's parish in Bath, taking care of the Anglican vicar, her dear brother Matthew. Now, she found herself in Scotland, once again alongside the stormy preacher, who had just taken a church in Huntly. And a Presbyterian church at that! What was the world coming to?

As if such a transition wasn't strange enough, she was now going to be a governess to the illegitimate daughter of a renegade earl! She lifted her eyes heavenward and didn't even bother to sigh. She hated sighs. "I suppose the answer to that question is really up to you, Mate. If you don't need me here to help get you settled, then . . ." She waited, watching him deliberate with himself. After all, thirty-five-year-old Miranda, an expert older sister, had been with him since he started in the ministry seven years before. She knew he'd have to think on it a minute.

Matthew's dark blue eyes focused on her steadily, and then he smiled. "It's time for me to let you go. Elspeth needs someone special, and you will understand her."

Miranda put her hand up to the large birthmark. "We'll make a frightful pair!"

Matthew took her hand. "I think you'll do wonders for the girl."

"One never knows, Mate."

"Oh, stop the nonsense, Mira. You've been taking care of people ever since I can remember. Elspeth only recently was reunited with her father, and she's lost him so soon."

"Not to mention that her mother is dead."

"Yes. She needs you."

Miranda regarded her brother, so handsome in his black clerical garb. "You'll be getting married soon enough, I suppose. You really don't need me anymore anyway."

"Now, Mira," he began, drawing his brows. "You know that doesn't make a difference. Sylvie and I would love to have you stay here with us."

Miranda pictured herself in the minuscule manse and shook her head. "No, thank you. I was planning on leaving anyway. I merely thought that I would go home to Leeds and care for Mother and Father. Now, I suppose God is calling me down another path. Not that it surprises me!"

Matthew rolled his eyes. "Nothing ever surprises you, Mira."

Three days later, Miranda watched in sadness as the body of Count Rene de Boyce was lowered into the ground. As warm as the weather had been the day he died, it was now quite cool, and the mourners pulled their shawls closer in the highland mist.

The situation was a complicated one, and she was still trying to understand how the young Frenchman's vices could have brought about the deaths of his wife's parents and brother. Because of his addictions to opium and gambling, he had been in a great deal of debt to a man named Claude Mirreault, and the de Courcey fortune seemed to be his only way out. When the money had failed to come to Count de Boyce through the death of Sylvie's father and older brother, Mirreault had taken matters into his own hands. Sylvie herself, now the owner of de Courcey Wines and vast vineyards in Champagne, had been condemned to die at the hands of one of Mirreault's assassins. But her husband had intervened in the end, for he was not an evil man, just weak. Rene had literally thrown himself between his wife and the bullet. And now he was being buried.

Sylvie stood alone near the coffin, holding their infant daughter, Eve, in her arms. No tears were falling from her eyes, but sadness had frozen her features into hard lines.

Miranda held her brother's hand. "I know you want to go to her," she whispered, pulling a stray lock of straight, blonde hair out of her eyes. "To comfort her."

"Yes."

The local minister prayed over the beautifully carved box. The count's mother stood weeping, having fought her son's burial in Scotland with all of her wiles. But Sylvie had been insistent, and Miranda understood. Eve must have her father near her as she grew. Rene would have wanted it that way.

Later, as the guests nibbled at comforting fare prepared by Pamela MacDowell, the castle cook, Miranda sat with her brother. Count Rene de Boyce had been Matthew's good friend from their days at Oxford. When Matthew had fallen in love with Sylvie before her marriage to Rene, and she with him, it was only his friendship with the count, his great sense of loyalty, that caused him to turn away from her, to come back to England.

"I will marry her soon," he declared in a soft voice only Miranda could hear.

"It is a good thing. And she loves you so. She always has."

They both sat and stared at Sylvie, who was comforting Rene's mother, dowager Countess Racine de Boyce. Miranda couldn't help but compare herself to the woman who would be her brother's wife. Tall and dark-haired, Sylvie looked Miranda eye to eye. But height was where their similarities ended. Sylvie's features were sculpted and distinct; Miranda always thought her own too delicate and childlike. She hated the way her cheeks had never lost all of their roundness. And if given the chance, she would have traded her long white blonde hair for Sylvie's dark curls in an instant. No wonder Mate loved her so.

"Sylvie's decided to send word to France regarding Young-blood's involvement in the death of her family." Matthew's voice was soft.

"I thought she'd do as much. She really has to. This isn't completely about forgiveness."

Matthew shook his head. "No. It isn't."

Miranda, who felt a strong pity for the missing earl, could completely understand Sylvie's viewpoint. "If someone killed our parents and we knew who it was, I don't think I could simply forgive and go on. I don't think that would be my right."

"Of course it wouldn't. Not only would it make a mockery of justice, it would trivialize their deaths. Sylvie understands this." He set down his teacup, the contents barely touched. Matthew Wallace was no great admirer of the earl of Cannock. "I think I'll go to her. She's sitting by herself now."

Miranda took a sip of her tea. "Take her for a walk on the moor, Mate. She could use it."

Her brother nodded and walked across the room.

Just then, Mrs. Wooten, the housekeeper, toddled over to her. "Miss Wallace? Might I have a word with you in the corridor?"

Miranda nodded, drained her teacup, then placed it just so on the tea table. "Of course."

The older woman led her out of the room. Her great brown eyes turned down in compassion. "It's Elspeth, Miss. She's cryin' inside the library. She's holdin' that copy of *Tom Jones* she was readin' with her father, and none of us can seem to comfort her."

"I'll go to her right away."

"Thank you, Miss Wallace," the housekeeper said, laying a hand on her arm. "You're heaven-sent, you are."

Miranda smiled, gathered a handful of brown skirt, and hurried into the library.

It was just as Mrs. Wooten had said. Elspeth sat slumped on the couch, hugging the copy of *Tom Jones* to her chest. Her eyes were shut tight and so lost was she in her grief, that Miranda had to clear her throat a bit.

She opened her gray eyes. They were deep and soulful, and were rimmed with very long, very black lashes. They truly gave testimony to the fact that the child was extremely intelligent, like her father. Her hair, another Youngblood trait, fell in long, glossy auburn waves to the middle of her back.

"Hello, Elspeth." Miranda sat down next to her and took her hand, assigning *Tom Jones* a less prominent position on a side table.

"Miss Wallace?" The words came out breathy and distorted, but Miranda concentrated, reading her lips carefully as though they were speaking the words of God himself.

"Yes, Elspeth, I'm here."

"What's the time?"

"Five o'clock."

Her eyes widened. "Time to stop this cryin'."

"Stay here longer if you like."

Elspeth sat up straight. "My maw always said ta me, 'Dinna waste the day, Bethie.'"

Miranda smoothed her hair from her forehead. "Do you miss your mother?"

Elspeth looked down. "No' really. She didna care much for me, ma'am. Once Papa came home, he made it all better."

"Tell me about your father," Miranda ordered softly, knowing instinctively what the girl needed. "I met him the night of his disappearance."

"He's a wee smasher, isna he?" Her eyes were bright. "An' awfu' smart!"

"Yes. I've heard that."

"Afore he come home, I was on ma own. Ma maw died a couple o' years ago, an' telt me ta come here. When I showed up a wee skinnamalink wi' a face like this, weel, they knew wha' I was sayin' must be right."

"You mustn't say such things about yourself, Elspeth."

Elspeth sat up very straight and looked a bit surprised. "Why no'? It's God's honest truth, so it is. I'm no' like everybody else, Miss Wallace."

Miranda smiled and touched her face. "Well, neither am I."

She began to braid her hair. "And ye've mythered along just fine for yerself, so ye have."

"I suppose so. I'm here with you, aren't I?"

Elspeth stood to her feet. "Aye, weel, maybees ye willna think so small o' me."

Miranda looked at her, a bit confused.

Elspeth explained. "Folk think I'm skelly all the way up to ma brain, miss. They treat the beasts better than they treat me sometime. But ye understand a bit what I'm aboot, doon't ye? No' tha' I'm sayin' yer skelly like me!" she rushed on. "But ye know I'm worth a bit o' somethin'."

Miranda put her arms around the child, feeling tears prickle her eyes once more. "Oh, Elspeth, you are worth more than just something, you are worth everything in the world, to God, to your father, and soon, to me. I'm looking forward to us becoming great friends."

"D'ye mean tha', miss?" she whispered, hugging her back tightly. Miranda had to strain to understand her, but she knew it would become easier with time.

"I certainly do. I'm not here just to teach you, I'm here to learn from you as well. Isn't that what friends do?"

Elspeth nodded, her head still against Miranda's chest. "Och, weel, I suppose it is. I've never really had a friend afore."

Miranda pulled back to look her in the eye. "Well, you do now. And I'll tell you more about another friend you can have, one who sticks closer to you than a brother."

"I've never had a brother," said Elspeth.

"I've got one," Miranda laughed. "And believe me, you can borrow him any time you'd like!"

"So ye'll tell me aboot this other friend o' yours, then?" Elspeth's eyes filled with tears.

"Of course I will, Elspeth. And he wants to be your friend as well." Miranda left it there for now. "Let's go up and get away from the crowd, and then we'll have a nice big supper to celebrate our new life together! Would you like that?"

"Surely I would," Elspeth responded, slipping her hand into Miranda's. "I'll show ye wha' I've been workin' on in the schoolroom too if ye'd like."

"Surely I would," Miranda laughed.

Hand in hand they wound their way through the castle, up the circular staircase, into the room that would most likely change them both forever. Perhaps in a large way, or maybe in a small way, but hopefully in a good way.

The sun was just beginning to rise the next day when Mrs. Wooten weaved into the room with a loaded tray. "I've got a bit o' breakfast for you, miss," she announced in her London accent, arms shaking under the weight of silver serving pieces, china cups, and a filled teapot. Miranda was braiding Elspeth's hair. "When you weren't in your own room," Mrs. Wooten explained, "I suspected I might find you here. You two are early risers this morning!"

Miranda eyed the teapot, but finished braiding Elspeth's long brown hair. "We both awakened when it was still dark, and when we took a look at the clock Elspeth suggested we stay up. It was already after five."

"Dinna waste the day!" they chimed together.

"Seems to me like the two of you will be getting along fine, then. Where shall I put this, miss?"

Miranda took the tray from her hands. Goodness, but it really was heavy! "You've got better things to do than wait on the likes of us, eh, Elspeth?"

The girl nodded and tied a white ribbon at the end of her braid.

Mrs. Wooten straightened her apron. "Thank you, then. I've got a busy day ahead of me!"

"More to do than usual?" Miranda asked, thankful it was a large breakfast beneath the domes. She was hungrier than an orphaned kitten.

Mrs. Wooten suddenly looked startled, then laughed a bit nervously. "Heavens no! Just the runnin' of the castle."

Miranda turned to Elspeth. "Oh dear, I do believe I've quite forgotten my handkerchief, Elspeth. Would you go and fetch me one out of my trunk?"

The girl obeyed without argument, and Miranda replaced the silver dome that had been sheltering the warmth of the eggs, blood pudding, and mushrooms. "I wanted to speak with you privately, Mrs. Wooten. How long will my post be? Is there any word from the new earl?"

The housekeeper scratched her ear and dusted the back of the chair in which Elspeth had been sitting. "Not yet. But the solicitors should be meeting with him today or tomorrow, I suppose, to tell him the news."

"And there hasn't been any word of David Youngblood?"

Mrs. Wooten looked at her feet, reaching into her pocket for her hankie. "Oh no, no." She wiped her eyes as she continued to look down. "They're presumin' him dead, miss. They're sayin' there's no sign of him at all. And with the way he was wounded ..."

Miranda experienced a sudden sadness at the news. She'd only heard bad reports concerning David Youngblood, but when she had met him, she had been filled with a kind of holy compassion, something given to her, surely, by God. She knew she wasn't capable of *that* herself. "Well, until I hear otherwise, I'll keep interceding with heaven on his behalf."

"I wish you would, miss. He was such a lovely, sweet little boy, once."

"Do you think the new earl will wish me to stay on? I want to know how attached to Elspeth I should become. To be forced to leave her after building strong ties . . . well, I don't know how she could take another desertion."

Mrs. Wooten smiled. "I knew you was the right one to bring over! Don't you be worrying about what Lord Tobin'll say. He'll be too busy with them songs of his to worry himself over who's teaching his niece."

"Songs?" This was intriguing.

"He's a composer. Writes the prettiest songs you ever heard! But he's a Londoner through and through. I doubt any of us will have to fret over the likes of him."

Miranda had never actually met a composer. "Maybe he'll come up to check on Elspeth's progress every once in a while."

Mrs. Wooten shook her head. "Don't count on it. I've worked for the Youngblood family a long time, miss. Lord Tobin's never even been to Greywalls. He's not like any of the rest of 'em. In fact, he even forsook Oxford and went to school in America. Wanted to get away from the whole sorry lot."

"America!"

"Yes, to Harvard!" For some unknown reason, this made Mrs. Wooten's chest stick out in pride. "His father was furious. And although they never forgave him, they didn't disinherit him, neither."

Miranda had to admire the fellow's spunk. "You seem to know a lot about these people, Mrs. Wooten."

"Oh, yes! The staff knows more about 'em than they do theirselves!"

"So you believe I'm here to stay?"

"That I do, miss. Now, is there anything else I can get for you before you begin the day's lessons?"

"Would another pot of tea in two hours be too much to ask?"

"But you've a hot pot right there," she pointed out.

"I've always said the two most important things in my life besides God, are my family and a cup of strong tea with lots of milk and sugar!"

"Then it'll be done," Mrs. Wooten declared. She backed out of the room with a smile. "Y'know, miss, it's going to be nice having you here. Greywalls could use a pretty face."

The woman was gone by the time the compliment registered. Miranda, figuring she had misunderstood, merely turned her back on the mirror and poured herself a cup of tea.

Sylvie came in thirty minutes later, while Miranda and Elspeth were just getting started on literature. "We're not going to read *Tom Jones* today," Miranda was saying as she looked over her shoulder at her soon-to-be sister-in-law. "Have a seat, Sylvie. We're just getting started on our studious adventure together, isn't that right, Elspeth?"

"I do so love ta be readin'," Elspeth said.

"And I do too," Sylvie said, pulling a chair over to the small table on which they had spread their books and papers. "I love Charles Dickens. He's my favorite."

"Ye read in English too?" Elspeth asked, inching her chair closer to the newest occupant of the schoolroom.

"But of course! My maid was English."

"Weel, ye can speak it awfu' good, I can tell ye tha'!"

Sylvie laughed. "Would you like me to teach you French? That is, if it is all right with Miss Wallace."

Miranda didn't mind. "I would welcome that. Mine isn't bad ... but it isn't good either!"

Miranda watched from the perimeters of the activity. As Sylvie started talking about *A Christmas Carol*, Elspeth's soft eyes widened with expectation. Miranda found it hard to imagine that this woman before her, this angular, yet somehow soft woman, was actually going to marry Matthew! What must she be thinking? Miranda chuckled deep inside, knowing that every sister, even though she might love her brother dearly, couldn't quite imagine anybody actually wanting to *marry* him!

But Matthew deserved a little happiness after losing his fiancée Isabelle years before. And Sylvie, after all that she had so recently been through, certainly deserved to find a love as strong and upholding as that only Matthew could offer.

It was decided they would read *A Christmas Carol*, Sylvie and Miranda going to the library to fetch a copy while Elspeth worked on some sums Miranda had quickly scratched out on a slate. They were among the stacks when Sylvie let out a long sigh.

"I can't imagine how you must feel right now, Sylvie," Miranda said, cued by the sadness in that extended breath.

Sylvie turned to her with tears in her eyes. "But for your brother and Eve, and you, Miranda, I don't know how I could get out of bed in the mornings."

Miranda thought of Sylvie's adorable baby, Eve, born only in June, now fatherless. Not for long, though. Mate would love her as his own. "But soon you will be part of a family again."

"It will be wonderful. My own family wasn't really much of one when I was growing up. Except for my brother Guy and me. And then Rene's family, well, the way his mother is . . ."

No need to say more about the countess Racine de Boyce, Miranda thought, remembering a women whose crazy love for her son blinded her to what was best for him. And now he lay in the grave. "We're glad to have you as a Wallace," Miranda said, nodding. "I've always wanted a sister."

Sylvie smiled. "You know, so have I."

"We'll get through these dark days together, Sylvie. The Lord is carrying you through now, too, although it may not feel like it."

Sylvie shrugged, looking very French. "At times I feel his presence most strongly, at times I feel alone." The clock on the library table let out a clunky burp. "Oh! Eve will be waking from her nap!"

"I'll find the book myself. You go tend to your little one."

Sylvie hugged her. "Miranda, you are a gift from God to me. I think of you as an angel."

Miranda smiled and watched her leave, thinking that if she listened to what people were saying about her, she just might sprout some wings! But she knew better than to believe that. She knew that there were times that she looked into the mirror and told God he had made a big, big mistake.

CHAPTER ✤ TWO

Tobin Youngblood sat down on the park bench and handed his lovely companion a newspaper full of fish and chips. He looked appreciatively at his own, ready to take a bite of the hot, crispy cod. But the familiar tingling sensation was beginning as he heard two birds singing to each other. A melody began to form as he thanked God silently for the food.

Daria thanked him for the meal, took a rather large bite of fish, and finished the tale that had been taking the better part of an hour. "And so I told Lord Heppleton that he could take such a preposterous proposal and throw it in the Thames for all I care! Can you imagine asking for a dowry like that when he would be obtaining such a jewel? It's ... it's *farcical!* The nerve of that revolting little man! Really! Who does that son of a nitwit think he is?"

But Tobin barely heard the colorful words of Lady Daria Christopher as she disclosed the latest matrimonial-seeking escapade of her daughter, Valentinia. The muse was pecking at him again. The melody he had been seeking for so long was creeping from the back of his mind to the front. The last thing he wanted to hear about was yet another disastrous marriage proposal hoisted upon the fair Valentinia. Yet, Daria, a widow for well over a decade, was a good friend who always supported his musical works with a fervent admiration. He shoved the tune aside, vowing to remember it later.

St. James Park was practically deserted, and he liked it that way. He took a bite of the golden fish. "Now you see then, Daria, that this is all coming back to haunt you. You are reaping what you've sowed for years now, refusing to marry me when you know we'd be a perfectly affable pair."

Daria threw back her head and laughed, spilling her fish and chips onto her lap. She leisurely piled the contents back into the greasy newspaper. "You're too poor, Tobin. You come from a banner family and all that rubbish, but the fact is, you inhabit a room above a gentlemen's club and only swarm about on the very limited inheritance your stodgy old dead father furnished you."

"At least you're honest about it, my dear." As if *that* had ever been a problem with Daria!

It was true that he had been asking Lady Christopher to marry him for at least the past eight years. They were highly compatible, it seemed. She was flamboyant, eccentric, and a true patroness of the arts. Her red hair mirrored the passion of her soul. Her vigilant eyes, so dark they were almost black, always spoke the intelligence of her mind and the truth of her heart. Not that her small, full-lipped mouth had any trouble saying how she felt. Not at all. Daria Christopher was a presence to be sure, and Tobin would have married her at any time. Not because he was in love with her, but because he admired her. There were very few women he admired. Very few men either, for that matter.

"Besides," Daria went on. "Why let marriage spoil a good relationship?"

She had a point. Where there were no expectations there were no disappointments. And as for that heady love one can only dream about, well, why bother to search for the romantic ideal for which he had been yearning all his life? It was impossible, he knew, to find such an overwhelming love. So why try?

The birds called to each other once more. There it was again, that melody. *Perfect for a prelude*, he thought, the tingling sensation in the back of his neck getting stronger.

"Oh, you'll never guess what that pompous old cow Mrs. Landsmount chortled to me the other day as I was being stuffed into a rather too small gown down on Bond Street."

Tobin heard her words from the outskirts of his consciousness, but the music was getting too strong to ignore now, and he wouldn't have chosen to do so even if he wanted to.

"Oh, dear, dear, dear," Daria ticked, swallowing the last bite of their hasty meal. "You'd better run along home now, little boy. I see that faraway look in your eyes. Go trap that rascal of a melody before it gets away for good. My maid will be polite enough to walk me home." She fingered the grease spot on her gown. "I may even decide to change my dress once I get there. Then again, I may not. I love the smell of street food."

Without a word or a backward glance, Tobin was on his feet, running for home.

He had never been so glad to step foot inside his club since he had joined almost ten years before at the age of twenty-seven. Pratt's was a club, a *gentlemen's* club, and right now he was almost prostrate with thankfulness that no women were allowed in the doors. None except for Mrs. Pratt, who ran the place. And Sophia never pulled him aside for a mindless chat before he was done for the day.

He hurried up to the room he took on the third floor, threw the remainder of his luncheon on the bed, and pulled off his coat. The melody had come into his head as they all usually did, at the most inopportune of moments. He sang to himself, the tune in his mind coming out with words that reflected his actions. "Pen, pen, pen. Where is my pen? Paper too, paper too." In the drawer of his desk, both were readily accessible. He deftly uncorked his inkwell, dipped the pen, and began to compose with wild scratchings and a swirling wrist.

Outside his window the day began to wane, but he didn't notice. The black notes ebbed and flowed across the transcription paper, the harmonies, the rhythm, all blending into a river of sound only he could hear rushing within his head. Tobin Youngblood was completely caught up in the tide of his own creation, forgetting the two lovebirds that had started the whole ruckus. When the room darkened, he lit an oil lamp without thought. When the breeze turned cool, he closed the window without realizing it. And finally, when the last note of the prelude was swimming with its predecessors, Tobin could hardly believe it was almost midnight.

Heavens. What a profitable ten hours!

He corked the inkwell, laid aside his pen, and examined the piece, hearing the music all over again. Yes, it was good, thank God. It was very good. It was what he had been searching for so long, and now it was down on paper. Tomorrow he would go over to the church and hear it. The organist at St. Martin's in the Field, John Clarkson, was a compatriot of his, a close friend, and always a willing party to the furtherance of his compositions. John Clarkson had prayed for him for years, Tobin knew, grateful that the organist had shared God with him in a way he had never heard before. It was after he came to trust the Savior that his music truly began a crescendo of greatness. Clarkson claimed first dibs on all his compositions, and for good reason, Tobin knew. There was no finer organist in all of Great Britain.

But for now, some supper. Certainly the leftover fish and chips coagulating on the bed wouldn't do, although he'd eaten worse in his day. Much worse. He was extremely hungry as he made his way down the steps and into the kitchen, where Edwin Pratt was cooking up a storm at the cookstove.

From the dining room the sounds of men chatting filtered through, latecomers on their way home from the theater or the opera, no doubt. A group of men were playing cards in a corner of the kitchen.

"Youngblood!" called Lord Percy St. Dennis, an overly civilized chap with slender hands, light brown hair, and a face that could top a statue of Adonis. "Care to join us at whist? Although, I must say, you do look a fright!"

Tobin caught a glimpse of himself in the mirror on the wall. Percy was right. His chestnut hair was sweaty and curled unruly above his eyes, and his normally ruddy skin was pale. Though he didn't play much, perhaps a good round of cards might be just the trick to restore him. "George!" he bellowed to one of the stewards across the room, "I'll just have a sandwich here at the table."

The steward, whose real name was Filbert, bowed and went to carry out the order. All the staff at Pratt's were addressed as George and had been for years. It made things much simpler.

Tobin filled the vacant seat with a loud groan.

"What, pray tell, was that all about?" the third person at the table inquired. His name was Frederick Dormerthwaite, a lawyer, a banker, and a man with a finger in every pie. His great girth gave testimony to the fact that he found his teeth in every pie as well, and every pudding and every roast and every cassoulet. Despite his size, there was a pleasing quality to the man, a heroic blend of size and beauty, not to mention hair perfectly silver and perfectly combed that had been making heads turn for years.

"Just finished up the first part of a new composition." Tobin picked up the cards as they were dealt. "My best work yet, I believe."

Percy elbowed him in the ribs, his light blue eyes twinkling. "Well, old boy, if the quality of the piece is in directly opposite proportion to your appearance, I should say our ears are going to partake of an audible masterpiece in church on Sunday."

"Clarkson, bless him, has first dibs as usual?" Dormerthwaite asked, the lamplight soaking warmly into his graying hair. Tobin had always liked the man. Some of the nobles disdained him for his humble roots, but the fact that he rose to the pinnacle of London wealth through his own wiles was something Tobin greatly respected.

"As always, my good friend John Clarkson will play it first. If he likes it, that is." Tobin turned his eyes toward the final member of the foursome, and perhaps the most quiet member of Pratt's, Hamish Smirke, a young man in quite the same circumstances as Tobin. Titled family, youngest son, devoted to something most people, especially his parents, couldn't understand. Yes, the two had much in common, though at twenty-six, Hamish was more than ten years Tobin's junior. Still, Tobin tried to look after the fellow, who had a propensity for too much drink and who could charm the women with his poet's eyes and well-formed mouth. The flawless teeth found within weren't something one came across every day either. "So, Hamish, how does your latest play go? I'm waiting to write the overture."

The light-haired young man smiled and shrugged his slim shoulders. "My father says I have six more months to finish up and sell it, and then the money stops."

"Well, cheer up, lad," Dormerthwaite huffed. "You never know whether fortune will set her sights on you. Bless me, I remember growing up so poor we ate cabbage soup for every meal. And then, life turned around in one day. One day!" He straightened his tie pin. "There I was clearing out the muck from the spring near the road when a lady, bless her heart, came by in her carriage. She cried out that her child was choking. Well, so I yanked open the door, pulled out the wee babe, and gave it a good whack on the back, bless him, and out came the offending bit of cheese. She was so grateful, bless her for all of eternity, that she pulled out her purse and just handed it right to me, the whole thing! I never even found out her name!" He puffed out his chest and hit it hard with both hands.

Hamish leaned forward. "What happened then?"

"Uh-oh. He's thinking up a new plot!" Percy said.

Dormerthwaite raised his brows and raised up an index finger. "What happened? Well, it was the beginning of my fortune!" His hands came together in a singular clap. "I left home then, was but a sixteen-year-old slip, bless me, and only came back once to get my family and bring them to London where I could provide for them. They're all gone now, though, bless every single one of them."

Tobin sat back and enjoyed the conversation. Unlike many of his artistic compatriots, he possessed a temperament that fed on the lives of other people; it didn't shut them out. While never described as the life of the party, he enjoyed conversations, he enjoyed being with people who could tell a good story, who had led interesting lives. The fact that they were by far the most handsome lot gathered at the club was something he enjoyed as well, though he wouldn't care to admit that out loud to anyone.

Percy threw down his cards. "I don't know about you, gentlemen, but I'm tired of cards."

Hamish nodded. "I simply can't afford them."

"And bless me if I'm not getting indigestion!" Dormerthwaite declared, stifling a belch unsuccessfully. "I'm going home. What say I carry you home in my carriage, Hammy?"

Hamish, grimacing at what sounded an entirely objectionable nickname, stood without objection to his feet and extended his good-nights as well.

Tobin's sandwich arrived, a beef sandwich with butter and cucumber. Percy eyed it suspiciously. "I'll warrant you wish you were over at the Beefsteak right now, eh?"

He took a bite, too hungry to wait, and spoke with his mouth full. "Not a bit of it. I wanted to talk to you anyway, Percy. Have you read any of Hamish's play?"

He took a sip of his drink. "No, no. Is it any good?"

Tobin nodded. "Quite good. You know, I don't mind being a man of little means when it comes to myself, but there are a hundred Hammies out there who just need someone to believe in their work. I can't bear the thought of him going back to Cornwall in six months without having sold his play. You don't think you . . ."

Percy shook his head. "No, no, no, my friend. Not *me*. I've enough to worry about without adding a starving playwright to the list. You know how my relatives are—graspers, every one of them. Not to mention what my wife's reaction would be!"

Tobin knew as much, but it didn't hurt to ask. "Just thought I'd inquire."

"Besides"—Percy slapped him on the back—"you know if I was going to air my pockets for the arts, I'd back that opera you've been working on for years."

Tobin chewed thoughtfully. "It's a shame Hammy cannot write the libretto. It's too bad I can't find *anyone* to write the libretto."

"You're too particular. If Dickens himself wanted to get his hands on it, you would turn him down."

Tobin laughed. "You're probably right there, old boy. I'm just searching for someone who truly understands my music . . . who understands *me*."

"*That* is a very tall order indeed, mate." Percy got up. "I'd best be off. My sister is coming into town tomorrow with her entire brood, Lord help me. I need to bolster up with a good night's sleep."

And a minute later, he was gone, off to fetch his coat from where it lay on the billiard table upstairs. Tobin was alone. He munched on his sandwich as the remainder of the club members filed out, greeting each man as he went by. Finally, an hour and three cups of tea later, they were all gone.

He wasn't the least bit sleepy.

Suddenly, Sophia Pratt herself appeared, ready to help clean up for the night. The rotund little peahen, with eyes that sparkled like pieces of jet, chose to sit next to him instead. "A good night here tonight, m'lord?"

He hated being called m'lord, had told the woman hundreds of times not to do that. "Yes, I suppose. I just came down around midnight."

"I enjoy this place, I do," she said, kicking off her slippers to ease her swollen feet. "All these dashing men. The duke of Beaufort wasn't around tonight, was he?"

"Not that I saw."

"Now there's a dashing gentleman if ever there was one." She smiled a wide grin that showed off a wee bit of parsley between her canine and her eye tooth.

Tobin Youngblood, keeping silent about the wayward herb, pushed back his plate. "As for myself, the duke of Beaufort has always rather reminded me of a ventriloquist's dummy."

Sophia Pratt almost spit out her tea at such an irreverent description of the man who had employed her late husband for years, the man who had begun in her kitchen the club she was now running. "He may not be much to look at, but he's a kind man and a true gentleman."

"True enough."

"You seem to surround yourself with the beautiful people, m'lord," she said, obviously in doubt as to whether her rebuke made its mark, Tobin surmised. "High born or low don't matter to you, sir. Just as long as they're pleasin' to the eye." She lowered her gaze as if she knew she had overstepped her bounds.

"In truth, I have given my life to the pursuit of beauty, Mrs. Pratt, in music and in my love for all the arts."

"Well, the duke of Beaufort has another kind of beauty, to be sure. He walked in here twenty years ago looking for something different to do, and turned my life upside down. Used to run just a boarding house, I did, and now I run a club. Life can take some funny turns indeed, Mr. Youngblood."

"So I keep hearing," he agreed, wondering if God was preparing him for a sudden turn. Certainly, he had many lessons yet to learn, if this conversation was any indication! He didn't realize his choice of fair friends had become cause for speculation.

The clock chimed 1:30 A.M. All the club members were gone, yet he was in no hurry to extend a final good-night. Of course, since he was one of the few members who took one of the upstairs rooms at Pratt's, he didn't have a long commute. As the younger son of an earl with little chance of inheriting the title from his nephew, a man only six years younger than himself, he wasn't privy to a vast storehouse of wealth. But he could afford the room, and the money it took to join the club. He was a member of Garrick's and the Beefsteak as well, a very good life indeed for a self-confirmed bachelor with a small inheritance on which to survive. But then, he was responsible to or for no one.

"Have you heard from your nephew lately?" Mrs. Pratt asked. "He used to come to these parts quite regularly."

Tobin immediately pictured David Youngblood. "I believe he's up in Scotland these days." His nephew was the earl of Cannock, the title Tobin's grandfather had passed down to his oldest son, who passed it down to David. Tobin didn't begrudge the man his position, for it was the way of things for younger sons to be passed over. Moreover, David could use the boon of being a peer. Born with a harelip, he had never been adored by his parents, or truly accepted by society. Tobin had never had any trouble with the lad, not that he had seen the fellow much. In truth, he wondered how David survived at all with a man like Tobin's older brother for a father! He shuddered at the thought of his brother, the late earl. Now there was a man to dislike. And yet the imperious earl had been cosseted by the social world. Simply put, they were a strange, cold brood, and always had been. But not David.

Tobin always regretted that he hadn't reached out to him more when they were children, but with that face of his . . .

"What's he doing in Scotland?"

Tobin pushed his plate further forward. "He's never been a real favorite at court, Mrs. Pratt."

She nodded. Everyone knew that. "And he was away in France for so long."

"Yes. But why he chose Scotland to settle down in . . ." He shuddered. Tobin could never really abide the cold weather. Now the solitude of those hills supposedly surrounding Greywalls, that was a different matter. He could enjoy that.

"It's amazing how much you two look alike, except for, well, you know."

"The deformity," he supplied rather irritably, then softened his words with a pat on her hand.

Mrs. Pratt stood up from the table and sidled over to the stove. "Can't sleep these days much. Not with Mr. Pratt gone."

"He is sorely missed," Tobin said. William Nathaniel Pratt had died only that year, having run the club for almost two decades. But Mrs. Pratt was bravely carrying on the tradition.

"Aye." She poured a cup of tea for herself and held up the pot toward Tobin. He declined the offer. "But me and Edwin will carry on all right."

"I'd say you and your son are doing an excellent job. That billiard room upstairs was a brilliant addition to the club."

"Well, Pratt's has never been stuffy, that's for sure. I'm not sure how much it's going to be used. Seems to be more of a coatroom than anything else. Most of our gentlemen just like to be together for a good meal, a good chin wagging about hunting and the like, and an occasional friendly game of cards. Oh, I remember the day when it all started."

Tobin could see she was miring down into one of her reminiscent moods, and he stood to leave. Normally, he'd sit there with her till at least two, but he had to get up early in the morning and visit his friend at St. Martin's. "I must retire, madam," he apologized.

"Sure you won't have a cup with me then, your lordship?"

He patted her shoulder. "Not tonight, Mrs. Pratt. And please, don't call me that. I'm just a starving composer hardly worthy of such an illustrious address as 'your lordship.'"

"Well, sir, that's what you are, and that's the way you'll stay. It could be worse"—she winked—"you could be the earl!"

He grimaced. "God alone help me if that were the case. Good night, then."

From the basement kitchen he climbed up the narrow stairs to the first floor where the billiard room lay empty, as well as the committee room. Finally he entered his quarters, shoved the fish and chips to the end of the bed, and lay down. Tobin didn't bother to light the lamp or change his clothes. The darkness was too soothing to chase away for just a minute or two.

He thought of the conversation with Dormerthwaite, how a man's fortune could change in an instant. And he realized he was quite content. Daria was a lovely companion, he enjoyed club life, and his music had never been better. His relationship to God wasn't all it should be, he realized, thinking of the Bible he hadn't opened in months. But in everyone's life there was room for improvement.

Come to think of it, he really could use a bit more money. That would be an improvement indeed.

⌒

Tobin straightened his rumpled tie for at least the tenth time as John Clarkson looked over the finished prelude. It was morning and the church was quiet. Clarkson's gray eyes flickered over the paper, darting quickly back and forth. His body, swaying slightly in the pew, was the only indication that he was reading music. It was his second go-through and he was still stuck to the edge of his seat. Finally, the last page was devoured, and he leaned his small wiry body back against the pew.

"Have you played it yet?" he asked, ironing a small wrinkle in the paper with his index finger.

Tobin shook his head and smiled. "Some compose, some play. *You*, my good friend, will do this far more justice than I."

But Clarkson shook his head. "That isn't true, you know," he whispered, his fingers caressing the paper as if it was the hand of a childhood friend. "But you know I'd be honored."

Truth was, Tobin wanted to actually *hear* it, simply close his eyes and listen without having to concentrate on the mechanics of the piece. This routine with Clarkson had been going on for years.

Clarkson seated himself at the great pipe organ on which he had been practicing when Tobin showed up earlier with a couple of hot cross buns and the manuscript. He had partaken of the baked goods, and now would partake of the remainder of his friend's morning offerings. Tobin was too nervous inside to eat just yet, so he pushed the sack of buns to the side and prepared himself by taking off his coat and loosening his tie.

He closed his eyes, lay down on the steps leading up to the high altar, and folded his hands across his growling stomach. Clarkson was now up in the organ loft, clearing his throat and arranging the music with an officious-sounding shuffle of papers. And then . . . silence.

"Can I help you?" Clarkson's voice shot Tobin to a sitting position, a complete disturbance to his well-being. What in heaven's name was he asking *that* for?

Silhouetted against the morning light, a man stood at the back of the church, his right arm weighed down by a heavy attaché case. He cleared his throat, and it sounded as if it was a young throat. "I'm looking for Lord Tobin Youngblood."

"I am he," Tobin volunteered, irritated and not afraid to show it. "How did you find me here?" He raised one knee and rested his arm on it.

Not bothering to answer the question, the intruder hurried up the aisle, his shoes squeaking noisily. He had already respectfully removed his hat, and he now carefully set the case down on a chair near the front of the church. Clarkson was coming up the nave now as well, obviously curious about the intruder's intent.

The man pulled out a document, a very foreign-looking document with David Youngblood's name written near the top. "I'm Barnaby Goodacre, a solicitor from the firm of Bowersly and Butterbaugh." He handed Tobin the paper, brows knit. "I'm sorry to be the bearer of such ill tidings."

Tobin tugged his fingers through his hair. "What are you talking about?" He hoisted himself to his feet.

"Your nephew, David Youngblood, the earl of Cannock, was wounded by gunshot in a very messy to-do in Scotland and has disappeared. He is presumed dead, I'm afraid. The authorities have given up the search, and so the estate proceedings will go on as if a body was found. There is a letter here from Mr. Butterbaugh which explains all that we know, which is at this point, I'm afraid, not very much."

"What if he's alive?" Tobin asked.

"He's wanted on murder charges in France, my lord."

"I can't believe it!" He sat back down on the altar steps. "What happened?"

"Read the letter, sir. It says as much as anyone knows."

"Do I need to go to Scotland?"

The young lawyer shook his head. "Only if you feel you must. A very capable staff is running Greywalls."

Tobin remembered his last conversation with his nephew before he had gone up to Scotland. There was a daughter, a deformed child with a dead mother. He couldn't remember her name. "What of the girl?"

"Well, of course there is provision for her in the will, but—"

"That isn't what I'm talking about! Is she being cared for?"

"The housekeeper, a Mrs. Wooten, I believe, is engaging someone. If that is satisfactory to you, of course, my lord."

My lord. My lord. They weren't exactly the words he wanted to be hearing right now. He didn't want to be hearing *any* words right now. "So I will be the earl of Cannock?"

"You already are."

"Oh, dear Lord," Clarkson muttered a quick, very sincere prayer. "Oh, Tobin." He sat down next to his friend. "I'm dreadfully sorry."

Tobin set the documents down beside him, putting off his feelings until later. "I suppose you'll need my signature?"

The man's brows drew together in confusion, apparently at Tobin's reaction, for he said, "Usually transference of a title is good news. But, yes, sir, we'll need your signature. It will allow us to go forward with the rest of the legal proceedings regarding the estates."

"Come up into my study and sign the papers there," Clarkson invited, and Tobin followed him up to the small room off the balcony. With each step, he felt he was leaving his old life behind. Life had changed in a matter of minutes, like Dormerthwaite had said it could.

He was now an earl, with vast estates and a seat in the House of Lords.

So why did he feel like jumping over the balcony?

CHAPTER ❖ THREE

God bless *her*, David Youngblood thought, spying the busty form of Mrs. Wooten as she crested the moonlit hill. Her short legs lurched from side to side almost as much as they were staggering forward, propelling her body in an alarming rate down the high mound. Alarming for *her*, that was. He had never seen the woman move that briskly in his life.

Throwing aside his newly won caution, he met her halfway up the hill and unburdened her. The basket was heavier than usual, and she had an extra blanket under her arm. Provisions for a rapidly waning summer.

"Forgive my tardiness, my lord, but I couldn't seem to get Mrs. Pamela out of the kitchen tonight! Even young Angus was pretending to be sick, but to no avail!" She patted her chest and gulped in vast quantities of air. "Oh, me. Haven't run like that since I was a slip of a thing!"

"What was Mrs. MacDowell doing down in the kitchen so late at night?" David took her elbow and helped her into the abbey ruins.

"Making trifle for Elspeth. Seems the girl is grieving something sorely for you, and Miss Wallace thought a treat might do her good. The lady is trying everything she can to cheer the girl up."

David marveled. For years he had lived a violent, luxurious life. He'd killed men for money, used women for pleasure, gambled fortunes out from under the feet of both sexes. He'd slid from one escapade to another with little inconvenience, no emotional attachment, with barely a thought for the consequences—having paid none. Until now.

For love had visited him. Love for Sylvie de Courcey had ripped wide his heart like a wild animal clawing into the dead body of its prey. It had changed him, quickened him somehow, prying open his heart to love his own daughter, the child he had ignored for years.

Oh, God, what have I done?

When did he allow the deformity of his face to corrupt his heart and mind? How old had he been when his soul began to mirror his mouth?

He silently allowed Mrs. Wooten to tend to his wound, her butterfly fingers comforting in a small way.

"It's healing nicely, my lord. As I said a couple of weeks ago, you'll soon be good as new!"

But he barely heard the words, and after she was gone, he left the food basket untouched. For the first time in over twenty years, David felt his eyes burn with tears, and then, the weeping began. He stumbled up the stairway, through the crumbling nave, and out into the fields. Away from God, away from himself.

But he knew that even if he ran forever, both God and David Youngblood would surely follow. After several miles, weakened by his injuries, he fell to the ground.

⁓

"M'lord! Stir yerself!"

David opened his eyes and craned his neck to view a little boy whose face was now coming into focus. He rolled over when he saw the lad's features weighted with a mixture of concern and fear.

Angus shook him. "Would m'lord respectfully stir his stumps? Yer no more than a mile from Greywalls! An' whit ye doin' here in the glower onyways?"

Blast it, but the boy was right! Out here in the open field he would surely be spotted. He was only about two hundred yards from the woods. He stood up and began to run. Angus, of course, followed him.

Once in the shelter of the trees, he placed his hands on the boy's shoulders and leaned down to look him in the eye. During the night he had thought about what he needed to do regarding Elspeth, and now was as good a time as any to begin. "I need you to fetch me two things, lad. And you must employ the utmost discretion and secrecy, of course."

"Aye, course, m'lord." His brown eyes went round and he nodded.

"Fetch me my large black cloak, the one with the hood, and the oldest, dustiest pair of boots you can find in my dressing room. But first you must speak to Elspeth. You must tell her I am alive and safe. But you must not, *must not*, Angus, reveal to her my whereabouts. Can you do this for me?"

The lad puffed out his chest. "I havena let ye doon yet, have I, m'lord."

David couldn't help but smile at the lad's simple pride. "Go now, I'll wait for you here. Remember, discretion and secrecy."

"Aye. I'll mind them both."

And the boy ran off like a tiny adventurer, looking as though he could conquer the world. David yearned for such innocence. He longed to be born all over again.

***

"What did she say? Were you looking at her face when you told her the news?" David was sitting with Angus just outside the ruins, near the fishponds. The sun was setting and he knew the boy was risking his parents' wrath to be out so late. But his loyalty to his employer prevailed.

Angus's eyes twinkled. "Och, m'lord, she was fair pleased. She was aw smiles—just like yerself, sir. An' her eyes were aw wrinkled up in gladness. A wee bit like yer ain now, sir."

David was never bothered when this boy referred to his deformity. Indeed, the lad seemed to think it was something special, something rare. "What happened then?"

"She wrote a wee note. I've got it on me now. But she stuck it into a bookie. A Bible. A wee, tiny one." He pulled the black leather book out of a knapsack he had slung over one shoulder and across his chest.

David took the precious offering. A Bible? This confused him. When had Elspeth become so interested in the Scriptures?

Angus pulled out a sack of scones. "I pinched these from the press, m'lord. The morrow's Sunday, an wifie Wooten winna be comin' doon on Sunday, so maybees ye'll get by 'til Monday."

David gratefully took the sack. "You're a good boy, Angus."

Angus nodded. "That's wha' Maw always say. She taught me a verse from the Bible, no' tha' I can read it much or anything yet, m'lord, aboot bein' Christian an' tendin' ta the widas an' the fatherless in their afflictions. Tha' wha' I'm doin' now."

And when have I ever done such? "So what is happening at Greywalls, lad?"

"Ah, weel, the count's funeral is over an' the investigation has moved over to France. They're pittin' the blame on some laddie called Claude Mirror or somethin' daft like tha'."

David felt relief. "And what do they say of me?"

"That ye were most probably pit ta death by some lackey o' Mr. Mirror. Mind ye, they say ye killed some folk over there yerself an' tha' it's in the hands o' the French now. There's no charges agin ye here in Britain. But I dinna believe all o' tha', m'lord. Ye've always been so kind to me an' mine."

David didn't say anything either way. "And what of Miss Wallace? How is she faring with my daughter?"

"Awfu' weel, m'lord. Yon Miss Elspeth just thinks the world o' her. Maybees she's got some kind o' kinship with her, on account o' all tha' lovely purple color she has on her face." Angus leaned forward. "I hear some o' the housemaids call it a blemish. If that's right, an' purple is such an ugly hue, how come all yon kings an' queens wear it all the time? Tell me tha'!" He leaned back and crossed his arms.

David patted his head. "I haven't any idea what you'll grow up to be someday, young Angus, but you've got a very special place in this world to be sure. So you like this Miss Wallace, then?"

"Oh, aye. An' she's great fun. She makes us clootie dumplins an' takes us for walks."

"Us?"

"Aye, m'lord. Ye see, I'm already six years old an' I canna read a single word, so I thought I might ask her ta teach me a wee bit o' readin'. Just enough ta let me get better on ma ain."

"And of course, the very colorful Miss Wallace said yes, and I assume you're learning more than reading now."

Angus was so excited he stood to his feet, gesturing wildly. "Readin' *an'* writin' *an'* countin' *an'* the stars!" He swept a hand across the heavens. "Last night we laid oot on the roof o' one o' the turrets an' looked at the sky. We counted five shootin' stars an' I saw the Big Dipper *an'* the Little Dipper! Next time we're gonna to find yon Pleiades, an' the belt of Orion! She promised."

And. And. And.

So much promise of so many things. David was glad Angus was given such a chance, especially after all the lad was doing for him. "So this Miss Wallace is a jolly sort?"

Angus was thoughtful. "No' cheerie like Maw, she's much more considered. But she's good fun, an' awfu' clever, an' she has a bonnie heart. Ye know, she says ta me every day, 'I love ye in the Lord, Angus, an' I love ye in ma heart.'"

"That must be a lovely thing to hear every day."

"An' she doesna let us get oot o' hand, neither!"

"How does she do it?"

Angus shrugged. "I'd feel sure ashamed hurtin' her wi' ma shenanigans. Seein' how she's tha' good to me, an' aw."

That was a different way of looking at obedience, David thought. Obeying not because one didn't want to be punished, but because one was loved and loved in return. He'd have to think on that one later.

Angus continued, "An' yon's wha' Miss Wallace teaches us aboot the Savior. Tha' he wants me ta do good things, an' be a good boy 'cause I love him an' am thankful fer all tha' he's done."

"So Miss Wallace teaches you about God?"

"Aye, sir. I'd hazard a guess that's where Elspeth got yon Bible. Although, wifie Wooten used ta teach us the Scriptures sometimes. An' she always prays so loudly, at all hoors o' the day, ye canna help but feel closer to heaven."

David laughed aloud. "Yes, that is Mrs. Wooten, to be sure. She did that when I was a child."

"Taught ye aboot the Scriptures?"

"No. My parents wouldn't have had that. But she used to 'pray without ceasing,' as she called it. All over the house."

Angus sat in silence for a while, then he spoke, tentatively so. "M'lord? Might I ask ye a question?"

"Certainly."

"And ye promise ye winna be gettin' angry?"

How could he ever be angry at Angus? "I promise."

"What kind of parents wouldna want their ain laddie to be taught the Scriptures?"

David shook his head. "You wouldn't want to know, Angus, and I certainly don't want to remember."

The sky darkened, until the stars that Angus mentioned were in plain view. They sat together until Angus rose to his feet. "I'd best be goin', m'lord. Maw'll be fashin' aboot where I've gone off ta if I'm not back for ma tea."

"Will you come again tomorrow then?"

Angus shook his head. "Most likely I winna be here until Monday evenin'. We're busy preparin' for the weddin' next week."

"Wedding?"

"Miss Wallace's brother, the preacher, an' the countess de Boyce. They're gettin' married right away. Ah, weel, I'll be seein' ye then, m'lord. Wifie Wooten said she'd be doon on Monday morn wi' a bit o' food for ye."

The boy left.

David felt his heart sicken with pain. So Sylvie and Matthew were getting married. It was all over now, wasn't it? There was really no hope. The only woman he had ever loved would never be his.

He remembered his grand scheme to make her a widow of Rene de Boyce. But he knew those days were over. They had to be. The evil had to stop. Someday he must seek her forgiveness. He could never live his life in peace without it.

CHAPTER ❖ FOUR

Matthew Wallace rose from his bed and felt that certain nip in the mid-August air that energized him for the day ahead. He couldn't wait to say his vows. Having conducted weddings many times, he understood the spiritual significance of such a commitment, and he relished the scriptural significance of the marriage relationship as it reflected Christ's love for his bride, the church. A light tapping sounded through the door to the tiny manse into which he was now settled comfortably.

"Mate?" The voice, though muffled, could only be his sister's.

"Come in, Miranda," he replied, buttoning his shirt.

The door opened and she stood there with a wide smile on her face. "Today is the day!"

He returned a very similar smile. "You're up and over early."

"I couldn't sleep! Think of it, Mate. A month ago we were in despair. We both thought you'd never be able to marry Sylvie, and now, it's the morning of your wedding! I'm so happy I could burst!"

Matthew wasn't surprised. Miranda was one of those rare people who could make others' happiness her own without feeling an ounce of jealousy. "How's Sylvie?"

Sylvie had been staying at Greywalls since the funeral. She had spent most of her time in her room, or walking the moors with Matthew. In truth he was worried about her, but she had, after all, experienced a great deal of trauma. Even the thought of their marriage wouldn't be able to take all that away.

"She told me the wisest thing she could be doing right now is marrying you. It will be almost medicinal to get her away from that castle, Mate. Away from those horrible images of Rene's death."

"And Youngblood's betrayal," he said, shaking his head. "I don't know which pains her more."

Miranda obviously knew. "The earl was her good friend, Mate. When she learned he killed her parents' for the sake of Mirreault, it could have quite done her in. Had you not been there," she quickly added.

"Sylvie is a loyal sort. There was a large soft spot in her heart for Youngblood, to be sure. I know I'm not the type of person who could truly forgive his actions, but I know Sylvie will. Someday."

Miranda, as no-nonsense as ever, said, "And certainly, Mate, we are commanded by God to forgive over and over again."

"Life is so simple for you, Mira."

She crossed over to the wardrobe and began laying out his coat. "It is as simple as we allow it to be. We humans tend to complicate matters that God intended to be elementary. And that's the truth of it. Now that you're a Presbyterian minister you won't need to be wearing your collar. Shall I set out the tie Mother finally sent you for your birthday?"

He nodded, glad that capable Miranda was taking over. "So Sylvie is happy?"

"As happy as she can be, considering the circumstances surrounding this wedding."

"That doesn't make me feel very good, Mira."

She crossed her arms. "Well, Mate, that speaks nothing as to the condition of her heart, it merely attests to the tragic circumstances. That she is so eager to marry you so soon should tell you everything you need to know."

He picked up the dark blue silk tie. "You know, Mira, you think more like a man than any woman I know."

"You just let your emotions get in the way, dear brother. And now"—she kissed his cheek—"I'm going to fix you some breakfast."

"I'm really not very hungry, Mira. Don't go to any trouble."

"Since when have you ever been any trouble?" she asked, and hurried down the hallway.

Mira's right, he thought, *this isn't going to be a very happy wedding, filled with gay sentiments and effusive congratulations*. In fact, some people would downright gossip about the marriage taking place so quickly after the death of Sylvie's husband. But he didn't care. Before God, he knew he should marry Sylvie today. And that was exactly what he was going to do.

***

"I've never shed so many tears at one time," Miranda whispered to Elspeth.

The two were standing in the castle chapel as Matthew's good friend, Reverend George MacDonald, conducted the wedding.

Elspeth took Miranda's hand and held it firmly. Miranda had seen quite a change take place in the girl, literally overnight. And for several days she had been happy, chatting about incidentals and asking question after question concerning her father. Mrs. Wooten was ready to scream, Miranda knew, but there was really no other person at Greywalls who had known David Youngblood as a boy.

And now, the child watched with a smile on her face as the wedding progressed. The bride was beautiful. Her dark hair curled down over her simple ink blue dress. In her hands was a bouquet of late-blooming roses. Fragile and pink, they served to echo the day in general. Indeed, though horrible happenings had preceded this wedding, God had been kind. Miranda had been praying that the wedding would somehow be a happy one, and that a heavenly reprieve would be extended for the bride.

The service was short, yet meaningful, and when her brother kissed his bride, his wife, Miranda stood to her feet and began to clap. At first the small gathering of guests didn't know what to do, but Miranda couldn't curtail her display of jubilation. It was so like the Savior to make something so beautiful out of something so dark.

"Bravo!" someone yelled.

"Excellent!" George MacDonald agreed with a broad smile.

Mrs. Wooten cried, "Kiss her again!"

Sylvie's eyes were shining, and she clung to Matthew's arm. Miranda could feel her joy. With tears in her heart, she handed her old post over to her new sister-in-law. Her days for caring for Matthew were over, and Sylvie was the perfect woman for the job.

And so the couple, so obviously in love, so full of joy and thankfulness, did as requested, falling into each other's arms with profound relief. The journey had been long and hard, but worth it now that it was over.

Later, after the bride and groom, as well as Eve, had boarded a train bound for London, the first leg of their journey to France, Miranda sat in the extensive library of the castle. In the corner a magnificent grand piano gathered dust. She put down her copy of *Jane Eyre* and walked over to the instrument.

Hesitantly she played a small piece she had learned during the two years she endured lessons. The piano was badly in need of tuning. Nevertheless, the music, so ineptly dabbled, was of comfort to her. She played a bit more, still softly. It was a shame, really, that this stunning piano rarely voiced a song. But she had run through her small repertoire. Rarely did she regret the fact that she had never put her heart and soul into her lessons, but this was one of those times.

Mrs. Wooten entered the room. "Did you know the earl himself could play the piano?"

"David Youngblood?" She could hardly believe it. After her brother's description of the man and his deeds, she could hardly imagine the soul of an artist resided within.

"Oh, yes. Not that he was ever given lessons, mind you." Her mouth curled down in disapproval. "But he would make up his own tunes, his own songs. They were like nothing any of us had ever heard, but they were beautiful, in a haunting way. Now, his uncle, the new earl, Lord Tobin, he plays more beautifully than anyone I've ever heard."

This intrigued Miranda. "Is he a pianist?"

"Oh, no. A composer. Lots of church music, but I've heard he is working on an opera."

Miranda held a hand to her chest. "An opera! I love the opera."

Mrs. Wooten smiled. "Well, it's too bad that Lord Tobin won't be coming around here then. At least he'd have you to appreciate him."

"Have you been around him much? He sounds like a very interesting man."

Mrs. Wooten whipped out a rag from her pocket and began to dust the piano automatically. "Depends on who you ask. We served the family for quite some time in London before coming here. Some people think he's arrogant and snobbish. Others say he's a genius. He's one of those artistic types to be sure. But he has a small core of devoted friends, so he must not be all that bad."

"Or his friends are just like him," Miranda laughed.

"I just remember him as a quiet type. It's been years since I've seen the man, though. A lot can happen to a person in that amount of time."

Miranda knew that was surely true. "Have you heard word from him as to my position here?"

Mrs. Wooten thumped her forehead with the heel of her hand. "Goodness, yes. He sent word last week that you are to continue in your post indefinitely."

Miranda felt relief wash over her, for she had come to enjoy life here at Greywalls. And since Matthew didn't need her anymore . . .

"We're glad you'll be a permanent part of us, love." Mrs. Wooten drew her into a quick embrace. "The Lord knows we could use a bit of sunlight here at Greywalls, what with the master disappeared and the new earl not bound to visit often. If at all."

"I'm glad to be here too." Miranda closed the lid over the piano keys. "Did you ever feel a sense of destiny, that you were where you were supposed to be, yet there was a lot more coming your way?"

Mrs. Wooten shoved the rag back into her pocket. "To be sure I have, love. But then isn't that the way God works? Isn't that what walking in his will is all about?"

The woman's faith was always comforting. "Yes, it most certainly is."

That night as she lay in bed, Miranda thought about Lord Tobin Youngblood. He sounded so intriguing, so elusive. The man was actually writing an opera. Hopefully he would find a good librettist. Miranda had only one quarrel with operas: their plots were usually full of holes! She thought that just for once, an opera should make sense on every level. And a story began to formulate in her mind, one she would very much like to hear set to music.

CHAPTER ❖ FIVE

B last!"

Tobin Youngblood, the new earl of Cannock, slammed his fist on the table, almost upsetting the ink pot. This wasn't coming as easily as he thought it would. Once again, he had been duped; a small victory had led him to believe he could win the war.

The prelude had been received at St. Martin's with all the acclaim it deserved. At least according to all the eligible young women who flocked around him after the service, grabbing his arms, fluttering their lashes, and gushing over his accomplishment. And he had thought to ride the wings of success right into the soprano aria of his opera. To no avail. The melody wouldn't come. It had to be filled with such beauty, such haunting beauty, that nothing he created was nearly good enough.

Apparently his musical muse wasn't as impressed by his new title as the marriageable ladies of London!

He put away his materials. *I'm to meet Daria in ten minutes.* Deliberating on whether or not to splurge and put on a fresh shirt, he decided against it. It was nearly as rumpled as it could be, but Daria might not recognize him if he was pressed and pristine like some of the other noblemen she was flirting with for the sake of her daughter. So he threw on his coat, grabbed the newspaper of fish, which was by this time as dried and hard as a brick, and hurried down the hall.

It had been a good day, otherwise. He was able to anonymously rescue Hamish's project after his father had been forced to cut off the boy's allowance prematurely and completely. And he had been fitted for a new suit. The first in four years. Daria would be mad as a hornet that he hadn't taken her along for some fashion advice. As he knocked on her door, having discarded the fish in the basement at Pratt's, he decided not to tell her. Besides, he was hungry, and he wanted to get to Brown's before the crowd.

"Oh, Tobin, you really are quite, quite the darling, aren't you?" Lady Daria Christopher exclaimed fifteen minutes later, opening the small bottle of French perfume. "You know how I adore the scent of lily of the valley."

Tobin reached into his pocket and pulled out two butterscotch candies. He handed one to Daria who was dressed in a very odd brown gown, decorated with silk autumn leaves, and wearing a hat with a small pumpkin at the side. She had told him upon arriving that evening that she was celebrating the arrival of October. Her eyes lit up even more at the sight of candy. Goodness, but he couldn't for the life of him figure out why a woman who loved penny candy more than expensive perfume was so worried about money. "I thought you'd like it. Personally, the purple color of the glass top sold me on it."

"I *adore* purple."

"And orange, apparently," he said. "It's quite an interesting ensemble you've chosen for tonight, Daria."

"You should see what I've got planned for Christmas! I designed it myself. It's like nothing you've ever seen."

He could certainly believe that!

They were now sitting in the dining room at Brown's Hotel, waiting for their order to be taken. Tobin, accustomed to such elegance as a child, was quickly getting used to it once more, now that he had the Youngblood fortune bolstering the constitution of his pocketbook. He was trying not to let it go to his head, but it was proving a bit difficult. Beautiful women, noble or not, were positively crawling out of the woodwork, and he had to admit, it was nice to be fawned over by such delectable, living works of art. "Have you decided what you are going to eat?" He looked down at his own menu. Though a slender man, Tobin loved a fine meal. A good chef was indeed an artist, he had determined years ago. He had already decided on a roasted capon.

"Oh, no. I'm not really very hungry tonight."

That was a warning sign. Daria usually loved to eat as much as he did. It was one of the reasons they got on so famously. "So"—he took a sip of water and winked at her—"am I going to have to pry it out of you, as usual, or will a sense of candidness rule your day?"

Daria unfolded her napkin and placed it in her lap. "Well, actually, there are two things bothering me tonight. First of all, it's Valentinia. She's being quite obstinate about Lord Dugley. Do you know him, by the way?"

He shook his head. "I've heard tell he's a bit of a bumpkin, but he's good-looking and rich."

"Yes, well, he's extended a perfectly good offer, but she will have none of it." Her mouth turned down severely, aging her a good ten years.

"What's the matter, then?"

"Nothing that I can speak of. He has had two other wives, but that shouldn't—"

"Two other wives?" Tobin blurted out. "She's only seventeen years old, Daria dear. What woman do you know who would want two other ghosts attending her wedding?"

Daria pursed her lips. "He isn't all *that* old, and he is, as you say, rather handsome." But her words were filled with doubt.

"And he'd take her off to the Lake District and you'd see nothing of her for months, possibly years, on end." Tobin took her hand across the table. "Be honest with me. Why are you so consumed with marrying the child off? Does she wish it to be so?"

"I don't know, Tobin." Daria rested her chin in the heel of her hand. "Sometimes she does, but other times . . . I really don't know. She just wanders about the house so . . . so . . . lost, and unsubstantial."

"Valentinia is merely a gentle soul. You don't understand her because she's nothing like you, Daria. But she is a good and proper girl."

Daria grinned. "Well, maybe that's the problem; I've never been viewed as all that proper!"

He laughed. "If she doesn't want to marry the man, then she shouldn't have to."

"You know, Tobin, you're not like any man I've ever met. You actually view women as people with minds, not just hearts and bodies."

He broke open a hot roll and began to butter it. "Some men wouldn't even concede you have hearts."

She rolled her eyes. "I know."

"It's simply that you've always told Valentinia she could marry for love, and yet you traipse all these gentlemen before her, my dear, and when she doesn't fall for them, *you* are the one who's disappointed. And you've been right persnickety yourself, when it comes to her suitors."

"Well, she is my only child, Tobin! You'd do the same!" she chided, her eyes indignant.

"Of course I would, Daria. Of course. But if this matter is bothering you so greatly, you should just stop worrying about it and let nature take its course. Valentinia is a lovely girl. Trust me, someday she'll meet someone gentle of heart who will truly love her."

"Let's just hope he has a lot of money." Daria pulled apart her own roll. "And I mean a *lot*." She gestured wildly, spilling her water glass. "Oh dear! I've spilled again."

But Tobin was already on his feet. A moment later, napkin in hand, he was on one knee mopping up the spill on the floor and the skirt of her dress. Daria was laughing. "You know you don't have to do such things anymore. After all, you *are* an earl."

"But I'm still your friend, Daria."

"You know, I like you in that position."

He looked up, his brows drawn. "What do you mean?"

"Down there, on one knee like that." Her red lips were smiling a bit too wide, he thought as he watched her unwrap the candy and pop it into her mouth.

⌒

Having pulled out all the stops, John Clarkson was attacking the organ like a gladiator fighting a bear. Tobin snuck quietly into the church and took a chair near the back door. The man was a marvel, truly. And although Tobin was quite accomplished, he knew he would never reach this level.

It had been a grueling week. October was barely upon them and he was no closer to discovering the melody to that aria than he had been months ago. It was rather discouraging, but since he had inherited his fortune, he'd been much too distracted. London was a wonderful city if one was wealthy. So much to do and see, so many places to spend money. He felt as if he was losing himself. Where had he left that place in his soul that yearned for simplicity and beauty and freedom. In the House of Lords? At all the parties he suddenly found himself attending?

Clarkson stopped in a mighty roar of airy pipe, and then silence. A deafening silence. Tobin cleared his throat.

"Is that you, my friend?" Clarkson ran his large hands over his balding head.

Tobin stood. "You found me out. It sounded wonderful, John. But, then, you do a Bach fugue better than anyone I know."

Clarkson's face reddened. "You're too kind."

"And you are much too humble." He pulled two apples out of his pocket and handed one to his friend.

Clarkson bit into his right away. "You have that look in your eye, my friend. You didn't just come here to listen to me practice, did you?"

Tobin followed suit and was crunching on his own piece of fruit. "I think I'm going away for a while. Up to Scotland."

"Really? For how long?"

"I want to see if I can finish the opera. London's too noisy now, too crowded."

John said he knew exactly what Tobin meant, although Tobin doubted it. John Clarkson was too simple of heart, too dedicated to one purpose to stand for a hectic life. Smart man.

"But in order to assure my friends that I'm not deserting them unduly, I'm having a house party at Greywalls in two weeks." The idea popped out of his mouth without warning from his head, as if his brain was sabotaging what he thought to be good sense. But then, what did he know? It might be just the ticket to a smooth transition. "Do you think you can make it?"

Clarkson looked doubtful. "I'll try. Are we going up by train, then?"

"Naturally."

"I've never traveled by train, Tobin."

"You'll do splendidly. And I shall tell you this, good friend, you will have the time of your life out there on those desolate moors. You might even find yourself a lovely Scottish lass to bring back home with you."

But Clarkson looked as if some convincing might be in order.

Daria was another matter altogether.

"Scotland? Now? Oh, darling, I absolutely *love* the idea!" Daria was fairly gushing at the invitation Tobin gave while eating chocolate truffles in her lime green parlor. "Is Valentinia invited?"

"Of course." He went over the list in his mind. The Christophers, Clarkson, Hamish, Percy and his wife, and he was even planning on inviting Mr. Dormerthwaite, the banker. Yes, a man like Dormerthwaite, not to mention his grand wife, would round things out nicely indeed.

Daria clapped her hands together rapidly. "Oh, yes. And the weather will be nippy, I suppose. I'll bring *all* my furs. I bought a cap from an American just the other day with a raccoon tail hanging off the back."

Tobin nearly spit out the candy he was just biting into. "A coonskin cap?"

"Why yes, that's exactly what he called it. Mentioned a fellow with an odd name, a Dannil Boone."

"Daniel Boone. The man's name was Daniel."

"Oh no! He said Dannil, I'm positively certain of that!"

This was going to be a very interesting time indeed. And then, when they had all gone back to London, at least five to ten pounds heavier than when they left, he would be alone at Greywalls.

All alone. But was he really good enough company? Even for himself?

CHAPTER ✦ SIX

Miranda and the Wootens congregated before the kitchen fire. Pamela and James MacDowell, Angus's parents, were there as well. Angus, of course, had already been tucked into his wee bed in the servants' quarters, and Elspeth had retired early. She claimed fatigue, but Miranda wasn't quite so sure. The child had been jumping around on nerves all day, so excited, and denying the fact from sunup to sundown.

Mrs. Wooten was busy buttering toast as Pamela sliced a sausage. James and Mr. Wooten leaned over a backgammon board, oblivious to the women's chatter. This homey convocation had become a nightly ritual since the days had begun to grow a bit cool. Here the five of them gathered, the higher servants of the castle, to have a late tea and gab about the day. Miranda cherished these times, remembering the evenings she used to share with Matthew. It was a vespers of sorts.

"I received a letter from my brother today," she said, pulling down cups and saucers from the wooden cupboard near the buttery door.

The others really didn't know Matthew well, but they had come to love Sylvie during her brief stay at Greywalls.

"And your new sister-in-law?" Pamela asked. "How's France?"

Miranda set the cups on their saucers and loaded them onto a tray. "There's been no trouble, thanks be to God. No trouble at all."

"What about that Claude Mirreault scoundrel?" Mrs. Wooten sliced off a square of butter and began spreading it on the toast in her hand. "Any news of him?"

"Mate says he's a slippery one. Nothing in the paper about him, and Matthew refuses to let Sylvie go to the man's chateau, even though she's begging him to do just that."

Pamela shook her head. "'Tis wise to leave such dealin's to the authorities."

Miranda laughed. "I think Mate is more frightened he'll get so angry he'll kill the man himself!"

Truly the situation wasn't a laughing matter, but Miranda was glad her brother was being so cautious. His temper and his fists got him into more trouble than was proper. "The Fighting Vicar." It was her own private nickname for him.

Mrs. Wooten arranged the toast on a Delft plate. "Well, let's hope it's all just a matter of the past now. There doesn't seem to be a way left for that man to try and grab hold of the de Courccy fortune."

"Oh, yes, that reminds me." Miranda held up a finger. "He also told me that she sold off the vineyard. Apparently, her father's finances weren't quite what everyone thought they were. In fact, Mate told me it was why she married the count so willingly even though her heart belonged to Mate. The de Courceys were hoping an alliance with the count would bring about a reversal of fortune, so to speak."

"So they were each weddin' the other for a fortune that didna really exist?" Pamela's mouth hung open as she placed the sausages neatly on a plate.

"I've never heard the like!" Mrs. Wooten wiped her pudgy hands on her apron. "Sounds like something straight out of the pages of a novel!"

The kettle screamed on the hob and Pamela went running. Miranda took hold of the tray and started toward the fire. "I'll just be glad when they're back home in Scotland, safe and sound."

"As will we all!" Mr. Wooten piped up, surprising them. "Then we won't have to listen to you ladies babble about like three hungry jackdaws!"

Mrs. Wooten patted his lean shoulder. "There now, dearie. If it wasn't for us, who would you have to eavesdrop on?"

James MacDowell respectfully stifled his laugh. And Miranda chuckled behind her hand. It seemed the housekeeper could always get the best of her husband, the steward of Greywalls.

Never mind about anything else now, she thought, a cup of strong tea in hand. She settled in a chair, closed her eyes, and took a sip. All was right with the world. At least for the next five minutes!

⁓

"I still canna believe I let ye talk me into this. Yer goin' to get me in a heap o' bother with his lordship tonight, Miss Elspeth."

Elspeth doubted that. Her father would never do anybody any harm.

They had been planning this escapade for the past week, buzzing quietly when Miss Wallace was out of the room. It had taken no small amount of persistence on Elspeth's part to convince Angus that he should take her to her father. But finally, when she promised to teach him Latin, he relented.

"Papa winna be angry with ye. In fact, I think he'll be fair pleased ye've listened ta my request."

"I could've asked him aboot it, m'self."

"But I wanted ta surprise him!" Elspeth reminded him.

Angus strode forward shaking his head. Elspeth hurried in the darkness to catch up with him. "Besides, I can sometimes bring food oot ta him, so ye dinna have ta be doin' it yourself aw the time."

Angus put his hands on his hips and glared. "Ye best not be thinkin' after *that* fashion, Miss Elspeth. 'Tis my job ta take care o' his lordship, an' I'll not be givin' it ta some . . . some . . . *lass*." He said the word like it was a piece of old candy, still intriguing, but definitely not edible.

Elspeth laughed, covering her deformed mouth with her left hand, as she always did. It was a habit her father had tried to break her of, but she just couldn't seem to drop it. "I'm fair surprised yer doin' such a good job, seein' yer nothin' but a . . . *lad*."

Angus kept moving forward, ignoring her return as any self-respecting male would do. "We'll be there in a wee minute."

"How long will the grown-ups be havin' their tea?" she asked.

"Maw never comes ta bed afore ten."

Elspeth calculated. "Grand. We still have more than an hoor afore we have ta be hame."

"Dinna forget the walk takes a half an hoor. We dinna have much time once we're there. I winna be gettin' in trouble with ma Maw over this, Miss Elspeth."

The closer Elspeth drew near to her father, the more excited she became. He cared about her, he truly did. It wasn't at all like her mother had predicted.

The abbey ruins materialized before her, and she ran down the hill toward the only other person in the world who understood what it was like to be so evidently imperfect. Miss Wallace, well, she thought she herself was so ugly, but Elspeth knew the governess clearly didn't understand the meaning of the word.

～

The backgammon game was set aside for the next evening's gathering, and the group settled in to eat the simple fare and drink cup after cup of tea.

Pamela took some knitting out of a bag and settled back into her chair. "I canna thank ye enough for what yer doin' for ma Angus, Miss Wallace. The lad will surely go far. James an' I never thought he would be havin' such a grand opportunity ta learn."

Miranda, having grown up the well-educated daughter of a rich woolen mill owner, was touched deeply by the woman's teary eyes. James's sober look echoed his wife's sentiments. "He's a joy to teach," Miranda replied. "So quick and bright. He already knows the entire alphabet and dozens of words."

James and Pamela looked proudly at one another.

"And when I'm not working with him, Elspeth is!" Miranda basked in the girl's loving, giving temperament.

Mrs. Wooten sipped her tea. "That one's a born teacher. 'Tis easy to see."

"An' yon way she's doin' so weel since her da's disappearance," Pamela said. "It was as if she was grievin' sore one day, an' the next . . ."

"I know," Miranda said. "There's no explanation for it."

Mrs. Wooten whooshed out of her chair and busied herself with another kettle of water. "All I can say is," she called over her shoulder, "we're glad you're here with us, Miss Wallace. And you're not like some of them snooty governesses who'll have nothing to do with us servants."

Miranda blushed. Truth was, she enjoyed being among the staff. Most governesses were caught in a lonely world, stuck in a twilight existence between the servants and the gentry. But Miranda refused to go unnourished by human companionship. "Well, you are such charming people, I have to wonder why you've allowed me into your little tea club in the first place!"

An hour later it was time for bed. The clock was chiming midnight and they'd stayed up later than usual, for when Pamela asked Mrs. Wooten how she made prayer such an all-day affair, the conversation seemed to grow legs that ran from one topic to another. Feeling spiritually refreshed, Miranda climbed the back stairway, a single candle in hand. She hurried through her nightly ritual, eager to light her bedside lamp and take down her Bible. Stepping out of her serviceable gown, she hung it back up neatly on the hanger. Her black leather boots she arranged at the bottom of the wardrobe. Next, Miranda sat at the small dressing table and took down her hair.

What a relief it was to feel it tumble down from its confines. The tingling sensation of her heavy hair going back in the direction it was supposed to bordered on painful, but it felt so good. She caught sight of her reflection. Mother had always told her that her features were quite lovely, but she could never see beyond the birthmark. Apparently, neither could most men. Looking at her bare left hand, she was certain a ring would never rest there.

Automatically, she brushed her hair now grown well past her bottom. One day, she threatened, she would cut off some of the length. But for now, it was the only bit of herself she truly thought was wonderful. Miranda allowed herself that small indulgence and felt not vain at all. After all, God created her completely. The good and the bad.

A soft, urgent knock rattled her door, and without waiting for an answer, Pamela entered the room, her face stricken.

Miranda stood to her feet. "What is it?"

"It's Angus. He's gone from his bed!"

"What? Is he in the house?"

"No' in the servants quarters. I thought maybees he'd be up here with Miss Elspeth. Would ye check?"

"Of course."

Miranda threw on a robe and hurried toward Elspeth's room. Taking hold of the knob, she opened the door softly. There lay the two children, moonlight spilling over their sleeping features.

"Oh, ma wee pet lamb," Pamela muttered in relief, taking her son gingerly from between the covers. "Crivvens, he's aw dressed!" The little boy's shoes and socks lay in a puddle of leather and wool nearby.

Miranda pointed to two fishing poles leaning against the washstand. "So is Elspeth." She shook her head with a smile. "Moonlight fishing. Goodness me!"

Pamela kissed her son on the forehead and left the room, her skirts swaying gently as she walked in a rocking manner to keep the little boy asleep.

Elspeth's breathing was shallow and even. Miranda kissed her forehead tenderly, caressed her pale cheek, and tucked the covers in around her. No, she may never have children of her own, but she had Elspeth, and in this she must be content.

A week later, Mrs. Wooten ran by her faster than a Corinthian on the road to Brighton. "Sorry, dearie," she yelled, "I just got word that his lordship will be here in a week!"

Miranda turned around and caught up with the housekeeper, who was on her way to the library. "He's coming in a week?"

"Oh my, yes." She rounded the corner, threatening to veer off into the wall. Miranda reached out a hand and steadied her. "And he's bringing a house party with him!"

"How many guests?"

"He said there should be about ten altogether. Oh, dearie, dear. What am I to do with such short notice?"

"We'll all do what we can to help you, Mrs. Wooten," Miranda assured her. "And my brother and his wife will be coming back today. I'm sure Sylvie will lend a hand."

Mrs. Wooten stood up as tall as she could, which wasn't very. "Now let's get one thing straight, Miss Wallace. I may do a little complaining—well, a *lot* of complaining, especially when a surprise is forced upon me like this—but I am perfectly capable of handling the situation without help from outsiders!"

Miranda nodded. "Do you want my help then?"

"I said outsiders. You're hardly that, Miss Wallace. Now come into the library with me and help me dust off this piano. He was especially clear that he wanted it in working order."

Miranda gasped. "Is there a piano tuner in the area?"

"Not that I know of. Is it in bad shape then?"

Miranda nodded and opened the lid. She played several notes of "Speak to Me Only with Thine Eyes."

"It sounds like it has a head cold." Mrs. Wooten shuddered. "What shall we do?"

"We'll have to send off to Aberdeen for someone."

"May I leave that up to you, then?" Mrs. Wooten asked. "It will be one less thing I'll have to worry about."

"I'd be horribly offended if you didn't. I shall get on it right away. Who shall I send the message with?"

"Oh, young Dougal, one of Mr. Wooten's men, a crafty, resourceful fellow. He always goes away to the city for us when we can't make do with what we've got around here. Dougal will find what you need."

And so Miranda found herself writing furiously to an unknown source, summoning a piano tuner to Greywalls. Once Dougal was on his way, looking all the happier for this brief holiday, she hurried back up to the schoolroom.

Angus and Elspeth were gone, and in their place was a note that said, "We've gone fishing."

Miranda rather doubted it. But she was too busy to do anything about it just then. *I will follow them soon*, she decided, wondering what it was about fishing that could possibly be so wonderful?

She ran back downstairs and found Pamela. "You've got a busy week ahead of you, then, I'll warrant."

Pamela was excited. "I canna wait. Aw the food we're gettin' in for the occasion will really give me somethin' ta work with! Did ye know there's ta be a dance on the last night?"

"A dance?" Miranda's mind began to turn. Elspeth had no fancy dresses. Neither did she, for that matter.

"Aye. I dinna ken Greywalls has seen its like for many a year."

Certainly, it would give the villagers something to talk about for a long time. Miranda ran for the door.

"Where're ye goin', miss?" Pamela cried.

"To Huntly. I've got to buy some fabric. I'm making Elspeth a new gown."

CHAPTER ❖ SEVEN

I have to tell you, Elspeth has taken every advantage of the free time she's had this week," Miranda said as she sat in the kitchen with Pamela. The cook was cutting up apples. There were so many apples harvested from the orchards, it would be a shame to waste them. And so the kitchen staff was working hard to lay up a good store of them for the winter. Applesauce, spiced apples, sweet, syrupy apples. Miranda was stitching away on Elspeth's new gown, her mouth watering all the while.

"Angus as weel. Off they go with their fishin' poles in the mornin', an' hame they come for tea with never so much as a minnow in tow. I wonder why they are thinkin' it's so grand." Pamela arose and took a mince pie out of the oven.

Miranda gathered the skirt of the pale rose gown, preparing to sew it onto the bodice. It would be a perfect ball gown for a young girl, and with the way she was planning to pile the child's hair in ringlets on either side of her head, how could anyone object to her presence?

"Do you think we might spirit away some of these goodies for Elspeth?" Miranda asked, looking around her at the various cheeses and meats, dried fruits and confections Dougal had brought back with him from Aberdeen. Along with the piano tuner, a surly man named Willie W. MacWilliams. Miranda was afraid to ask what the W. stood for.

"Why, certainly! She's the earl's niece, after aw, albeit from the wrong side o' the sheets."

Miranda had been troubled all week regarding this new relationship that was about to be hoisted upon her charge. Would he call for her? Would he pay her mind? Or would he demand her out of his sight?

Miranda shook her head. "Even the most well-meaning person could find himself repulsed by her. Some could overcome their revulsion, but not everyone is that strong, or that sympathetic." Miranda had experience of such people firsthand.

"Aw we can do is ta wait an' see, Miss Wallace. My heart aches fair sore for the child." Pamela wiped a stray tear from her eye, leaving a swipe of flour across her cheek. "It's a grand thing m' Angus is the lad he is. She'll find acceptance from him."

Miranda agreed and almost let out a sigh, ready for a change of subject. "I was more than surprised that the earl extended an invitation to my brother and his wife to join their party."

"Why?" Pamela put her hands on her hips. "She's a countess an aw. It's no' surprisin'. A house party's been one matter, but puttin' on a ball, with all o' the local gentry invited, crivvens, but I dinna ken if I can cook up *that* kind o' storm!"

Miranda laughed. "You'll do wonderfully! Your tarts are quite the best I've ever tasted. Sylvie said she hadn't any finer in France."

Pamela blushed. "Scotland was closely aligned with France for years. The dishes were passed doon from one o' my great-grandfathers who cooked for one o' the clan chiefs doon near Perth. Guess it's just in ma bones now."

"Well, wherever it comes from," Miranda said, "I, for one, am glad it's there!"

From the library above them, the sounds of the piano being tuned vibrated through the ceiling. Mrs. Wooten sauntered in, her arms full of clean bed linens. "It will be nice to hear his lordship play again."

"Have you heard him play much, then?" Miranda asked, surprised.

"Oh, my yes. He was quite a bit younger than his brother and sister. When his father died and his brother inherited everything, he would come to London for the holidays. Rather a quiet lad. But when he'd sit down at that piano, heavens me!"

"It's the only aspect of this whole party I'm looking forward to," Miranda confessed as she laid aside the finished skirt and began to embroider what was destined to be the front of the bodice. "What does he look like?"

Pamela shrugged, and Mrs. Wooten was quick to answer. "Like Lord David does"—her eyes rounded—"*did*. Like Lord David did, without the harelip. A beautiful man, I'd say, though not in the conventional way."

"Ye seem sore interested in him, Miss Wallace," Pamela remarked.

"I'm sure he has his fair share of admirers without adding me to the queue."

Mrs. Wooten poured herself a cup of tea and sat down for a rest. She slid off her slippers and groaned. But, as always, she wasn't too tired for a chat. "He's long been an admirer of Lady Daria Christopher, and she's quite fond of him, I hear."

"Why have they never married?" Miranda asked.

"Don't know." Mrs. Wooten sipped her tea.

"I thought the servants knew the masters more than they did themselves?" Miranda joked.

Mrs. Wooten waved away her comment. "I guess some are just more mysterious than others!"

~~~~

"There really isn't any point in setting to work today," Miranda told Elspeth and Angus in the schoolroom. "We're all too anxious about the guests."

"Does that mean we can go fishin'?" Angus shouted as he bounced in his chair, his dark eyes practically popping out of their sockets.

"I suppose so." Miranda shook her head. This whole fishing business was almost a mystery. Not one fish had come home with them yet. "In fact, I think I shall go with you myself!"

Both of them shot up out of their seats. "Och naw!" Elspeth cried. "It's awfu' cold the day—"

"Aye, it's freezin'!" Angus interrupted, his eyes darting like mad.

"An' we get awfu' hungry . . ."

"Well, I'll bring a picnic!" Miranda wanted to laugh at their discomfort. "It will be fun!" She clapped her hands for effect. The poor dears.

"It's only fishin'," Elspeth said.

"And we never get so muckle as a bitie!" Angus pointed out. "There's no' any fun in *that*."

Miranda drummed her fingertips on her chin. "What fun indeed? There must be something amusing about it, the way you two are always out there whenever possible."

Angus assumed a very serious look, like a little man. "Honest, Miss Wallace. Ye widna have a bit o' fun."

"An' that's the honest truth, miss," Elspeth offered softly, although Miranda could tell she was growing increasingly uncomfortable. Best to leave things as they were for today. Getting Elspeth out of the house and into the fresh air was probably the best thing she could do, with the earl arriving and all. Who knew what would happen after that?

Miranda crossed her arms and looked at them sternly. Every once in a while she forced herself to play the governess as the role should be played. "Well, then. You may go, but"— she held up one finger—"I'm giving you an assignment. I want you each to draw and name two fish that you see." She turned around to the cabinet and pulled out two blocks of watercolor paper, a set of paints, two brushes, and a jar. "Fetch a clean rag from Mrs. Wooten or your mother, Angus. Be back no later than five o'clock. The guests should be arriving around four, and I'm sure you won't be called for until at least six, Elspeth."

Her eyes rounded in horror. "D'ye think he'll call for me, Miss Wallace?"

"Of course I do."

"But I thought . . . I thought . . ." She couldn't seem to get the words out. "All those bonnie ladies, an' aw."

Miranda got down on one knee and held the girl to herself. "You have nothing to be ashamed about. Do you hear me?"

"But ma face . . . an' . . . I'm no' a Youngblood. No' really."

"It isn't your fault that you were born on the wrong side of the blanket, Elspeth. You mind that. And mind this as well: if someone is incapable of looking beyond your outward appearance to the real Elspeth inside, then you don't want to bother yourself with them!"

"Aye!" Angus piped up. "Mother says ye have a bonnie soul, Miss Elspeth, an' if ye want ma tuppence worth, there's nothin' in this world bonnier than that!"

Miranda ruffled his hair. "Listen to the lad, Elspeth. For he is wise beyond his years. Go now. Fetch some food from the kitchens as well, and remember, five o'clock."

Angus took Elspeth's hand and led her from the room. "I'll look after ye, Elspeth."

Miranda watched them wander down the hallway, went back to her room, and began to pray. She remembered how thankful she had always been that Matthew was there to stick up for her, to think she was wonderful.

"But I get so tired of people staring at me, Mate," she had cried. "They never look me in the eye. Their heads always turn as I'm walking past. How can I bear such unpleasant scrutiny for a lifetime?"

Matthew had held her hands. "Show them your joy, Mira. Show them the love of God. Don't you realize, you have a way of getting people's attention far greater than almost anyone? And when they look at you, help them to see God."

The words had stood her in good stead for years, and she had tried to live by them. Miranda wasn't a Bible scholar like Matthew; she didn't have large portions of the Scriptures memorized like he did either. But she prayed joyfully, gave thanks, and showed God's love as best as she could.

While she lay on her bed, Mrs. Wooten entered the room. She had ceased bothering to knock weeks before. "Good morning, Miss Wallace. I trust you're feeling well? You're not ill, are you?"

Miranda sat up. "Oh no! The children begged to go fishing, and being the soft-hearted individual I am, I let them."

Mrs. Wooten automatically began dusting the dresser. "You're doing a fine job with those two. I'm sure the earl will be quite pleased with Elspeth's progress."

Miranda crossed her legs beneath her skirt, pulled Elspeth's new gown onto her lap, and started to baste the final sleeve. "Do you think he'll take an interest in her at all?"

"No. To be honest, I do not."

"I don't think she really wants him to."

"Maybe not. In any case, it isn't as if he'll be living here. It will probably be best to stay out of his way."

———

David Youngblood sat near the abbey fishponds. He wondered if the children would be coming today as well. What a wonderful week it had been. Miranda Wallace must be a gem to give them a holiday while the house was in such a ruckus. He pulled the small black Bible out of his inner pocket.

He remembered the man he had been less than three months ago. How enjoyable all the trappings of wealth had been. The fine clothes, the rare wines, the delicacies of the palate. Beautiful women would congregate near him, despite his face, in hopes of going home with him, in hopes of a precious bauble he would toss their way once he cast them aside. All this had given him security of sorts.

And now, sitting in the quiet of the hills, he realized that it had all meant nothing. *He* had meant nothing to all of those people. The world was revolving just as it had before. His universe had imploded and nobody really cared. He had nothing. Nothing but the love of a daughter, the affection of a small lad, a crypt for shelter, and a basket of food each day.

I've never felt more free. He opened the Bible and began to read. Remembering how that Matthew Wallace fellow was always quoting from the New Testament during their Oxford days, David had started there. He was already into the book of I John. "If we walk in the light," he began, reading out loud, "as he is in the light—"

"Papa!" Elspeth and Angus were cresting the final hill between the abbey and Greywalls. He stood to his feet and spread his arms open wide.

Chapter ✦ Eight

Well, we should be thankful the engineer was able to stop the train in time!" Lady Daria consoled Tobin, as they sat outside by their railroad car. A large oak tree had fallen on the tracks just north of Perth. The conductor had sent a porter off to the nearest town to hire some help. But right now, the officials were arguing over whether they should chop it up or go back and get a pair of oxen to pull it off. Tobin was getting more out of sorts with each man who felt the need to speak his piece.

"We're not going to get to Greywalls until at least midnight if something doesn't happen soon," he grumbled.

Mr. Dormerthwaite, sitting nearby and casually smoking a cigar, tipped his hat back. "Enjoy it, Youngblood. Bless me, but I relish in the moments when I can do nothing but relax. Normally, I'd feel guiltier than Guy Fawkes, God rest his soul, whiling away the hours like this."

"At least you've got a good cigar," Percy said with envy, looking over at his wife who sat with a scowl on her face. Lady Sharon hated cigars, even outdoors, and she looked in no mood to have her wishes disobeyed by someone like her husband.

Lady Daria kissed Tobin's cheek. "You poor dear. Always in such a hurry to create beauty, you don't appreciate it when it's staring you in the face. Look around you, man! Look at this countryside! It reminds me of the time—"

"Please Daria"—he held up a hand—"no stories. Not now."

Dormerthwaite exhaled a cloud of smoke. "Listen to the lady, m'lord. That stone wall over there"—he pointed to his left— "is worth at least two songs."

Hamish, quiet as usual, piped up. "I agree. You know, this is the first time I've been to Scotland. But it certainly won't be the last."

Daria laughed. "There, you see? We'll have a wonderful time. We'll simply begin the party right here. We need some music."

Percy stood. "What was that song you learned at Harvard, Tobin? From the Negro man?"

Sharon grimaced. "Do sit down, Percy. You're embarrassing me."

Lady Daria clapped. "Oh, but I simply *adore* Negro spirituals. Do sing it, Percy, won't you?"

But Percy sat back down, making eyes at Dormerthwaite's aromatic cigar.

"What about you?" Daria asked Tobin. "Why don't you sing it? Please, darling?"

Tobin felt ridiculous, but there were only a few other passengers who had chosen to exit the train. Even Valentinia herself was not with the group. "Why not?"

"Can you sing it like a Negro?" Daria asked him.

Tobin raised his brows. "I don't know that I've ever really tried to sing like a Negro."

Lady Sharon stood to her feet. "This is quite ridiculous. Why would any of us want to hear a song sung by Negroes? Come, Percy, let's get back on the train."

Percy rolled his eyes, but followed. Long ago Tobin had cast aside any sackcloth and ashes he had ever worn on behalf of his friend. Percy was half as much to blame.

Tobin inhaled through his nose and winked at Dormerthwaite. "'Go, tell it on the mountain. Over the hills and everywhere,'" he began to sing, trying to push his pipes down to an all time low.

Dormerthwaite hurrahed. "I know this one!" And he joined in, his raspy bass blending with Tobin's smooth baritone.

John Clarkson pulled out a harmonica, and looked hopefully at his friend.

"D, A, D, G, D, A, D." Tobin quickly gave him the simple chord progression. Clarkson would figure out the verse on his own.

Red-cheeked and happy, Mrs. Annie Dormerthwaite, a lubberly woman tented by a voluminous black dress and red cheeks, began to clap in time to the music. By the end of the chorus, she was yodeling along with her husband, her great bottom swaying like a pillowed pendulum.

"'While shepherds kept their watching, o'er silent flocks by night,'" Tobin sang the verse alone. No one else seemed to know the verses. Clarkson was playing at the pace of a reel. The mood was buoyant and free of care.

And then the chorus came around again. By the time Tobin had dispatched the last verse, everyone knew the chorus. Not only the Greywalls party, but the rest of the train passengers as well who had congregated near the group.

Annie Dormerthwaite yanked her husband to his feet and they began to dance a merry trot, their feet pounding the grass, their laughs bringing a smile to all who watched. And when they had sung the last "Jesus Christ is born," John transitioned into a rousing Scottish march.

> *"March! March! Eskdale and Liddesdale!*
> *All the blue bonnets are over the border!*
> *Many a banner spread flutters about your head,*
> *Many a crest that is famous in story.*
> *Mount, and make ready, then,*
> *Sons of the mountain glen,*
> *Fight! For your homes and the old Scottish glory!"*

Tobin pulled Daria into his arms and they wheeled around, laughing. He couldn't remember when he'd had this much fun. To feel such liberty, such youth.

As the tree was hauled away to the side of the tracks, and they were instructed to return to their seats, a disappointed protest erupted. When Tobin looked across the moor, now glowing yellow with gorse and the dying day, he felt a sense of destiny take his hand. He examined the golden fields, a halo for the earth itself, feasting his eyes on their beauty as they illumined the way before him.

"They should have been here two hours ago!" Mrs. Wooten thundered, her nerves getting the best of her. She had dusted every polished surface in Greywalls. Three times.

"Oh, oh." Mr. Wooten ducked as she picked up a vase. "I've seen that glint in your eye before, Mrs. Wooten."

Wiping it off, she handed it to Miranda who had just returned with an armful of mums, asters, and heather. "Don't worry, I'm not going to throw anything, Mr. Wooten. I feel like it, though."

The three of them stood near the main entrance to the castle. It was an unassuming entryway, having never been changed from its medieval birth, and so they sought to cheer it up by lighting as many candles as possible. Miranda quickly arranged the flowers for the long table in the great hall where the party would be dining later on that evening.

"The children have yet to return." Worry tickled Miranda's already guilty conscience. "It will be getting dark soon." *What kind of a governess am I anyway?*

"I don't know what poor Pamela is thinking," Mrs. Wooten fretted, oblivious to Miranda's comment. "Her dinner will be ruined, I'm sure."

"Now, you shouldn't be worrying about our Pamela," Mr. Wooten advised. "On her worst days she's a better cook than even the Buckinghams had."

"You're right. Still, this is most distressing!" Mrs. Wooten pulled out her rag and started dusting her husband's spotless collar.

"Mrs. Wooten!" He drew himself up proudly, the quintessential steward. "What, madam, are you doing?"

Mrs. Wooten's mouth opened in horror, and she stopped circling her rag.

Miranda held a hand up to her lips and began to chuckle. Heavens, but she couldn't help it. Watching those two was like observing two blue jays dicker in the treetops. Mr. Wooten yanked once on his lapels, turned sharply on his heel, and walked into the great hall.

"I did it this time," Mrs. Wooten said softly. "Oh, I've really done it this time."

⌐⌐⌐

David Youngblood lit a small fire near the stairs, its ready warmth lifting his spirits further. "It's getting late, I know. But just have a bit of cheese and bread to strengthen you for the walk home."

Elspeth was more than willing to extend their visit, but Angus wasn't so sure. "Maw's goin' ta make mincemeat o' me if I dinna get hame soon."

"*Amo, amas, amat*," Elspeth began.

Angus looked up and crossed his arms. "Och, go on, then. But just for a wee while, Miss Elspeth. Ye know how Miss Wallace'll get aw fretful. I dinna want ta have her mytherin' over us!"

"*Amamus, amatis, amant!*" Youngblood finished the conjugation with a laugh. Angus was beat and by the lad's expression, it was clear he knew it.

But fifteen minutes later, having refused all offers of food, Angus stood his ground. "Miss Elspeth, I've no better pal than ye, but I'm leavin' now, wi' or wi'out ye. It's gettin' dark."

Elspeth was about to protest, but Youngblood laid a light hand on her shoulder. "Be a good lass," was all he said. He knew the child would obey.

David handed the pair their sketch pads, one containing a picture of a perch, the other a brown trout. He'd done the outlines himself and let them do the painting. They were rather good, he had to admit, even Angus's, which ended up looking something like a squirrel the way he got so carried away with the upper portion of the fish's tail. Elspeth's work was beautiful. It seemed she inherited the artistic sensitivities, and hopefully not the artistic *insensitivities*, of his side of the family.

He watched as they headed out of the ruins, fishing poles resting on their shoulders, sketch pads tucked tightly under their arms. These two children were having a miraculous effect on him, to be sure, and autumn wasn't over. And yet, the nights were growing colder, and he knew he could not stay in this haven of tranquility forever.

Miranda hurried across the bailey and out through the great gatehouse of the outer palisades. The inner wall that had divided the inner bailey from the outer bailey had been demolished a hundred years before, when another Lord Youngblood decided to put in a track to run his thoroughbreds. But now the grass had grown back in place, and it was a wide expanse between the keep and drawbridge. It was evident by its design that Greywalls had been built by an Englishman, with its vast palisades and dry moat.

The sky possessed very little color now, and the smell of the fires in the village did much to mellow the darkness. Miranda, while never having been much afraid of the dark, nevertheless preferred taking her walks in the sunlight. She could see by the bent vegetation the direction the children had taken, and was puzzled when she realized they weren't headed to the stream. Of course, she reasoned, she wasn't an expert on the lands surrounding

Greywalls, and Angus probably knew the area well. There were probably scads of streams.

She strode on, deciding that she wouldn't allow another fishing excursion for quite a while! Not that they ever brought home any fish. Goodness, but she hadn't been prepared for children's complete ability to make no sense whatsoever! Even Mate hadn't been this mysterious as a child. But she pictured their faces when they were in the schoolroom, heads together, so eager to learn, and she knew she would forgive them anything.

The moor seemed to lengthen beneath her feet, and thanks to the light of a full moon she was still able to follow their trail. Fifteen minutes passed, then twenty, and she quickened her pace as the night temperature plunged below comfortable.

"Elspeth!" she cried, hand cupped to her mouth. "Angus!"

She heard a small cry over the crest of a hill. Picking up her skirts, she ran forward. "Here we are," Elspeth was shouting. "We're over here!"

Finally, Miranda could see the pair. Elspeth was standing, helpless and crying, and Angus lay on the ground.

CHAPTER ✧ NINE

W hat happened?" Miranda asked, breathing in hard and fast from her exertion.

"Dinna ken, Miss Wallace. We were walkin' home when aw of a sudden he said he didna feel aw that good, an' then he just fainted clean away. No' two minutes afore ye came."

Miranda knelt down beside the lad. "Angus?" She stroked his forehead. No response. She became more insistent. "Angus! Wake up. Can you hear me?" She patted the boy on his cheeks and chest, took his hands and rubbed them between her own, then shook his arms. "It's growing too cold for him to be out here like this. Go get some water from the burn, Elspeth. We'll try to revive him that way."

"Wha' burn, Miss Wallace? There's no burn around fer a mile." Then, realizing what she had said, Elspeth put her hand up to her mouth.

Miranda allowed her anger to show. "You've got a lot of explaining to do."

"Let me," another voice dove into the scene, and Miranda could hardly believe it when a silhouette belonging to David Youngblood fell across the moonlight.

"All right then." Miranda's concern for Angus far outweighed her surprise at the sight of the renegade nobleman. "But get him to shelter as you talk. From the looks of you, my lord, you have a lot more to talk about than these two children."

"As you wish." David scooped up the lad and held him tightly to his chest.

"Where are we going?" Miranda asked, and David told her about the abbey ruins. "There's a small burn near there. We'll try and revive him by the fish ponds."

"An' he *is* breathin'!" Elspeth piped up with false optimism.

"So, you've been hiding yourself there, eh?" Miranda kept up with him step for step. "Things are making more sense now."

"I had to tell her I was still alive," David said without apology. "When Angus told me how distraught she was, how she couldn't be tempted even with Mrs. MacDowell's trifle, I knew I could not let her believe me dead any longer."

Miranda took Angus's limp hand, shaking it as she walked along. She conceded to Youngblood's course of action. "Yes, you did the right thing."

The abbey came into view and the three fishponds, each leading into the other, latticed by the bright moonlight. David Youngblood knelt down with Angus in his arms, while Miranda cupped her hands and dug them into the cool, dark liquid. It came down with a wet slap onto Angus's face, and he sputtered as his eyes cracked open to slits. "Wha . . . ?" he breathed, then his eyes opened further, and realization that all was not as it should be pounced upon him. Then, seeing Miranda and David Youngblood, he muttered, "Och, jings . . ."

Miranda kept on her governess face, although she wanted desperately to laugh from relief as well as from humor. "Are you all right?"

He sat up in David's lap. "Wha' happened?"

"You fainted!" Elspeth cried. "It was terrible! One minute we were walkin' back ta Greywalls, an' the next, ye were doon on the ground!"

"I can mind feelin' awfu' hungry an' dizzy, an' then ... weel, I canna mind anythin' after that."

Miranda helped him to his feet. "Can you walk?"

"Aye." The little boy nodded. "But I'm no' feelin' so grand now, Miss Wallace."

"Come then." She put a hand out for each child. "We'll get you home and into bed. You both have worried enough people for one day."

David Youngblood stepped forward, looking thinner than when she had last seen him, but obviously fed. He pulled a book out of his pocket. "I have a feeling this is yours," he said softly. "I apologize if it was taken without your consent, as I fear it must have been."

"My little Bible! I wondered what had happened to it!" Miranda had chalked its disappearance up to her own carelessness. She turned to Elspeth. "That was in my nightstand, wasn't it, Elspeth?"

"I'm sorry, Miss. It's just tha' ye were talkin' aboot man not livin' just by bread, but by God's holy Word, an' I knew ma da needed help, an' I knew tha' he'd need a copy o' the Scriptures. I couldna ask ye or ye'd know why I needed it."

Miranda felt rebuked, even though the girl shouldn't have gone into her things without permission. David still held out the book. She pushed it back toward him. "Keep it, my lord," she whispered, remembering the man's reputation, and all men's need for a Savior no matter how sullied or unsullied their past was. "I trust it is giving you much comfort."

"Oh yes, it is." David's answer surprised her greatly. "Your brother and I had many discussions regarding the Scriptures during our days at Oxford. Mostly my trying to tear it apart. But all these years later, those talks have come back to haunt me . . . in a benevolent way." His eyes spoke that something was indeed happening inside of him, and he wasn't quite sure what it was.

"It has always stood me in good stead." Miranda suddenly felt awkward and stiff, cursing the doubt that flowered in her mind. She couldn't imagine a man of his morals finding peace from God's Word. In her own heart, she had written this man off years ago, doubting if even God would go to such trouble for a headstrong sinner like David Youngblood. Apparently, he would, and once again she was reminded how far she had yet to go in her mission to be more like her Savior. "Come, children." She began to walk forward. David's slight touch on her arm stopped her.

"Will you keep my secret?"

Miranda stared into his eyes, lit to a silver gray in the moonlight. "I want to come back to talk to you before I promise anything. And I want to hear the truth from you. All of it."

"Come back whenever you like."

"Can I come an' aw?" Elspeth cried, obviously delighted at this turn of events.

Miranda couldn't help but smile. How could she deny these two people the only comfort they truly had in life right now? "Yes, you may. Now then, let us be off. The party should be here by now, and they'll be wondering what has become of us."

"A party?" David Youngblood asked.

"Yes. The new earl, your uncle, is bringing some guests to Greywalls. It's truly put the staff in a dither!" she laughed.

David became solemn, his gaze searching her face and coming to rest on her birthmark. "He's a good man, Tobin is. A hard fellow to understand at first. Don't judge him too harshly if he doesn't treat you like he should."

Miranda's hand shot up involuntarily to her cheek. She quickly lowered it, faced with the blatant physical imperfections of the man before him. "Why, my lord, it isn't up to me to judge him at all. Good night, then."

"Just a moment. Let me get Angus something to eat along the way." He ran down into the crypt and emerged a minute later with a hunk of bread. "It isn't much, but with those spindly legs of yours, Angus, I believe you need all the help you can get!"

Angus obviously knew better than to refuse the snack this time.

They started forward again, and this time weren't detained. "It will be eight o'clock soon," Miranda stated. "Hopefully they'll be sitting down to dinner when we get there. That way we can sneak in. Do you understand that what you've been doing has been deceitful?" She turned to each of the children, Angus's cheeks becoming an alarming shade of bright red. "I'm truly disappointed in both of you. For each lie you've told me, you'll scrub one floor."

"Aye, Miss Wallace," Angus said softly, as if his heart was breaking. "Will ye tell ma maw?"

Miranda shook her head. "No. But you will, Angus."

"Aw, come on, Miss—"

"No, no, Angus. You must be brave. It is the way with sin. Making up for it is so much more difficult than withstanding it. You might remember it next time." She knew she sounded preachy, matronly even, but she just didn't care. She wasn't about to let one of these "teachable moments" pass them by. Come to think of it, it was what she was paid for.

"Aye, miss." He breathed in quick gulps of air, trying not to cry.

"And as for you, Miss Elspeth," Miranda said sternly, "you will not only scrub the floors, but you will write a ten-page essay on the worst possible outcomes of your lies."

Elspeth must have known better than to argue, for she merely nodded her head. "I'm awfu' sorry, Miss Wallace. I'm sorry for lying ta ye."

Miranda stopped and turned Elspeth to face her. "Child, it didn't hurt me so badly that you lied to me. We are all human, and I understand that you and I, and everyone under the sky, will sin. It's why Jesus died for us. What hurts my heart is that you wouldn't trust me with the truth about your father."

"I've known aboot this from the start!" Angus wailed, the truth spilling out of his mouth. "I was wi' his lordship the night o' the slayin's! I've been takin' his food ta him aw these months."

"Does your mother know this?" Miranda asked.

"Nay, miss. But wifie Wooten does. Although I probably shouldna be tellin' ye tha'. I'm sorry, Miss Wallace. I didna mean ta hurt ye. I'd never want ta do tha'."

Miranda threw her arms around him and held him close. "I love you in my heart, Angus, and I love you in the Lord. You've disappointed me, but I understand you were thrown into a situation in which no little boy your age should be."

"I promise I willna lie ta ye agin!" he gushed, hugging her neck tightly.

"No, lad," she whispered. "Don't promise me that. It's better not to promise at all than to break it later on down the road. Just assure me you'll try your hardest to always be honest with me."

The lad pulled back, tears of remorse streaming down his face. "Aw right, miss. An' I'll even do the great hall as one o' my rooms ta scrub."

Miranda laughed and pulled the two children into her arms. They were so warm, so real, so sweet. She knew that God had given them to each other. "I'm glad you're all right. Why do you think you fainted like that?"

"I was fair hungry, miss! I havena eaten' anythin' aw day! It's been a day like tha'! Miss Elspeth sayin' 'Angus, go here. Angus, go there.'" He rolled his eyes as though he were married to her.

Miranda laughed out loud.

They began walking again. Miranda was surprised when the moon was quickly shuttered by a front of clouds. "Let's hurry on then, children. It feels like rain."

"I'm so tired, Miss Wallace." Angus's breathing was getting heavy.

"I know, lad. As soon as we get home I'll get you something good to eat."

And so they stepped up their pace. But half a mile from Greywalls the clouds gave way beneath the weight of a mighty downpour. In no time their clothes were filled with rain. But just as quickly as it had come, the rain stopped. Laughing at the frightful sight they made, they hurried toward the gatehouse and the warm fires of the kitchen.

The house was quite a sight. All was in apparent readiness for the guests. Large lanterns swung on iron posts, the breeze strong enough to catch them up in its arms. A large wreath of purple heather hung in welcome on the door.

The three of them gasped at the peculiar loveliness of the scene, the wind doing its best to make it one of movement and dance. Miranda almost wished she could be one of the arriving guests. It would be a most welcomed sight for them after such a long journey from London.

"Listen!" Angus cried. "I hear somethin' comin' up the rood."

Elspeth gasped. "Maybees it's them! I canna see anything for the darkness."

"I don't know who else it would be. Let's hurry, children."

They began to cross the drawbridge, but the carriage was closer than anyone had thought, the wind distorting the distance of the sound.

"Watch it!" the driver yelled, and Miranda tugged Elspeth out of the way. But she lost her footing, and they all went tumbling down, legs over heads, into the dry moat, which was no longer dry, but muddy and slippery.

"Oh, dear!" she cried, picking herself and the children up. Angus and Elspeth, obviously unhurt, were already picking up handfuls of mud and slinging them at each other. "Out of the ditch now, please," she ordered. And they were all no worse for the wear as they climbed out of the trench, losing their footing half a dozen times.

Another carriage came rolling along, and Miranda was thankful for the darkness that hid them from the occupants. The house party had arrived, and there was nothing for them to do but follow in the carriages' path. She had to get these children out of their wet clothes. Some hot tea would be nice for all concerned.

Hoping to go into the back entrance of the keep, Miranda quickly ushered the children away from the main entrance.

"Excuse me!" someone yelled, pointing in their direction. Miranda ground to a stop and looked his way. The man's face was heavy with exhaustion. "What do you want here?"

"I—" Miranda began.

"Oh, Tobin, I know you're tired," a red-haired woman interrupted, "but they're just beggars. Leave them be. They might be going to the kitchen to get a bit of food."

Miranda felt herself stiffen, and the contrary side to her nature stood up to be counted. "I am Miss Wallace." She walked forward, propelling the children with her. They all looked ridiculous, so muddy and wet, and the lantern light did little to pretty them up. "This is your niece, Elspeth, and Angus, her friend. And we were out walking in the rain." Miranda felt the children press their bodies closely against her. And no wonder, the frown on that man's face was enough to put anybody off!

She raised her chin and her eyes met the earl's. She didn't mean to be defiant. In fact, she had meant to soften things so as to pave a smooth way for Elspeth, but she couldn't help it. There he stood in his beautiful clothes with a stunning woman on his arm who, apparently, was more gracious than he was. To be certain, he was a handsome sort outwardly with his auburn curls and the Youngblood eyes ringed with exhaustion. She couldn't vouch for his spirit, but she could certainly wager a very educated guess, that his insides didn't match his outsides. To be given so much only to use it thus, Miranda thought, was downright shameful!

He shook his head, averting his eyes from her frosty stare. "Get into some warm clothes. Those children will catch cold, Miss Wallace." His voice was stern and lacking patience.

And he turned on his heel, and strode into the keep.

"Nice to meet you as well, my lord! I'm sure Elspeth must feel the same way!" she felt like shouting, feeling her birthmark tingle with the heat of anger. But the door to the castle was closing.

Really, Miranda thought. *What a boor!* The first time he is confronted with his niece and that was the best he could do? Terrible. Absolutely terrible! Inexcusable, in fact. But it wouldn't do to show her frustration to the children. She pasted a sweet smile on her face, feeling extremely false-hearted.

"Come along, children. Let's go in and have a nice warm bath, and then, well, I'm sure your mother will make us oatmeal with lots of sugar and cream, Angus."

"An' a lovely wee cuppa for ye, miss!" Elspeth chirped, oblivious to the fact that she had been slighted.

CHAPTER ❖ TEN

And this, my lord, is your bedchamber. Legend has it that Robert the Bruce, William Wallace, *and* Bonnie Prince Charlie all slept here." Mrs. Wooten whipped out her dust rag, then put it back into her pocket with a self-conscious laugh.

"Good heavens, Mrs. Wooten." Tobin looked around him at the masculine wood-paneled room. "They'd all be furious that an Englishman has come to stay in their bed."

He was trying to be pleasant, but it was proving more difficult by the minute. It wasn't that he didn't appreciate the woman's pleasantries. Normally, he'd be thrilled to hear the lore of the house, but all he wanted was a hot bath and some peace and quiet.

"Postpone dinner for an hour, if you would." He knew his order would give the cook cause for a fit, but realized there wasn't any possible way he could face the group just yet. "We'll eat at ten."

Mrs. Wooten closed her eyes briefly, then nodded. "Yes, my lord."

"That bath will be drawn shortly?"

"Right away, sir. I've arranged for a valet for you during your stay. He's in the dressing closet putting away your things. Charlie!" she called. "Come meet his lordship."

Tobin repressed the distinct need to shake his head in dismay. A slender young man, prematurely gray and only as tall as Mrs. Wooten, entered the room and bowed with respect. The necessary introductions were made and when the valet said, "Your bath is ready, sir, and your evening clothes are laid out," Tobin knew he and the fellow would get along just fine.

And so it was that he found himself alone and in the bath. The warm water was soothing, but he was troubled. Daria had been distancing herself the past few days. They had been subtle maneuvers, to be sure. Ignoring his hand on their walk, not kissing him good-bye on the cheek in her usually friendly manner, taking Valentinia with them everywhere they went.

Not that he didn't like Valentinia. How could one not like the child? Sweet and compliant and quiet, she was a weak man's dream and a threat to no woman. She was pretty enough, quite lovely actually, if you liked downcast eyes and perfect hair. It certainly was strange the way he had found himself alone with her on more than one occasion. He had come to Daria's townhouse for tea three days earlier, and ended up chatting with Valentinia the entire time. The girl was intelligent, it seemed, if you could get her comfortable enough to open up her mouth so wide as to let her thoughts flow out. Well, he reasoned, after having to sit with her most of the way from Perth, he had the right to sandwich himself right between Mrs. Dormerthwaite and Daria during dinner. And speaking of dinner, he was quite hungry. Why in the world had he postponed the meal until ten? Never mind, there was time now for a quick nap.

As he fell asleep, he remembered his great-niece, standing there covered with mud. And the governess as well. Half of her face looked as if it had collided with a bowl of raspberries. Not much else to see about her, unfortunately. Too dark. And who on earth was that skinny little boy, again? Was he responsible for that urchin as well?

Now Elspeth was another matter altogether. He had no idea she'd inherited her father's physical shortcomings to such a grotesque degree. Well, the fact was, she was just a child, and he certainly wasn't expected to take her under his wing in any way but a financial one. She'd be up in the nursery with that Miss Wallace most of the time, thank goodness. With the way her father was, she was lucky she hadn't ended up on the street!

Tobin didn't know how to handle himself around those less fortunate. He found he laughed at the wrong things, or worse, stared in a curious horror at the malformation. It would be best to simply keep Elspeth away from the guests. Why subject the child to humiliation? Besides, a woman like Lady Sharon would have no mercy.

He'd have to talk with this Miss Wallace tonight before supper. And with that decision made, he fell asleep.

⌒

"Pardon me?" Miranda felt extremely tired. It was late by her standards, and the poor guests were still fifteen minutes away from eating. "I don't believe I heard you correctly."

The new earl of Cannock sat before her on the library sofa, eyes unreadable. "I believe you did, Miss Wallace." His eyes slowly scanned her face, then stopped to rest on her birthmark. "I said I wish for the child to stay cloistered out of sight for the next three days during the party."

How could he be so blatant about his distaste regarding Elspeth? Best play ignorant. She opened her eyes wide and smiled. Her smile, she knew, would have been quite fetching without her blemish to detract from it, and she flashed her straight white teeth. "Oh, I assure you, my lord, Elspeth is an extremely well-behaved young girl. She wouldn't cause a fuss. I could guarantee you that."

He briefly looked at the floor. "I would have expected a wild streak in her, being the daughter of my nephew."

"Oh no, sir! She's quite docile, a lamb really. And so intelligent!"

"Well, that's no surprise. Her father is a genius. A *diabolical* genius apparently, but a genius nonetheless. I'm not sure I can trust her. Not yet."

He seemed too relieved about the excuse. Miranda decided to push his lordship a bit. "Well, there's only one way to find out if she is able to behave well in a social setting. And the sooner the better, I'd say."

"How do you mean?"

She crossed her arms and paced before his sofa. It was impossible not to notice what a handsome man he was with his wavy chestnut hair and those round, deep eyes. His brows were thick, but arched and well-defined. Yet it was his hands that truly caught her attention. The hands of a musician, she thought, suddenly piqued at the mental diversion from the topic at hand. "You hold the keys to Elspeth's future."

He nodded. "Yes. She came along with the title, I suppose."

And so caring too. "Well, my lord, by inviting Elspeth down to visit with the guests, you will be administering the ultimate test. If she comes and behaves herself, then obviously she is willing to try and be the niece she ought to be. If she doesn't come down, well, then you've got nothing to worry about."

"What if she comes and makes a scene?"

"I tell you, Elspeth isn't the type. And if she does, I promise to be nearby and will take her out of the room immediately."

His eyes flickered, and she stopped pacing, looking straight into his eyes. "She's just a young girl, my lord. She needs a family."

He stood to his feet and shook the creases out of his pant legs. Or tried to. "I think you've rather had much too much to say about this matter, Miss Wallace."

Miranda realized that the tales of his arrogance were not unfounded. And she had never seen someone more visibly uncomfortable. Or rumpled. She could hardly believe he had just put on that suit! "Oh, my lord, do forgive me. But I feel as if I have been placed here to be Miss Elspeth's advocate. She has no one, really, and she was obviously given to you by God—"

"Is that so?"

"Why, yes, it is. Doesn't God give us all good things?"

His brow uncreased and he casually sat back down on the sofa. "Yes, he does, Miss Wallace. I've always found that to be the case. But what of the bad things? The things that some people are forced to bear through no actions of themselves?"

"Like Elspeth?" She wasn't willing to be impertinent, but was quite willing to turn his own remark around on him. "Or . . . me?"

He was clearly uncomfortable, playing suddenly with David Youngblood's packet of cigarette papers that had been sitting on the table where he left them long ago. "Well, yes."

"Do you remember the story of Joseph? How his brothers sold him into slavery . . . a very bad thing done through no fault of his own."

"He was an arrogant little devil, though!" Tobin declared.

"Through no *great* fault of his own," she corrected. "And he ended up saving the entire nation of Israel from starvation when a massive famine struck the land."

"Yes, I know. But what does that have to do with you? Or Elspeth?" His eyes rested on her birthmark again.

Miranda felt her face go hot and covered her cheek with her hand, but she continued bravely. "Had I been a more attractive woman, no doubt I would be married by now, and would have forfeited many wonderful chances to serve God."

"Isn't serving a husband a worthy calling, honored by God?"

"Of course. But I need more than that, perhaps. Or less. Only God knows which." Miranda had conversed with herself many times along these same lines.

"Is it worth it, then?" He threw the rolling papers down beside him.

"It has to be, doesn't it? And on the days when it is not, I make it so. You shouldn't smoke these things." She picked up the rolling papers. "They smell up the house, your clothes, everything."

"I don't smoke them." His eyes widened with a glimmer of grudging admiration. "Where do you come from, Miss Wallace, with all your lofty opinions and ideas?"

"Leeds is where I grew up. But I was recently in Bath. Swainswick actually."

"And you believe God brought you here? To serve him?"

"Yes, my lord, I do. Do you serve God?" she asked, unafraid of being so bold. The man needed her right now. Finding another governess would be a great deal of trouble. "Do you love him?"

He looked into her eyes, and the haughtiness faded, leaving behind a human being. "I do. Not as much as I ought, Miss Wallace. And there are many areas in which I am a constant disappointment to my Creator."

"Aren't we all that way, though?" She was still unsure as to his true spiritual state. Did he really know the Savior, or just want to? "If we were perfect, Jesus' death wouldn't have been necessary."

Someone burst into the study just then, an extraordinary-looking woman, a woman like none Miranda had ever seen. Her red hair flamed in large loose ringlets around her face, and she was dressed in a breathtaking evening ensemble of gold and purple. It was made in a gypsy styling, with large loose sleeves, a laced bodice, and a patched skirt. The patches were embroidered with gems and pearls, and below the billows of petticoat underneath, a golden, jewel-encrusted slipper peeped out. Oh yes, the woman who had defended them by the main entrance.

"I've heard a vicious rumor that supper is almost ready! You know what they say about Scottish cooking," the woman laughed, suddenly realizing she was interrupting. "Oh, dear. Forgive me. I thought to find his lordship, and—"

"Don't be silly, Daria," the earl said. "Miss Wallace and I were just finishing up here, weren't we? Miss Wallace, this is Lady Daria Christopher, a very good friend of mine."

"Miss Wallace! But you must be the governess Tobin told me about!"

Apparently the woman thought everything was cause for jubilation. "Yes, my lady, I am governess to Miss Elspeth."

"Of course! I haven't met the child yet, but if she's anything like her father . . ."

The earl took Miranda's arm and began leading her to the door. "Miss Wallace assures me she's not, other than she obviously shares his malformation."

"Well, thank goodness she's tame." The pretty mouth spoke with a bit of a pout. "But I did always like David, deformity and all! People's shortcomings have never bothered me, even your birthmark, Miss Wallace. Although I'm sure it bothers you greatly. Actually, it goes quite well with my ensemble. Perhaps we should trade gowns! I've never dressed up as a governess before."

The earl breathed in sharply.

Miranda tried to explain, setting down the rolling papers. "Actually, Lady Christopher, it doesn't really—"

"Yes, well, Daria," the earl interrupted, fiddling with his coat button, "we're finished our discussion, so good Miss Wallace can get some sleep."

Daria plopped down on the sofa and picked up the rolling papers. "Then you should be thankful for her, Tobin. She's taken on a great responsibility, raising a deformed child and all. Will we be meeting the girl?"

"That's what we were discussing," Tobin admitted. "I thought it best not to bring her down."

Daria sighed, suddenly looking bored and somewhat tired. "Perhaps you're right." She wrinkled her nose at Miranda. "She'll put a damper on things, you know. Not for me personally, mind you. But Percy's wife, Lady Sharon, now there's a real corker! She'll make mincemeat of the child in one glance."

Miranda had to respect the woman's honesty, if not her opinion. She turned and walked through the door. The earl followed. "I'd like a final word," he said.

"Of course, sir. You *are* the lord of the manor." Miranda knew she was being disrespectful, but she also knew he deserved it. She prayed her tongue wouldn't get the better of her.

"I hope you understand my decision."

She refused to look at him, choosing to focus on his tie instead. "You know I don't. You know I can't."

He spread his hands wide. "What would you have me do? I cannot force her on my guests and expect them to have a good time."

"Then you might stop and consider just why these people are your friends? Or, you might stop and consider if you are really being honest. Is it really about your guests, or it is about you and what you can and cannot tolerate. I've heard you are a great lover of beauty."

He leaned against the door frame and scraped a hand through his hair, but said nothing.

Miranda continued, "I know we're not the most beautiful creatures, Elspeth and I. And if my heart doesn't ache for myself, it surely does for her. I've worked all week on a gown for her reception by her uncle. She's never worn such finery, my lord. It's a beautiful gown, I assure you."

"I'm certain it is." His voice was soft.

"You don't have to be beautiful to create beauty."

"I'm sorry."

Miranda looked up in his eyes then, wanting to feel anger, but feeling only pity. "I am sorry too, my lord. Sorry for you, that your soul is so shallow it can only receive what comes in through your eyes and your ears." She gathered her skirts in her hand. "I will do as you ask and pray that God would teach you to listen with your heart. Good night, then." She turned and began down the corridor.

"Miss Wallace," he called, but she picked up her skirts and quickly made for the stairs.

CHAPTER ❖ ELEVEN

Pamela's meal was now but a memory. Most of the guests praved over the spiced squash soup, stuffed pheasant, buttered potatoes, apple ragout, and breads accompanied by various delicious relishes and chutneys. Dessert was an affair of its own, with mince tartlets, a chocolate torte, and a brandied custard. Lady Sharon's grudging admission that it was an adequate spread did more to let Tobin know the dinner was a success than all the highly audible "bless me's" and sighs of contentment being blown across the table by the Dormerthwaites.

"Would anyone want to join me up in the library for some games?" He stood up. After that nap he had enjoyed earlier, he was far from ready for bed.

Percy jumped to his feet. "I could keep myself awake for a few hands of whist."

"You'll do no such thing!" Lady Sharon said crisply, not bothering to pick up her napkin which slid to the floor as she stood. "We're retiring now. Come along."

"Count me out." Clarkson pushed out his chair and followed suit. "I'm exhausted. All that harmonica playing."

Mrs. Dormerthwaite took her husband's hand. "I believe I'm ready to retire. What of you, Mr. Dormerthwaite?" She winked at him slowly and a saucy smile spread on her lips.

He shot to his feet. "No cards for me tonight!" he cried in an excited voice that echoed against the rafters of the room. "We'll say our good nights, then. Good night." Tobin wanted to laugh out loud. He'd always heard the Highland air was good for matters of the heart. Apparently, it was true.

"Valentinia?" Daria patted her daughter's hand. "What of you? You're such a good backgammon player, I'm sure you could win handily against his lordship."

And so it was he found himself together with Lady Valentinia in the library, Daria and Hamish having both pleaded exhaustion. He began to set out the game pieces. This wasn't exactly how he had planned to end the evening, but he didn't want to hurt the girl's feelings.

"Don't bother." Valentinia sat down at the game table. "I actually don't like backgammon much."

Tobin looked up in surprise. It was the first time he'd heard Daria's daughter utter an opinion contrary to her mother's. "But your mother said you did well at the game."

"I do. But it's *her* game, not mine. I'm much more interested in cards."

He laughed and pulled out a deck from the thin drawer of the card table. This was certainly a new side to the girl. "What then? Whist?"

"Oh no!" She reached for the deck. "Poker. Aces wild."

"Poker!" he chuckled. "Where did a young woman like you learn that game?" He pulled a container of chips from the shelf behind him.

She shuffled like a pro. "I have some friends in the theatre Mother knows nothing about. I learned the game from an American actor. Do you know how to play?"

He sat down opposite her and cracked his knuckles. "Used to play at Harvard."

"I'll deal." The cards slid out from her fingers, landing in neat piles.

"You surprise me, Valentinia."

"Call me Val." She rearranged her cards in her hand.

"*Val?*"

"Yes. Valentinia is such a Daria name. Val is what my friends call me. I think the shorter name suits me better. Mind if I smoke?" She reached far behind her to the end table and skimmed off David Youngblood's rolling papers.

Tobin could hardly believe his eyes. "I don't have any tobacco."

"That's all right." She opened the drawstring on her evening bag and pulled out a pouch of sweet-smelling tobacco. Her deft fingers proceeded to roll a thin cigarette.

"Does your mother know you smoke?"

"Of course not. She doesn't know much about me at all, my lord. It's such a Daria way to be. Oblivious, that is. I'm surprised you didn't catch onto me years ago."

"*Years* ago? You're only seventeen, Valentinia."

She looked at him harshly.

"I mean *Val*."

Lighting the smoke, she inhaled deeply. "That's better. I'm so glad the others went to bed. Except for Hamish. I've had my eye on him for quite a while now."

"*Hamish?*" When would the surprises stop? "I take it you met him while with your theatre crowd."

"Yup."

Yup? This girl was a shock a minute! "Have you spent much time with him?"

She merely pouted at him. "There wouldn't be enough hours in the day to spend with a man like Hamish. But Mother has other ideas. Of course."

"Naturally. I'll take two," he said, pointing to the deck and sliding his discards across the table. In the course of three minutes, Valentinia Christopher had gone from saint to siren.

She exchanged the cards. "And I'm taking one."

"Well, you must have been lucky."

Her smile, just above the cards, was mature and almost seductive. "I'm always lucky, my lord."

"Yes, well." He cleared his throat, dreading the next surprise. "That seems only natural."

She flipped open the case of chips. "So, do you want to really gamble or just play for fun?"

Trying to picture Daria's face if she knew what was going on, he said, "Just for fun. I'd be a cad to call in for money on a seventeen-year-old girl."

"Woman," she corrected him. "I'm not the little girl Mother thinks I am."

"And why are you showing this side to me now, Valentinia?"

"*Val!*"

"Val. Aren't you afraid I might go back to your mother and tell her everything?"

She divided the chips evenly between them. "Oh, no. I've known you for years, my lord. You'd never do anything like that. But believe me, I've got a reason for telling you all of this. You need to know who I really am before you hear Mother's proposition. You start the bidding. I'll keep score."

"What proposition?" He set his cards down and threw a white chip on the table.

"Only one chip? My, my, mustn't believe in that hand. I'll see your one and raise you five. A marriage proposition."

"I'll see your five and raise you ten." He wouldn't be outmaneuvered by a child! "So your mother has finally begun to come around. I've been trying to get her to marry me for years, you know."

"I'll call." She slid over ten chips and took a deep drag from her cigarette. "Yes, I do know. I've been trying to talk her into it myself. It would be nice to have a man about the house. We girls do get lonely. Full house."

"Pair of tens."

"Oooh, goody," she gloated, setting down the smoke in an ashtray and pulling the pile toward her. "Anyway, we'll be glad to have you around, that's for certain."

"And you're worried that I wouldn't want to marry your mother if I knew she had such a wayward daughter?"

"Marry *Mother!* Who said anything about marrying my mother?"

This was confusing. "Well, then, what are you talking about?"

"Mother wants you to marry *me.*"

His head shot up. "What?"

"It's the case, I assure you. Now do calm down and I'll deal another hand."

She sat there so calm, so matter-of-fact. And he felt absolutely dumbfounded. The girl was almost twenty years his junior—age-wise, that was. He guessed now that she could teach him a thing or two in other areas. What could Daria be thinking?

"It really is quite abhorrent to me, if you'd like to know the truth. I know I said all that about having you around the house. But it was true only if you were Mother's man, not mine." She inhaled once more on the cigarette and stubbed it out.

His vanity got the better of him. "*Abhorrent?* Isn't that a little strong?"

"Well, maybe it's overstating it a bit, but the point is the same. May I have a glass of brandy? Even whiskey would be fine."

"No, you may not! Now, I want more of the story. You can't just spring news like this on a man and expect him to swallow it without a few questions in return."

"Go ahead, then." She shook her ringlets back over her shoulders. "I suppose you deserve to know it all."

"When did all this come about?"

"She got the idea soon after you inherited your fortune and your title. At first I was rather agreeable to the situation. You have no idea how horrible it was to be paraded around Almack's like a performing monkey, eating stale orange cake and drinking weak tea."

"You *did* have many offers, didn't you?"

"Oh, yes. But she's turned most of them down, or I have. And with good reason."

He had to admit that was true. "And so she saw me as an acceptable prospect for you."

"Naturally. And you should take it as the highest of compliments. People will settle with far less for themselves than they will for their offspring, you know."

He examined her sitting there, so worldly-wise and self-assured. It was only a matter of time before Val sprang out for good and Valentinia was no more. Poor Daria. "So that is why we've been pushed together so much of late?"

"Yup."

"And you are against it completely. Hence this display this evening."

"Oh, it's no display, I assure you. This is me. This is who you'd get. I thought it only fair to let you know. I won't give up my friends or my activities, and I won't be a dutiful wife—if you know what I mean—and I most certainly won't live up here in these forsaken Highlands." She shuddered. "I cannot get back to London soon enough!"

He looked at her frankly, stopping her when she went to deal another hand. "So, how do we break the news to your mother? You don't want to marry me, and quite honestly, Val, I don't see us as a good match at all."

She sat up very straight. "What do you mean? You don't find me attractive? I know I'm a bit of a libertine, but I assure you, I've always behaved quite proprietously in those delicate areas."

"You mean to tell me you've never taken a lover? I don't believe it."

Her eyes widened in shock. "Of course not! How can you say such things to me?"

So it was true, then. "This *has* all been an act, hasn't it?"

"Well, no. I really do smoke and I really do play cards and I really do—"

"Not want to marry me," he finished, suddenly feeling very sorry for the girl who had dropped her guard and mistakenly laid bare what little innocence was left. "Why, Val? Two months ago you were picking out men at all the balls."

"I wish to marry Hamish." Her eyes challenged him.

"You mean it's gone that far? I never knew you really even were acquainted with him before tonight. You positively ignored each other on the train."

"Precisely. Mother introduced me to him as a friend of yours at Brown's one evening. I caught him down in the theatre district not two days later, and we've been meeting in secret ever since. It's been positively *murder* staying away from each other during this trip." She pulled out another rolling paper and set to work.

He said nothing for a long time, merely sat and watched her as she smoked. It must be terribly difficult for her to have her future be bandied about, and in such an incompetent manner at that! He remembered being that age, a lad who was allowed to make his own choices as far as whom he loved and when. He hated to admit it, but he had been a charmer, and there weren't many women who refused him. Of course, those days were over now. His decision to follow the Savior had changed all that. At times, though, it had been extremely difficult not to yield to the pleasures of the flesh. He'd had some very close calls.

"This is such a Daria thing to do," Valentinia whispered, finishing up her smoke and assaulting the ashtray with the glowing butt. "I'm quite angry with her, you know."

"To be honest, so am I." He took her hand. "Hamish, eh? Truly?"

"Oh, yes. His writing is so brilliant."

"But a man is more than his talent, Val. It's why I've always cared about your mother. She admires me for who I am inside, not just the music I create."

"My lord." She squeezed his hand, then let go. "Hamish is my heart. I cannot imagine life without him. If he never wrote another word, I should still love him."

"Artists can be temperamental. Hard to live with."

She nodded. "Yes."

"Do you want me to talk to your mother about him?"

Her eyes flew open wide. "Heavens, no! Just propose marriage to her, seriously this time. If she accepts you, fine. If she rejects you because she wants you to marry me, you can tell her you'd rather not, and that leaves me free to love Hamish."

"You'll have to tell her someday, Val. Especially if you're planning on marrying the fellow."

She looked down. "Yes, I know. But I'm not ready to yet."

"Your secret is safe with me," he assured her.

"So you're going to propose to Mother?" Her eyes sparkled with mischief once again.

"I guess so," he sighed, wondering for the first time in years if it would be the right thing to do. Daria was more full of antics than he'd realized, and he thought he had seen them all! "You're as bad as your mother when it comes to matchmaking, Val."

She got up from the table and threw her arms around him. "Thank you, my lord. Or shall I say 'Daddy'?"

He laughed as the clock chimed one. "What we should both say is good night."

CHAPTER ❖ TWELVE

With a child to the left and to the right, Miranda set out for the abbey, wondering just what she was going to say to the true earl of Cannock. His reputation was well known, even by the common people of the land. And to think he had murdered Sylvie's parents. Had just aimed a pistol at their heads and pulled the trigger.

She felt Angus's hand in hers, and Elspeth's, and could hardly imagine holding a gun in them, much less holding it up against live flesh and bone. Much less believing that pulling the trigger was anything she had a right to do!

What was in this man's mind? What skewed sense of conscience resided in his brain, tinting reality to a darker shade than normal? Well, something had died within him a long time ago, she was sure. For David Youngblood was anything but normal, anything but able to view life from a proper perspective.

Not to mention his skills at manipulation! He'd ruined Rene de Boyce, for heaven's sake, and extorted the fortunes of who knew how many others? What did she think she was going to accomplish by talking with him? He'd just play her with the skill he'd garnered over years at the gaming tables. Reading her eyes, the hesitation in her voice, each gesture, each word. He'd said he'd been reading her little Bible, but that could have been a ruse as well. A way to make her comfortable with him, then use her to further his plans.

But she had a job to do. Elspeth was her charge and she had to see to her best interest.

She tried to force herself to think on the bright side. He certainly didn't seem to be the monster everyone said he was, and he certainly seemed to be a loving father. Seemed to be. Seemed to be.

That was the problem. David Youngblood seemed to be a lot of things, but no one could really say who he actually was. Not Sylvie, who had loved him more than anyone had before. For he had betrayed even her.

The abbey came into view, and with each footstep toward it her heart filled with dread. She prayed for peace and the words to say. Better people than she had probably confronted David Youngblood. She wasn't going to be the one to change him, that much was certain. Only God could do that. She just had to make sure Elspeth was safe in his presence.

He sat on a windowsill, looking out over the fishponds. He didn't look menacing or brooding. He looked quite safe as he lifted a hand and waved at them.

She waved back, a small, insipid wave.

The children ran forward and jumped up into his arms. He whirled them around and set them down as Miranda stopped in front of him.

"Miss Wallace," he said, after greeting the children, "you came. I'm glad."

"Go ahead and play in the meadow, children," Miranda said. They gladly complied, having already begun a pretend game of Bonnie Prince Charlie and Flora MacDonald.

Miranda, forgetting all the opening lines she had rehearsed, trying not to look afraid or even nervous, handed David a sack of food and some extra blankets. "Here. It's starting to get quite cold at night."

"I've got enough blankets now, though." David's tone was optimistic.

Miranda felt far from optimistic. Nauseous was more like it. "But always being cold does something to your morale, I've found." Stupid thing to say.

"Well, I know a bit of something about bad morale."

Miranda knew she had more to discuss here than morale. She'd always been straightforward, direct. There was no sense in straying from that course now. "My lord, we both know why you're here at the abbey."

"Yes."

"And we both know what happened in France."

"No use trying to defend myself against it. There is no defense for me, really. None at all, Miss Wallace."

"Is it something you'll ever talk about?"

He shook his head. "Not anymore. I am a murderer, Miss Wallace. I admit it. Discussing the details is useless once the confession is known."

Well, at least he was admitting he was wrong. Not that it began to make up for anything. Not that it might even be how he felt. "Some would say it was your deformity that made you like you are."

David Youngblood was looking through the sack of food. Apparently hungry, he pulled out a leg of pheasant and began pulling the meat from the bone in very small pieces. "I've heard that all of my life, it seems," he said.

"I've heard you didn't hail from the most loving of families."

"You've heard correctly. And then, to be born like this." He pointed to his mouth. "But then, you know somewhat of what it is like to be stared at."

"It's about more than being stared at," Miranda said. "I, at least, had the blessing of a loving home. It never mattered what I looked like there, I was always accepted."

"You were indeed blessed, then."

"My parents have always loved God, so it was easier to love me."

"Mine loved only themselves. Even my sister, a lovely girl, never measured up. Although they didn't scorn her as much they did me, they never really cared much about her. We weren't raised really, my sister and I, we simply grew up. And in separate households as well."

"Did you find acceptance from anywhere?" she asked, her heart breaking. He must have been a sweet child, with a mop of curly auburn hair and those large gray eyes. Matthew would tell her that David was playing with her now. But Matthew didn't know what it was like to be rejected for what you look like.

"Not really. Only from Mr. and Mrs. Wooten."

"They're wonderful people. So dedicated to the Lord."

"Yes, they tried to share his Word with me. But I wouldn't listen. I've always been so angry with God at the hand I was dealt."

Miranda could understand that. She had been through it herself. She nodded.

"So you understand that, I see?" he asked.

"Oh, believe me, I do. I remember crying alone in my bed, night after night, staring up at the stars outside my window, and thinking how in heaven's name could God make those beautiful heavenly bodies and make me too. I remember smashing all of my mirrors when I was ten."

"I did the same thing!" David cried. "Only when I was seven."

"From what my brother said, you had no trouble getting the ladies."

He snorted. "It depends on how you define the term 'lady.'"

"I've never had a man really interested in me. Well, that's not true exactly. There were two. But they soon found other prospects."

"I don't know why that's the case. You're a beautiful woman otherwise."

She laughed, not bitterly, but because he could come out and say it so freely. But then, he deserved to. He had paid more than his fair share of dues, and looking at his face, and remembering Elspeth's, she knew she was indeed blessed to have gotten off so lightly. "It's amazing how few people can get by the birthmark, though."

"It will be good for Elspeth to have you with her," he stated. "You'll understand, somewhat."

"Yes. I believe God sent me to her. In fact, I was telling that to your uncle just yesterday."

He was finished with the piece of meat. After looking into the sack once more, he pulled out a thick slab of crusty brown bread. "Care for some?"

Miranda was feeling a bit peckish, and she still didn't think she could eat. She shook her head.

"So you've met Tobin? And how did you like him?"

"It really isn't my place to offer an opinion of my employer." She bent down, picked a blade of grass, and began to dissect it.

He took a bite of his bread. "Oh, come now. It's me you're talking to, the true earl, and a man with a reputation for irreverence as long as Hadrian's Wall. I will take no offense."

Miranda didn't like to share negative opinions, but being in David's company was doing something strange to her. It was as if she felt comfortable for the first time in her life. Here was someone who couldn't secretly look down on her or despise her. Here was someone who couldn't laugh at her face and be justified in doing so. "Well, if he's anything like the rest of your family, it isn't a wonder you chose to live in France all of those years."

"I was kicked out of the house. I *had* to go to France."

"You would have ended up there eventually, I'll warrant."

He smiled, and it was beautiful and gruesome at the same time. "You're probably right. England was stifling me."

"Perhaps you could have used a bit *more* stifling in some areas."

He saddened. "You know, all my life I searched for acceptance and love. And one day, I found it. Do you know who loved me like that first? Who never stared at my mouth with dismay, or kept an iron lock on my eyes to keep from looking down?"

"Sylvie?"

Miranda was shocked when tears filled his eyes. "And I destroyed it. And for what? Money? Power? I do not even understand it myself anymore."

This was the real David Youngblood coming through. Miranda knew it somehow. Knew there was no manipulation going on here, only truth. "Sometimes we get caught along in a flow of events."

"I wish I could claim it was that. It would be easy enough. The fact is, having money made me feel good. I could buy joy. I could buy friendship. I could buy love."

"Joy is possible to buy, but only temporarily," she said. "Friendship can be bought, but only in the form of companionship. As far as love is concerned, I don't think it can ever be bought, no matter who is selling and who is buying."

Youngblood pulled out an apple, then took a penknife out of his pocket and sliced into the crispy fruit. "The funny thing about it is, I've got nothing left. I've destroyed my life, and I've never felt more at peace. It's as if God has pulled me away and has given me only himself."

"That's true. But he's showing you his love in many ways, even now." She thought of the children who had been visiting him with startling regularity.

David's eyes misted again. "When I think of all the years I wasted, away from Elspeth . . ."

"And Angus's admiration for you is genuine."

Almost as if on cue, Angus looked up and waved, his wide smile practically dividing all the freckles on his face in two.

He smiled and waved. "Yes, it is. The boy, I would swear, is really an angel sent down to all of us frail specimens of humanity. He's a beautiful child, and yet he loves being here with Elspeth and me in all our ugliness."

"Angus has one very divine quality in particular," Miranda stated. "He looks on the heart, and sees a person's beauty there."

"How I wish someone would have done that for me years ago. But that is all water under the bridge. I can only go on from here. But where?"

Miranda wondered how far he had read in her Bible. "God will show you. Especially if you're reading his Word. I've found wonderful insights in the book of Proverbs."

His eyes lit up. "Oh, yes. To be sure. Now Solomon is someone I can relate with a bit. All of those women!"

"How far have you read?"

"The entire thing," he proclaimed.

"Already? How so?" She'd heard of hungering and thirsting after righteousness, but this was amazing. Especially considering it was David Youngblood, of all people!

"I've nothing else to do. As I said, God has brought me out here."

"Then"—Miranda hesitated somewhat—"have you given yourself to him?"

David shook his head. "Not yet. All the terrible things I've done . . . Miss Wallace, when I search deep in my heart, I still see the black and terrible monster clawing to break free. I feel him there, and it frightens me. I no more deserve God's goodness and forgiveness than Judas himself."

"Oh, but that's not true!" Miranda took his hand. "Don't you see that forgiveness is the very point of salvation? God forgives more easily and more readily than you or I ever will. It's cheating him to assign him our grudging ways."

"I know all that in my head, Miss Wallace. Accepting it is another matter altogether."

Elspeth and Angus came running in, their cheeks reddened by the crisp breeze blowing over the sunsoaked moors. "Papa!" she cried as he jumped down, throwing her arms around his neck though they had parted company only ten minutes before. "I love it here."

He returned the hug, then helped Miranda down from the sill. "I'm glad, Bethie. But it's time you should be going. Miss Wallace was good enough to bring you here, but she said you could only stay a little while."

"Oh." Elspeth's voice dropped down an octave in disappointment. She turned to Miranda. "Can we come again tomorrow?"

"I don't know why not!" Miranda straightened her skirts. "After all, the house party is going on, and we want to stay out of the grown-ups' way."

David Youngblood's eyes darkened. "Run along, Elspeth. Miss Wallace will catch up to you shortly. May I have a quick word?" he asked Miranda as they strolled out of the ruins. He took her arm.

"Of course." Miranda liked the feel of his strong hand around her wrist.

"Was it an order? Staying out of the guests' way?"

"Yes." She wished she could reverse time for just a minute to come up with a more plausible excuse. As it was, she could only answer him truthfully. It was his daughter, after all.

"My uncle's order?"

"Yes."

Youngblood cursed. "Forgive my language. I just wanted life to be different for Elspeth. I can't blame Tobin entirely. If I had been the man I should have been . . ."

Miranda put her hand over his. "I won't let him hurt her. I promise."

"For some reason, I believe you when you say that." David lifted her hand to his mouth, then dropped it. "You were sent here by God, after all."

"Yes, I most certainly was." She turned and left him, walking quickly up the hill. His lonely, gray eyes haunted the vision of her mind.

⌒—

"Sylvie! Matthew!" Miranda picked up her skirts and ran across the bailey to where her brother and sister-in-law were alighting from the carriage. "You've come for the party?"

Matthew reddened in embarrassment. "Yes, being married to a countess and all. Not quite the normal function for a simple country parson."

Miranda laughed at her brother's description of himself. Matthew could never be described as a simple *anything*.

"Ex-countess," Sylvie corrected, pulling Miranda into an embrace. "We've only been married two months, and I already have him trained to perfection! It's so good to be back home," she breathed.

"I've missed you." Miranda pulled away. "And now you're here at Greywalls. I have to tell you they had a dreadfully calm night last night. You didn't miss a thing. They arrived late, ate at ten, and went to bed."

Matthew pulled his lovely young bride close to his side. "Sounds good to me!"

Sylvie chuckled. "He's a bad boy, your brother. I do not know how you put up with him for so long!"

"I bless the day you took him off my hands, Sylvie," Miranda joked.

Matthew looked wounded, his dark hair blowing unruly in the wind. "It's nice to know my company is so much in demand."

They were at the front steps now, and Miranda knew she was supposed to be keeping out of sight of the guests. Matthew would be furious if he knew, and so she kept the matter to herself. The last thing Tobin Youngblood needed was a black eye from her brother. On the other hand, it might just do him good.

"I must see to the children's supper in the kitchen." Miranda excused herself. "You go on in, I'm going round back."

Sylvie looked disappointed. "You mean you won't be down tonight? How terrible."

Matthew stiffened, instantly suspicious. "What's this all about, Mira?"

Miranda tried to laugh naturally. "You must remember that I'm just a governess now. One that must keep her charge from the festivities. Unfortunately, everyone expects her to be a female miniature of her father!"

Sylvie looked down.

"I'm sorry," Miranda said. "I didn't mean to mention him. It just popped out." This was ridiculous! Keeping all this a secret from the people she loved the most, from the people that truly deserved to know.

Matthew waved a hand. "Don't fret, Mira. Sylvie's coming to terms with it all a little more each day. Aren't you, my love?"

Sylvie nodded.

"Do you think you will ever come to forgive him?" Miranda asked, hating the way she sounded so genuine, when she knew she was being as manipulative as David Youngblood had once been. She just hated to see these two people, David and Sylvie, suffer so.

"What does it matter?" Sylvie shrugged. "David Youngblood is dead. And what's done is done. I cannot bring my family back . . . or him."

"I'm sorry," Miranda said. "Would you bring him back if you could?"

Nodding, Sylvie took the handkerchief offered to her by her husband and dabbed her eyes. "The heartbreaking part of the matter is, I truly loved David. Not like I do Matthew. But his act was such a betrayal, I often wonder if I will ever get over it completely. Unless he crawls back to me from the grave and begs my forgiveness, I doubt if it all will truly leave me."

"He just wanted you for himself," Miranda said.

"I am not a woman to be owned," Sylvie declared, sounding more like her old self than she had since the night of the shootings.

"That's my girl." Matthew patted her between the shoulder blades. "You have a right to feel sore."

Sylvie tried to brighten up. "Let's save the melancholy for another day. It's my first supper party in ages, and I want to enjoy myself."

They walked in through the door for perfect people, and Miranda went around to the back.

CHAPTER ❖ THIRTEEN

Tobin looked at himself in the mirror and didn't at all like what he saw. It bothered him that he couldn't reach out to his niece. It bothered him that he had been so rude to the governess. And yet, he couldn't do anything about any of it right now. The order of the day was a marriage proposal. Here it was almost seven o'clock, and he had yet to get Daria off by herself. After much mindful deliberation last night, he decided that yes, Daria would be a good match for him. She understood his temperamental ways, his strange working hours, the fact that he would practically kill himself trying to get to pen and paper before a melody was lost. Daria understood all of this and more. He wasn't getting any younger, and he certainly didn't wish to die alone. Besides, if you couldn't marry your heart's ultimate love, then surely your best friend was a close second.

The party had been going splendidly so far. After a morning of shooting with the other men, they all joined with the women in the drawing room for a cozy, fireside breakfast. The sausages were fresh and so were the eggs. Mrs. Dormerthwaite declared that a ride would be lovely, and so they found themselves on horseback, riding over the moors. With an arrogant tilt to her head, Lady Sharon left them all in her dust. Percy had turned to him, breathing a sigh of relief. "Thank heavens she's gone."

They had all laughed.

"Next time, don't tell her where you're going," Hamish ordered his friend.

"Here, here!" Dormerthwaite clapped. "What do you say we turn around and head back? We may get an hour or so to play cards before she realizes we've left her."

"She *was* going off at quite a clip." Percy tapped his riding crop against his thigh. "She'll be furious with me."

Daria poked him in the side with *her* crop. "Sharon is *always* furious with you. You might as well give her a reason to be."

Percy looked as if somebody had hit him over the head. "Good heavens. You are right, Daria. Absolutely right. Let's go, then!"

And so they all turned tail, back to Greywalls. They laughed over backgammon and whist, and to Tobin's delight and Daria's horror, Valentinia suggested poker.

"My dear! A lady doesn't play poker!" Lady Daria gasped.

"But Lord Youngblood taught me, only last night. I don't want to forget."

"Tobin! I know I'm very modern in how I raise this child, but . . . *poker!*"

"I think it's utterly charming." Hamish looked down at his hands.

Daria grimaced. "I don't remember asking your opinion, young man. Tobin, I think we need to talk about this."

"Oh, come now, Daria." He wasn't about to give Valentinia away. "There's nothing to talk about. We were only having a little fun."

The group sat down to the cards and played until Lady Sharon stormed in, her pale, chapped lips bleached by anger to a more startling shade of white.

"What is going on?" she grated.

"Just a few hands of cards, darling!" Daria butted in cheerfully. "Do sit down, Sharon."

She wound the scarf of her riding hat around her forearm. "I will not. Percy, come now. We must change for dinner, whatever the slop set before us tonight!"

"Bless me, but I've enjoyed the food!" Dormerthwaite chortled.

"I seem to remember a verse in the Bible, lovey," Mrs. Dormerthwaite added, "about not casting pearls before swine."

Lady Sharon inhaled sharply. "Are you trying to imply that—"

"I'm not implying anything, love." Mrs. Dormerthwaite smiled boldly as she arranged her hand of cards. She looked Lady Sharon directly in the eye. "I'm saying it outright. For all your fine airs and haughty ways, what with your criticisms and cutting barbs, a pig has more gracious manners and treats those who feed him far more kindly."

"Oh!" Lady Sharon huffed. "Why, you fat, common—"

"That's enough, ladies." Tobin stood to his feet. "Perhaps we should all get ready for the meal."

"Bumpkins!" Lady Sharon whirled around and out the door. Percy followed her, looking alarmingly nauseous.

Clarkson shook his head. "I don't know how he does it. Or even why. Year after year with that woman. The poor man."

Tobin shrugged. "We all make choices, my friend." But his own words did little to comfort him. He had been wanting to take Daria aside, to ask her the biggest of all questions. But she had successfully evaded him all day.

Well, she won't any longer, he thought, up in his room as Charlie put away his riding clothes. He straightened his tie to no real avail, flicked a piece of lint off of his evening coat, and went straight to her chamber.

After a loud knock on his part, Daria's maid answered the door.

"I need to speak to your mistress right away," he ordered.

The girl dropped a curtsy and left him in the hallway. Three seconds later, Val hurried out, one finger to her lips as she disappeared, obviously on her way to a secret rendezvous with Hamish. Finally, Daria appeared, dressed in a velvet gown of white. On her head was a halo of glittering, jeweled stars.

"You look angelic." He wondered just what she would come up with next. To Daria, it seemed, every party was a costume party.

"Thank you, Tobin. Now, what is all this fuss about? Appearing here at my chamber door and all ... well, it just isn't your normal bill of fare."

"We have to talk and the sooner we do so, the better it will be for all of us. Would you like a candy?" He pulled a butterscotch out of his pocket.

She took the candy and popped it into her mouth. "Oh, lovely, yes. I do love butterscotch." She wrapped the satin ribbon of a small evening bag around her wrist as she walked beside him. "I'm still a bit upset with you over that poker tutoring session."

"I must ask you to forgive me, then. You know how it is with Val ... entinia, Daria."

That Daria didn't bother to ask what he meant spoke the truth of what Valentinia had been saying. "Well," she pouted, "I suppose it will be all right. At least we know she won't be sneaking off with a group of cardsharps!"

Tobin wanted to howl with laughter, but he didn't. Instead, he showed Daria through a back passage and led her into the chilly garden. The last thing he wanted was for someone to overhear his conversation ... in case she turned him down. Which was a definite possibility!

The moor was misty, and the moon was a fuzzy orb, out of focus and ethereal. He took her hand and led her to a fountain of Pan playing his pipes. "You've got to stop being so obvious, my dear," he said with a chuckle to soften the coming accusation. "Did you really think I'd fall for it?"

She took a sudden interest in the fountain. "I don't know what you're talking about, Tobin."

"Oh, yes, you do, Daria. You know perfectly well. I've spent more time with your daughter in the last three days than I have since I've known the both of you. Now, I believe you have a confession to make, and you might as well be straightforward about it."

Daria crossed her arms to form a warming X over her bosom, refusing to look at him. "I *still* don't know what you are talking about."

He laughed. "Going to be difficult, are we? I had a hunch you would be. Let me spell it out for you, then. I don't wish to marry your daughter, Daria."

"Why ever not," she said, becoming defensive, forgetting her feigned ignorance, forgetting her interest in the cold water near her feet. Her hands slapped onto her hips. "Valentinia is a lovely girl. She'll make a wonderful wife!"

Tobin gently led her to a nearby bench and laid his arm across her shoulder. "For someone else, Daria. What, in heaven's name, gave you such an idea!"

She shrugged. "I don't know. I was lying in my bed one night . . . the night you brought me those fresh muffins, and I thought it was such a sweet thing to do. I thought then, what a perfectly lovely husband you'd make. How could I be so selfish to take you for myself, when Valentinia needs a man like you?"

He put both of his arms around her and looked down into the sweet, beautiful face he'd come to know so well, the face of his good friend and companion of years. "You're a silly woman, Daria, standing there looking like an angel, and talking like one too. You once said you'd marry me if I was a rich man. Well, I am a rich man now." He slid off the seat, bent down on his knee, and bowed his head for several seconds as his mind formed the words.

"Oh, do get up, Tobin!" Daria cried, pulling him up by handfuls of hair. "This is ridiculous! Down on one knee. Heavens!"

"Ouch! Stop that, Daria." But he remained on his knee. "Will you marry me, Daria? Really?"

"I'm not in love with you, you know," she said honestly. "I love you, but I don't get that delicious feeling in my stomach when I'm with you."

He stood to his feet and grinned. "Well, to be honest, you don't do that for me either."

"And, although I've never told you this before, I'm past the stage of giving you an heir."

He considered that for a fraction of a second and decided his second cousin Charles was truly the man for the job. "There are more than enough Youngbloods to go around, Daria. What do you say? We enjoy being together, we like the same foods, the same music, the same plays, the same operas . . . we both adore parades and flower shows."

"A match made in heaven?" she asked, trying not to laugh.

He winked. "Well, let's not go that far! What do you say, old girl?"

She tapped a finger against her chin for several seconds, then smiled. "All right, then. But I want a grand wedding, Tobin. I want loud, grand music, flowers galore, and I want a wedding gown that will set the tongues of London wagging for years!"

He pulled her to her feet. "Somehow, I don't think that is something you'll have to try very hard to do!"

"And I want the reception to be a masquerade ball! No stodgy old wedding breakfast for us!" Her round eyes were blazing with newfound excitement.

Tobin laughed and hugged her to him. So dear, she really was so dear to him. "I can't believe you even entertained the idea of marrying me off to Valentinia."

"I know," she chuckled, not moving from the circle of his arms.

"There are a lot of roles I'm capable of, my dear, but being your son-in-law is not one of them."

Daria pulled back and began laughing uproariously. "My son-in-law! Oh dear, Tobin. If I had thought of it in those terms, I should have cast aside the idea immediately. How ridiculous I am."

"Not ridiculous, my dear. Charming."

She placed her hands on his shoulders and smiled an endearing, lopsided grin.

"Shall we seal our engagement with a kiss?" he asked, knowing it was probably the right thing to do.

Daria put out her hand. "For some reason, darling, I think we should just shake on it."

The kitchen brigade was taking in their nightly ritual much later these days due to the party. But no one wanted to forsake the warm, homey time by the fire.

"I declare," Mrs. Wooten sighed, putting her feet up on an old ottoman. "I'd forgotten what a lot of work these house parties in the country can be. Poor Pamela"—she patted the cook's knee—"I'm sure you've cooked more in the last week than you have since you took on the post three years ago."

Pamela nodded, then took a bite of bread and butter sprinkled with sugar. "Weel, it's true enough. For so long it was just the staff up here, until the late Lord Youngblood took up residence. We were taken aback at that. But, Mrs. Wooten, we were glad ta be put ta use. Most of us onyway."

Mr. Wooten cleared his throat and scratched hard at his left eyebrow. "The two footmen were rather upset at our arrival, I daresay. You would have thought I had requested they run ten miles backwards when I told them we were going to polish up all the silver!"

James MacDowell was busy carving the fine details in a small, ornate pediment for a music cabinet the new earl had requested. "'Tis an honor to be doin' such fine carvin' an' cabinetry. Ma fingers have been itchin' for such a task for a long time."

"Well, there was muckle work needed ta the ootbuildin's," Pamela reminded him. "An' ye did that weel."

Miranda thought she'd find out a bit more about the very intriguing David Youngblood. "The last earl, what was he like, Mrs. Wooten, as a child?"

The strain on Mrs. Wooten's face immediately softened. "He was a lovely boy. Tried so hard to please his parents, until he was about ten. It was then he realized that not only did they not love him, they despised him."

"Och, that's awfu'!" Pamela gasped.

Mrs. Wooten agreed. "Mr. Wooten and I were busy with our own brood, and I always regretted I didn't have more time for the lad than I did."

"You loved the boy well, Mrs. Wooten," said her husband. "He knew it, and he loved you in return."

"But my love wasn't enough to save him. He started to gain his terrible reputation when he turned sixteen. Got in all sorts of fights and brawls, and to make matters worse, he was an excellent fighter. I don't know how he learned to be so resourceful with his fists, but he was always stronger, better than the other lads. Finally the teasing stopped, but he was never accepted into respectable social circles."

Pamela shook her head sadly. "I guess he never learnt the difference 'tween earnin' respect an' demandin' it."

"How could he?" Mrs. Wooten defended him. "Born like that, he never had a chance of being respected any other way."

"And then to die so tragically," Mr. Wooten added sincerely.

Miranda was quite surprised that the housekeeper had kept her secret even from her husband. "I don't agree with you, I'm afraid. From what I saw of the man, his intelligence, his

135

strength, and even his capacity to love, I'd say he could do wonderful things. I'd say he could earn the respect of the nation."

Mrs. Wooten looked at her sharply, but only got up to pour herself another cup of tea. "I prayed for him for years, you know. When I think of the sinners that have been saved by God's grace, I always had hope for him."

"That's right, Mrs. Wooten," Mr. Wooten agreed, "the power of God can do amazing things, things which we can hardly believe."

"And the softening of a hardened heart is the chief of miracles," Miranda said. "It no longer surprises me when I hear of folks being healed, or dire circumstances straightening out. I take for granted the changing of the seasons, and the sun rising and setting each day. But when I hear of a hardened sinner falling to his knees before God in true repentance, I am filled with awe and am assured once again that the Lord I serve is indeed a great and mighty God."

"Amen!" Pamela rocked softly in her chair. "It's fair true, Miss Wallace. God changes hearts every day, but when we hear tell o' it, we rejoice."

James MacDowell set down his chisel. "The angels hold nothin' o'er us. There's nothin' so bonnie as hearin' o' a sinner washed in the blood o' the lamb."

A bell from upstairs began to ring with a vengeance. Lady Sharon. Of course.

Mrs. Wooten barked an irritable, "For the love of all that's decent, what's she want now?"

Lady Sharon had already become the open sore in the staff's collective foot. It seemed she had a talent for ruining a good time, even when she wasn't in the room.

The gathering broke up as Mrs. Wooten, who had already sent all the housemaids off to bed, groaned to her feet and left the room. Miranda followed her up the steps but kept ascending to the top floor. A very light snow was falling, nothing that would last for long, she knew, but her thoughts turned to David Youngblood, alone in the abbey on such a cold night.

Her heart grieved for him, and she lifted her face in prayer to the Maker of all, beautiful, plain, or ugly. She felt a closeness to the nobleman as she had never felt with another man. She felt comfortable in his presence. She felt accepted and understood. Miranda prayed for David until her fire died and the room grew cold.

CHAPTER ✦ FOURTEEN

D o ye really think I look beautiful?" Elspeth's soft gray eyes shone in the lamplight of Miranda's room. It was the night of the ball, the night that they had both been looking forward to, the night when Elspeth would wear the most beautiful dress she had ever owned, a dress she never thought would adorn the likes of a girl like her. "Do ye really think I look bonnie?"

No wonder her eyes were shining. Miranda fastened the last button on the rose-colored gown she had been working on after hours in the presence of the kitchen brigade. "Yes. And I have to admit, this is quite the loveliest little gown I've ever made." It was the best handwork she'd ever done, the flowers a play of texture and color that could only be described as masterful.

"Where did ye learn ta sew like tha'?" The girl fingered a long, walnut ringlet that sprouted with several others from a coordinating ribbon.

"My mother taught me. She said it's good to have a skill you can always count on. 'You never know where life might take you,' she always said." She began to tie the sash.

"Do ye think ye can teach me ta sew like tha'?"

"I was planning on it!" Miranda answered, making perfect loops of satin and pulling them taut. "In fact, I had a length of wool delivered just the other day from my father's mills. It's soft and the color of sweet cream. We're going to make a cloak for you."

"A real fine lassie's cloak?" Elspeth's voice was full of wonder.

"Oh, yes." She turned her charge to face her, inspecting the getup with a critical eye and deciding her creation was good. "We're going to embroider the yoke too, with black silk frills. You'll be the talk of the church!" Miranda watched closely for her reaction to the last sentence.

"Kirk, Miss Wallace?"

"Yes. In Huntly. You remember my brother, don't you?"

"Course. The man with the feisty eyes an' the sunny smile. I liked him weel enough. An' he liked me an' aw, I think."

Miranda chuckled and began hanging up the child's everyday gown. "Well, it's time we ventured out on Sundays, don't you think? Together."

"Do ye think it will be aw right?" Elspeth looked fearful.

"I'll never let go of your hand. You'll see. There are lovely people in the church there. They'll be glad to see another person come to worship the Lord. And you do sing so prettily, Elspeth. A voice such as yours is always welcomed."

"Can I wait 'til the cloak is finished? An' will ye put a fine deep hood on it?"

Miranda nodded.

"An' may I keep ma hood up, even inside?"

Miranda nodded again, and pulled the child in a close embrace.

A muffled voice, unmistakably female, interrupted the silence. "May I come in?"

In the doorway stood what appeared to be a knight with a chain mail hauberk, and a steel helmet with intricate carving along the mouth guard. Over the hauberk was a white, sleeveless tunic with a red cross.

"Enter into our chamber, Joan of Arc!" Miranda invited in a "hark thou" voice and a flourish and a bow.

Elspeth began to laugh hysterically as another equally shrouded head appeared around the corner. The head of a fierce dragon.

The dragon roared a gravelly "Rhrrrrgh," then spoke as if horribly offended, the voice more civilized than usual. "Joan of Arc? My dear woman, that is none other than St. George him— I mean, *her*self!" The dark blue eyes visible through the wide, round nostrils could only belong to Matthew Wallace.

Miranda had expected no less of her brother and his wife. Suddenly the drab little schoolroom became a storybook land as newlyweds entered gauntlet in claw.

"And what is going on here?" Sylvie asked as she lifted off the helmet. Her usually glorious waves were scraped back into a tight bun. Even Miranda had to admit the hairdo did her little justice. But Sylvie seemed as comfortable with herself as ever.

"We're just getting ready for the ball," Miranda explained. "Not that we're going to the main festivities, but we've got a lot planned."

"Such as?" Matthew pulled off the comical papier-mâché mask.

Elspeth jumped right in. In the past two days, Sylvie and Matthew had been up to the nursery several times. They had dubbed her their honorary niece and had shown the girl so much kindness and love in such a short time, Elspeth had already placed her heart next to theirs. "First off, we're goin' up ta the top o' the barbican ta watch the guests arrive. Then we'll sneak across the inner bailey in these great big, black cloaks we found in an old trunk in one o' the storage rooms."

Sylvie raised her brows and elbowed Matthew in the ribs. "Sounds like more fun than we're going to have."

"But that's not aw. Mrs. MacDowell is packin' us a wee piece, wi' chicken an' aw, an' we're puttin' it up where the pipes for the organ are. We're goin' ta watch the ball from behind the screen."

"Until your bedtime," Miranda reminded her, feeling very spinsterly as she said the words. "Or, maybe a *bit* later." And that was even *more* spinsterly.

Matthew scooped out his pocket watch from the folds of his costume. "It's time you should both be going if you're going to catch the grand entrance of the local gentry!"

Elspeth wasted no time in grabbing the old cloaks laid out neatly on the bed. "Hurry, Miss Wallace! We dinna want ta miss anything."

"This ball has been the talk of the town for the past three days," Sylvie informed them. "The church is all abuzz with the news. Some of the more prominent members of the congregation are coming, hence"—she kicked at the inside of her skirts—"my decision not to wear hose! I'm sure Saint George would be mortified to know I am impersonating him while wearing a skirt."

"Oh, I don't know, my love," Matthew quipped, "they all wore robes back then anyway."

"What's young Angus doing tonight?" Sylvie asked as they descended the stairs. "I thought surely he'd be joining in on your festivities."

"He's helpin' ta serve the night," Elspeth said.

"That's right," Miranda agreed. "All hands on deck."

Sylvie kissed them both before sliding her helm back over her head. "I'll look up to the screen behind the organ every so often and wave," she promised.

"So shall I," Matthew said. "Or I may breathe fire in your direction."

"Oh, please, no!" Miranda chuckled. "We wouldn't want you to melt the pipes!"

Miranda and Elspeth hurried further down the spiral staircase and out into the dark night. As expected, the previous night's snow was already gone, and it was actually quite mild. Looking like characters in a gothic novel, they raced across the courtyard, the cloaks flapping around them. Already they were giggling uncontrollably at the melodrama of it all, but neither felt foolish, only adventuresome.

"Did ye bring the spyglass?" Elspeth asked, once they were settled on top of the great stone wall of the inner bailey. They were crouched low, their faces peeping in between the crenellations.

"Yes. In fact, I brought one for each of us." Miranda slid one from either pocket of her skirt and handed a fancy white one to Elspeth. "What luck to have found these in that trunk with the cloaks. I wouldn't be surprised if you have a pirate ancestor or two, Captain Youngblood."

The first carriage rolled through the gatehouse, and the procession began. Six large torches lit the entryway, and it was easy to see each of the guests as they alighted from their vehicles.

"Let's count them," Elspeth suggested.

"And let's keep track of how many Cleopatras, Marie Antoinettes, and Queen Elizabeths there are!"

Actually, the group was a bit more creative than they expected. There was only one Marie Antoinette and not a Cleopatra or a Queen Elizabeth to be found. Among their favorites were David and Goliath, Chanticleer, and a couple dressed as a pair of dice. He was dressed totally in black, she completely in white, and atop their heads were two large, cube-shaped hats complete with the appropriate markings. It wasn't a masked ball, but it didn't matter, really, for Miranda and Elspeth didn't know anybody anyway. "Probably a good thing," Miranda said. "That way it won't ruin it for us. You know how it is with those who are contrary, no matter what they do, or how lovely they look, their personality spoils it!"

"Wha' I widna give ta be bonnie like tha' lassie there." Elspeth pointed to a replica of William the Conqueror's wife, Matilda.

"Me too." Miranda focused her spyglass, then laughed. "I love the way she has that copy of the Bayeux Tapestry wrapped around her neck!"

"I ken. I'll bet the real Matilda felt like doing tha' at times an' aw! I canna imagine sewin' those wee men and the same shields an' helmets, day after day."

"She loved her husband dearly, Elspeth, and wanted to honor him with the work of her hands."

The spyglass was still glued to Elspeth's eye. "Like we should honor God."

"Exactly. 'Whatever thou findest to do, do it with all thy might,'" she quoted.

"So, the Lord can be glorified in the smallest, most menial of tasks."

"That is the case. Even the most wonderful of accomplishments are mostly made up of day-to-day duties, consistently carried out, faithfully executed." It was a lesson Miranda needed to remember herself, she realized. "Matilda wasn't perfect, though. She put her son Robert, a ne'er-do-well if there ever was one, before her husband." Might as well put in a little history lesson.

"Och, look!" Elspeth pointed, clearly taking in nothing Miranda was saying. "There's the last o' the carriages."

They were delighted when a Little Miss Muffet and a very tall, skinny brown spider emerged.

The music from the hired musicians began spilling forth into the chilly air, and so the ball began. Elspeth didn't wish to miss a moment. "C'mon, Miss Wallace, we'd better fly, just like we said we would!"

Miranda agreed, and they climbed down off the wall by a set of narrow stairs. It wasn't long before, goodie basket in hand, they entered the loft where the pipes were kept.

From below, local musicians played on fiddle, pipe, harp, flute, and drum. Reel after reel echoed down in the great hall, candles and torches blazed, and the guests were dancing with abandon.

"Now this"—Miranda reached into the basket for a tea biscuit—"is what I call a successful party. My mother always measured her party's success by how many smiles she could count at one time!"

Elspeth's eyes couldn't be dragged from the view before her. She was enraptured with the spectacle, mesmerized by a scene she couldn't possibly imagine being part of, Miranda supposed. "Were ye allowed ta go ta the parties at your grand hoose?" Elspeth asked, obviously remembering Miranda's tales of growing up as the daughter of a wealthy woolen mill owner in the city of Leeds.

"Oh, yes! Matthew and I were always present until eleven. But we'd sneak in behind the plants near the service entrance to the ballroom and watch from there."

"Did ye never get caught?"

Miranda chuckled. "No. Although, now that I'm older, I'm sure Mama knew we were there. Parents *do* have eyes in the back of their head, you know."

When "Lily Bolero" began to play, she jumped to her feet. "It's ma best tune, Miss Wallace! Can we dance, now, please?"

"You and I? Right here?"

"Aye. Right at this minute, if ye please?" Her lovely eyes pleaded, and Miranda would have no sooner turned her down than she would have pronounced it was bedtime.

"All right then." She climbed to her feet. "May I have this dance, Miss Elspeth?" She bowed.

Elspeth curtsied sweetly. "Ye certainly can, Miss Wallace!"

And they joined hands and began to jump softly around, their feet skipping in circles. The music was happy and lilting with a strong one-two rhythm. The drum beat forcefully; the flute played joyfully and quickly in rapid triplets. On and on, it swept them into its harmonies, and they danced with more abandon as the song wore on.

And Miranda began to laugh. She threw back her head, feeling her usual inhibitions slide away with the ending of each phrase. This was fun. Wonderful, innocent fun. And looking down into Elspeth's face, so free and full of joy, made her feet pound harder and her laughter more raucous. She was free to dance wildly, without being conscious of who she was and what she looked like.

A movement caught the corner of her eye as they circled around, their hands joined together. A throat was cleared.

Miranda stopped. Elspeth practically fell, but caught herself.

"My lord." Miranda smoothed her skirts. When had the music died?

He cleared his throat again. "The meaning of this, please?" His eyes didn't move from Miranda's face. He completely ignored his niece, who shuffled uncomfortably next to Miranda. She felt the girl's hand go into hers.

Miranda stood at an intersection, a choice to be made regarding importance. Was it more important to be ingratiating toward her employer, or was it more important to take a stand for Elspeth? There really was no choice. "We didn't wish for the dress to go to waste."

He was clearly puzzled.

Miranda fingered the puffy sleeve. "We spent hours on this dress for this very evening, m'lord."

Lord Tobin still refused to look at Elspeth. The beauty of the gown was wasted on him, this supposed lover of beauty.

"Do you see the dress?" Miranda asked, keeping her voice at a calm level. "Do you even care to?"

"You were causing a ruckus. I will not have my guests disturbed," he said. "Back to your quarters immediately."

Miranda knew she had made her point and merely responded with a respectful, "As you wish, my lord."

"I will not be disobeyed again." He turned on his heel and was gone.

The music continued. A new song with a tune fiery and wild. Miranda felt her face flush to a deep red. Embarrassment, anger, and indignation filled her like hot air into a balloon. But Elspeth held a hand up in front of her mouth, her shoulders hunched in amusement. "Just goes ta show ye, Miss Wallace, some people dinna ken how ta have fun!"

"Let's go back, Bethie. It's time for bed, anyway." She took Elspeth's hand and led her down the hallway to her room.

Disobeyed. Who did that man think he was, anyway?

Elspeth slipped her hand into Miranda's as they entered the girl's small chamber. "Even if I *do* get into bother, it was worth it." She turned to face her teacher. "It was a braw night, Miss Wallace. I never thought I would see the like in aw ma born days. Thank ye."

Miranda shoved back the tears. "It was worth it to me too."

And it was. Just to see the happy abandon on her charge's face was worth it all. Still, she wasn't looking forward to the morning. Not even one bit. *I'll have to spend a lot of time in prayer tonight*, she thought, knowing if she didn't, her temper would probably get the better of her. Unfortunately, she knew she'd probably fall asleep as soon as the pillow caught her head.

They knelt down together, and Elspeth folded her hands, closed her eyes, and began to pray. "Dear Lord in heaven," she began, her voice growing stronger with each word. "I pray for Miss Wallace, and I pray that his lordship winna be too angry with her so that she will stay here with me at Greywalls. Bless Papa an' Angus an' the MacDowells an' the Wootens. Amen."

Elspeth climbed into bed and Miranda tucked the sheet and eiderdown close to her chin. "You're a lovely child, Bethie. I'm glad God brought us together."

"Me an' aw, Miss Wallace."

"I thank God every day for you."

The girl smiled and patted her hand. "No' half so much as I thank him for ye."

Miranda kissed her on the cheek, turned down the lamp, and quickly retreated to her room. The incident had upset her far more than Elspeth could have realized. Far more. She felt humiliated and shamed, and she couldn't begin to fathom how Tobin Youngblood could be so callous, so cold.

Now David Youngblood was another man altogether. She had never seen a father so tender with his daughter. He was a man who understood all too well that people weren't perfect, that they needed love and warmth and a chance to prove themselves. Elspeth had so much to give, and that snooty Londoner wasn't even willing to stop for a moment to see what a gem was hidden within Greywalls. What boorishness! What ... cheek! Really!

Right then, Miranda Wallace couldn't get far enough away from the likes of a self-absorbed prig like Lord Tobin Youngblood. She yanked open the door of her wardrobe and pulled out her cloak.

CHAPTER ❖ FIFTEEN

*Y*ou *have got to be one of the most boorish, selfish men that has ever* *existed! She's just a child, and that governess is only trying to do* *her job.* Tobin berated himself. He didn't completely understand what was happening to him. Achieving status and wealth in so short a time had turned him into a true Youngblood, and he didn't like it one bit.

"I thought I was above that," he confessed to Clarkson later that night.

The ball was finally over and they were sitting before the fire in the library, drinking a pot of tea. The sun was due in a few short hours, and he would have to face the formidable governess. He had to admire her courage. And her forthrightness. There was no guessing with Miss Wallace.

"It's understandable, Tobin," Clarkson assured him. "Most men wouldn't be able to bear up under such a reversal of fortune."

"I'm not most men."

"That's what we all say."

That was true enough.

"In any case," Clarkson continued, "the bulk of us are leaving tomorrow, and you won't have to worry about what other people think. Is the child so deformed?"

"It's heartbreaking."

"Ahh." Clarkson filled up his cup again. "Then she needs my prayers. Life is tough enough when you *don't* stand out."

Tobin agreed. "It's so hard for me to reach out to people that aren't—"

"Like you?" Clarkson finished. "And yet, you entertain all sorts of abhorrent qualities in people."

"What do you mean?"

"Take your new betrothed, for instance. Her fashion sense is downright kooky, Tobin. She respects no man or woman and plays with her daughter's life as if it is a chess piece—but she's beautiful. Percy, while fun to be with, is a coward, unable to stand up to Lady Sharon—but he's dashing and handsome. Hamish is a self-flagellating, weak man who relies on others to further his cause—but he's comely."

"And what of you?" Tobin asked, not unkindly.

"Although I am a man of average face, hardly beautiful, we make music. And, I suppose that is enough for you. Now, if I was deformed, I wonder if you'd spend so much time at St. Martin's in the Field?"

It was honesty, pure honesty, and Tobin knew it and respected it. "You're right. I'd like to think it wouldn't be so, but I cannot say for sure. I've searched for beauty all of my life and have found it in many ways. But the quest has become more important than the meaning. How did it ever get this way?"

Clarkson added a small amount of sugar to his cup and stirred thoughtfully. "It's not for me to say, really."

"Yet God is the creator of all beauty. The ills and deformities of this world are a direct result of the Fall." He picked up the tattered pack of rolling papers and ruffled through the leaves.

Clarkson nodded. "And yet, wouldn't you say it's an even more difficult, more glorious, more *divine* task to create beauty from offensiveness?"

"Of course. You are right."

"You must give the child a chance, Tobin. God has placed her in your path."

"But she shouldn't be my responsibility! She's illegitimate, for heaven's sake! It was her own father's irresponsibility and, yes, evilness, that has put her in my path."

"All the more reason for you to reach out to her. She didn't ask to be born." He rushed on. "I know it isn't easy, but you cannot turn your back on her while you are in this house. Or the governess either, for that matter."

"The governess?"

Clarkson nodded. "I've seen her with the child, out while I was walking. She's lonely too."

Tobin had never been lonely. Not really. In fact, at times he rather enjoyed solitude. "She's coming to meet with me this morning. I'm certain she'll be furious."

"Don't forget, you're the ruler of this household. I doubt if she'll give you much trouble. Besides, she appears to be a woman with a good deal of circumspection."

"Not like Daria!" Tobin joked.

"Definitely not like Daria. And who knows what kind of good company the two of them will turn out to be?"

Tobin couldn't imagine a Highland girl who had never been out in public and a spinster governess as good company. "Well, I am here to finish up my piece. I won't be able to expend too much time."

"Every journey starts with the first step," Clarkson said. "Open up your heart."

And therein, Tobin realized, lay the real problem.

"I'm sorry for getting your daughter into such a situation," Miranda apologized, stifling a yawn. Dawn would soon arrive and she knew she should be heading back to Greywalls, but the thought of facing Lord Tobin hardly encouraged her to leave St. Ninian's and its inhabitant, who was a far more engaging, accepting companion.

Half of David's face was lit by a shaft of moonlight shining through the barren tracery of a window. They sat together in what was once the cloister. "I'm glad she had such fun beforehand, though. Do you think she realized what was really going on?"

"Not exactly. She just didn't want to be in trouble. You know how it is with children."

"Good. You know, I'm surprised I misjudged Tobin like I did. I always thought he was a bit different from the rest of the Youngbloods."

His voice was extremely calm, but Miranda noticed how his fists were clenched.

Miranda took his fist in hers and uncurled it, setting it back on his leg. "You hide your anger well."

"I learned to hide my emotions at a very early age. But that is a topic of discussion for another day. Elspeth must be protected at all costs, Miss Wallace."

"Yes, I am aware of that."

"You must keep him away from her."

"I agree with you."

He looked out over the breaking darkness. "I'll not have her chasing rainbows, Miss Wallace, looking for love that isn't there, looking for reassurance from people who despise her. She must be strong in her own right."

"She has people who already love her dearly," Miranda pointed out.

David stood to his feet, so tall and strong now that his wound was completely healed. He was walking the moors at night,

Miranda knew, and if the food baskets she alone had brought were any indication, he was eating well. "To think that he sits there in my home, attended to by my servants, with my money . . . and then refuses to allow *my* daughter free access, makes me more angry than I can say."

Miranda rounded her words with a soothing tone. "You have every right to feel the way you do."

"Sometimes I just want to storm up to Greywalls, grab him by his coat collar, and drag him bodily off my property."

"This must all be terribly frustrating for you," she agreed. "Why do you stay here? Why not go back to France, or to anywhere, for that matter?"

He leaned down on his haunches and took her hands in his. She felt their warmth and realized that this was a man who was looking God in the eye and trying desperately not to blink. "I don't want to leave Elspeth. Not now. Not ever."

"You would live here for the rest of your life?" Miranda asked with incredulity.

"If that is what it takes, yes."

"She's become your lifeline."

David turned slightly and rose to his feet. "Incredible, isn't it? I don't know what I would do without you, Miss Wallace. That you take care of her and protect her and teach her gives me great comfort."

"Is it because of my own deformity that you feel this way?"

"To be honest, yes. You understand her. And, somehow, you understand me."

Miranda had to agree. "Our upbringing was so different, though."

"But you know what it is like to not fit in."

Miranda realized this was true. It was something she always tried to deny, something her parents had insisted wasn't the case. But it was true. "Well," she said cheerfully, "you understand me as well, so I suppose we'll call all that a draw."

He laughed. "You've been around me too much, Miss Wallace. Speaking in gambling terms now, are we?"

She returned his laugh with her own as she stood to her feet. "I should be going, it's very late. If I'm not back by breakfast, poor Mrs. Wooten will be beside herself with worry."

"Have you any news of Sylvie?" he asked suddenly, detaining her exit with a hand.

"I saw her tonight, in fact. She's well."

"And happy in her new marriage?" His eyes were guarded, and his voice too light.

"Yes. Very. My brother is a good man, my lord."

"And did you talk of me at all? Do you think she would ever find it in her heart to forgive me?"

"In time, perhaps, my lord. But as it stands, she thinks you are dead."

He pulled the small Bible out of his coat pocket. "It's something I must ask for someday. I must pay for my deeds."

Miranda crossed her arms, suddenly cold. "How will you ever pay for your deeds if you are here?"

"I do not know, Miss Wallace. But I must get her forgiveness first."

"It may be too much to ask of her."

"Nevertheless, it is something I must do." His face displayed his determination.

"And have you forgiven yourself?" she asked.

"No, but God has."

Miranda laid a hand on his arm. "You believe that? Truly?"

He nodded slowly, his eyes welling with tears. "I did what I should have done a long time ago. The Savior gave me so many chances, Miss Wallace, but finally I have given myself to him, heart, mind, body, and soul. If I had listened to his call when he first extended it, how different my life would be."

Miranda could hardly speak, the sudden rush of joy was so great. Spontaneously she threw her arms about his neck, pulled

153

him into a firm embrace, and kissed his cheek. "What wonderful news!"

"I wanted to tell you when you first arrived, but I didn't know how to bring it up." His face filled with joy as well as he pulled back. "I have no idea what is going to happen next, though," he admitted, extricating himself, face red with embarrassment.

"Trust him. You know you can." She could hardly believe it, David Youngblood was blushing. Truly God dealt in miracles.

"Yes, I know that. You know, God used you in my life. You were willing to let him do that. You've come, day after day, talked with me, cared for me. And I thank you . . . Miranda."

Miranda felt her face redden. "It was an honor, my lord," she said, kissing him again on the cheek.

As she returned to the castle, Miranda was given a fresh perspective. God was on the throne, and he was even now working in the midst of all of them. She had no idea what was going to happen next, but she was sure it would be impressive.

Chapter ❖ Sixteen

"Well, I suppose I might just as well meet my doom." Miranda pushed down on the arms of her chair and stood. They had decided to go against tradition and eat their breakfast downstairs with the staff. In truth, Miranda needed their support more than ever before. And going without sleep the night before, well, she could only pray she wouldn't burst into tears during the confrontation.

Mrs. Wooten ordered one of the maids to begin clearing the great table of its bowls and spoons. It had only been an oatmeal morning, so there wasn't a great deal to gather. "You know," she said, leaning her elbow on the surface, "I really don't believe you'll have too much trouble with him."

She sounded so decisive, Miranda had to ask, "And what makes you so sure?"

"I believe God is working on him."

"As he's workin' on every mother's son o' us, ma'am," Pamela said from where she stood at the cast-iron stove.

"No, in a different way. Remember how he didn't want our Elspeth around the guests, afraid her ugliness would be a disturbance to them?"

They all nodded.

"Well," she continued, "the truth of the matter is, that it would be a disturbance to *him*."

"That's true enough, Mrs. Wooten," Mr. Wooten agreed.

Angus rose to his small feet. "Miss Elspeth is the bonniest lassie I've seen in aw my days." And he meant it. "I dinna ken wha' all the puff an' bluster is aboot. We were grand enough up ta now." He left the room, the talk obviously too disturbing for him.

James MacDowell drained his tea. "The lad doesna take kindly ta change."

"An' yet he did weel enough when the last earl was aboot the place," Pamela reminded him.

"*Anyway*," Mrs. Wooten said, clearly not done with her summation of the situation. "Think about it, a man unable to accept physical imperfection, a ward with horrible deformities—"

"A governess with an unhideable and rather large birthmark," Miranda said, because she knew no one else would and it furthered Mrs. Wooten's point.

Pamela spooned up her final bite of oatmeal. "Aye, I know what ye mean. It sounds just like the Lord to bring a talented man like his lordship here to show him what true beauty is."

Miranda slid her chair back. "I really am going this time. Say a prayer."

Lost in her thoughts and worries, she was surprised when she put her hand to the library door and a burst of music sounded from the piano. A flourish of notes coursed out in a pattern so exquisite she found herself thrilling to its beauty, taken captive on a river of emotion. Pictures crowded her mind of a Greek warrior and a maiden, lost in the wilderness, lost in their love. She couldn't stop the story as it played behind her eyes: the hot sun, forbidden love, an angry god, a wise fool, and a finally, a lover's promise extending beyond death. Beyond the Elysian Fields—fields of everlasting life. Fields of gold.

What is happening? Not understanding this burst of joyful creativity, she lifted her hand back away from the knob. To enter now, as the heated wonder of his musical tale was splayed against the cold stone of the castle, would almost be sacrilege. "I will come another time," she whispered to him more than herself. And grabbing a handful of skirt, she hurried upstairs to pen a note.

Not wishing to disturb your composing, I am leaving this note in my stead. If you please, I will come at your bidding at a more convenient hour for you, my lord.—M. Wallace.

Miranda slid the note under the door to the library, and soon was engaged with Elspeth and Angus and the dashing Sir Walter Raleigh. But Miranda's heart was not with her task. She was remembering the music of her employer and wishing with all her heart that she might be a wee mouse in the corner of the great library, silent yet filled with the beauty of Tobin Youngblood's song.

⌒

"I always loved the color of the leaves in the autumn and then their graceful descent, swirling with the wind, down to the forest floor."

Miranda stared at David Youngblood in awe. The man never ceased to amaze her. How he could have ever been the monster he by all accounts had once been was cause for stupefaction. He fascinated her in a way that no man had, and although she had learned long ago not to deeply ponder her feelings, she had found herself wandering in the direction of St. Ninian's for the past three nights. She joined him for his walks, and they talked of God mostly, of redemption, of human frailty. But it was daytime now, and Miranda had taken her two pupils out for some fresh air. Of course, they begged to come see David.

"One day, not more than a few years ago," she confessed as they sat by the fish ponds, "I realized that I thought of the leaves in a strange way. I seemed to think that each leaf was somehow reincarnated, that it came back again, each year replacing itself with itself. And then one day, at eye level, I saw a leaf fall from an oak tree. I realized that each leaf had only so much time on earth, before it fell to the ground with the rest of its kind." She reached into the sack of food and pulled out one of David's tartlets. "It made quite a change in me."

"You suddenly felt like a leaf, eh?" His motions echoed hers, and he bit down into a tartlet himself.

"Exactly. I will not replace myself. I will fall to the ground with the rest of my kind and that will be it. But the difference between myself and a leaf is that I can make so much more of my existence. I don't have to simply hang there. I can choose to sow good or evil. I can choose action or complacency. I can choose obedience or rebellion."

"Up to a point," he said. "I was just reading in Romans this morning, the words of St. Paul. 'It is not of him who willeth or runneth, but of God who sheweth mercy.' Whether you're going to be a good leaf or a bad leaf is really up to God in the end, is it not?"

"You sound as if you've been speaking to my brother!" she laughed. "He's always told me I sometimes forget the extent of God's sovereignty."

"But the point is the same, isn't it? I was determined to be a leaf used for destruction, but God saw otherwise fit to pull me from despair. I ran from him for so long, only to be ground to a halt, ground to nothing but dust. And so he re-formed me thus. Every day I am more and more amazed at his generosity . . . his . . . tenacity."

"God certainly isn't one to give up easily."

Angus and Elspeth ran in quickly to grab a snack and then were as quickly gone.

"Shall we walk a bit?" David asked. "I doubt if we'll be in any danger of being spotted."

Miranda agreed, and soon they found themselves in the woods, followed by the children. They talked of the news of Greywalls: the engagement, the composing frenzy, the way the guests all left without their host bidding them good-bye.

"He was in such a 'musical maelstrom,' as his valet called it, that he didn't even bother to see them off. Not even his new betrothed was given so much as a fare-thee-well."

David's eyebrows raised. "So Tobin has finally decided to marry? Lady Christopher, I assume."

Miranda remembered what they had looked like at the masquerade ball. Lady Daria was dressed as the North Wind in iridescent shades of blue and gray. And her escort made an impressive show in whites and ivories as Old Man Winter. Not that he could really look old, Miranda thought. "They are both quite inspiring in their own way, are they not?"

"It's that artistic personality," David drawled.

"Well, with their looks, they are made for each other. Does such a handsome face run in your family?"

"I suppose so. My grandfather, Tobin's father, was quite an astounding-looking man. Almost too good-looking, if you know what I mean."

"Does his portrait hang at Greywalls?"

"Oh, no! He was an Englishman to the core. Never set foot in the place!"

"So that's why your father sent you here as a child. To them it was remote and far from their world." It was so easy to be candid with David.

He nodded. "It's funny how differently Tobin turned out from my father, though raised by the same man. There was quite an age difference between them. Tobin was the son of his father's old age. My grandfather was quite active socially when my own father was growing up, and hence, my father was the same. With Tobin it was very different."

"What happened?"

David moved a branch aside and allowed her to walk forward on the path. "My grandfather became ill. Horrible headaches. It happened after the death of my grandmother. He married his nurse not a year later. The headaches ceased, and not long after that Tobin arrived, and the man doted on the child. People suspected my grandfather was not truly the father at first, but when the Youngblood hair grew in and the gray eyes we all have matured, well, it was easy to see he was the legitimate offspring of the earl of Cannock, though conceived on the other side of the marriage bed! Not that he knows of that, of course."

Miranda tucked *that* bit of news away for later. "You two look so much alike."

"Except for . . ."

"Well, yes, that goes without saying. But he lacks your spark, and your strength. At least I think so, from what little I've seen of him."

David's voice, coming from behind her as he followed her up the path, was filled with a smile. "You are a lovely woman, Miranda Wallace. These last few weeks we've known each other have been remarkable. I've never felt so good about myself in all of my life!"

She liked the sound of that. "I'd say we're souls akin, my lord."

He came up beside her on the narrow path and stopped her. "Please, call me David. I feel like I've known you all my life. I feel like I've found a friend in you that I've never had before."

Miranda felt a bit disconcerted at the request. After all, she was a mere governess. "My lord, I—"

"I mean it . . . Miranda. May I call you Miranda?"

"Of course."

"Well, then, extend the same privilege to me."

His face was so calm and interested, so assured and friendly. She relented with a chuckle. "Oh, all right, then. David it is."

"Good."

She was still intrigued about her new employer and not about to let the subject go just yet. "So, Lord Tobin was raised in the quiet of the country?"

"For many years, until my grandfather died and his mother moved to the London house. He was about twelve then, I suppose. I was six at the time, but I remember hearing the news from Mrs. Wooten. He was nice enough to me, but by then, he was already exhibiting such promise with his music that he had little time for anything else."

"What about his mother?"

"Well, being a commoner, she never quite fit in with the rest of the family. She stayed to herself, learned how to raise orchids and lilies, and my father did what he could to include Tobin in the social scene. But he was always a bit too eccentric for the garden-variety peer. He's popular in his own circles, but most of society is a bit intimidated by him."

"I can see why!" Miranda said.

"Don't judge him too harshly just yet. Tobin is a man with a soft heart, but he doesn't always know how to show it."

"Another Youngblood trait?"

"Precisely! You're learning, aren't you?"

They came upon a small clearing in which a rock formation had been pushed from the earth who knew how long ago. The leaves were almost completely gone from the trees now, and the ground appeared as if it could use a good snow.

"So, then, I assume you have not yet talked to my uncle regarding the mishap at the ball?"

Miranda shook her head. "I will assure him, however, that we will do our best to stay out of his sight. Don't you really think that is for the best?"

"Definitely, I do. If he isn't going to reach out to the child, it's best for her to stay out of his way, to save her from an emotional attachment she might imagine herself to feel. Does she mention him at all?"

"Not really. She has you, David. At first, when I found out that she was coming here, that you were alive, I wondered if it was best for her to be privy to what could be dangerous information. But I think it's saved her so much grief and pain. She might have tried to seek out his affection, but she knows you are here, and that you love her."

"That I do." He hesitated for a moment, then indicated a boulder, inviting Miranda to sit down with him. "Does she know the . . . extent . . . of my past?"

"No. The staff has sheltered her from all of that."

"She never asks what happened that night . . . why I am hiding."

"Elspeth is a smart child. She doesn't ask what she doesn't want to know."

He brought his hands, fisted in frustration, forcefully down on his thighs. "I know I need to do *some*thing, Miranda. I know I need to beg Sylvie's forgiveness, own up to the truth in France, and go to the guillotine to pay for my crimes and my sins. You call me strong, but I am hardly that, for I cannot seem to leave this remote life."

"If going to your death was easy, David, it wouldn't be a punishment for murder. It's not any wonder you feel the way you do. It would be easy for me to say now that you have the Lord it shouldn't be hard to do the right thing, but I don't believe that for a minute. In my experience, life gets harder when you follow God faithfully. Happily, though, he provides the strength you need."

"He's certainly helping me now," David agreed. "He's visited me many times through you, Miranda."

"It's truly been my privilege," Miranda said without artifice.

"Still, something has to change, and soon. I can't stay in the confines of St. Ninian's forever. I don't believe God wants me to."

"Where do you believe God has called you to be then?"

"France."

"France? Really? But if you go back there—"

"I know. God help me, I know, Miranda. And yet I feel constrained."

"Well, if you feel you must . . ."

"But I haven't the strength!" He shoved his fists in his pockets. "And there's Elspeth to consider as well. What good am I to her as a dead man? I'm the only one in this world who truly understands her. Oh"—he waved a hand—"I know you come close, but being realistic, your birthmark can hardly compare to her mouth. You see the bad hand you were dealt as something that will keep you from marriage, but Elspeth's malformation is something that will keep her from humanity. She needs me, Miranda." His words were filled with pain. "She needs me to show her that God makes no mistakes. Is it truly honorable for me to turn my back on her for the sake of justice?"

Miranda couldn't begin to answer that. All her life she had been someone people came to for comfort, for a word of advice. But sometimes there were just no words to be found.

That night, sleep refused to entertain Miranda. She had prayed for everybody she knew, had caught up on the letters she had been putting off writing for the past two weeks, had even washed out her stockings and hung them neatly before the peat stove in her room. She was too antsy to read, too agitated to merely try and settle into the bed.

But she wasn't too nervous to think. And unfortunately her thoughts were centered on two men, both with the surname Youngblood.

David Youngblood had been on her mind with increasing frequency. He fascinated her. The fact that he had murdered, philandered, stolen, and blackmailed his way through French society repulsed her on one hand and excited her on the other. It was so foreign to her, almost exotic. Perhaps that was what attracted her to him, the way he had experienced so much of what she had been taught to fear, to shun. It was that part of her that was born inside of her—that part that would never be wiped clean until the day she saw the Savior face-to-face—that was intrigued by such a life.

To look upon one's life as a dandelion gone to seed, to be picked, to be blown apart. There was a freedom to it. But she knew all too well where such freedom led, and she suddenly understood why some women, chaste and pure and innocent, allowed themselves to be snatched up by an exciting ne'er-do-well.

Yet there were other aspects of David Youngblood that fascinated her. He was a polished man with the ability to do anything he wanted. And now that he had given himself to God, the possibilities were indeed endless.

Tobin Youngblood, on the other hand, wasn't faring so well in her thoughts. Talented, creative, and yet so removed, he seemed anything but strong. Driven, yes, he was, but at what expense?

You're not being fair, she chided herself, *you've hardly even spoken to the man.* Was his need to create, to bring forth the music of heaven out of nothing to the neglect of all else, really a weakness? In some ways yes. But Miranda was forced to admit she had no idea what it was to be compelled into such a fury, such an overwhelming need to express the inner workings of the heart and soul. She had no gifts like that, no burning desire to make a mark upon the world that would never be erased.

There was no use in trying to go to sleep now, she realized, looking at the wind-up clock at her bedside. The face of David Youngblood materialized clear in her mind's eye. Never before had she been this interested in a man. She was highly intrigued, to be sure, but she had to wonder if it was because he was the only man she had ever met of whom she felt even remotely worthy. Her birthmark was a lovely sight compared to his mouth. Was it this fact that made her feel as if she could rightly give him a piece of her heart?

By 4:00 A.M., Miranda was dressed and ready for the day. She knew Pamela would be most grateful if the fire was already started in the kitchen before she came down at 5:00, and Miranda was needing a strong cup of tea. She pulled her shawl around her shoulders and proceeded down the steps.

Down the corridor on the second floor she stopped.

The music.

Again, it had the same effect on her.

She remembered what Mr. Wooten had said about the small door which opened out into the upper floor of the library that circled the main floor, a loft of sorts, what the servants called "the mezzanine."

Praying for the ability to keep silent, praying that the door, only four and a half feet high, would not screech and moan, she pulled up the handle, disengaged the latch, and pushed inward. A slight scraping on the floor was all the noise that accompanied the movement, and the earl was playing loudly, attacking the keyboard with a vengeance she could hear, if not see. His back was facing her, and she watched in fascination as his hands covered the keyboard with a power and a strength she had never before witnessed in a musician. Close to his body, his hands would hide themselves from her view, only to dash outward into the upper treble and lower bass octaves. Back and forth, loud and soft, the song was a juxtaposition of opposites, a hurricane of sound that somehow lifted many raging notes up into the air to settle gently into her heart. The meaning of his music was apparent to her, and she realized, startled, that the man was indeed praising God with the works of his hands.

She wept. Holding her hands against her mouth at the beauty of his praise, she lifted up her soul to the one who loved his creations with such an overwhelming love that he enabled them to create beauty on a scale she had never before experienced. He gave to them a small piece of himself to fulfill them even as they offered it back.

The piece ended, and his chin dropped down onto his chest in apparent exhaustion. He swung his legs out from beneath the keyboard, pushed his hands down on his knees for support as he rose, then collapsed onto the couch. Less than three minutes later, Miranda could hear a soft snore, and she quietly exited the room as a stillness settled, a content silence, a benediction of rest and peace.

"Has Lord Tobin emerged yet?" Miranda asked Elspeth two days later. They had finished their afternoon tea, then had walked briskly around the bailey while Angus cartwheeled and popped handsprings beside them. And now they were digging their books and slates out of the desks, preparing for a lesson on the Greek gods.

"No' yet. But he's askin' for more an' more pieces, an' is drinkin' more an' more tea."

Miranda threw some peat into the stove. She had gone back the night before, taking a blanket and a pillow, and lay down amid the rows of books. No sleep came, nor did she wish it to, for as the night progressed she had penciled a story inspired by the music. "Sounds like it's only a matter of time now."

Elspeth didn't respond. She merely closed her eyes, her face soaking up the heat of the renewed blaze. The matter regarding the ball ceased to be of grave importance to both of them. After all, if the earl himself deemed it of such insignificance that he had failed to call Miranda before him for four days now, in how much trouble could they find themselves?

Not much, Miranda decided, somewhat relieved, somewhat dismayed, that matters were unresolved. "Did Mrs. Wooten tell you what kind of sandwiches he's been asking for?"

"A bit bread an' beef, with nippy sauce on."

"Well, that would keep anyone awake, would it not?" Miranda retrieved a volume of history from the shelf beside her. "And have you any idea who first came up with the sandwich?"

Elspeth shook her head as she opened up the small drawer in the table and pulled out a pencil.

Oh good. The tale of the earl of Sandwich would provide a twofold lesson: the importance of ingenuity and the evils of gambling. Unfortunately, Angus, who helped his father in the afternoons now that the new earl dreamed up various wood-working projects, wouldn't be around to hear it.

A knock rattled the nursery door. It opened and there stood Mrs. Wooten, the inevitable dust rag polishing the brass knob. "He's called for you."

"Is he . . . upset? Still?" Miranda quickly stood to her feet and grabbed a woolen shawl from the back of her chair. The castle was so cold these days.

"He looks terrible. Like he saw death and was too tired to run for it."

"It's probably not a good time for us to be talking," Miranda surmised.

Mrs. Wooten just shrugged. "I wouldn't keep him waiting if I were you."

"You're quite right. Elspeth, go over those square roots, and when you've finished them, you may get out that length of embroidery we've been working on, and then, if I'm not back yet—"

"Are ye goin' ta the Inquisition, Miss Wallace, for it ta be takin' so long?" Elspeth asked.

Mrs. Wooten stifled a merry hoot and left the room.

When Miranda got to the door she heard Elspeth say, "An' after ye come back, could we finish yon jiggin' from the other night? It was awfu' rude o' him ta come bargin' in like he did!"

"Why, Elspeth," Miranda said, very pleased, "you've got quite a lovely sense of humor. I didn't realize it before now."

"I always crack jokes when I'm feart," the lass said, hardly making Miranda feel any better.

CHAPTER ❖ SEVENTEEN

He knew he should have waited to have the woman brought to him. Tobin knew he wasn't at all in the proper mood for a confrontation. Spent of all his resources, he was tired.

Best to get it over with. He prayed that God would give him a heart of love and compassion, considering not only what the poor woman looked like but the fact that she was generally decent and kind and could teach him a thing or two about common decency. Right now, he just wished he was back at his old room in London, waking up to the smell of Mrs. Pratt's roast beef after an evening of work, feeling refreshed and hungry. *Strike the beef idea.* He grimaced, having eaten more than enough roast beef sandwiches in the past week. A nice chicken, baked to a crispy gold with rosemary and stuffed with sage and bread-crumbs would actually do quite nicely. Roasted potatoes and some peas would round out the meal delightfully. He would tell Mrs. Wooten to let Mrs. MacDowell know he wished such fodder for supper.

A light knock sounded on the library door.

He breathed in deeply and squared his shoulders. *This is it.*

"Come in!" he called, knowing she would hear without any trouble. Spinster women like Miss Wallace always had hearing as sharp as a pin, having never developed the need to ignore the bleatherings of spouse and offspring.

A woman was backing in through the widening space of the door. She was tall and slender, and her hair, a magnificent shade of blonde, shimmered in the afternoon light that spilled from between the drapery panels of a nearby window. Tobin couldn't help but notice the slimness of her waist, or the way her back curved so gracefully from a long neck. As she turned, he noticed the hand that curved around the handle of the tea tray. It was fine and sculptured, the fingers slim and long. His gaze returned upward, to the sweet point of her chin, the profile of shapely lips and a small nose. The eye looked downward, and then . . . she turned to face him, the birthmark on the other side of her face in full view.

"Oh, Miss Wallace," he acknowledged, all complimentary thoughts pushed from his mind by the realization that it was only the governess who was entering the room after all. "Let me help you with that."

"Mrs. MacDowell sent it up with Angus just as I was coming down the hall. I told him it would be no trouble to deliver it to you myself."

He moved to take the tray but to no avail. "I'll just set it on the table by the sofa," she said. So far she had not looked him in the eye. But she sounded cheerful enough. Perhaps she wasn't going to spend the next few minutes telling him how superficial, shallow, and completely devoid of compassion he was.

"Ah, Miss Wallace," he began. "It's been several days since I had originally thought we would talk and I must apologize. I've been—"

"Composing. Yes, I know. We *all* know!" Her hands were flutters of graceful yet self-conscious movements as she arranged the cups onto the saucers.

He wanted to laugh when she rolled her eyes, then began to pour tea into his cup. She handed it to him confidently, without sugar or milk. "How did you know—"

"How you take your tea?" she finished. She crossed her arms and looked up for a few brief moments. "You probably will think I am quite daft, but I can tell by looking at people how they take their tea. You know how some folk can read a man when they enter a room. They can tell whether he's hard or compassionate, honest or deceitful, kind or selfish. Well, I have the gift of instinctively knowing how someone takes his tea."

This was amusing indeed! "And have you ever been wrong?"

"Of course, on occasion. But I would estimate I'm right at least eighty-five percent of the time."

"Extraordinary." He sat down on the sofa and indicated that she should do the same. "And when did you realize you had this gift?"

The governess sat down at the extreme other end of the couch, her back stiff as a poker, her bottom just at the edge. A perfect lady, he noted. How could he have missed that hair? Its shading was quite lovely; the silver light of the moon sparkled along each strand. It was a cool shade, and judging from the width of the braid that coiled into a knot at the back of her head, it was extremely thick and heavy. She looked longingly at the teapot before she answered.

"I was twelve. My mother had a group of women over for tea—the wives of all my father's foremen, to be exact—and she told me to pour. Without even thinking to ask, I fixed each woman her cup, and to everyone's amazement I had made up only one cup in error."

"Extraordinary," he said again, because it was. People surprised him every day. "I'd definitely say that's a talent not usually heard of, let alone displayed."

She blushed. "That's nice of you to say, my lord, considering you are a man of true talents."

He sat forward and began pouring her a cup of tea. "Did you hear any of the music I've been playing over the last few days?"

Her eyes lit up, he was glad to see, but he wasn't sure if it was due to the recollection of his pieces or the fact that she would soon be the partaker of a cup of tea. "Sugar?" he asked.

"And milk. Lots of it."

"I see I don't have your talent. I took you for no milk and just a smidge of sugar."

She laughed. "I'm new to governessing, my lord."

He immediately apologized. "You must forgive me. I have not your talent. I am afraid I assume all women in your position are . . ." He fought for the word.

"Frugal and austere?" she provided easily.

"Exactly." He busied himself with the sugar, glad for something to do.

"You don't have to fix my tea, my lord," she said, "my being a governess and all."

Was she joking? He couldn't tell. "No matter. Employing my hands will keep me awake. I am truly exhausted."

"An overabundance of roast beef and horseradish will do that to anyone," she said, again not smiling. "Or should I call it 'nippy sauce'?"

Tobin didn't quite know how to take her. Was she joking with him? If so, it was most impertinent, but if not . . . well, he could hardly reprimand her for a simple opinion, could he? "Did you hear anything I was playing?" he asked, his ego getting the better of him. The piano concerto was the most magnificent piece he had ever written. It had flowed from him like a massive bolt of lightning, striking the composition paper with a bright, almost dangerous, force.

Her face remained guarded. "Yes, of course. Your activity has been the talk of the castle since you holed yourself up inside here."

"And?"

"Well, we were all wondering if you were going to make yourself sick on so little sleep and so many sandwiches!"

"As you can see, I am fine." He spread his arms wide, wondering if she missed the point of the conversation on purpose. "Did you listen to any of my music as you were walking by?" He didn't know why he asked such questions of people, for truly they made him miserable, waiting for the answer, hoping against hope that the torture he had subjugated himself to was worth it, that he had created something that uplifted them on all levels, body and soul and spirit. And this woman was taking her precious time answering his question.

She still refused to meet his gaze. "I didn't hear much as I walked by the door, sir, no. I'm sorry to say it, but being so busy with Elspeth, there's little time for dillydallying in corridors."

"Now you *do* sound like a governess!" he announced in almost triumph, thinking that, yes, he had read the woman right after all.

She drained her cup and set it down gently on the tray. "My lord." She cleared her throat. "About the other night—"

"All forgiven," he rushed out, knowing he should apologize, but trying to remain "earl-like" in her eyes.

"But—"

"That's what I wished to tell you." He suddenly remembered what she looked like when she was dancing with the girl. How gracefully she had moved, how abandoned she was as her feet whirled them too fast. Indeed, this woman seemed to be a study in contrasts. Intriguing, indeed. Definitely more than met the eye at first glance! "So you can continue on as before with the child. You'll have no interference from me."

Her eyes snapped open wide, then shut a bit. He could tell she forced herself to remain sweet as she stood abruptly to her feet. "We'll not be in your way, my lord. I'll do my best to make sure you aren't inconvenienced in any way by our presence at Greywalls. May I go?"

He nodded, staring up at her, thinking she would have made a wonderful Viking woman. So forthright. Stalwart.

Her bright blue eyes finally bored into his own, and he could feel the painful passion of her words as they fell upon him like hailstones. "For someone who creates such loveliness, such beauty, I find it hard to believe you don't really understand the true meaning of the word."

And then she was gone. Wishing he could follow her and do the ensuing conversation justice, he nevertheless stayed where he was, feeling her absence, smelling the subtle sweetness of her perfume.

He was spent. In all ways now, exhaustion had overtaken him. His head drooping forward on a neck whose muscles had suddenly relaxed, he padded up to his room and proceeded to fall into a long, hard sleep. He would think about what she had said later.

CHAPTER ❖ EIGHTEEN

David knelt down and added some dried branches and bracken to the small fire he had made near the stairwell in the crypt of the abbey. Miranda couldn't help but notice the powerful muscles in his thighs as he balanced on his haunches. It was hard to believe that his only family had never seen what a beautiful specimen of God's creation he truly was. His bodily proportions were the closest to perfect she had ever witnessed, his eyes were beautiful, and his hair was thick, glossy, and soft. She should know about that, for she had just given him a haircut and felt the silky strands between her fingers.

"Winter is setting in for good." He threw his cloak around his shoulders. "You should be back at Greywalls in comfort."

"Whoever said a castle was comfortable in winter?" she responded. "I much prefer the coziness of a small cottage."

"Still, the snows will be falling soon." He searched through the daily knapsack and pulled out a fresh shirt and pair of pants. "I see Mrs. Wooten was going through my wardrobe again!"

Miranda laughed. "I tried to convince her that dirt and grime had its own warming capacities, but she refused to listen."

"Mrs. Wooten knows me too well," he said. "If you can't be pretty, you might as well be clean."

"I've always been accused of being overly fastidious. We take what steps we can to make ourselves more presentable, don't we?"

"Always. So," he said, sitting down and crossing his legs, "how is Elspeth doing with her schoolwork?"

Miranda put her hands out toward the small blaze. "As they say, 'The apple doesn't fall far from the tree.' She is highly intelligent. You should be proud."

"Oh, I am! If I ever thought God had completely forsaken me, I was mistaken. Elspeth is a gift beyond price, a rare jewel straight from the mines of heaven."

"She's especially doing well at Latin. I think she has a particular aptitude for languages. Who knows where that ability will take her?"

"I always loved languages myself."

"Well, then you can teach her as well. Sylvie comes in one day a week to teach her French. I can speak the language myself, but it's so much better to learn it from someone who grew up speaking it."

At the mention of Sylvie, his eyes warmed yet further. "So she has come to care about my daughter, then?"

She nodded. "You know Sylvie. Never one to let a little deformity get in the way."

"She's a wonderful woman," he agreed.

"You need to go to her, David. You know that."

He nodded, suddenly sober and quiet.

"I'll talk to my brother," she offered.

"Be more specific this time, Miranda. Tell him where I am."

Miranda looked at him sharply. "Are you certain you want me to tell him?"

"Yes. He's a good man, a man of God. I know that now. He'll know whether or not Sylvie is able to take such tidings."

David reached out and took her hand, his expression earnest and filled with gratitude. "I thank God for you every day, Miranda. Do you know that? I don't know how I could make it through these days without you. You must know that I will someday do all that is in my power to thank you properly."

"The fact that you talk to God at all, David, is thanks enough."

He leaned back on his hands. "I remember reading from Julius Caesar, and when he said 'To die will be a very big adventure,' I thought him foolish. I still think it now. Certainly, to *live* is the greatest adventure of all."

Miranda agreed. "And to live in the adventure of God's will is even more worthwhile."

~~~

Miranda had always loved Sundays. But now they had continued to be her favorite day for yet another reason. After escorting Elspeth, wearing her beautiful ivory coat, back to Greywalls, Miranda would return to Huntly and laze away the afternoon with Sylvie, Matthew, and Eve.

Dinner was over, the dishes were cleared and washed, and she sat before the hearth with her family, enjoying the sounds of the breezes that whistled over the top of the chimney, the soft, high creak of Sylvie's rocker. This was peace without responsibility, love without condition, rest without worry. Her times at the cottage bolstered her for the rest of the week.

"We have some wonderful news for you, Mira," Matthew said on a Sunday nearing the end of November.

Miranda could guess what it was, but she didn't wish to spoil the announcement.

"We're going to have a baby!" Sylvie brought her hands up to her mouth, excitement lighting up her brown eyes.

Miranda felt a broad smile explode upon her face. "I knew it wouldn't be long! How wonderful!"

Her sister-in-law sat on the arm of her husband's chair, Matthew's arm around her waist. "You should have another niece or nephew to dote on come spring."

"You couldn't bring me better news."

Sylvie's face became serious. "I just want you to promise me you'll be there to deliver this one as well."

Miranda remembered the night Eve arrived into the world, born in circumstances so adverse and challenging, and yet here they were, together in this peaceful home, God's love in evidence all around them. "You can be certain I would be no place else!"

Sylvie leaned against Matthew, satisfied. Now that Miranda knew, the signs were obvious. Her sister-in-law had seemed more weary than usual and had touched very little of her supper, obviously fighting the queasiness of early pregnancy.

Sylvie announced it was time for a nap, and taking the baby to cuddle with, left Miranda and Matthew to sit before the fire.

"Congratulations, Mate. You'll make a wonderful father."

"I thought I already was one!" He pointed to one of Eve's booties left on the table.

"I stand corrected." Miranda picked up the scarf she had begun knitting earlier that day. "This is certainly a day for big announcements, I suppose, for I have one of my own."

Matthew sat forward in his chair.

"David Youngblood is still alive," she said quickly, knowing there was no easy way to broach the subject. Her needles clicked furiously now.

"What?" He went pale, obviously remembering the man's diabolical plot to make Sylvie his own. "Are you sure?"

Miranda set her work in her lap. "I've seen him myself."

Matthew sat back hard against the cushion of his chair, unable to speak. Miranda could almost see the thoughts swirling in his brain.

"He's come to know the Lord, Mate."

Matthew's expression told her he found that even harder to believe.

"I assure you it's true."

"Where is he? Was he in France?"

"Oh, no. He's hiding out in St. Ninian's abbey, about two miles from here."

Matthew scratched his head. "And he's been there all this time?"

"Yes."

"You've been aiding him?"

Miranda nodded. Matthew always knew when she was lying.

"Mira! The man killed Sylvie's parents. How could you do such a thing?" His dark blue eyes filled with fire. "He's a devil. I don't know how he's convinced you otherwise, but I've been in the ministry for far too long to know that some people just *don't change.*"

Miranda could completely understand her brother's point of view, but she wouldn't concede. "I know when a man has changed. Would you deny Christ's power to heal a man like David Youngblood? Would you deny that the blood of Christ could cleanse even a heart as black as his?"

"Well, no, but surely—"

"I tell you this, Mate. David Youngblood is no longer the man you knew him to be. God has taken hold of him as firmly as he did you and me."

Matthew still looked doubtful. "David Youngblood is a much more slippery fish!"

Miranda licked her lips. "I was in ministry with you for years, brother. Do you not trust me to know when someone is truly awakened spiritually, or just playing a game?"

"I suppose so, Mira. But . . . *David Youngblood?*"

"David Youngblood." She shoved her yarn and needles into a cloth bag.

He blew out a heavy breath and lifted a shaky hand, raking it through his dark curls. "I can hardly believe it."

Miranda stood to her feet. "I'll make us a pot of tea. It might help to calm you down."

"Oh, I'm calm. Believe me, I'm calm."

"Well, then humor me. I could use a cup myself."

Ten minutes later she was back with a proper tray, and he was quick to accept a cup once the tea was steeped.

"So why are you telling me all this?" he asked. "I assume you've known for quite some time."

"You assume correctly, Mate."

He blew on the cup and took a small sip. "It has something to do with Sylvie, doesn't it?"

She nodded. "He wants to beg her forgiveness."

"Absolutely not!" Matthew shouted immediately. "No. I will not allow the man in my house."

"But why? I told you, he's changed. If God has forgiven him, why won't you?"

Matthew shook his head. "This isn't about forgiveness. It's about Sylvie. I swore to protect her, Mira, and that is exactly what I will do."

Miranda thrust out her chin, expecting her brother to react like this, but feeling defensive all the same. "Don't you think the decision should be left up to her?"

"In her present state? No. I don't think so for a minute. See here, Mira." He set down his cup. "Sylvie just found out she is expecting. It's the first time I've seen her eyes truly light up with joy since Rene de Boyce was killed. How can you ask me to destroy that now? Don't you see? It's just another one of Youngblood's ploys to throw us all back into the misery in which he himself has become accustomed to living."

"I disagree."

"I see he has you under his spell, then."

Miranda set down her own cup. "Do you really believe that?"

"It's obvious, isn't it? There he is, alone and seemingly vulnerable, so deformed and rejected. And you come along, the savior, seeking to heal wounds that have been festering since the day he was born."

"I understand him!"

"No, you don't. You could never understand a man like him. You merely see him as even lower than yourself. You look upon his face and compare it to yours, and for the first time in your life you feel beautiful. He's used your disfigurement to manipulate you, and you don't even realize it."

Miranda could hardly believe she was hearing these words, and from her own brother. Despite her wishes to the contrary, tears filled her eyes. "I always thought you were on my side," she said quietly, crossing the room to grab her cloak from a hook by the door.

He shot to his feet. "Wait, Mira, I didn't mean   "

"Oh, you were clear enough, Mate. Perfectly clear, in fact." She yanked open the door.

He ran across the room and laid a hand on her arm. "Mira, please. Don't go like this. I only meant to help you see what you've got yourself into. You know I don't care about your birthmark."

"That's obvious to me now," she bit back, pulling the cloak tightly around her and running for home.

It was hard to think in the deepening chill of the evening. Her heart was painfully bloated with such anguish, such rage, that all she could do was feel. Tearing in through the door of the castle nearest the kitchen, she flew up the steps to the second floor. And as she passed the small door that led to the loft of the library, she stopped.

Coming from inside was music so soothing, so compelling, she found the tears pouring profusely from her eyes. Quietly, she opened the door and sat down to listen. The song washed over her, bringing her a respite from her anguish, and she fell asleep.

CHAPTER ❖ NINETEEN

Everyone at Greywalls knew Miranda was upset. Her sunny disposition and dependable ways had become so commonplace that when she had failed to show up Sunday evening for the nightly gathering in the kitchen, they knew something was wrong.

Miranda was a bit amused at the way Angus was sizing her up the next morning, his one eye squinting as he cocked his head. "That's what they're sayin', Miss Wallace. But ye canna see e'en a whit o' difference."

Elspeth was sober. "Miss Wallace, ye winna yersel' at breakfast, an' ye didna say yer prayers last night like ye meant it."

Miranda took Elspeth's hand in her left hand and Angus's in her right. "Neither of you has a brother or sister, so you may not understand what has pained me so much. I found myself in an argument with my brother yesterday, and to be truthful, it hurts my heart so much, I can hardly think of anything else. I feel betrayed and sad, as if I've lost the only ally I ever really had."

Angus looked deep into her eyes, turned their hands around, and tucked hers as firmly into his small one as was possible. "Ye know tha' it's fine ta be sad, aye?"

Miranda couldn't answer. She tried to live by the edict to give thanks in all situations, to be happy in her salvation at all times. "Truth be told, Angus, I feel like a failure. How could I let one argument with Mate do this to me? Shouldn't the Lord be enough?"

"All I know, Miss Wallace, is yon Scripture ye gave us aboot Jesus healin' the heartsore. If hearts didna get sore, he'd have nothin' ta do!"

"Aye, right enough," Elspeth said. "Hearts are broken every day. An' I dinna ken tha' it's only the hearts o' those who dinna love the Lord."

Miranda squeezed their hands. There was much wisdom in their words.

A light rapping sounded at the door. All three of them were delighted to see Sylvie's face appear in the crack between schoolroom and corridor.

She dispensed wide, warm hugs to the children, presented them each with a small, brown bag, and then turned to Miranda. Her embrace was welcome and reassuring. She handed Miranda her knitting bag, left in Huntly after the argument.

"Won't you come in, Mrs. Wallace?" Miranda asked, her warm voice belying her formal words.

"But of course. I was hoping we'd continue with our French lessons."

The children squealed over the candy within the sacks as she took off her cloak and pulled over another chair.

"That sounds like a perfect way to start the day's lessons." Miranda closed the book from which she had been about to teach.

"And when I am finished, I was hoping we all might go out for a bit of fresh air," Sylvie announced.

"We all could use a walk." Miranda stood. "Why don't you start the lesson, and I'll order up some tea, then start my knitting again. I'm making Elspeth a scarf to go with that new coat we've just finished up!"

Miranda had already knitted ten new rows by the time the tea arrived. Pamela MacDowell brought it herself, along with a plate of sandwiches. "Just thought I'd look in on wee Angus. I'm so proud o' the boy an' aw he's learnin'."

Miranda whispered, "Sit down for a while, rest your feet."

"Och, no!" she said softly, almost in horror. "I've already got too much ta do this mornin'. His lordship was quite specific aboot his dinner this afternoon. He knows exactly wha' he wants ta eat an aw. Never seen anything like it afore!"

Miranda chuckled. "I always thought artists cared little about what they ate."

"This one isna like tha'. No' a wheen. I do believe he views food as art." Her eyes twinkled.

"Then you must enjoy being in his employ."

"Och, I do, weel enough! It's grand to be appreciated for what ye can do, e'en if the loon who does the appreciatin' is a wee bit daft like! I best be runnin' along now, onyways." She was out the door, blowing a little kiss to her son before disappearing altogether.

And so the morning dissipated like the steam from the teapot. What had begun as thick and oppressive had ended pleasantly and with the aroma and warmth of friendship and cozy wintertime comfort. Chilly winds blew outside, but the schoolroom was sheltered and snug. The calm murmur of Sylvie's French was soothing, and it was then that Miranda forgave her little brother even though he had not yet asked for such. Knowing Matthew, it wouldn't be long before he came himself.

Soon the dainties were consumed, and the children looked as if they needed some exercise. "Go on out into the bailey for a while," Miranda ordered. "I'll come and get you in thirty minutes."

Needing no other prompting, the children grabbed their coats and were gone in a clatter of laughter and pounding heels. Miranda almost let out a sigh. Instead she tidied up the tea things. "I suppose Matthew told you everything."

Sylvie busied herself as well, stacking up plates and saucers. "Yes. He didn't want to, but I forced it out of him. It isn't like you two to fight."

Miranda couldn't help but laugh. "Oh, you didn't see us growing up! We fought all the time. Now we just save it up for the really important matters!"

Sylvie, however, remained sober. "I think Matthew was wrong in what he said about David. I believe you when you say he's changed."

Miranda felt a true spark of hope. "Oh, he has, Sylvie, believe me. This couldn't be an act. I've been raised a Christian and have been around them all my life. What he tells me of his heart can only come from a person who has truly been made whole by the Savior. Of course"—she sat down and began folding the soiled napkins—"Matthew doesn't believe me. He thinks I'm being fooled. But I know, Sylvie, I know as much as anyone can know, that David belongs to God now."

Sylvie nodded, her eyes filling with tears. "I cannot see him yet. I want to, but I cannot." She sat down in her chair and leaned her elbows on the table, looking into Miranda's eyes. "Jesus says we are to forgive, but I can't yet. *Juste ciel!* It isn't only that he killed my parents, Mira, it was that he betrayed me by doing so. I thought he was my friend; I thought he truly loved me."

"He does, Sylvie. Too much."

"I suppose you're right. Perhaps that was what drove him to do what he did. He knew my father was less than the man he should have been, he knew my mother had been putting her needs above mine for many years—"

Miranda grabbed her hand. "The truth is, Sylvie, David is not your normal man. Years of living with his deformity—"

"That doesn't absolve him from taking responsibility for his actions!" Sylvie cried.

"I never said it did. And I can't expect you, a beautiful woman, to understand what it is like to grow up with something so glaringly wrong with you, something less than normal, the very presence of which naturally draws the attention you do not want and can ill afford."

Sylvie dropped her eyes.

"Do you believe in the power of God, Sylvie?"

"Of course I do. I've witnessed it many times in my own life."

"Then is it so hard to believe that God can even turn the madness of years around, that he can heal David's heart and mind?" Miranda asked.

"No. And I believe that he has done so, Mira. I know I can trust your word on that. It's just that I'm not ready. Now that I'm expecting . . ."

Miranda patted her hand. "I understand."

She looked up. "You'll see him soon, then?"

"Probably tonight. Do you wish for me to tell him anything?"

Sylvie shook her head. "No, not really." She looked thoughtful for just a moment, her eyes becoming hard. "Actually, you *can* tell him something for me. The man responsible for so much of this havoc, the man who may still seek my life and most probably still has his sights set on my fortune, is Claude Mirreault."

Miranda nodded. "He's a dangerous man."

"I will forgive David for what he did under the hire of Mirreault, if he makes sure Mirreault never harms my family again."

"He wants to turn himself in, but the thought of leaving Elspeth keeps him at St. Ninian's."

"I can't fault him for that. He would feel he was deserting her. But he must make restitution, Mira, he must!"

"And implicating Claude Mirreault would suffice?" Miranda didn't know why she was so desperately seeking a way for this man to live, but she knew he must. She didn't think God would bring David to him so he could die right away. David had been given an infirmity and a past that would, combined with the knowledge of God, ultimately strengthen him for a monumental task. When Angus had said the earl was special, he was right. Anyone who looked closely enough could see it.

"There would be almost no greater joy in my life than to see Claude Mirreault walk up the scaffolding to the guillotine!"

"May God make it so." Miranda brought her hands down onto the table. "But in doing so, David may implicate himself."

Sylvie's eyes remained steady. "Then it's a risk he'll have to take if he ever wants to speak to me again."

"You drive a hard bargain, Sylvie."

Sylvie lifted her chin proudly. "I'm not Armand de Courcey's daughter for nothing, Mira."

Several minutes later, Miranda walked Sylvie to the gatehouse. "Are you sure you don't wish for me to call a carriage to take you home?"

"Oh no. I need the fresh air, and the exercise will do me good. I got much too fat when I was expecting Eve."

Miranda snorted. "No, you just got average."

"Oh, I almost forgot!" Sylvie cried. "The other reason I came today was to tell you that there's a member of the congregation who bought one of those new velocipedes! He cannot even begin to get his balance, he says, and wondered if Matthew had any use for it. We immediately thought of Elspeth."

Miranda clapped with delight, recalling a picture she had seen of the peculiar two-wheeled vehicle a few months before. "She would love it! Would you like me to send someone around to fetch it?"

Sylvie shook her head. "Matthew wants to bring it himself." She shrugged. "A peace offering, you know."

"Tell him it will be graciously received."

Sylvie looked at her sister-in-law in earnest. "These situations are hard for him. He doesn't take it well when he's hurt someone."

"I know, Sylvie. He never has."

"The velocipede won't arrive until December," Sylvie informed her.

"Tell him he's invited to tea tomorrow afternoon."

The two women embraced, and Sylvie was on her way, a solitary figure on the wide, cold moor. Miranda found the children and decided to join in on their footraces, much to the delight of the stable master and his grooms. Soon they had a small version of the Highland games going, wood and large stones flying through the air.

That night, she felt too exhausted to go to the abbey, but it was her evening to take the daily provisions to his lordship. Feeling she didn't have a choice, and knowing she should tell David about her conversation with Sylvie, she set out after dark, the chilly breeze invigorating and able to spur her on at a quicker pace.

David Youngblood wasn't as well-receiving of the news as she thought he would be.

"What do you mean I must implicate Mirreault before she'll forgive me?" he shouted in the crypt of the abbey. It was night and the light of the small fire turned his features into an eerie mask.

Miranda set down the parcel of food she had brought. "That's what she said, David. I don't believe there's any deeper meaning to be drawn here."

"Do you have any idea what she's asking me to do?" His anger was making him agitated.

"Not really. I'm just a governess, you know." She pulled the sack closer to her and opened up the drawstring. "Pamela put in some lovely—"

"Don't change the subject, Mira," he barked. "If I go over to France, I'll be arrested right away. And with this face, it isn't as if I can go about in anonymity."

She placed her hands on her hips. "I'm just the messenger, David. You're shooting the wrong person."

All the anger left him suddenly, and he rushed over to her, taking her hands in his. "Oh, Miranda. I know, I know. I just loathe myself so much right now. All this . . . this . . . retribution I must pay, it's all my fault. I have no one to blame but myself, therefore, well . . . it doesn't matter. It isn't at all unreasonable, what Sylvie asks, is it?"

Miranda shrugged. She could forgive David anything just then, looking at him so strong and filled with emotion. The fire on the floor caught the copper in his hair and warmed his gray eyes.

"And it isn't just what Sylvie asks," he reasoned softly, more to himself than to Miranda. "It's what is required of me by God."

Miranda nodded, squeezed his hands, and let go. "He will give you the strength and the resources."

"The resources?"

"Why, certainly. If God wishes you to bring down the evils of Mirreault, he will provide all that you need."

David looked at her, examining her as he rubbed his chin. "Do you . . ." He hesitated, shook his head, then continued, "Do you really believe God is in this somehow?"

"Oh, most definitely!" The answer leaped out without her even thinking it over. "Claude Mirreault is an evil man. He must be stopped. And who better to stop him than you?"

David sat down on top of his pallet, resting his elbows upon his bent knees. "What of Elspeth?"

"He'll take care of her too."

"But will you?" he asked unnecessarily.

Miranda smiled and sat down beside him. "You know the answer to that, David."

He nodded. "I'll wait until spring. It will be better then."

"You'll winter here, in the abbey? How can you?"

"I'm surviving just fine," he assured her.

"But it will grow much colder in January. Now would be the right time."

"But Elspeth needs me."

"That's true. But she'll always need you. If you go to France and take care of things as you should, you'll be home all the quicker, ready to take her wherever it is you want to go, and with Sylvie's forgiveness and blessing yours to claim."

David raised a hand. "I need more time to think this through. To formulate a plan."

"Do you know anyone with the Paris police?" she asked.

"Do I!" he laughed. "They're the most corrupt lot of them all!"

CHAPTER ❖ TWENTY

Miranda's world began to settle into a very satisfactory routine. Lessons, intensely rendered, were dealt with in the morning. Then dinner with Elspeth. Long jaunts with her charge in the afternoon and a visit to David Youngblood. Tea in the schoolroom and the instruction of womanly arts. Reading. Bed for Elspeth.

Congregating in the kitchen with the rest of the staff still took up some of the dark hours. But her most cherished time of the day occurred when she snuck into the library with a blanket, some paper, and a pencil. Then the music of Tobin Youngblood would disturb, soothe, caress, and jostle her, and she would sit silently, drinking it in as if it would fuel her for the coming day.

She loved his music.

It enlarged her soul and spurred in her a creative force she had never known before. When his music settled deep inside her heart, her pencil would scratch across the paper, filling the blank space before it with words so winsome and fitting, words that waltzed in perfect step with each note it accompanied, she knew God had breathed, and set for her a new course, a fresh way to glorify him and enjoy him.

Over and over again, she would hear the opera on which Tobin was working, the concerto, even the requiem. She knew the melodies by heart now, each lilting phrase, each pounding beat of the bass chords, and she wrote the story of a Greek woman, heroic and wise, straining to emerge, her movements harmonizing with Tobin's.

There she would fall asleep, only to wake up in the cold, dark silence. Miranda would make her way back to her room, refreshed yet ready for more sleep in the comfort of her bed. She thanked God for this life she had been given. And her existence continued along in such a comforting pattern, until a week before Christmas when the velocipede finally arrived.

⁓

Oh, Tobin could just *hear* Daria's voice as her loopy black writing leapt off the page and barraged his eyeballs with its staccatoed tidings. He never realized handwriting could actually be loud!

Darling!

Darling, darling, darling. Details, details, details. The dress was being made even as she was writing, not in any normal color, but in a "violent pink." Violent pink? He couldn't even begin to imagine what Daria meant by that. And would he be surprised by the trimmings on the gown! He was certain he would.

They weren't going to get married in a church, she had decided, but on a barge floating down the Thames. They'd land in Richmond where there would be a reception on the lawn at Richmond House. She'd already received permission from the queen who would, by the by, be happy to attend. Tra-la-lah!

Good heavens, Daria! What's next?

Oh dear, a circus theme for the reception, apparently.

He rolled his eyes as he pictured the lions and elephants she was describing, all wearing "violent pink" headpieces with giant feathers. There would be acrobats and jugglers, of course, darling. And it would all be so festive and so ... so ... "darling, darling."

"I know you told me to try and not make it a circus, darling," she wrote. "But that statement set me to thinking ..."

And to realize he had no one to blame but himself!

Not able to bear it anymore, he set the letter down on top of the piano and decided to read the rest tomorrow. Or maybe the next day. He was surprised that the peacefulness of the Scottish countryside had so infiltrated his senses that even Daria's letter was simply too cacophonous to endure for an extended period of time.

Still, it made him think. She truly had accepted his proposal. With Daria one could never be certain. She might have said, "yes darling," then continued on with the status quo until he was forced to gently remind her. But not this time. The dancing bears and spinning elephants attested to that! The fact that she had set a date was further reinforcement that she was serious. A June wedding. "That I've decided on the mundane as far as dates go," she had written, "will come as a complete surprise to everyone in London!"

And that was another thing. He realized suddenly that he wasn't missing life in London at all! According to Hamish's latest communiqué, he and Valentinia were all but married, planning to elope on Christmas Eve. His play was almost finished and he didn't even mention liquor, which wasn't necessarily a good sign. Percy was now staying in London exclusively, having gladly complied with Sharon's wishes to have the country estate in Kent to herself. He was having a marvelously good time with John Dormerthwaite, and Pratt's was especially amusing these days. Percy didn't say why, but Tobin suspected it had nothing to do with the new billiard table.

Even the remembrance of his life in the city made him yearn for some fresh air. He walked over to the window, opened it, and was immediately swallowed up in the loudest, most raucous laughter he had ever heard.

Why, there was Miss Wallace, straddled on one of those new-fangled velocipedes, speeding toward the stable! The wooden contraption seemed to be shaking her to the very bone, the large front wheel vibrating with every bump on the dirt path that led from the gatehouse to the stables. Her hands held firmly onto the handles, and her entire body jumped with each rut. It was amazing she was keeping her balance so well! That Miranda Wallace had a propensity for athletics came as somewhat of a surprise to him.

"Watch oot, Miss Wallace!" Angus was yelling, adding his shrill voice to the din. "Ye'd better curb yer speed, or ye'll be sorry!"

"I'm fine!" she shouted back, her feet pushing the pedals in a mad circle. "This is the most fun I've had in years!" And she laughed some more. The sound of it, so uninhibited, so ... brave ... was utterly surprising to him. She had always seemed like such a cautious soul. Not that he'd had much conversation with her other than ones that were destined to point out his short-comings. Come to think of it, maybe she wasn't cautious at all!

"Miss Wallace!" Elspeth hollered. "Look oot for yon—" And she put her hands over her eyes.

The governess hit a rock that protruded severeal inches from the ground. The boneshaker came to an abrupt stop, but she kept going, sailing through the air in a silent, wide-eyed billow of skirt, petticoat, and hair.

Good heavens!

The children began running toward her even before she hit the ground. And when she did, landing first on her arms, then rolling over from her head to her back, she lay perfectly still, eyes now closed.

Tobin ran out of the room. Where were the stable hands anyway? Didn't they see her down there? He ran out the main doorway, the chill of the December air unhampered by his shirt.

The children skidded to a stop, then leaned down over her.

He ran faster, watching as Elspeth said something to Angus and pointed to the castle. As the lad began to rise to his feet, a pair of long arms shot out and with a loud "boo!" Miranda pulled both of them down on top of her.

Tobin stopped near the well house. Again, she laughed and laughed, full, deep, and throaty. "I got you!" she cried. "And I got you good!"

"Miss Wallace!" The children's mirth, high-pitched and musical, harmonized with their teacher's as they rolled over and over in the dusty courtyard. Tobin pulled in his breath. He knew then, he had never heard a more beautiful sound in his entire life. Mesmerized, he watched the group until they tromped back into the castle twenty minutes later, both children having been given a ride on the vehicle with a careful Miss Wallace holding them up.

Tobin thoughtfully made his way back to the library and sat down at the piano, the tune of Miranda's laughter fairly exploding inside his heart. He felt bemused by what he had just experienced. A deformed child, a marred woman, and a spindly-legged little boy had inspired him in a way most surprising.

His fingers found the keys and seemingly on their own painted a melody like nothing they had ever played before. A strange beauty was layered into the melody, a haunting harmony deepening the composition. He called it "Lady of Gold."

⁓

Miranda awoke to a silence more dense than usual. The light that shone softly through her window was paler, more white than the normal blue of the night. It could mean only one thing.

Too excited to even put on her slippers, she jumped out of bed and ran to the window, the floor so cold she felt it in her ankles. The land was softly swaddled in a magnificent white so vast and pristine it could have come only out of the heavens. Not bothering to awaken Elspeth, she shrugged into her clothes, teeth chattering, then went into the schoolroom to start the fire. Angus was already there tending to the job himself. "It's a bonnie way ta shake a leg, is it no', Miss Wallace?"

"Aye, Angus. It is. I see the silence woke you up too?"

He nodded. "Aye, yon, and more besides." He jerked his head in the direction of Elspeth's room. "Ye'd maybees want ta be havin' a look yonder."

Miranda felt her eyebrows draw together, and she quickly crossed the room. When she opened the door and found the bed empty, she was hardly surprised. She looked at Angus. "Gone to see her father?"

"Who else?"

"Thank you, lad."

"Ma da says it's a heavy sky tha' winna stop snowin' fer days."

Miranda felt alarmed. "I'll go fetch her back home then."

He stood to his feet and met her gaze with a purposeful nod. "I'm goin' wi' ye. Ye'll need a fine man like me wi' ye on such a day. Especially wi' it still bein' dark an' aw," he added, the six-year-old shining through.

Miranda knew there would not be any sense in arguing, and she certainly enjoyed the laddie's company. "Let's be off then, shall we?"

The snow was only a few inches deep, and the going would be easy enough. But Miranda had to agree with James MacDowell; it didn't look like the storm would be letting up any time soon. Elspeth should have known better than to sneak off like that, she thought with consternation.

They found Elspeth with her father, who was cooking several sausages over the small fire in the crypt. How the man survived day after day in the cold was something Miranda couldn't fathom. Yes, he had plenty of blankets, warm clothes, and a nip of brandy every now and again to warm his innards, but to never be truly warm . . . well, she would never want to be in his shoes, that much was certain!

He was delighted to see them and added more sausages to the pan. They enjoyed a hearty breakfast together, David gladly sharing his food. But Miranda was insistent soon after that they needed to get back to Greywalls. Elspeth clutched at her sleeve. "Oh please, Miss Wallace, please let me bide a wee minute, Miss Wallace."

Time to act like a governess. "Absolutely not! You took a chance in coming here, Elspeth. And with the storm setting in now, it's too dangerous."

David Youngblood crossed his arms over his chest and picked at his teeth with a sliver of wood. His eyes twinkled in a way that made Miranda recall the rogue he had once been, and she felt herself blush a bit. "Do as Miss Wallace says, Bethie. And you must promise me not to come back here until the snow has not only stopped but is melted from the ground."

Miranda realized his easy demeanor was just an act.

"Och, no, Papa!" Elspeth protested. "That could be the spring!"

"Do as I say, daughter," he said in a mock-stern voice. "Now give me a hug."

She threw herself into his arms, and Miranda watched David's face as his eyes closed. This child was his only earthly cause for joy at this point. No wonder he couldn't leave for France, no wonder he couldn't leave her yet.

Several minutes later, after the children said their good-byes and scampered on up the hill, throwing snow at each other, David laid a hand on Miranda's arm. "Have you any word from Sylvie?"

"Nothing new. She still comes and teaches French to the children."

"And she is well? The pregnancy uneventful?"

Miranda wondered if David Youngblood would ever belong to anyone but Sylvie. "All is well."

"Good. Perhaps I should leave for France. Perhaps it is time."

Snowflakes fell onto his auburn curls, and the slight wind blew cold against them. "Yes, David," Miranda said. "It is time."

"Do not tell Elspeth I have gone. I will be back before the snows melt."

Miranda felt a hollow dread come over her heart. Surely the man was going to his death. "I will take care of her. Always."

His eyes burned suddenly. "No! No, Miranda! I said I will be back. I . . . will . . . be . . . back."

She nodded, picked up her skirts, and turned. "Good-bye, then."

When he made no move to embrace her, to say a word of thanks, Miranda knew the feelings which had been developing inside her for this man had been for nothing. But instead of her heart breaking, she felt free. There would be no true rejection, then, would there?

On the jaunt home, climbing up hills and down into vales, she realized she had only wanted to be in love. That this man was the first one she had met who would not spurn her for her face. But wanting to be in love, and actually finding oneself immersed over one's head in the state, were two vastly different matters. It was, indeed, something she might never fully understand. And perhaps that was just as well.

Tobin lay on the leather couch of the library as if he had been turned to stone. On his chest, laid bare for the world to see, sat Miranda's papers. Her strong handwriting, slanted too far to the left to be proper, was in such direct contrast to Daria's it was almost laughable. But the words she had penciled down were anything but funny. *Amazing* would be a more accurate description.

How surprised he had been to come upon the small stack of vellum hidden behind a dusty spittoon up in the mezzanine. It was even more of shock when he realized the words belonged to Miranda Wallace. Some notes were mere musings of her heart, peripheral jottings off the topic at hand.

"I thrill. The music which he plays drowns me like a flood. But instead of fearing the loss of myself, I willingly breathe each phrase into my lungs as though it is breath of another kind, another state of being."

He hardly knew what to think. Each statement brought a happiness to him, as if someone finally understood what he was trying to say, who he really was, and was giving it back to him in her own unique mode of expression. It suddenly brought a validity to his own gift when he realized God must feel the same way when the talents of his children were given back to him.

He smiled, reading a very small note written in the corner of what appeared to be the beginning of a story. "How can such beauty come from a man who is incapable of seeing the inner beauty of God's creations?"

That stings a bit. He was feeling sheepish about his initial attitude toward his nephew's child. He still hadn't reached out to the girl, though he knew he needed to.

"You'd think his own vanity would spur him to at least talk to the child every once in a while, to make it somewhat appear like he's a decent sort."

She's hit the mark with that one!

"Yet, I suppose he is so consumed with his work that he doesn't give Elspeth so much as a thought."

"She's wrong there," he whispered. He'd felt guilty about it since he'd arrived, but he hadn't experienced a creative flow like this in years, and all he wanted to do was compose and play.

Curving his arm behind his head, he began to read the story. Though she didn't write down which melody went with which poem, he instinctively knew. The images she had conjured reflected almost exactly what he had pictured in his mind as he wrote. Of course, the details of the story, the easy plot, were her own. But they were perfect. A strong Greek woman, a beautiful Greek man. And which one of them was destined to live out eternity in the Elysian Fields? He knew his mythology as well as anyone classically educated, and he realized this was destined to be a tragedy.

"She knows my heart," he said to himself, not beginning to even understand how. Yet he knew it to be true. "Even if she does not yet realize it herself."

How could a governess, a simple woman with a port-wine stain over half of her face, understand beauty and reverence in a way that he, always considering himself so sensitive and appreciative, could not?

It appears then, that there's much I can learn from this woman, and that she—he fingered the pages—*has much more to give than I could have ever dreamed.*

CHAPTER ❖ TWENTY-ONE

It's Christmas!"

Miranda could hardly contain herself as she threw off her covers. It was her favorite day of the year, a day her family had always made special. The other servants had never heard of such hoopla, especially the Scottish born who were looking more forward to Hogmanay, but she soon had them as excited as she was. Nights leading up to the holiday they were all in the kitchen working on some sort of present or other. Miranda embroidered, Pamela canned, Mrs. Wooten knitted, James MacDowell carved a chess set, and much to everyone's surprise, Mr. Wooten drew beautiful snow scenes with charcoal.

She shivered into her clothes, adding an extra layer of flannel undergarments to ward off the day's chill, and ran downstairs. Elspeth could sleep a little longer.

Down the corridor she flew, thinking of the Yule log they'd throw into the hearth down in the kitchen. Hoping the large log would truly catch, she remembered how it almost never did back in Leeds. She veered into the kitchen, expecting to enter a dark, cold room but was surprised to find the fire lit and the Yule log burning like a giant torch cast aside by some wayward Titan.

She gasped at the sight, touched by its simple beauty. "What a lovely sight! Pamela!" she called, turning around, surprised the cook was already awake.

"Sorry." A deep voice came from the darkened portion of the kitchen. "It's not Pamela."

"My lord?" Miranda peered into the gloom. "Is that you?"

He stepped forward into the warm firelight. His beauty was striking. The masculine, yet perfect features, the copper curls of his hair. More slender than his nephew, he was, nevertheless, well proportioned. His hands, so strong and yet so sensitive, stretched toward her, holding a small gift. "How long before the others come down?"

Miranda shook her head. He didn't look as if he'd been to bed yet. But then, Tobin Youngblood always looked as though his clothes had journeyed to the far ends of the earth and back again. "Not long. Half an hour maybe."

He placed the gift, clumsily wrapped and topped with a wrinkled satin ribbon, in her hand. "For Elspeth."

"Shouldn't you give it to her yourself?" She wanted to laugh at the forlorn little box, the way it was dressed much like the man who had handed it to her.

"I don't know. After all this time . . . would she even accept it from me?"

Miranda said nothing, setting the gift on the worktable. "I'm just about to make some tea. Would you care for a cup?"

"Yes, thank you."

The atmosphere between them was stilted and awkward, but Miranda didn't want to part company with him just yet. "You know, children are quite forgiving."

"I've not much experience with them, I'm afraid."

"No. That much is evident."

He laughed. "You can be quite candid, can you not?"

She shrugged as she reached for the porcelain teapot. "I've found it best not to beat around the bush."

"So you see yourself as quite the no-nonsense lady? No frills or pretensions."

"I've gained quite a reputation for it, actually."

He watched as she pulled down the tin of tea and began measuring it in spoonfuls, feeding the round belly of the pot with the small, dark leaves.

"Would you mind pumping out some water?" she asked, forgetting he was an earl.

"Of course. Forgive me," he said, obviously forgetting the same thing. "I should have offered."

They worked together for the next few minutes in silence. He fired up the stove while she sliced some bread and put them in a toasting iron.

Not about to let the subject go, Miranda said, "As I said, children can be very forgiving."

"I'll have to take your word on it."

They stood side by side at the worktable, Lord Youngblood leaning back against the edge, Miranda facing its surface, preparing the tea tray. "Give her the present yourself, my lord. Please. It won't really mean anything if you don't."

He inhaled deeply. "It's difficult, you know. I mean, when someone is born in such a way as Elspeth, everyone thinks about how difficult their life will be. But no one is allowed to say how difficult it is for those around them. Not to stare, not to wish it was different, not knowing what to say."

Miranda turned to face him. He kept staring into the fire just across the room. "Look at me," she commanded him.

"What?"

"Look at me."

Slowly he turned his head, his eyes first resting on her birthmark, then quickly moving to her hair.

"My lord," she began. "Right now, all you see is my birthmark, because there isn't much more about me that you know to look for. I can promise you, my brother, his wife, my family hardly sees it anymore. They see me . . . Miranda."

His eyes widened. "Miranda? Is that your name?"

"Yes."

"It's beautiful."

"I know. It's why my mother gave it to me. She wanted to ensure that something about me was beautiful."

He gave a nervous chuckle.

"You see?" she continued. "Even my own mother was repulsed at the very first. It's natural you should feel the same way as well. And with Elspeth, I have to admit, it took some getting used to even on my part."

"Really?"

"Oh certainly! Just because I have a birthmark doesn't mean I have learned to immediately overlook someone else's deformity. It's a long, gentle process. But it's worth the effort. You really ought to give it a try."

He smiled, and it lit his eyes with an uncommon warmth as he reached for the small gift and placed it back into his pocket. "When is her Christmas dinner?"

"At two, after the servants have served you."

He nodded. "When is my dinner?"

"Noon."

"Tell Miss Elspeth that she is expected to dine with me. As are you."

By this time the tea was made and poured. He took his cup, said, "It's time we ran this house properly," and exited the kitchen leaving behind a flabbergasted Miranda.

⸻

"He really wants to sup wi' us?" Elspeth was in awe, then suddenly suspicious. "How?" She sat down on Miranda's bed and straightened the lace on her cuffs.

Miranda was fixing the hem of her own gown. "I think he feels badly about his previous behavior."

Elspeth shrugged. "He wasna a patch on ma da onyways." She began to brush her hair. "I still canna understand how he told me no' ta come back ta the abbey until spring."

"He said until the snows melted." Miranda put the thread up to her mouth, bit down, and pulled. "There, good as new." She stood up, letting the hem journey back to its rightful latitude. "Are you ready to go down?"

Elspeth nodded. "Might as weel get aw the gawpin' oot the way."

"Me too," Miranda laughed, placing the girl's hand in her own.

They were halfway down the cold corridor when Elspeth asked, "Do ye think he's hurtin' aboot not seein' me fer his ain sake, or fer mine?"

"To be honest, probably a little of both."

"Yon's awfu', then. Usin' me to ease his ain guilt." It was the first time Miranda had heard bitterness in Elspeth's voice.

Miranda put her arm tightly around her charge's shoulders. "Bethie, ninety percent of all good that is done is motivated by guilt in one form or another. When it isn't, well, it's truly a gift from God. Don't despise him for being a perfectly normal human being. Rejoice that he's trying to rise above it, for whatever reason."

But Elspeth said nothing. She simply crossed her arms over her chest and tilted her head at an "I'll wait and see" angle. Miranda had a feeling that she was going to be doing all the talking. She wanted to heave a sigh, but of course didn't.

Lord Tobin Youngblood was waiting for them by the fireplace in the great hall. "Merry Christmas, ladies."

"And to you, my lord," Miranda responded, nudging Elspeth.

"Aye, m'lord. You an' aw."

The voice was so small and weak, so pathetic, Miranda felt her heart breaking for the child. She held tightly to her hand.

Lord Tobin held out his hand toward his great-niece.

"Go on, child," Miranda whispered. "Go greet him like a proper young lady. It will be all right."

Elspeth lifted tortured gray eyes to her governess, but Miranda only nudged her forward. Unfortunately, life would be full of these moments for Elspeth. The sooner she got used to it, the better.

The thought sounded cruel to her ears.

Lord Tobin met her halfway across the hall, where she took his hand and dropped a very sweet, very graceful curtsy.

"Nicely done, Elspeth," he said graciously, and kept hold of her hand. "May I escort you to dinner?"

Elspeth nodded mutely and Miranda, suddenly the outsider, watched the two walk away from her toward the table. The hair color was the same, and even something about their build spoke of family ties.

It was a start.

*

"Well, what did you think of his lordship?" Miranda asked long after the uncomfortable meal was over with and Elspeth was getting ready for bed. It had been just as Miranda had suspected. She had created the majority of the conversation, which ranged from the Prime Minister to why God saw fit to give people eyebrows.

"I miss ma da," Elspeth said simply. "He minds me o' him, ye know."

"I did notice that. And he could never deny you are a Youngblood."

Elspeth smiled her gruesome grin. "Aye, maybees. I canna caw mesel' the name Youngblood, but I am one fer aw that."

"What is your last name?" Miranda asked, shocked that she hadn't thought to ask sooner.

"Farquarson."

"Now *that's* a mouthful!"

Miranda handed Elspeth her nightgown and watched her pull it over her head. "You never talk about your mother, Bethie. Would you ever care to?"

Elspeth tilted her head to the side and shook it. "Ma isna abody worthy o' mindin' really."

The remark sliced through Miranda, whose own mother was a loving, godly woman worth praising. "How long has it been since she died?"

"Three years. That's when I came ta Greywalls. An' jist as soon as I met Mrs. Pamela an' wifie Wooten, it made aw the difference."

"So that's where Angus gets it from, eh? I thought so."

Elspeth jumped onto her bed. "Och, aye. Miss Wallace?" she asked, her tone of voice indicating a change of subject was coming. "Is ma da really still the earl, or other yon loon?"

"I really don't know, Bethie. I'm not a lawyer."

Elspeth was silent for a moment, staring at her hands resting on the white eiderdown. "He did somethin' awfu', no?"

Miranda didn't quite know what to say. "Child, I—"

"Nay. Dinna say a word, Miss Wallace. I know fine tha' he must o' done somethin' awfu' bad to be hidin' like he is. An' with no one to see 'im on Christmas too. Is he still gettin' food?"

"Yes, I'm sure he's eating just fine. I was wondering what was bothering you today. You've been even more quiet than usual. So you're feeling sorry for your father."

Tears filled the child's eyes, and she looked into Miranda's. "Aye, miss." She dropped her face into her hands and wept.

Miranda immediately sat down upon the bed and took her hand. "Oh, Bethie, don't cry. Your father is a grown man, a wonderful man. He's all right tonight, I promise. He can certainly take care of himself, you know."

"I know. Och, I miss him somethin' terrible, Miss Wallace, so I do. An' the thought o' our first Christmas together bein' like this an aw!" She began crying again.

Miranda cursed herself for making the day more special to the child than it would have been otherwise.

Yet even as Elspeth fell asleep, Miranda was left thinking about their conversation and hoping against all reason that David Youngblood would indeed make it back safely to his daughter. Safe and free.

CHAPTER ❖ TWENTY-TWO

France

David Youngblood paid the fisherman handsomely from a fine leather purse. "You'll tell no one you brought me here."

"Aye, aye, sir." The old mariner, missing three fingers but making up for the loss of tissue with the many scars on his face, offered David a grisly salute and a rotted smile.

"You'll come across again, in a month's time. The remuneration will be doubled if your boat is waiting when I get here."

"Aye, bu' I'll ne'er leave, then," he wheezed.

"No, you must go back to Scotland. I wouldn't want to arouse suspicion."

"Jist as ye say, mister. But I'll no' be away till the mornin'. I'm goin' ower to yon bothie an' get bleezin' drunk, an' then I'm gonna sleep like a dead man. An' *then*, I'll be goin' back."

Youngblood gathered his duffle bag and slung it over his shoulder. "In a month, then, Kenny."

And he was on his way, on the road to Paris. He had sailed from Aberdeen to the coast of France, two miles north of Cherbourg, in the disguise of a common worker. Brown pants, a gray, heavily woven shirt, a warm wool coat and hat, and his favorite old boots served to take away a bit of his physical dignity. Only a bit, mind you.

Camille won't even recognize me at first, he thought, pulling his hat down low and rolling up his collar. It was imperative that no one see his face. For there was none like it in all of Paris. None that he knew, anyway.

He breathed in deeply, muttered a prayer, and began to walk down the dark road. But God was with him, he knew, and instead of feeling he was a man headed for destruction, he knew he was a man who had finally decided on a narrower path, harder on the feet, but easier in the end. Maybe he'd pick up a few crowns along the way, even if that meant hearing the words, "Well done," a bit sooner than he had planned.

"Joyeux Noel!" a passing cartsman called to him.

David waved his hand in greeting and answered likewise. *Merry Christmas, Elspeth*, he thought, looking out over the sea. For the first time in thirty such holidays, he finally realized the meaning of it. Looking far up into the heavens, his eye caught sight of the North Star, and he remembered the Star of Bethlehem which led the Magi to the Christ child. *Well, I may not have a star guiding me*, he mused, *but I do have the Lord himself, no matter where the path may lead*.

Indeed, somehow, though he was alone and far from home, it was the first merry Christmas he had ever known.

⁓

The music had a softer quality to it than usual, Miranda thought later that night as she crept through the small door into the library loft. It was definitely Christmas music, and it definitely put her in a pensive mood.

She took out her pen and paper, remembering the day, the dinner, the way Elspeth had left his present unopened. No matter how much Miranda had prompted her, the girl refused to unwrap the dilapidated little gift. It amazed Miranda that Elspeth had hidden her resentments so thoroughly for all of this time. "He canna give me a present an' expect me ta think tha' his scunnerin' me was aw right, Miss Wallace."

"You must forgive him, Elspeth. That's what this present is all about, you know."

Elspeth had jutted out her chin. "If'n he asks me, maybees I'll forgive him."

Miranda realized that Elspeth would not be convinced. She penned a quick note about forgiveness and the importance of it not only for the transgressor but for the transgressee, and tucked it into her pocket. Tomorrow she would talk about bitterness to Elspeth. She had fallen into it herself for a time. Oh, how she hated being responsible for the spiritual well-being of a child at times. She felt so preachy and obvious. *I don't know how Matthew does it.*

The earl was playing softly now, and Miranda decided to do nothing but listen tonight. No writing, no stories, no unasked-for librettos. Just to let the music wash over her was enough. Softer the music played, and yet softer, and finally, it faded.

She waited for it to start up again. These pauses were normal. Perhaps he was penning something to paper, or looking out of the window. She knew better than to make a move, or even breathe too heavily during these moments, lest she be found out.

"Caught you!"

Miranda, startled, rose to her knees with a loud cry.

There standing in front of her was a triumphant Tobin Youngblood, a grin almost as broad as his face lighting up his eyes.

"My lord!" Miranda huffed, feeling her face redden. "You shouldn't go sneaking up on a lady like that!" She began to straighten her papers.

"And you shouldn't go skulking around library stacks, listening in secret to someone who has no idea of your presence!"

"Well," Miranda said, flustered, "if you didn't play such beautiful music, I wouldn't have been here in the *first* place!"

He crossed his arms. "So it's really all my fault, is it?"

"Absolutely."

He bowed and extended a hand. "Then all I can say to that is, thank you."

She allowed him to help her to her feet. "Forgive me, my lord, I shouldn't have been here without your permission. I will go."

"No. No. Stay, please. Come downstairs and let me play a song for you. It's a new tune, written only yesterday . . . during the day . . . so you probably haven't heard it."

"Let me just collect my things."

He leaned down with her, gathering up bits of paper, some pencils, even an empty teacup. "You have quite a little camp set up here, don't you?"

Miranda nodded, but didn't know what to say. She wasn't about to retrieve the blanket and pillow she had stuffed behind the chair. Following him down the spiral staircase onto the main floor of the library, she allowed him to show her to the leather sofa.

"Now, you just sit there and listen, and then tell me what you think."

She obeyed, only because she wanted to. Anticipation dried her throat, and she eyed the empty teacup with dismay. Soon the music started, and when Tobin opened his voice and his heart and began to sing, Miranda could hardly believe what she was hearing.

"Elysian Fields, Elysian Fields,
follow me my love.
For though your beauty is not for the eye,
your heart is made of gold.
Fairer than all the goddesses
are the deeds of your hands, my dear.
Elysian Fields, Elysian Fields,
follow me my love.
Follow me to fields of gold."

Miranda stood to her feet. "My words!" she gasped. "How dare you take them without me knowing! How dare you read from my papers!"

Unruffled, Lord Tobin stood to his feet. "Don't you like the song?"

"Yes, but that is clearly not the point! You stole my words!"

"Oh, believe me," he drawled, his normally bright eyes quickly going flat, "I'll give you all the credit if that's what you're worried about."

Miranda was outraged at his remark. "No! I don't care about that! But you read my papers, you read my thoughts, you read my heart! How dare you presume such intimacy."

Tobin Youngblood walked forward. "Dear Miss Wallace, I *am* sorry. I thought you'd be excited, I thought this would be what you would want."

"How much did you read? Be honest, please."

He sat her down gently, paused. "All of it."

"Oh blast, I wish I was anywhere else right now!" she cried, dropping her forehead into her waiting hands. She had never felt more foolish. "Daddy always warned me never to write down anything which might come back to haunt me."

"I read all of the things you said about me. Every single entry."

Miranda had never been so embarrassed in all her life.

"And," he continued, a smile in his voice, "I believe you were right about me."

She raised her head. "What did you say?"

"You were right. I thought I understood beauty. But obviously, I don't. Those words you wrote, Miss Wallace, that story. Do you know I've been searching for years for a libretto for my opera? No story has ever been good enough, beautiful enough. Until now."

"My story?"

Excitement ignited his eyes, and he took both her hands in his. "Yes. The perfect-looking Greek man, the wise and good woman who is not beautiful—it's wonderful. How they live their lives together, loving each other, and when it is time for them to die, he goes on to the Elysian Fields because he is fair to the eye, and she is doomed because, despite her good works, she is not beautiful."

Miranda actually felt flattered, though still a bit piqued. "You did read it all, didn't you?"

"Every word of it. Miss Wallace, you are a genius! And think of how beautiful this will be when set to music, not to mention what the sets and the costumes will be like . . . so Grecian and flowing. I never thought of my music being set to a tragedy, but I don't see why it can't be."

Miranda took her hands from his. "But it isn't a tragedy, my lord."

"What? Well surely it is. They are parted. She meets damnation."

"No, sir. The story is not finished."

"Really?" he sat forward, waiting to be told the rest.

Miranda decided not to make it easy on him. Obviously he was one of the beautiful people who were handed everything and then some. No. She wasn't ready to tell him what she had been planning. "Maybe soon," she said vaguely.

His brows raised. "You can't possibly mean you're not going to tell me the rest?"

"I certainly do."

"But your story has spurred me on. I need to know how it ends to create the right score."

Miranda smiled and stood to her feet. "Maybe soon," she repeated, "when I know the ending myself."

That seemed to placate him for the time being.

"Would you like some tea?" She was ready to change the subject. She knew where the ending was going actually, but she didn't want to commit to anything.

He conceded. "All right, then. Have it your way, Miss Wallace."

She chuckled, thinking this man might not be so bad after all, and left the room to go get the tea. As she trekked down to the kitchen she caught a glimpse of the night sky. No stars. More snow? Hopefully not.

They enjoyed their tea together. Tobin Youngblood played various pieces for her, asking for her opinion.

"You don't really want my opinion, my lord. It truly means nothing."

"I don't believe that for an instant," he said earnestly. "I do not write just for myself, Miss Wallace. I write for God and to uplift the human spirit."

"Well," she laughed. "I'm feeling very uplifted, then."

"Good."

He played for a while longer, finally joining her on the sofa for a second cup of tea. "Did Elspeth open my present?"

Miranda shook her head. "She can't yet. You understand, don't you?"

"I guess I do. You know, reading your story was a bit of an eye-opener, I must say."

"Really?"

"Yes. I mean, what is the purpose of creating beauty if you fail to see it in others? Yes, beauty and its appreciation separates us from the animals, I know all that. But there is beauty of another kind. I want to discover that, Miss Wallace. I want to be that hero, that man that can love, despite the outward, what is so wonderful regarding the inward. Your story made me yearn to be better."

"Uplifted you?" she asked with a smile.

"Well, yes. Or it will, if I can just get over my fears."

That was an interesting remark. "Fears? What do you mean?"

He sipped from his cup, then set it down. "There is a reason Elspeth frightens me, the way she looks, how I respond."

Miranda waited patiently as he gathered his words.

"I could pass it down. The disfigurement may not be on my face, but it may be in my body, Miss Wallace. David's father, my older brother, was not possessed of a harelip. Far from it. He was one of the most handsome men in England when he was young, before he became . . . well, we won't go into that . . . I've heard it's bad luck to speak ill of the dead."

"If you believe in luck."

"Well, it's bad manners, then. Anyway, there you have it. I'm scared of passing it on to my own child, and then, not being able to deal with it once I am face-to-face with it."

"And this is why you've never married?" Miranda asked.

"I didn't realize it was until the past few weeks. When Daria told me she didn't want to have children, I was far too relieved, as if my mind was only looking for an excuse."

"But what does this really have to do with Elspeth, my lord?"

"She's a reminder of all that. She's a true Youngblood, Miss Wallace. I worked hard all of my life to get away from them."

"So it isn't just her mouth?" Miranda wondered if she should ring for more tea.

"Initially, yes. But it set me to thinking. I've been evaluating myself, the entire situation for weeks now. And I have to say, I completely agree with your assessment of my character. Not very flattering."

Miranda softened. "Oh, my lord. Don't be so hard on yourself."

"I'm thirty-six years old, Miss Wallace. I should be far beyond this in wisdom, discretion, and kindness."

The fire in the grate was dying. "Why don't you stir the fire up a bit, my lord?"

He complied, bending down on his haunches before the glowing embers and reaching for another log nearby. "I now believe I was brought up here by God himself. There's so much I need to learn. And you and Elspeth are the ones to teach me."

"You might try looking in little Angus's direction too, my lord, if you want to learn by example."

"I've been terrible to my niece," he confessed. "I should have called her to me long ago."

Miranda nodded. "Yes, you should have. But you can do so again. And I have a suggestion for you that may help."

"Anything," he said.

"Tell her you're sorry. That's all she wants. To hear it directly from you. The present wasn't enough."

He looked down at his hands, then spread them just above his knees. "I'll call her to me tomorrow after breakfast."

"Better yet," Miranda said cheerfully, feeling suddenly tired, "why don't you join us for breakfast in the schoolroom?"

He looked doubtful. "That's rather early, isn't it?"

Miranda cocked her head.

The earl laughed. "All right then. But you must promise me it will not be before seven o'clock."

"I promise." Miranda joined in his laughter. She stood to her feet. "Well, my lord, the teapot is empty and it's just about to strike midnight, so I suppose Christmas is officially over. I should retire."

They said their good-nights, and Miranda took the tray down to the kitchen. The fire was banked for the night and the others had gone to bed. It was one of the few times she had missed the nightly gathering. But she didn't regret it. Miles of ground had been covered that evening, and hopefully, tomorrow would be a brighter day. Not that the dark sky would help as far as that went.

On the way up the spiral staircase leading to her floor, Miranda looked out of the window. Rains were falling, the air had obviously warmed, and the snow was already gone. The land was black and deep, slippery and barren-looking.

"Elspeth!" she cried, and ran, frightened, to the child's bedroom, remembering David Youngblood's words. "When the snows are gone ..."

CHAPTER ✦ TWENTY-THREE

Tobin knew something was very wrong by the look on Miranda's face as she rushed into the library without knocking.

"My lord!" She slid into him.

He grabbed her shoulders. "What is it, Miss Wallace?"

Fear gripped her expression. "It's Elspeth. She's gone!"

"What?"

"Her bed is empty."

"She's not in the castle?" Surely the child had only wandered away from her room.

"I don't think so." She was shaking her head from side to side. "Her coat is gone, and her boots. Believe me, she left Greywalls."

"All right, then." Tobin realized there was no time to be wasted. The conditions outside were terrible for a healthy, stalwart man to be out in, let alone an eleven-year-old child. "I'll get my cloak. Do you know where she might have gone? Any favorite places?"

Miranda nodded. "Yes. Shall I call for some horses?"

"Do that. I'll be back down as quickly as possible."

Once up in his room, Tobin pulled on his riding boots and a warm jacket. All he could think was, *This is my fault.* He should have reached out to the child. Daria was always telling him how he understood people, how kind and gentle he was. Hah. Well, now he would prove her right.

He ran as fast as he could down the stairs. By the time he got to the entryway, Mrs. Wooten, Mr. Wooten, and Miranda stood there, whispering sharply to one another. He cleared his throat.

"My lord!" Mrs. Wooten shouted, startled. "We didn't realize you were there."

"Are you ready?" he asked Miranda, choosing to ignore their open-eyed glares.

"Yes." She nodded. "Mr. Wooten ordered the horses brought round."

"And you ride?"

"Of course."

Wooten handed him his hat, glaring at Mrs. Wooten while she wound his scarf around Tobin's neck. "She's quite a horse-woman," she said. "At least that's what I've heard."

"Well, there's no time to be lost," he said, taking control of the situation. "Miss Wallace?"

"I'm ready." The governess breathed in deeply, saying, "Oh my," as Mr. Wooten opened the door and the chilly, wet air barraged them. "Let's be off then."

He helped her up on a small, yet sprightly gray mare and was pleased to see how well Miranda sat upon the animal, how comfortable she was. Then, swinging himself up on his own horse, a stallion called Mister Socks, he patted its flanks. Despite its silly name, it was a magnificent bay, and it caught his attention the first time he walked through the stable.

"I see you've taken a liking to Mister Socks?" Miranda called through the rain. "Angus named him, you know."

Tobin thumped his heels lightly against the horse's flanks. "Let's find that child, Miss Wallace."

She clicked in agreement, her horse following along. It was only a few seconds later that she caught up to him. But the rain was coming down so hard, and the mission was so dire, that conversation was nil. Instead, he settled in for the ride, content to let her lead him in the search.

"Where are we going?" he finally shouted above the pelting rain.

"To the abbey! St. Ninian's Abbey," she returned, not flinching against the downpour.

He'd never heard of it. But he supposed an abbey would be a natural place of intrigue for the child. "How much longer?"

"Ten minutes!"

"Let's step up the pace!" he shouted. "It's growing colder, I fear."

"I thought so too," Miranda called over her shoulder.

"It will begin sleeting soon." He cursed himself for forgetting to bring a blanket in which to wrap the child.

They both tapped their heels against the horses' flanks and galloped faster.

Finally, they crested a hill, and he could barely see the hulking outline of a ruined abbey.

"This is it!" Miranda called, spurring on her horse to an almost dangerous pace.

He followed suit. "I'm right behind you!"

By the time they careened into the abbey they were soaked through to the bone, but Miss Wallace noticed nothing of their discomfort. "Down to the crypt!" she yelled.

Tobin didn't like the sound of that, but he dutifully followed her down the steps and into the dense darkness. They stopped at the bottom landing and listened, breathing in shallow wisps of still air. Miranda turned, her heel crunching as it revolved.

Then . . . a gasp.

A light sob.

And then, "He's gone, Miss Wallace. He's gone."

"Oh, Bethie." Miranda hurried toward the sound of the voice. "Let's get you home. A storm is coming our way, and it may turn to sleet, or even ice."

"He said ta come when the snow was awa'. He said he'd be here." The words were filled with tears, and said through swollen lips.

Tobin was mystified. "Who is she talking about?" he whispered to Miranda.

"Not now," the governess's voice hissed through the darkness, obviously upset. "Let's just get her home and in bed, she's frozen to the core. Please pick her up, my lord. I don't think I can carry her up all of these steps."

Eyes adjusting, he walked toward their dark shapes and easily scooped Elspeth into his arms. "I'm sorry I was so horrible, Elspeth," he said right away. "I'm sorry you ran away. I'm sorry I didn't give you a better reason to stay with us."

But the child said nothing, merely dropped her head against his chest and began to cry afresh. They hurried up to the horses, the night indeed growing colder.

"Here," he said to Miranda. "Take her just until I mount. I'll carry her home with me."

Elspeth lifted her head and stopped sobbing. "Mister Socks?" she said. "He's the most bonnie of aw the horses."

"I think so too," Tobin whispered, and swung himself up. Reaching down, he lifted Elspeth gently up to sit in front of him. Miranda handed him a blanket, which he wrapped around the girl. Then she handed him another, and he did the same.

"You are quite the prepared woman, aren't you, Miss Wallace?"

She smiled and handed him yet another blanket. "And one for you too."

He raised his brows, pleased, very pleased. "And have you one for yourself?"

"Naturally. Why do you think I brought these in the first place? Now, let's be off. We could all use a warm bath and a hot cup of tea. Both of which will be waiting for us."

"The poor Wootens must be beside themselves with worry," he remarked as they started forward.

"And so they should be!" the governess snapped. "Elspeth!"

Elspeth turned her face further into Tobin's chest and suddenly pretended to sleep.

"She's sleeping, I think," Tobin called.

"And well she should be!" Miranda shouted. "I can tell you that tomorrow will not be an easy day for the child."

He hugged the girl closer to him. "Go easy on her, Miss Wallace. She misses her father."

"Aye, I do," a small voice whispered up into his neck. And once again Elspeth began to cry.

Tobin's heart broke, and he cursed himself for having been so remiss, so consumed with his own work, so . . . cruel. *I'll make it up to you*, he thought, *I'll make it up to you both*. Yes, even to Miss Wallace, riding beside him with her brow creased in worry, so faithful, so responsible, and yet for all of that, still a bit of a mystery.

It was only a few hours later, after breakfast, that Lord Tobin knocked on the schoolroom door. Elspeth was in bed, fighting a low-grade fever but sleeping quite peacefully, and Miranda was working on a poem.

"Come in, my lord!" she called, knowing it had to be her employer. After all, nobody else knocked anymore.

He entered, looking bemused. "I see your instinctual talents include knowing who is on the other side of doors as well as how they take their tea!"

She laughed.

"How's Elspeth this morning?"

"A bit of fever, but other than that, no worse for the wear. My midmorning tea should be up shortly. Would you join me?"

"I would love to. Thank you for not holding me to our 7 A.M. appointment." He sat down on one of the small chairs, his knees up to his chest. "Goodness, but I haven't sat in a nursery in years!"

"Schoolroom," Miranda corrected. "Bethie insists on calling it that. When they get past a certain age, they want nothing to do with babyhood."

"I remember that. And being the only child around our house . . . well, I guess I can understand Elspeth's wanting to grow up. There's so much expectation of you when you are the sole act, as if you live under a magnifying glass that has absolutely nothing else to look at."

Miranda set aside her pen and peered frankly at Lord Tobin. "I don't think that's Elspeth's problem. I think she believes that if she is grown up, life won't hurt so badly."

"Is she in for an unpleasant surprise," the earl said, reaching for Miranda's journal.

She batted his hand away. "My lord!"

"Sorry," he said, picking up an eraser. "You're just so intriguing to me, Miranda, I mean, Miss Wallace. No, actually I mean Miranda. It's too beautiful a name to go to waste. May I call you Miranda?"

What could it hurt? "As you wish, my lord."

"And as for all of those 'my lords—'"

"Don't even think about asking me to call you anything else!" Miranda piped. "What kind of example would that be for Elspeth?"

He cleared his throat and opened his mouth, about to speak. But he hesitated, then said, "I'll put some more peat into the stove."

Miranda secretly enjoyed his discomfort, considering how arrogant she had perceived him to be when he first came to Greywalls. "All right." She nodded. "It would be most appreciated. I'm not the warm-blooded type."

"It's the same with me," he said over his shoulder as he set to the task. "I wondered about myself, coming to Scotland for the winter, if I had finally gone daft."

"I see you had the piano moved so your bench is in front of the fireplace."

"Oh, yes. It hasn't been quite so bad now." He came back to the table and sat down.

"Why don't you just get it over with?" Miranda suddenly said.

"What?"

"You want to ask about last night, don't you?"

He nodded, eyes troubled. "David's alive, isn't he?"

Miranda looked at her hands, knowing there was no easy way to do this. "Yes."

The earl blew a long breath from between pursed lips. "I knew it had to be that. I've been up all night thinking about it. Who else would be there, at a ruined abbey? Who else would Elspeth risk so much to see?"

"He's gone now. He told her he'd be back before the snows left. He thought it would only take a few weeks, and no one expected those rains to come and take the snows all away."

"You don't know much about the weather around here then, do you? It's very temperamental. Can be snowing one minute, sleeting the next, back to snow, and then to rain."

Miranda shook her head. "I'm new to these parts, remember?"

"Yes. But Scottish weather is infamous. I'm surprised David didn't know better."

"He was just hoping, I suppose."

The earl raked a hand through his hair. "Where did he go? France?"

Miranda nodded. "I promised I wouldn't tell anyone any-thing."

"Oh, come now, Miranda. I should know this information. I am his closest relative."

"He's in danger," Miranda said reluctantly. "There's so much you don't know about the night he disappeared."

"Tell me."

"Trust me, my lord, you really don't want to hear this."

He gently set down the eraser and placed a hand on her arm. "Will I be in danger of losing my title?"

She shrugged. "Possibly."

"Then I want to know."

For one of the few times in her life, Miranda allowed herself a long, hearty sigh, then began to tell the tale of the de Courceys, the de Boyces, David Youngblood, and Claude Mirreault.

CHAPTER ❖ TWENTY-FOUR

It hadn't been an easy trip to Paris. He traveled in almost every manner of transportation known to mankind except, perhaps, a rickshaw, and so when the City of Lights cast her illumination upon a twilight sky, he was more than eager to find shelter. There was only one place where he would be welcomed.

He knocked on Camille's door, throwing his hood as far forward as he could. A minute later, there she stood, looking as beautiful as he remembered, her long, curled blond hair falling in ringlets over her bosom and down the front of her fancy dressing gown. One of the most celebrated courtesans in Paris.

"Say nothing!" he hissed. "Don't react. It's me. David."

She looked both ways down the street, then pulled him by the hand into the place Sylvie's former husband, another of her many contracted lovers, had bought for her the previous year. "Come in."

In two seconds the door was closed behind him and he threw off his cloak.

"*Mon cher!*" she cried, throwing herself into his arms and pressing her mouth to his face. She had never charged David even so much as a franc for the love she had given him, physical and otherwise.

The familiar fires stirred within him, and he yearned to kiss her back in the sensuous way he always had. For although he had never loved Camille as he should have, he was attracted to her beauty, was drawn to her evident love for him. He gently pushed her back. "I need your help."

"Are you all right?" she asked. "Where have you been? You've been the talk of Paris for months now."

"Have the servants retired for the night?"

"A few minutes ago. Come warm yourself. I was down in the kitchen making soup."

That she didn't seem anxious about housing a fugitive wasn't unusual. Camille, embroiled deeply in the affairs of Claude Mirreault, had basically become quite unflappable. Her life had always been a pendulum, swinging the way of good fortune one moment, bad the next. She was just glad to be hanging there at all, David knew. After all, he had introduced her to Claude Mirreault in the first place, when she had been homeless and living on the streets. Because of her hunger, she had been able to entertain suggestions she wouldn't have been open to a month before. "I wasn't always this way," she told anybody who cared to listen to her story.

She continued talking as she helped him out of his coat and took his hat. "I want you to know I didn't believe you had died for a minute, my lord." She led him back to the kitchen from which the wonderful smell of onions, garlic, and chicken was wafting. "I heard you had disappeared. That you were presumed dead. Didier came back to Claude with the full report. Well, as much as he knew anyway. And Yves is dead."

David nodded. "Yes. Shot by Rene."

"Yves had it coming to him, *mon chere*. I've never cared for his sort. A violent man from the cradle, no doubt. And so, you come back to Camille, eh?" Her vermilion lips, now dyed to a permanent red by countless applications of color, smiled. She had grown even more beautiful, he couldn't help but notice. *Camille*. He hadn't realized that he had missed her until right now.

"I need your help."

She shrugged, all shoulders and neck. "So I assumed."

Walking over to the stove, she pulled off the lid to the soup pot and stirred the bubbling contents. He followed her, leaning over to smell what he considered just then to be an edible masterpiece. "I forgot you knew your way around a kitchen so thoroughly, Camille. I'm so hungry. It was a long trip."

"So I gather." Camille immediately retrieved a bowl from the cupboard and filled it, setting it on the small wooden table used for the few staff who ate their midday meal at her home. "There you go. I'm glad you came to me, though. As much as I hate to admit it to you, I'd have it no other way. Once more, we see that I can fill a hunger no one else can."

David ignored the double entendre. "How long have you been with Claude Mirreault?"

"You were the one who found me on the streets, my lord. You know better than I do."

David shook his head. "I honestly don't remember the year, Camille. I'm trying my best not to remember myself during those days. But my point, regardless of when you found yourself in his employ, is this. How would you like to finally get out of his clutches?"

She sat in the adjacent chair. "Don't raise up a girl's hopes, my lord."

"If you're interested, I have a plan."

"I hate that man. I've always hated that man."

And so he began to explain, realizing he hadn't much to say. He didn't know what he was really going to do other than go to the authorities and offer his services.

Not much longer, Camille was laughing still over David's audacity. "To think you will take him down without a viable plan? You must be mad! Do you really think this will make you immune to the guillotine?"

"They'd much rather have Mirreault's head than my own."

"And do you really think the authorities will believe there's nothing in it for you?"

"Oh, there's plenty in it for me, Camille."

She looked triumphant. "Such as?"

"Forgiveness. Redemption. Something. I don't know what, completely. But I've got to do something."

"Do you have any idea who you will talk to? Who will take you seriously?"

David shook his head, feeling ridiculous, vulnerable for the first time in front of this woman.

She clicked her tongue. "Poor thing, that all these years should pass between us and you've finally come to the place where you need me. Now"—she held open her arms—"come back to Camille. Come to my bed, and let me love you as I've always loved you."

David sat still, wondering if he was strong enough to resist, praying he would be.

～

She had spent all day in the library with him. They had laughed until they cried, written together—he music, she words—and had joined in a communion of creativity that was so stimulating, Tobin could hardly believe such warm camaraderie existed.

She sat next to him on the piano bench, singing.

"Oh, Zeus, forbear!
Decline from your law.
Give me my maiden forever.
You may be merciful to me
for the beauty of my form,
be merciful to Xena for the beauty of her heart."

He stopped. "You know, you have a lovely little voice."

She shrugged. "It isn't much, really. A choir voice is all."

"Well, I find it quite pleasant. Sorry for the interruption, do go on."

As he began the portion of the opera again, he looked over on the couch where Elspeth sat bundled up reading *Tom Jones*, a broad smile on her face. "I'm not trying to replace him, you know, " he said to Miranda.

Miranda followed his gaze. "No, you're not. You're being a good uncle. And that's all anyone ever expected you to be."

The song began afresh, and Elspeth stayed put. Angus wandered in and out, and even the servants found excuses to enter the room. Tobin had never felt so domesticated in all his life. He couldn't imagine going back to Pratt's after experiencing life on a plane such as this.

Late that night, when he finally lay down to sleep, a most welcome thought came to him. He'd been with Miss Wallace . . . Miranda . . . almost the entire day, and had barely thought about her birthmark.

⁓

"Camille, there's something I must tell you."

God had been kind. He had pleaded exhaustion and made his escape, Camille pouting all the while.

"What is it, *mon chere*?"

They were breakfasting, just bread and cheese and coffee, for Camille ate simply despite her lavish surroundings, despite the elegant satin and lace robe that dressed up the occasion.

And so it was that David Youngblood began to fulfill the work laid out for him in the Bible. He'd read passages exhorting him to tell others of the marvelous works God had done for him. He told Camille of God's love through his Son, Jesus Christ. He told her of his death upon the cross. And he told her of the gift of salvation. He told her what God had done for him.

Camille sat motionless, eyes wide, incredulous. And when he finished, she shook her head. "I thought you were joking at first, *mon amour*. But you're not, are you?"

David took her hands in his, practically spilling her cup of coffee as he reached across the table. "I've wronged you, Camille. Over and over, I've used you and exploited you. I've lied to you more times than I can remember, much less count. But believe me this once, and from this day on, I'm more serious, more truthful, than I've ever been."

Camille pulled her hand back. "So you will not come to my bed? Ever?"

"I cannot. Though my body is screaming at me to do so, God help me, but I cannot." He took her hand again, persistent, realizing for the first time that Camille had truly been a friend to him. Had given without having received much of anything in return. Always.

She examined him closely. "So, then, I am supposed to help you take down Claude Mirreault. And it will be like before, eh? *Zut alors!* I give of myself to you, and in return, I get nothing. It will be just like old times!"

David knew he deserved much more than she was giving him. "I need you, Camille. I need you to pave the way for me."

She stood to her feet, paced to the window, and looked outside over the dawning day. "It is quite strange, in light of what you say about your God and your Christ, about how he guided you to himself, and eventually moved your feet down the right path."

"Why is that?" He stayed where he was, wondering where it would go from here, trying not to rush her, but wanting to get on with the reason he had come, wanting to get things over with.

"It looks as if he's sent you to the right place once again, my lord. Not that you deserve it. Not that I deserve it, either, for once again, it is at my expense." Her voice was softer than the pale peach of the new sky, and there was a quality to it that made him ache, made him see her, after all these years, as a woman with not just a heart, but a soul, made by God, and made so beautifully at that.

"Tell me, Camille. How am I at the right place?"

Her smile as she turned to him was tight-lipped, grim. "I was once the mistress of the Minister of Justice. Evariste Lyell is still a very good friend of mine, in fact."

"I can't believe it. This is such a coincidence!"

Camille raised her brows. "Coincidence? Hardly! I could say that about most of the officials in Paris, thanks to you, David Youngblood."

⁓

"What do ye picture if ye try ta imagine the Elysian Fields?" Elspeth asked at the schoolroom table the next morning.

Miranda was intrigued. So the girl had been listening after all. "Why don't you tell me first? Obviously you've thought this out."

Elspeth nodded, her teeth chattering a bit. It was so cold outside, the little stove wasn't doing much to keep them warm. Poor Angus had been carrying wood and peat in all morning for the various heating contraptions found within Greywalls. "I see fields o' pure gold, Miss Wallace, bonnie fields that go on an' on forever. But I dinna see 'em like in yon story. They be for onybody who's nice an' braw, not just for the bonnie lasses and lads."

Miranda reached out across the table. "It's what I picture too, Elspeth."

"Is yon how heaven would be?"

"Well." Miranda chuckled. "Heaven is a different matter. We don't go there because we're beautiful *or* good. We go there because the Savior has paved the way and set our feet on that path. But I picture heaven all gold and beautiful."

"Me an aw," Elspeth said, her eyes downcast. "It's braw to know tha' God forgives oor sins, aye no?"

"Why do you say that?"

The child was fighting for words, so Miranda tried to help her along. "Go on, Bethie, you can tell me what's on your heart."

"God has muckle to forgive me for just now." Her head was still bowed; her hands were clenched together. "Aboot ma uncle."

"Bethie, you made it seem as if it wasn't important whether he took an interest in you or not."

Elspeth fought back the tears. "It wasna true. Wha' he did hurt me inside. An' I couldna forgive him fer you. Och, Miss Wallace, I feel so clarty inside an' so ashamed!" She let the tears flow, and Miranda arose and put her arms around her.

"It's all right, Bethie. You're tenderhearted. You had every right to feel hurt by his callousness. But he wants to make it up to you. He wants to make things right if only you'll let him."

The girl nodded, her head still tucked against Miranda's chest.

"Well, then"—she stroked the child's hair—"the first thing I suggest you do is open up that Christmas present! Where is it?"

Elspeth shot out of her chair. "In a drawer in ma room! I'll go fetch it!"

"You do that! And I'll ring for our tea. We'll make this a celebration."

Miranda pulled on the bell while Elspeth scampered off. Mrs. Wooten would know without even sending up a housemaid what it was Miranda was ringing for. Two seconds later, Elspeth returned, her fingers shaking.

"Go ahead!" Miranda laughed. "Open it!"

She undid the rumpled ribbon and the haggard paper, then pulled off the lid. Inside was a scarlet velvet pouch. Miranda was curious now. "Go ahead, Elspeth. See what's inside."

Elspeth opened the pouch and put in two fingers. "Oh." She felt the contents, and gasped as she pulled out a chain. "Yon's a necklace. An' there's somethin' on the end."

Miranda licked her lips waiting for the prize to be revealed.

"A key!" they said simultaneously.

"I wonder what it goes to?" Miranda asked, reaching forward and letting the beautiful gold key slip between her fingers. "It's perfectly lovely."

"I suppose I'll jist have to ask him, aye no?" Elspeth's gray eyes sparkled with enthusiasm.

CHAPTER ❖ TWENTY-FIVE

Like some medieval lord, Claude Mirreault surveyed the countryside before him. He was a large man with big hands and feet. His face appeared as though it had been laundered violently in its tender years, the weave of his skin scarred and pocked. And yet his movements, graceful and lithe for a man his size, served to tell anyone who observed him that he had lived in luxury and wealth for more years than not.

Now, if one knew Claude Mirreault personally, well, one knew he wasn't born to such privilege. Even now, on this January day, he thought about the man he had been, the man he had become. He thought often about the odyssey of his life. A bear above a teeming pool of trout—that was how he saw himself. One swipe of his hand . . . and mayhem would result.

He loved it that way.

A small dark man, his friend of many years, and the legs to his infamous operation, joined him at the window of the massive chateau Mirreault had seized as debt repayment fifteen years before.

"Didier," Mirreault greeted him. "A fine day."

"*Oui, monsieur.*" The man's voice shook a little.

"And did you find the information I was seeking?"

"Uh . . ." He looked wildly around him, a little man with a big task. "*Oui.*"

"And they are still living in Scotland?"

"*Oui.*"

He rubbed his bullish chin. "And what of the de Courcey fortune?"

"Safely tucked in a bank in Paris. Ready for her daughter upon her thirtieth birthday."

Interesting, thought Mirreault. *So Sylvie wants to instill a little responsibility in the child prior to inheriting so much wealth.* "How much is there?"

"Two million francs!"

"Ahh." Mirreault was unruffled. "That's what I wanted to hear."

"Sir." Didier set his list on a dainty carved table by the window, "there must be some other way. I'm not comfortable with the new arrangement."

Mirreault turned away from his kingdom and pulled tight the tassled ends of the cord that held his silk dressing gown closed. "I do not wish to be privy to your reservations, Didier Vachel. I simply wish you to carry out our plans as you always do, quickly and orderly and secretively. You've been a good man to me for many years, do not spoil it now."

"But kidnapping, sir?" Didier said softly. "The child isn't yet a year old!"

Claude shook his head and picked up a beautiful brooch that he used as a paperweight. It had once belonged to Marie Antoinette. How he loved his royal objet d'art! He was trying to collect one item from a crowned head of every country in Europe, and he was two-thirds of the way there. "Didier, you are growing soft. I never thought I would see the day. The death of

Yves did something strange to you, did it not? I see in your eyes now, my friend, that you do the work, but you love it no longer."

Didier sighed, pulled a handkerchief from his pocket, and wiped his brow. "I'm getting old and tired, Claude. I do not know how much longer I can go on."

Mirreault knew this day was coming. He just hadn't expected it would be so soon. "This is the last job I will ask you to do. Bring the child to me, and that is the end of it for you. The ransom will be paid, and you will be free to take all that you've accumulated over the years and go."

Didier inhaled, a bit shaky. "You promise me? This is the last request you will ever ask of me?"

Claude, hardened against all of humanity, all except his oldest, most loyal friend, put forth his hand. "I promise you"—Didier took his hand—"that kidnapping Eve de Boyce will be the last criminal act you will do for me."

"The last criminal act I will *ever* do!" Didier declared passionately.

"As you will," Mirreault conceded. "Now go. The sooner you finish, the sooner you can say good-bye to this life you've chosen. And Didier . . . no ransom note yet. Leave nothing. The longer her precious child is away, the more she'll pay for her return. Besides, I want the de Courcey wench to suffer for the torture she's put me through to get to her money."

Tobin, embroiled in working out the harmonics of a particularly difficult passage, nevertheless heard the key turn in the lock. He smiled and said a soft "Thank you, God."

"Uncle?"

"Yes, Elspeth." He turned to face her. "You opened the present, I see."

She walked slowly, shyly, over toward the piano. "I did. I came ta ask wha' it meant, but I got ma answer. It is a key ta the library."

He nodded. "And only you have one. You may enter any time you like, day or night, while I am in here."

"Aye?" The way her eyes jumped to life made him feel even more ashamed of his behavior before Christmas.

"Absolutely. So you will come and visit me, then?"

She nodded.

"And you know," he continued, "I've still not had a proper tour of this castle! From what I've heard, you've explored it down to the last corner."

"Aye, an' aw the round walls an' aw!"

He laughed. "Elspeth, would it be too much to ask if I might give you a hug?"

"No, it wouldna!" she cried, jumping on his lap and throwing her arms around his neck. "When ye asked for ma pardon yonder, an' I didna give it ye . . . I'm sorry. I do forgive ye."

Tobin felt his heart warm to the child like it never had before. Truly, she was a part of his family, his great-niece, a Youngblood. And one of the nicest Youngbloods ever spawned in a long line of scoundrels and cads! He held her to him closely for several seconds, then looked her full in the face, examining her.

She grew red.

"Don't be embarrassed," he said. "I'm getting to know you now, Bethie. The sooner I look at your face, the sooner I grow used to it, the sooner I see only *you*, child!"

"That's jist the way it is, I suppose." She sighed, but smiled.

"Unfortunately, you're right."

"An' if I want ta meet life head-on, I might as well just get used to it." She leaned in close. "It's jist like ma maw always said. Maybees the only canny thing the wifie e'er said."

Tobin realized just then how truly remarkable, how innately beautiful Elspeth really was. "Do you want to meet life head-on?" he asked.

"No' aw by mysel' I dinna!"

"As long as I'm living, child, you'll never be alone." He took the necklace dangling from her hand and placed it around her neck.

Elspeth grimaced. "I'm sure Lady Daria willna be able ta hide her wheest about that!" she joked.

Good heavens! he remembered. *Daria.* Why, he hadn't thought about her in two days!

Didier Vachel had one of those faces one didn't really notice at first meeting, one didn't remember at second meeting, and at the third meeting only a vague recollection occurred.

It was one of the reasons he was so good at what he did.

He blended into the crowd down on one of the wharves of Calais. A ship was waiting, one of those new steamships. He couldn't say he was exactly looking forward to getting on such an untried vessel, but it was the quickest way over to that miserable island across the channel. Yes, a miserable island full of miserable people eating miserable food and wearing miserable fashions.

If someone had looked at him askance at that moment Didier would have toppled him like a child's tower of blocks. His mood had never been darker, or more anxious. Something was going to go wrong here. He could feel it, and he only hoped that when it occurred, he was far away or near a clear way of escape.

This life was turning bad.

Truth was, he had felt that way for a long time. But he comforted himself now that this was his final job. *Just get the child and get out*, he kept telling himself over and over again. *Get out.*

He ended up on the deck, seated next to a man who, judging by the strong odor that snaked its way out of his clothes, hair, and breath, had been having a love affair with the garlic bulb for much too long. Unfortunately, he could see no other empty seats, and he wasn't about to go below deck. Talk about smell! *Ciel!*

Between the voyage and the train trips, Didier figured he would be there in three days, maybe four. Though he despised the British, he certainly loved a few things about London: St. Paul's Cathedral, the Tower, and a walk through St. James park. Even in winter, he remembered the flowers that he'd seen there last spring when he had been combing the city for Sylvie de Courcey.

The wind began to quicken, the crew started rushing about, and all the passengers were ordered below deck.

Didier ran for the stairs, heaving back and forth from the waves that were strengthening with each gust of ragged air that bore down from the west. Knowing his propensity for mal de mer, he sought an empty corner, plonked his head against the side of the wall, and fell asleep.

Over the course of the next few days, Miranda found herself in the library on the earl's request.

"Have school down here," he ordered kindly when he came to the schoolroom with Elspeth after he placed the key around her neck. "I've heard of the keen intelligence of this Youngblood, and I'd like to see it for myself."

Elspeth winked. "No' ta mention ye'd like ta get Miss Wallace ta give ye a wee hand wi' yer opera!"

"She *is* smart, isn't she?" Miranda laughed. "All right, then, help us gather our books, my lord, and we'll set up shop in the library."

Elspeth moved in flits and flutters, truly excited.

Miranda watched as the earl helped his niece. He joked with her. Pulled on her braid as Elspeth showed him all of her favorite books and toys. "Course, I dinna play with toys much anymore," she said.

He nodded gravely. "I should say! A great girl like you?"

Miranda turned away from them, hiding the broad, involuntary smile she felt spring to her lips. She gathered her own things in her arms. "All ready, then?"

"Comin'!" Elspeth chimed, halfway to the door.

And so, lessons were interspersed with music. They even had their dinners before the fire. Miranda brought down one of her blankets from the loft, much to Lord Tobin's amusement. "That was convenient," he piped up. "Anything else up there in Camp Miranda?"

"Hush, my lord," she chided, hoping Elspeth would not hear her impertinence.

No such luck. "Ye two sound like an auld married couple!"

Miranda felt herself redden, but said nothing.

"Now then." The earl cleared his throat, blushing as much as Miranda. "Let's begin our new routine."

Looking back a few days later, Miranda realized what a wonderful situation this was turning out to be, not only for Elspeth, but for herself. To work alongside a man like this was stimulating, to say the least.

"So," he asked one evening, long after Elspeth had gone to bed, as they sat before the fire and enjoyed their farewell-to-the-day cup of tea, "how do you like working with me?"

"I'd say we work well together."

"Of course, you were already used to working with a man. After all, you were with your brother for years at his parish, were you not?"

"That was a bit different, though," Miranda said, eyes glued to the blaze of the fireplace. "By caring for Mate's physical needs and his home, I enabled him to do God's work more efficiently and effectively. But I never really helped him much with his actual calling. With you . . . well, we're working on the same project. It's been a lovely experience, really."

He reached out a hand and turned her face toward him. "I should say." He looked into her eyes. "You are quite a remarkable woman, Miranda Wallace. So different from who I first thought you were."

"It's nice to see you've finally learned that good things come in odd packages." She hated the nervous laugh that squeaked out.

He would hear none of that sort of talk and he told her so. "And it sounds like you're fishing for compliments besides!"

"Me?" Miranda couldn't believe her ears. "Hardly!"

"Oh, it's true. You know you're a lovely person."

She twisted her mouth. "Despite my birthmark?"

He raised his hand again, reaching forward to that purpled side of her face. She instinctively drew back. "No. Please."

"Does it pain you?" he asked, his face so beautiful and unblemished, yet full of a strange sort of wonder which she couldn't quite grasp. His eyes were telling her something, but she couldn't understand their language.

"Oh, no. It's just that I'm not used to people touching me."

His eyes closed, and when he opened them they were misted and sad. "Miranda, Miranda. To be so giving and loving, so caring and good, and yet untouched. It is a sad thing indeed."

Miranda shrugged, looking back toward the fire. "I've become used to it over the years."

"Please don't turn away," he petitioned. "I feel like I know you so well, Miranda. Your words come from a heart of passion and love and they flow so freely. You've done a remarkable job with Elspeth. It's as if you've given your entire life away to others so that you don't have to live it for yourself."

"My lord, perhaps giving my life away *is* for myself. Perhaps it makes me happy."

Lord Tobin went to the piano. "I wrote a tune for you, Miranda. Would you like to hear it?"

Miranda felt her heart begin to beat heavily, a mad thumping. "Of course," she said, remaining outwardly calm.

"Of course." He laughed, imitating her tone.

And so he began to play a soft tune. It was so simple and yet it spoke directly to her heart. In the strong, yet lilting melody, his heart was calling to hers in a way that frightened her as well as stroked an innermost portion, an area never touched by anyone before.

His eyes closed as his fingers artistically found each note, each chord. He swayed back and forth on the bench, playing softly at times, a bit louder at others, but never tumultuous or harsh.

And then it ended.

Miranda had watched him the entire time, his eyes closed, his head shaking with each rise and fall. It was the most beautiful experience to which she had ever been privy. A tear fell down her cheek and onto her hand as the final note died out completely.

"It's beautiful," she whispered, her heart full. "No one's ever—"

"Hush," he said. "No one's ever seen your heart before this, have they?"

Miranda shook her head, beginning to weep. She ran from the room, love storming after her, catching up and capturing her heart. Up the stairs and down the corridor she hurried to her room, head swimming, eyes overflowing.

CHAPTER ❖ TWENTY-SIX

It was all Tobin could do not to run after her, not to pull her into his arms.

What is happening to me? he thought, feeling a sensation of such happiness that any emotion he had ever had paled when remembered. It was a rush of joy, of gladness, of completeness. She was the woman he had been searching for. Someone kind and good, someone who could only be appreciated by experiencing. That was it. Miranda wasn't simply a woman . . . she was an experience. A warm, sweet whirlwind, a refreshing stream, a starry sky. Miranda was all of these.

Hadn't he tried to say as much in his song?

It was so easy to write for her. She inspired him.

He felt as though he floated up the stairs and into his bedchamber. *I felt compelled to come to Scotland. And now I know why.*

Charlie helped him out of his clothes, yawning all the while. "Did ye have a grand day, m'lord?"

"Oh yes, Charlie, an excellent day."

"Did ye get much music made doon yonder?" Charlie hung his waistcoat on a hanger.

"More than ever before."

"Aye, grand."

The conversation ebbed as Charlie busied himself with the earl's clothes. Tobin realized he knew nothing about the fellow.

"Are you married, Charlie?"

The man shook his head. "Och, no, m'lord. Thought aboot it once, but och, weel, I suppose the lassie found greener pastures."

"I'm sorry to hear that."

Charlie hung Tobin's trousers up next. "I'll tell ye this, m'lord, ifn' I ever fall fur a lassie again, I'll no' dance a reel like I did wi' Gillian. I'll have her off her feet afore she knows what happened, right doon to the front of the kirk with a ring an' a minister!"

"So that's what happened? You waited too long?"

"Aye. A muckle great mistake, if ever there was one, m'lord. Gillian would be mine the noo if I hadna dragged m'feet across all o' Scotland! It's one o' those times in ma life I wish I could go right back an' mend."

Tobin vowed he wouldn't make that mistake. Not with Miranda. He'd attack quickly and quietly, before she could do too much thinking.

Charlie finished up his tasks and left. Tobin was glad to be alone, but he found, as he lay down and stared up at the darkness, that he was incredibly hungry. Before he left the room, he grabbed his Bible off of his night table. He'd failed to keep this appointment for far too long. Wanting to resume a close communion with his Savior, Tobin eagerly made his way down to the kitchen. He stacked bread and cold chicken into a sandwich, stirred up the fire, and settled himself into Mr. Wooten's chair. It was time to reacquaint himself with a very old, very dear friend.

"Darling, Wooten!"

The distinctive voice echoed through the entry hall of the castle all the way back to the library. Tobin could hardly believe it. Daria had come. He immediately looked in Miranda's direction. She was presently helping Elspeth with mathematics, but her head had jerked up at the sound and her eyes rounded like two large plates.

It was as if they were sharing the same thought, he realized, as if they had forgotten that he was a man betrothed to be married. Well, he hadn't forgotten really, he had pushed the matter back as far in his mind as he could, realizing he had until the beginning of spring to act on it.

"She's here," he said simply.

"Yes."

"Miranda—"

She held up a hand. "Don't say anything, my lord, please. Just go to her."

"You must know the parameters of our engagement."

Her face looked harder than he had ever seen it, her eyes shuttered and clouded over. "It's none of my business, my lord, and it never was."

With swirling skirts and snatching fingers, nails clicking against the surface of the table, he watched her react. And he knew without a doubt that she was a storm of emotion as she picked up books, slates, and pencils. "Come, Elspeth, before her ladyship arrives."

"Miranda, please!" he yelled when she hurried toward the stairway leading to the loft. "You don't understand."

Now halfway up the steps, she set a hand to the railing and turned around, her face stricken, its right half extremely pale. "It's not my place to, my lord. We'll keep to the same arrangements as when Lady Christopher was here before."

He could hardly believe what she was saying. Elspeth looked befuddled and suddenly worried. "No!" he said with strength, stopping her motionless at the top step. "You both will be down for supper at eight o'clock, and that is an order."

Miranda only nodded, and soon disappeared through the small door in the far wall.

Blast! Tobin thought. *Blast! Blast!* Matters weren't supposed to have moved along this quickly! He had made his plans the night before and they were good ones, blast it! They'd work together during the day, sharing their hearts and souls, and then, he'd suggest they dine alone, after Elspeth had gone to bed. He'd open up yet further and ask her all the questions that had been milling about in his head since he had first read her writing. Slowly, but not too slowly, he would bind her to him, and he would freely offer his heart. And *then* he was planning to take a train to London and break the news to Daria.

This wasn't how he had planned it, blast it all!

He pressed his hair into something remotely resembling order, pulled down on his waistcoat, and straightened his lapels. Footsteps clicked on the stone flooring outside the room, and a jolly laugh mixed with Wooten's deep chuckle.

Tobin couldn't help but smile. After all, Daria had been his friend for well over a decade. They had never let love come between them before, and hopefully they wouldn't start now.

Love?

Tobin froze. Was that what this was? He pictured Miranda in his mind, the hideous birthmark, yes, that was there. But so was the long, blonde hair that made up a braid as thick as his wrist. And the blue of her eyes, startling and clear. Not to mention the full, sweet cherubic cheeks or the pretty lips that he found so fascinating to watch as she sang. Was this love? This feeling of immense comfort and well-being, this instinctual knowledge of each other's hearts?

Daria breezed into the room like a ship at full sail. And, indeed, perched on her blue hat was a miniature Spanish galleon, complete with hoisted sail and taut rigging. "Tobin, my darling man!" She held out a hand heavy with even more rings than he had remembered. And one in particular, that he had placed there, winked at him with disapproval.

"Daria! This is a surprise!" *Act natural, old boy.* He hurried over to her and kissed her hand. "What brings you to this forsaken wilderness?"

She laughed. "We heard about the rains and how things were unseasonably warm up here, so we decided to come and surprise you."

"We? Is Valentinia with you?"

"Oh, just speaking in the royal sense there, darling. No, it's just poor little me, mind you. Valentinia insisted she'd rather be dead than bound for Greywalls. And I thought as this was the first real stand she's ever taken with me, I would honor it. The girl is getting old enough to make a few decisions, and once we are married—"

Tobin tuned out the rest. *Once we are married.* He realized what he needed to do, but there she was before him, lips moving faster than a life-size version of the ship on her head during a high wind, babbling about wedding plans and how much fun she was having.

"—and, darling, I do believe I've rather gotten used to this idea of holy matrimony now that the plans are coming together more and more each day. You will foot half the bill, will you not? Of course you will. Now, I'm famished, and if I know you, you've got food stashed away somewhere. There! I do believe I've said everything!" She flipped a cascade of ringlets back over her shoulder and spied a plate of tea biscuits on the table before the fire. "Lovely!" she pronounced them, picking one up and waving a dismissive hand in his direction. "Do play something, darling. I could use some calming down."

He couldn't help but laugh and tend to her bidding. "I should say!"

It was just what he needed, to escape into his music. Daria would listen for hours, claiming there was nothing that could calm her so well. And that is what happened that afternoon, thankfully. After an exhausting, all-night ride on the train, it wasn't long before she was curled up on the couch, a snoring, blue satin ball with a capsized ship foundering atop her head.

Miranda had never felt more dowdy or more ugly in her life. She wanted to cry as she stood before her wardrobe and saw only three dresses there. One was a muddy brown, one was a faded navy blue, and the third was black, the only garment even remotely resembling an evening gown. Sighing, something she found she was doing far too often lately, she took down the black dress, laid it on the bed, and stripped off the gray one she had worn earlier that day. Mrs. Wooten had ordered a warm bath drawn for her. *At least I'll be clean and fresh*, she thought.

Oh, that was Miranda, all right. Clean and tidy and so pleasant. Dependable, sweet, and always ready to help.

Blast, she thought, realizing her exclamatory vocabulary had been far too influenced by the Youngbloods. But at that moment, she wished for all the world she could be someone else. Someone flamboyant and charming with a flair for conversation and the ability to make men go wild.

Her reflection made her want to cry for the first time in years. Oh, that face. That wretched face! The world was right for turning away from it in embarrassment. It was ugly and sad. There was nothing appealing or worthy about it. Even the hair she had always been so proud of looked pale and insipid and served only to accentuate the port-wine stain.

Whoever thought of that name? she wondered, not for the first time. Port wine. Such a nice drink. A warming beverage taken by men in back rooms. Hah! How different could she be from *that?* She slapped a flat hand against her reflection, thinking maybe she would decline. Lady Daria surely wouldn't mind. She was probably only too eager to have her fiancé all to herself, Miranda thought, shaking her head.

"You're an idiot."

She didn't know whether she was saying it to her reflection, or her reflection was saying it to her. *Oh, Lord Tobin*, she yearned, *why have you done this? Why have you taken my heart for your own?*

All her life she had been so careful to keep it close. True, there had been a scare or two, such as David Youngblood, but nothing along these lines. Nothing before could measure up to this. And it was now swallowing her like a whale swallows a minnow. The question was whether or not she could swim free from in between the beast's teeth. She rather doubted it. True love wasn't something one could escape from. It simply *was*.

She brushed a small amount of rouge on her "good cheek" as she called it, and fastened a filigreed pearl brooch to her dress.

"Miss Wallace!" Elspeth pirouetted into the room in the lovely rose-colored gown Miranda had made for the ball last autumn. "I'm ready!" she called in singsong.

Miranda couldn't help but smile. She held out her hand. "You look lovely, Bethie."

Elspeth grasped her teacher's hand in hers. "Let's be off then."

Miranda looked seriously at her charge. "What would you think if I just had a tray sent up for me, and you went down and enjoyed the evening with your uncle and his fiancée?"

Elspeth crossed her arms. "Ye think ta yerself tha' I'm too green to know what's what, don't ye?"

Miranda said nothing.

"Well noo, I could take it tha' aw the fine words ye've been sayin' ta me aren't fit fer yersel' an' aw? Ye know, aboot bein' proud o' all the things ye've done, an' aw yer talents an' that?"

Miranda pasted on a smile. "You're right." There was really no way out of it. "Let's be off then. Maybe Mrs. MacDowell's food will make up for my severe discomfort."

Several minutes later they found themselves in the great hall waiting for Lord Youngblood and Lady Christopher. Strangely, however, the table wasn't set and the room was cold and uninviting.

"Do ye think we misunderstood?" Elspeth asked.

"Miss Wallace!" a voice suddenly trilled from the doorway. "Elspeth, darling!"

Miranda turned to face Lady Daria, who was dressed up like a milkmaid. Laced bodice, flowing white chemise, a full skirt daringly baring a bit of ankle. Of course, the fabrics, silk damasks in shades of plum and moss, were nothing a mere milkmaid could afford. She even wore her curled hair in a long braid that hung over one shoulder. With such a severe hairdo, Lady Daria should have looked less entrancing. But Miranda couldn't help but notice that she was even more striking, for her features were truly beautiful and could stand up just fine on their own, thank you.

"You must be wondering what is going on?" She crossed the room with a slight skip to her gait.

Elspeth stood with her mouth gaping open, looking even more unattractive than usual. But Daria seemed not to notice. She pulled the child into her arms. "We're having a storybook party in honor of you, my dear!"

Miranda chuckled inwardly. Elspeth was reading Homer now. But the child was excited, nonetheless.

"Who are ye?" Elspeth asked.

"Why, Little Miss Muffet, of course!" She turned around for them. "Do you like it?"

"It's nigh as bonnie as yon Snow Princess."

Lady Daria stifled a humorous gasp. "Oh, my word. I heard about your little escapade up there in the pipe room! My, my.

You *are* a brave girl, aren't you?" She leaned close to Elspeth. "Your uncle was furious about the disruption at first, you know. But I have to say, I admired your spunk right away!"

"It was aw Miss Wallace's idea," Elspeth whispered.

"Really?" Lady Daria stood up straight. "You didn't *seem* like the average governess when I met you during my last stay."

Miranda felt herself redden. "Thank you, ma'am."

"No. When I saw the way you stormed at Tobin, I thought, Now there's someone who will give that man a run for his money!"

Heavens! Miranda thought with dismay. *But I truly like this woman!*

"Well, let's get into the library, we've got the entire evening planned. And you, my dear"—she put an arm around Elspeth's shoulders—"are the guest of honor."

Miranda followed them down the corridor. The governess. She was merely the governess.

Tobin knew Miranda couldn't possibly know how endearing she looked as Mother Goose with the polka-dot bonnet on her head. And Elspeth, with a wig of long gold curls that fell almost to the floor, was a charming, if not embarrassed, Curly Locks.

"And wha' are ye, Uncle?" Elspeth shouted, her voice overloud from excitement.

Daria interrupted. "I couldn't convince him to be Baa Baa Black Sheep," she said, pulling out a hilarious boiled wool hat with sheep-shaped ears sprouting out the side.

"I told her since my suit was blue, I would be Little Boy Blue, and we would just leave it at that!"

But Elspeth would not be put off so easily. "Och, go on, Uncle Tobin. Put on the hat. Dinna be a muckle great spoilsport!"

Tobin looked first to Miranda for support. She only dropped her gaze and pretended to fluff out the bow of her bonnet. He looked at Daria. "Help me? Please?"

"Oh, no!" she gloated, clapping her hands with delight. "You got yourself into this mess, and you'll just have to get yourself out of it!"

He knew he was beat. "Oh, all right! If it will just get the three of you off my back, I suppose I'll be Baa Baa Black Sheep."

Feeling like a fool in front of Miranda, he pulled the cap down over his head, stuffing his curly hair, which had been flattened against his eyes, up into the recesses of the headpiece. He couldn't even begin to imagine what he looked like. "There! Are we satisfied?"

Daria and Elspeth let out hoots of laughter. Even Miranda, understandably subdued—if her feelings in any way matched his own—cracked a smile.

"Would ye like ta see yersel' in yon mirror?" Elspeth asked, more than willing to lead him over to the decorative mirror above the mantle.

"No, thank you, I would not!" He was going to play the disgruntled lord to the hilt with this one, he decided. "How in the world I let you two women browbeat me like this, I cannot even begin to guess."

The food arrived. They started off with a bowl of curds and whey, which Tobin only pretended to eat. Then Pamela outdid herself with a blackbird pie. "And we made sure she put exactly twenty-four birds in the pie!" Daria shouted. Goodness, but he never realized quite how loud the woman actually was!

They sat on a blanket before the fireplace. Tobin had to admit he was having somewhat of a good time, but Miranda had said practically nothing. She was uncomfortable, but there could be no help for it. The thought of not seeing her from the time she left the library this afternoon until only the Lord knew when, wasn't something he wanted to entertain.

The comparison between Miranda and Daria was striking. Both women were magnificent in their own right, and for different reasons. But Miranda knew his heart, she understood him, and in some ways needed him in a way that Daria never would. He'd never seen her subdued like this. Before God, he would put a smile upon her face again.

They rounded out the meal with a Christmas pie and some "Knave of Hearts Tarts" as Elspeth called them. A charming display.

He was surprised to see how Daria was reaching out to the child. He'd thought she'd react far differently. She kept trying to bring Miranda into the conversation, to no avail, and when the governess excused herself after the final cheese and biscuits, he wasn't at all surprised.

I will catch up with her this evening, he promised himself.

But she didn't come down later on after the others had gone to bed and he sat down at the piano. He waited for an hour, the clock striking midnight. Finally, wondering if he should do so, but deciding there was no other course of action, he went to her room.

He felt like a schoolboy again as he stood outside of her door several minutes later, afraid to knock. Then he remembered the castle was his for the time being, he was the earl of Cannock, and she was in his employ.

He raised his fist and knocked four times.

No answer.

He sighed, expecting as much. A feeling of dread twisted his stomach and he knocked again. There was no sound from within. So carefully, slowly, so she wouldn't awaken if she was already asleep, he pushed open the door.

The bed was still made up.

"She's away," a voice sobbed in the darkness. Elspeth's.

"What happened?" he asked, now spying the girl's silhouette in the doorway to the schoolroom.

"I dinna ken. Her cloak's away too. Miss Wallace wouldna bide wi' a body like me forever."

Tobin hurried across the room and held out his hand. "Oh, Bethie. Don't say such a thing. You know Miss Wallace loves you with all of her heart."

Elspeth placed her hand in his. "She was awfu' sad tonight, Uncle. I heard her in yonder gettin' undressed. Grumpin' aboot stuff I didna know aboot." Tears flowed freely from her eyes.

Tobin embraced her. "Elspeth, do you know where she might have gone?"

"Her brother's hoose in Huntly, I think." She wiped her eyes with a lace-trimmed hanky. "Can we go off an' get her now?" Her words were hopeful.

"You get back to bed, Bethie. It's very late. I'll try to have her here in the morning, when you wake up. Go back to bed," he said again. "I will find her. And rest assured that she didn't leave because of you. Do you have any other idea why she was so upset this evening?"

Elspeth's large eyes were wise and sad. "Och, come on, ma lord. Surely ye know Miss Wallace loves you, with all her bonnie heart."

CHAPTER ❖ TWENTY-SEVEN

Camille opened a secret door in the paneling behind the Minister of Justice's desk. It was very late, but it was Thursday. What had once been their evening. The light from the gas sconces shone softly on his balding head, and he didn't appear to notice her as she silently shut the door. He had been more than eager to allow her audience with him when she suggested she bring by some supper for them to share together. "I have a matter of importance to discuss with you, dear Evariste," her note had said. He had sent a speedy reply saying he'd be delighted to see her again and how it had been much too long since they had last parted company.

"*Chéri,*" she sang softly, and he turned.

"Ah, Camille. You've come." He was a kindly man, soft-spoken, and not at all suited to his post. Far too merciful, a famed peacemaker, Evariste Lyell was slight in proportion, shy with friends, and wont to drink only on special occasions. The fact that he needed to sleep with Camille wasn't something he was proud of, he assured her the first night he summoned her to him.

"But I am a lonely man," he had said, and then proceeded to tell her of his wife, recently deceased, for the rest of the evening, not touching her again except to twine her hair through his gentle fingers.

His suits were ill-fitting, his knuckles too hairy, and yet there was something so benevolent and appealing about his eyes that one forgot just how awkward the man was. Camille loved him like one would an old friend of one's father. In their short time together she had become severely protective of the gentleman. The time that he had needed her sexually was brief, but their friendship endured, and she did all she could for Evariste to help him make the transition from married man to widower. She remembered the many nights she would simply lie next to him, take him into her arms, and sing him to sleep. Except for Thursday nights when he stayed late, working at his desk. Then, she would bring a basket of dinner and rub his head as he finished up paperwork. She'd never had an easier assignment in her life. And this one had had nothing to do with Claude Mirreault. That in itself was a wonderful thing. She wasn't going to ruin this man, as she had so many others.

Of course, she would have no qualms in seeking help for David Youngblood, the true love of her life. Her feelings for David had always been something she likened to an incurable disease that progressed with time but never killed.

"What did you bring for us tonight, little love?" he asked, eyeing the basket hanging from the crook of her arm.

Camille sat down on his lap, just like old times, and placed the basket before him on the desk. "Simple fare tonight, *monsieur*. Just pâté, cheese, and bread. And a bottle of wine." She pulled the length of bottle, containing a fragrant red, out of the protective toweling and did the same with two glasses.

"You used to care for me so well," Evariste said gratefully. "I miss you, Camille, and I bless the day you came to me. Do you remember the first time I saw you?"

"Of course." She began to set out the small spread while he opened the wine, obviously in a mood for reminiscence. "I spilled wine all over you at a party!"

He laughed. "Yes. And then the duc de St. Dennis introduced us and told me all about you."

"And you said 'Hired!'"

His eyes clouded. "You must not talk like that about yourself, *chérie*."

She slid a knife into the crock of pâté. "It's who I am, *monsieur*. We've never pretended with each other before."

"It's hard for me to think of you that way now, Camille."

"You paid the bill, though."

He took her hand, kindly. "I suppose we all do what we must to survive. Myself included."

"That is true. You were no lily in this matter. Now"—she took a sip of her wine—"enough of this talk. I am hungry. Let us eat."

"Someday your figure will catch up to your appetite!" He laughed the easy chuckle of an old friend.

It wasn't long before they were finished, Evariste recounting his day, calling her his sweet pet, telling her she had kept his old age from becoming the nightmare he thought it would be. And then, of course, as she always had before, Madame Lyell came to the fore of the conversation.

"And will she be canonized soon, *monsieur*?" Camille joked, rubbing his shoulders now.

He chuckled and placed his spectacles on the bridge of his nose, looking beneath the nest of paper on his desk for his pen. "The point is well taken. I will speak of her no more if it pains you."

"Of course it doesn't pain me," she assured him. "I think it's lovely that you loved her so."

"Tell me," he said, still not looking in her direction, still looking for a writing implement, any one would probably do, pencil, pen, it didn't matter. "Have you not been in love? Do you not know what it is like to be consumed with someone?"

Honestly, no one had ever asked that question of her before. None of her "clients" had ever cared to. "Yes, *monsieur*, I do."

"Really?" So surprised was he by her answer, he turned around in his chair. "*Really?*"

She put her hands on hips. "You think that because of what I do, I do not have a heart?"

"Well, no, *chérie*, it's just that, well . . . I'm sorry, I suppose I shouldn't have said—"

She couldn't bear to see him so uncomfortable. "I will not always do what I do."

He nodded. "No, I don't suppose you will, sweet Camille. So tell me about him. Do you love him still? This man?"

Camille raised her head high and proud. "I will never stop loving him. I wish I could. There are nights I pray to, but my prayer is never answered. I wake up and my heart is still full of him. I hate it, *monsieur*, indeed at times I hate him because I love him without reason or logic."

"Will you tell me who it is?"

She filled her lungs with breath before letting it out slowly. This was the right thing to do. She hated to use dear Evariste this way, but there was really no other choice. The time was right, and now she must go on. "David Youngblood."

"Oh, dear!"

"And he is still alive."

"Oh dear, oh dear!"

Camille rushed around and sat again on his lap. "You must help him, *monsieur*." Her words came out in a rush.

"Help him? How can I, Camille? If he's not dead, then surely he has disappeared?"

She grabbed his hands. "Not only is he alive, he is in Paris."

Lyell sat up straight. "No!"

"I assure you it is true."

"Oh, Camille, my sweet pet, if you are protecting him ..." He waved his arms in a gesture filled with helplessness.

Camille removed his spectacles and took his face between her hands. "Did you ever see a beautiful ring in the window of the jewelers, look down upon the finger of your own dear wife to see the humble bauble upon it, and wish you could simply go in and trade the one for the other?"

Lyell couldn't help but smile. "Many times, *chérie*."

"How would you like to trade the life of David Youngblood for the even bigger, blacker life of Claude Mirreault himself?"

The Minister of Justice examined his mistress carefully. "And what's in this for you, pet?"

"Freedom. You see, I am chained to Claude Mirreault myself."

"Then that is all that I need to hear. What do you wish me to do?"

___

"You are the most incredibly stupid woman I've ever heard of!" Miranda said to herself as she walked westward toward Huntly, toward her brother's manse. Always having prided herself on her intellect, always having clung to the fact that she could think better than any of those women with perfect skin, Miranda berated herself as she hurried along.

Thankfully, the rains had stopped and the moon shone down upon the pools of water in the roadway. Surely her feet would be soaked by the time she arrived, but she hadn't lost her footing or gone sliding down any embankments.

Miranda couldn't wait to get to Huntly. Back to Matthew, the man who hardly ever let her down. *I was a fool to have left him in the first place*, she thought, knowing how much of a help she had always been. And now with Sylvie pregnant, well, they could use her around the house, that much was certain.

The warm lights of the manse appeared in the distance. Sylvie was a night owl, Miranda knew, and would welcome her sister-in-law's intrusion. Which is exactly what happened.

"Miranda!" she cried, when she saw her standing on the doorstone. "You are soaked clear through to the skin. Get in here right now!"

Miranda smiled and allowed herself to be mothered and jostled and warmed and even fed, for she had eaten no more than a few bites at dinner. And all the while she confided to her brother's dear wife.

"I suppose God is teaching me a lesson about pride," she said, having confessed to Sylvie the new complexion of her heart. "I thought I was above love, that I would never fall prey to its wiles."

They were sitting before the fire. Sylvie leaned forward and patted Miranda's knee. "Love is a ravenous beast. It eats every single part of you once it truly attacks. Oh, Mira"—she leaned forward and put her arms around Miranda's shoulders—"God isn't punishing you. You can't believe that."

Miranda shook her head. "No, I don't really believe that. Not really. I'm just trying to understand, Sylvie. I'm trying to settle this in my head. I'm seeking a reason for the pain."

"Miranda?" Matthew's voice came out from the bedroom. "Is that you?" A moment later, he was standing at the doorway in his nightclothes. "Are you all right?"

At the sight of her brother, her compatriot, her dearest friend, Miranda broke down and cried. Matthew took her into his strong arms and nodded to Sylvie, who left the room. He sat down with her before the fire, and Miranda let him comfort her.

⌒

David Youngblood was waiting. Camille would surely be back soon. He hated that the thought of her entertaining the Minister of Justice bothered him. All of those years he had taken Camille for granted: her beauty, her grace, the way she practically worshiped him despite his many flaws.

He looked over at the brandy decanter she had placed on a table near the settee. At one time he would have thought nothing of ingesting all of the contents, but now . . . well, things had changed. He knew he could no longer anesthetize himself against himself.

Camille returned several minutes later, breathless from her run up the steps. "My lord!" she breathed. "Hoo, what a run. Yes, it will all be all right."

David stood to his feet and held her by the shoulders. "What did he say?"

"He said he'd rather have the entire bowl of soup than a mere mushroom."

David raised his eyebrows. "He said that?"

She shrugged out of her coat. "Well, not in those words. But the point is the same. He will lessen the punishments for your crimes in order that Claude Mirreault will find his."

"So I will not see the guillotine?"

"No."

"Did he say what he will do instead?"

"No. He wishes to talk to you about that himself."

"Oh, dear. I—" Suddenly weak in the knees, suddenly realizing that his life was not over, that it was only just beginning, he sat back down in his chair. "Camille." He didn't know what else to say. "What would I do without you? What would I do now?"

Camille pulled off a dainty hat and set it on the table. She laid a small, well-manicured hand upon his shoulder, her fingers restless against the crude weave of his shirt. "I used to ask myself that question many times regarding you. But then you left and I found out and I survived."

"And you survived," David echoed, the words more reassuring to himself than to her.

"I will always survive. As will you. And now . . . now that you are so religious . . ." That shrug again.

David turned his face so that he might see her eyes. "What do you think of me now, Camille? I am a murderer, a thief, and committer of countless other sins and crimes. What do you think of me now?"

Camille's green eyes filled with tears, and she turned away from him. She spoke, always honest, but not comfortable. "I believe I love you even more, my lord. A thought which is very much painful to me, for now that you have God in your heart, a woman like me will never be allowed in it as well."

For the first time since he had known this stunning courtesan, David's heart broke for her. This woman, who would have done anything for him, was a truly worthy creation of the Lord of the universe. He put his hand upon hers, scooped her fragile fingers into his own, and brought it to his mangled mouth. Her eyes closed at the brief physical contact, and he watched in fascination the effect he had on her.

Could I ever love this woman? he asked himself. And the answer, as her eyelids fluttered open, and he remembered all the nights she'd comforted him with her body, all the days she'd lingered by his side, all the kind words, the selfless deeds in his name, was a resounding *yes*.

So surprised and amazed by this revelation was he, that he took her into his arms and kissed her.

She kissed him back hungrily, pulling up his shirt. But he stopped her. "No, Camille. Not like before. Please, not like that."

"But, my lord," she began to argue.

"Expect more from me, sweet Camille. I am not who I once was, thank God."

Camille pulled away, crossed her arms, and examined him thoroughly. Her head shook in bemusement, but she did not look away. Indeed, it seemed as if she could not. Finally, she pointed to the pot of tea on the table, her face almost grim.

"May I join you for a cup, then?"

"I would consider it an honor." He pulled out the chair for her and attended to her needs. The realization that he would never stop apologizing to this woman for all the pain he had meted out wasn't grievous. Rather, he decided firmly, he was excited by the prospect.

Purposefully he banished Sylvie de Courcey Wallace from the portion of his heart she once owned. It was a decision he had to make, a decision not of the heart but of the mind, of the will. He would open his heart to another, perhaps to Camille. But he would pine no longer. Not when the true love of a woman like Camille was his for the taking.

CHAPTER ❖ TWENTY-EIGHT

It didn't take Tobin long to get to Huntly. He jumped off of his horse, wondering what he was going to say. He'd already heard tales of Matthew Wallace's overprotectiveness regarding his sister. And for good reason, Tobin realized, knowing how heartless children could be, knowing Miranda had most likely suffered uncountable cruelties in the years when the heart is left tender and exposed and altogether too forgiving.

The door opened and a masculine face appeared. Matthew only nodded, overpowering him, though he was quite a few inches shorter than Tobin. "Come in, my lord."

Tobin nodded in return. He took off his gloves and shoved them into his pocket as he stepped into the warmth of the small homey cottage. Looking around him, he couldn't help but yearn for such simplicity. "I've come for her."

The preacher shook his head, shut the door. "No."

Tobin took off his scarf and threw it over his forearm. "She is here, then."

"Arrived about an hour ago." Matthew shuffled his feet restlessly. "Can I get you a cup of tea?"

"No, thank you, it's late. I'd like to speak with your sister."

Matthew Wallace shook his head again. "Asleep by now, I'd guess. She's been through enough today already."

Tobin looked down. "It's all been a dreadful misunderstanding."

"I'm sure it has. And yet, Mira knew of your engagement. She's old enough to have known better."

"I never—"

"I think you'd better go. If she hears your voice, the wound will go that much deeper."

"But—" Having barged into the man's house in the middle of the night, Tobin felt at a loss.

"It is enough, my lord. I won't have my sister's heart broken anymore than it is already." His deep blue eyes were serious, yet held a protective threat. Tobin decided not to argue right now. It was obvious Wallace was doing his best to control himself, and Miranda was asleep. Tomorrow would come soon enough. "What of Elspeth?" he asked.

The preacher's eyes softened. "Miranda will return to Greywalls when you return to London, my lord. In the meantime, you are free to send Elspeth around here for her lessons. Angus too, for that matter." His voice softened as well at the mention of the lad everyone loved.

Tobin put his scarf back around his neck. "As this is your home, I'll do as you ask for now, Wallace. But I will return shortly. Tomorrow afternoon, in fact."

Matthew laid a hand on his shoulder. "Give her several days, my lord. Please. You couldn't possibly understand a woman like my sister. She's lived through more pain than you or I could begin to understand. She needs time before she can face you again."

Tobin wanted to yell, *But I love her!* Yet he couldn't. He'd never voiced the words yet, even alone. And the revelation came as such a shock, he was gently ushered out of the house, the door already closed behind him before he quite realized he was alone under the wintry sky.

I love her, he repeated to himself, eyes closed against the breeze, heart singing with joy.

⁓

Tobin watched as Daria and Elspeth sat up in the library loft, giggling over what? He didn't know. The two had become fast friends overnight. It wasn't that the child had already forgotten her beloved Miranda, but she was experiencing love and acceptance from someone beautiful. He had to admit, he hadn't expected such fortitude of character from Daria.

Of course he was happy for Elspeth, but now, it made it much more difficult to break things off with Daria. He had chosen wisely in Daria, it was painfully evident. But now, he loved another. He was crazy for another. *Oh, Miranda!* he cried within. Her face, imperfections and all, he recalled, so lovely to him now. The voice, the soothing voice she owned. How he longed to hear it say his name one day. *Tobin, my love.* Yes. But so far, only "my lord" and "your lordship" had been directed at him. How wonderful it would be to hear her tell him she loved him.

And yet, I am unworthy of such a love, he realized, recalling his monstrous treatment of both Miranda and Elspeth upon his arrival. He hoped Elspeth was right when she told him Miranda had given her heart to him.

Only two more days and he would return to the Wallace household. If she wouldn't willingly come with him, he wasn't quite sure what he was going to do. For one thing was certain, a woman like Miranda Wallace would not be forced or even coerced into doing anything she didn't wish to do.

He had to talk to Daria.

More laughter bounced down from above, and two faces peered over the railing, looking like clowns. Literally.

He put his hands on his hips. "Daria, wherever did you find that makeup?"

"I brought it with me, of course. You don't think I'd be caught this far from home without some greasepaint, do you?" She was perfectly serious.

Tobin couldn't help but laugh. "You are two of the most divine little clowns I have ever seen. The flower pots are a nice touch, dear. What do you think, Elspeth? Are you ready to go away and join a circus of gypsies?"

But Elspeth just grinned, wide and wonderful. "Ye know somethin', uncle. I fair like Lady Daria, so I do."

"Well, I don't suppose that is a surprise. It seems you two have much in common. You've not grown up yet, Elspeth, and neither, apparently, has Daria."

Daria raised her head proudly. "Thank you, Tobin. I take that as a compliment."

The two disappeared and more laughing was heard. Tobin shook his head, wondering how in the world he had backed himself into such a corner.

Evariste Lyell spoke softly. He wished he could simply pardon the man standing before him, the man already sentenced to a life of difficulty by the deformity he had borne since birth. But the sense of justice in him, coupled with the sense of mercy, was impelling him to act with both.

"Your story makes sense on all levels, my lord, and I don't believe you to be a liar." He held up the paper on which he had jotted the list of crimes David had confessed. "You will be spared the guillotine, but I cannot do justice to the office I hold, to the people I serve, without punitive action being taken. You understand this, don't you?"

David Youngblood sat at ease on the couch. He had already graciously thanked Lyell for whatever mercy he would deign to show. A gentleman through and through. "Of course."

"I've been thinking of ways to punish you for your misspent years. Exile isn't enough, I've decided." Lyell hated to do what he was about to do. Clearly this man would do no harm in the future, but he couldn't let it go and live with himself; he couldn't set a precedent, even in his own mind, for such policy. Just because someone has turned to God, and God has forgiven his sins, Lyell reasoned, does not mean that he does not have to pay society back for his deeds. People had died. Justice must be served. This was his simple and straightforward policy.

Youngblood sat forward, eyes respectful.

Lyell continued, leaning his backside against the edge of his desk and crossing his arms. "Have you ever heard of Devil's Island, my lord?"

The English nobleman's eyes grew round, then closed. He nodded slowly. "The penal colony in French Guiana."

"Precisely." Lyell noticed the way the fingers of his lordship's left hand curled into the upholstery of the arm of the sofa. "You will be sentenced to five years on Devil's Island."

"But how—"

Lyell held up a hand. "It will be as though you have disappeared from the earth. The only people who will know of your whereabouts will be Camille, myself, and the emperor, or anyone else you wish to tell. You have a daughter, yes? That matter, of course, is up to you. But I must tell you, my lord, not everyone survives Devil's Island." He stared long into Youngblood's eyes, wanting desperately to offer another road. "That is what I have for you. It is the best I can do for you. And in the end, whether you live through Devil's Island, or die on it, will be up to God. In the end, his justice will prevail."

David Youngblood's hands came down onto his knees and he stood. "I have no choice but to accept, no recourse but to say thank you for sparing my life. But I must ask you this. Why the secrecy?"

"I have another condition. One you must humor an old man regarding." He pushed off from the desk and stood directly in front of Youngblood. It was a matter most dear to his heart and it must be understood. "If you make it home, I wish for you to take care of Camille. I wish for you to make her a lady, your lady—Lady Youngblood. She deserves that."

"But how will my name be cleared? My deeds have been well-publicized in France. England too, for that matter."

Lyell scratched his sideburn. "I have a plan, but it will cost you dearly."

"I have more money than I know what to do with."

Lyell sat on the couch and indicated that David Youngblood should sit back down. "I know of a man, a very sick man, named Alan Richelieu. He is poor and he is dying painfully. He will confess to the crime and go to the guillotine for you."

"What?" David became immediately agitated.

"Be still, *monsieur*. Matters like this happen all the time in high affairs. We're just proficient at keeping them secret from the general public. He wishes for a merciful death, a release from his pain, and enough money to see his family live in security for the rest of their lives."

"Where did you find him?"

"Why should that matter to you?"

"But how can he agree to such a thing?"

Lyell regarded Youngblood thoughtfully. "You've never had to skip a meal, have you, my lord?"

The earl shook his head.

"Then you cannot know. Will you accept the arrangement?"

"Only if I can talk to the man myself."

"As you wish. Georges!" Lyell called to his secretary, who immediately entered the room. "Give the earl of Cannock the address of Monsieur Richelieu's home."

David Youngblood stood.

"Actually," Lyell continued, "the arrangements have already been made. Richelieu has already made his confession to me. He will be taken from his family tomorrow."

"Why are you doing this?"

"For Camille."

"Do you love her that much? Still?" David asked.

Lyell pulled off his spectacles and began cleaning them with the tail of his coat. He would swear the man was jealous. Good. "Not in the way she loves you, my lord. But I care about what happens to her, and I am willing to go to great lengths to see that one day she is as happy as she once made me. She deserves that, don't you think?"

"Yes." David shrugged into his coat.

"Go then. There's much to be done, much to be arranged regarding this matter."

David Youngblood exchanged a good-bye with him and was gone. Lyell stared out the window for a moment over the icy Paris street as the earl of Cannock emerged in the darkness, the breeze blowing through his hair, a gray muffler wound around his mouth. He couldn't imagine what the hardened convicts of Devil's Island would try to do to this man, but he knew one thing. David Youngblood was definitely a man who could take care of himself.

He immediately set about writing a letter to the emperor. An hour later, having explained the details of the situation, he locked the document in a desk drawer, turned out the light, and went home.

David Youngblood breathed in through his nose, feeling the air whoosh down through his cleft palate, swirl around in his mouth, and slide down into his lungs. He had forgotten how cold Paris could be.

The small hovel in which the Richelieu family resided had been almost as cold as it was outside. The man was laid out in bed, full of sores, quiet in front of a small stove. His family attended to him and obeyed him instantly when he asked for privacy, gathering ragged shawls and mufflers and stepping outside.

David couldn't think of anything to say but "I am David Youngblood."

The dying man nodded. "So you are. Who else would you be?"

He got down on his knees beside the bed. "You must hate me. I'm sorry." It was the most awkward moment of his life, kneeling there before the man who would give what was left of his life for his family. He was grieved his behavior had given Richelieu this opportunity. "I don't know what else to say."

Richelieu apparently didn't have much to say either, and a voice within David said, *Look on this man. See a man who is willing to die for love.*

And so he did, his eyes slowly traversing the sunken face, the skin, yellowed like a dying daffodil, the eyes with whites gone to the shade of well-creamed coffee, the irises bleached and thin and dull.

"How old are you?" David asked.

"Forty-one."

The man looked seventy.

"How long have you been sick?"

"Not as long as you might think."

"And the doctors, they don't know what it is?"

The placid eyes narrowed. "Listen here, your lordship, don't think about redeeming me. Don't think about doing a good deed and sacrificing my family on the altar of your guilt. I'm dying. I'm dead." He painfully pushed himself up on an elbow, eyes now ignited. "I AM DEAD!"

He lay back suddenly, the movement exhausting him. His eyes were closed, his voice almost inaudible. "Let me die in peace, my lord. Let me die knowing that even in my death I have served my family."

David shook his head in wonder. "How can you do this? How can you leave them so easily?"

Richelieu opened his eyes. "Do you not see? Are you not an educated man? I'm already gone. This is not Alan Richelieu you see wasted before you. This is another man, a sick thing unable to so much as relieve himself without help. This is not Alan Richelieu who would drain his family, who would concern them all the day long with matters of bodily functions and pain, teeth and hair and sores. I welcome you, my lord. For you are my angel of death, the execution of this man who has taken over Alan Richelieu."

David stared at the man before him, and he understood. Somehow he understood that this man needed to do this. The single part of David that yearned to call in a physician kept him from doing so. "You will not spend your last night with your family in this place," he said with authority. "You will see for yourself that they are well taken care of, that they will live in comfort."

"Then our deal ... will stand?" the dead man asked.

"It will."

Three hours later the Richelieus were settled in a moderate, well-kept home. The fire was warm and a good supper was passed around a new table. Confused wonder filled the family's eyes. Alan Richelieu smiled in contentment from his bed as he watched his family. David knew this because Camille had been there. Dressed in a serviceable gown and claiming to be the wife of a mysterious philanthropist who had provided it all, Camille had been their guide to a better place, a better way of living. They had clucked over the fine butter, gazed at the thick soup and crusty bread Camille had made for them. They had stared at each other in amazement. And Alan Richelieu smiled.

The next morning the paper told of his confession to the murders of the de Boyces. But Alan couldn't have read it, even if he had known how. He had slipped away quietly during the night, off to find the man he once had been, nobody knowing where he had truly gone. Least of all David Youngblood. Where was Alan Richelieu now? Where was he now?

The next day, David hired a horse and set out toward Versailles and that pretentious show of wealth belonging to Mirreault. Actually, Youngblood had to give the man credit. The moneylender didn't go to extremes in his luxurious surroundings as most men not born to wealth and privilege would be wont to do. He did have good taste in furniture, if nothing else. And as regarding his dressing gowns, well they were a bit garish in fabric, but brilliantly executed. *Certainly his taste in women isn't up to snuff*, Youngblood thought, a quick parade of Mirreault's flopsies dancing the can-can across his mind's eye. *Except for, perhaps, Camille.*

But that matter was for later pondering. Camille was beginning to get under his skin. A prostitute with a heart of gold, he laughed, and shook his head at the typical way in which she could be categorized. But truly, a woman like Camille would fit into no real category. She was too precious for that. Like a diamond scraping at glass, her beauty, her tenacity, her kindness was etching away his sharp edges, ones that had been exposed by his conversion, the edges he had hidden for so long under the crust of anger and disdain. Certainly he owed the girl more than just a profuse number of apologies. The fact that she could forgive him so easily showed him that she was far ahead of him already in exhibiting Christ's love, though she did not yet love him herself.

As I said, a matter for future pondering, he ordered himself, wanting only to be focused and assured at the coming meeting.

God is so good, he realized as he rode along, remembering the passage he had read earlier that morning. "Be still and know that I am God." Yes, God was in control of everything. He had to be, for this was a matter only the Divine could handle, a battle God alone could win.

"Do justice, love mercy, walk humbly with thy God." Now *those* words were a bit more specific. A list of orders he could live with, even though it would take the rest of his life to do so with any real grace. It was enough to guide him in the grace and mercy of the Savior, all the way to Devil's Island, and all the way home. And he *would* be coming home.

The chateau appeared in the distance and he spurred his horse on faster, the cold wind biting at his face. He didn't care. It was time to fell the grisly house of Claude Mirreault, and he would do so, not by might, not by power, but by the grace of God.

He reined in his horse as it sped into the courtyard. After jumping down, he slid that morning's newspaper from his inner coat pocket and pulled on the great gonging doorbell.

A manservant answered, brows raised. "Lord Youngblood?"

"In the flesh!" He spread his arms wide. "Is he in his study?"

"*Oui, monsieur*, but—"

"No need to worry, I'll find him myself."

"But—" The servant stammered behind Youngblood, all the way down the corridor to the masculinely sumptuous room at the back of the house, a paneled, wainscoted wonder.

David pulled open the door. "Mirreault!"

The servant hopped and popped behind him from one foot to the other and back. "Sir, I tried to—"

"It's all right, Henri." Mirreault held up a hand. "Just be a good man and fetch the earl some tea. Judging by the shade of his lordship's nose and ears, I'd say he could use a warming up."

The man disappeared instantly and Mirreault, nonplussed by Youngblood's appearance, went for the brandy decanter. "A pre-warm-up warm-up?" he asked.

David held up a hand. The last thing he needed was brandy muddying up the works. "I'll wait for the tea."

"Never thought I'd behold the day when you'd refuse a more than decent libation. A side effect from your disappearance, no doubt."

Without commenting, Youngblood held up the paper. The headline, in thick, black letters, was easily readable from across the room. "Alan Richelieu confesses to murders of Armand and Collette de Courcey."

"Who, pray tell, is Alan Richelieu?" asked Claude, either disguising his surprise, or feeling none. David couldn't tell which.

"The question this morning is, 'Who *was* Alan Richelieu?' He died last night, a very sick man," Youngblood said with an easy shrug, his relaxed words tasting like sour wine behind his teeth. "He would've rather gone to the guillotine for me, died quickly, and known that the money I paid him would see his family in good stead for years."

"He defeated you royally at your own game, though, eh?" Mirreault raised his glass in a salute to the dead man. "Expired before he was relieved of his head."

Mirreault examined David closely, eyes flat. David maintained a steady breath, praying for calm. "You are quite the man, aren't you, my lord? Brilliant strategy, absolutely brilliant."

"Yes, well, at least all that money spent on my education wasn't for naught."

"So when does the cocoon burst open and you officially flutter back into society?"

Youngblood cracked his knuckles and grinned. "I find the straight and narrow is boring me, Mirreault, and remaining incognito has its fair share of advantages. I will return in good time, not necessarily quick time. Depending on you, that is."

Mirreault shook his head. "Why should I admit you back into the inner sanctum after you betrayed me by failing to carry out my will regarding the de Courcey girl?"

"Because we are two of a kind and Didier is getting old."

He raised a brow. "You'd leave England for good, then?"

"Who said I have to leave England for good? The pickings there are plentiful." David leaned forward. "Everything you've heard about our women is a lie. They are ripe and waiting for someone like me to come along, give them love, and take their fortune." He smirked.

"You returned with your style intact, I see." Mirreault lifted his glass again. "*À la vôtre.* So, you've yet to inform me what good you will be to me?"

"Oh, believe me, Mirreault. I can work wonders for you. Absolute wonders!"

The tea arrived and was poured by the same manservant who had answered the door. David raised his cup. "To success in the very near future," he said as a toast, meaning every word in a way Mirreault would never guess. At least that was what he was hoping, praying. Could he pull this off? Could he really pull this off? Doubt clutched him, fear slewed its way through his mind.

"To success," Mirreault echoed, toasting to the beginning of his downfall. "So tell me, my lord, what is the first thing you would like us to do together?"

David made his eyes go hard and cold. "I want revenge on Sylvie de Courcey."

"All in good time," Mirreault purred, raising his brows. David wondered what was happening behind those eyes. He couldn't tell whether he was the cat or the mouse in this game they were playing together. But one thing was certain, he had to see this thing through to the end, whichever way it played out. His life was extended, a gift from a man named Alan Richelieu, a man whose name would be forever blackened. He would not allow it to be for naught.

Youngblood felt his heart shudder, spin, and he did his best to quell the nausea in his stomach, to quiet a mind gone frantic.

CHAPTER ❖ TWENTY-NINE

Here, have some tea, you look *horrible*." Sylvie Wallace handed Miranda a brimming cup.

Miranda gratefully accepted. She sipped, waiting for that feeling of well-being to envelop her. It didn't. Nevertheless, she drained the cup, knowing she needed to keep going.

Matthew walked into the room and kissed her cheek. Her bad one. "How are you this morning, Mira?"

"I honestly don't know, Mate."

He put an arm around her, kneeling down next to her chair. "Stay strong. Don't let yourself spiral down."

"I won't," she whispered. "I can't."

He began to help Sylvie with the simple breakfast of scones and cheese. Sylvie still wasn't feeling well, and the smell of eggs was too much to bear. Miranda knew she should get up and help, but she just couldn't.

"His lordship will be by tomorrow, Mira. Have you thought about that?" Matthew asked as he worked.

"I've thought of nothing else."

"I assume he's going to try and get you to go back to Elspeth."

Miranda was assuming the same. She nodded.

"What are you going to tell him?" Sylvie asked softly.

Miranda shook her head. "I honestly don't know. I'm so torn now. The last thing Elspeth needs is for me to desert her. And yet, to watch him with Lady Daria . . ."

Matthew and Sylvie just looked at each other, sadness apparent in their eyes. Love for her plainly exhibited as well.

"Are you sure he gave you no real reason to believe he had more serious intentions regarding you, Mira?" Matthew was obviously ready for a fight.

"None other than the fact that we got along so well, and he was always calling for me. Oh, you should have heard the opera we were working on."

Matthew's brows raised. "Truly? You were working on his opera with him?"

"Yes. The libretto."

Matthew smiled, proud. "Father always said you had a way with words, and with the way you're always reading poetry, I can't say I'm surprised."

"I'm sure it was a beautiful story you wrote." Sylvie sat down at the table with a fresh cup of tea and a piece of dry toast. "Oh, Mira." She put her hand out and placed it on top of her sister-in-law's. "I feel responsible for all of this."

"You?" Miranda and Matthew questioned together.

"How so, my love?" her brother asked.

"I've been praying for months now that Miranda would find love, and now see what has happened."

Miranda felt herself warm a bit. There was so much love in this house. "Thank you for your prayers, Sylvie. God knows what is best. That is the only hope I have right now. And sometimes that doesn't even seem like enough."

Later that day, when Sylvie and Eve were napping, Matthew built the fire up higher and asked for Miranda to make some tea.

She gladly complied, and several minutes later they sat together at the table, Matthew's sermon notes scattered over the surface.

Matthew looked her squarely in the eye. "You need to either go back, Mira, or explain to Elspeth why you've left her. You owe the child that much."

Miranda knew he was right. "It's just so hard, Mate."

"I know, Mira. It's difficult when love is lost. But you've got to decide whether you can face your pain and go back to Elspeth. She needs you."

Miranda shook her head. "Not really. Lady Daria is wonderful to her."

"Miranda." His tone was accusing. "You know it's true. The child loves you."

"But if I leave now, it will be easier on her," Miranda made the excuse. "I certainly won't be going to London after his lordship marries. I can't see myself as that sort of brokenhearted appendage dangling painfully about."

"Then at least go to her and explain. Don't let your pride get in the way of what is right for her."

Miranda felt more desolate than she had ever felt before. "Mate, how can I tell her the truth, that because of my deformity, love will never come to me, and because I love her uncle and he doesn't feel the same way, I must leave? Where does that leave Elspeth? What would she think regarding herself?"

Matthew sighed. "Perhaps his lordship will have a solution we haven't thought about. Let's wait and see what tomorrow holds."

Didier was ready for the whole matter to be done with. The whole sorry way of existence. This wasn't life! This was scraping by—on a golden floor, mind you—but scraping by all the same. *J'en ai marre!*

The small manse was settled down for the night, quiet and cozy. A thin tendril of smoke from the banked fire in the kitchen stove skewered the frigid atmosphere. They were all under their mounds of quilts, most assuredly, sleeping and dreaming of the day to come. A bright day, oh joy, for people like this could not know what it is like to walk in darkness.

He shook his head, wondering if he should just quit the scene entirely, whether he should flee the entire mess—the joke even—his life had become. But he knew that would be ridiculous. All his hard-earned money was back in Paris, back at Mirreault's chateau. It was listed carefully in the old brown ledger book Didier himself had been keeping for years. And down in the basement of the castle, dug into the thick stone wall at the east end, was the treasure room. The wealth held inside its recess was beyond the belief of most of the world's inhabitants, and not even Claude, who trusted Didier implicitly to manage all of the mundanities of his affairs, realized just how vast his fortune truly was.

Now, to the task at hand.

He felt disturbed the moment he squeezed in through the doorway. As if he was desecrating something holy and good. The glowing coals, dying down in a neat mound in the hearth, cast a red, faint light in the main room. Such meager surroundings. A cookstove, a drysink, a cupboard, and a table and four chairs. Doors carved into the wall to the left announced there were two other rooms. He knew the front one was where the vicar and his wife slept. The other was a study where the sister was now sleeping, the one with the appalling blemish. Yes, he knew the layout perfectly, for he had come the night before, as silent as he was now. In some ways he wished he hadn't. In some ways he wished he hadn't had a day to think about these people, to allow them feeling flesh and living bone. But he was nothing if not thorough.

He sighed, a thin, slow sigh. Soundless. White.

It wasn't going to be easy, snatching up the child from between her parents, but there was no other way to do it. An extra quilt would be folded neatly on the window seat in their chamber. It would do nicely to wrap the babe in for their escape.

Silent as a single, fluttering leaf, he stole into the room, shaky with nerves, his breath loud in his ears. Carefully lifting the blanket, he let its folds drop open, a patched puddle of cotton on the crude floor. It would keep the child warm on their ride to the carriage waiting several miles away. Nevertheless, he was a careful man. Reaching into his coat, he felt the weight of his derringer, warmed with his body heat, lying snug between the waist of his pants and his shirt. The weapon was an extension of himself, just another piece of Didier Vachel. Taking chances wasn't an option. He had to be ready for a fight. Ready for whatever would come—and he knew by experience that anything could come.

He circumnavigated the bed, blanket ready to receive the baby. Reaching out, he gently unwound the de Courcey woman's arms from the child, fingers graceful, his touch light. A beautiful child, yes, sleeping like she should be—mysteriously fragile, absent from the cares her elders had been worn down beneath years of living. And looking so much like her father. Didier remembered Count Rene de Boyce with disdain. Too protected for his own well-being, too beautiful for his own good.

Misjudging the corner of the bed, his thigh brushed against the wooden frame.

The vicar's eyes opened and he sprang to his feet. "Who are you?" he said in a thick voice, reaching around him, toward the headboard of the bed.

Under the covers, Sylvie stirred, murmuring, "What is it, Matthew?"

Didier didn't hesitate a second. He pulled out his derringer, aimed, and shot. The vicar, hit in the shoulder, spun around from the force. It knocked him down, sending him crashing against the bedside table, the small lamp, books, and papers spilling onto the floor.

Sylvie sat up at the sound of the shot. At the sight of the man with the gun, she gathered the baby to her. "No! Do not hurt us! Matthew!"

"I'm here!" The vicar groaned, holding his hand against a profusely bleeding wound.

Didier panicked. He had to get this baby out of here. Where to go, where to go. Think. Think. Now.

The sister was now standing at the door like Lot's wife, gruesome, white-haired, and bloodless with fright. He reached in vain for the child, the mother's arms gripping her hard. The derringer fired again, an extension of his will, the bullet discharging into the woman's leg.

It was easy to grab the baby now. Both parents were wounded. The vicar was still on the floor and the woman was struggling on the bed, holding onto the baby with one hand, while trying to staunch the pulsing flow of blood on her wounded leg. He lifted the child easily, its mother severely weakened. "No!" she screamed. "No!"

But the sister was back now, charging at him with a poker from the fireplace. Easily evading her wild swing, he shoved her against the window, folded the baby in the quilt, and ran out of the cottage. The night would suck him into her darkness, as she always did, receiving her child, hiding him beneath her shadowed mantle of silence.

⁓

Miranda, picking herself up off the floor, rushed over to the bed.

Gripping the nightshirt around him, Matthew rose to his feet. He ran through the bedroom door and out into the darkness. Sylvie screamed hysterically, losing blood from her leg. Miranda pulled her into her arms. "Lay down, Sylvie," she commanded. "Matthew's going after him."

"Eve!"

Miranda had never seen such devastation on a human face. "I'm going for help."

"It's Claude Mirreault," Sylvie gasped, losing blood. "He has something to do with this. I saw that man before somewhere. In Paris . . ." Sylvie's eyes closed, and Miranda knew unconsciousness had rescued her for the time being. She threw on a gown, stuffed her feet into her boots, and swirled into her cape. Matthew was coming back through the door. "Eve's gone. He rode away on horseback. There wasn't any way I could catch up. Not like this."

He began to sway, and even in the darkness Miranda could see that all his color had drained from his face. "Tend to your wife. There are clean rags in the cupboard drawer. She's bleeding heavily. And then, tie up your own wounds, Mate. I'm going to Greywalls for help."

Miranda ran, her skirts prohibiting her movement, the frigid winter air whooshing into her lungs like a million tiny knives as they heaved and breathed. Suddenly her problems, her own heartaches, meant nothing. Sylvie might die. Matthew as well. Eve was gone. She drove her legs faster and faster, praying for strength, praying for speed, praying for God to extend his mercy to the ones she loved. For only he could meet their needs this terrible hour.

The castle was pulled from the darkness by her frantic gaze. Dark, large, hard.

Home now.

Minutes later, lungs aching, she ran through the gatehouse, across the bailey, and up to the main entrance. It was locked up tightly for the night, as Greywalls always was. It had once made her feel safe, now it constricted her throat in panic. She yanked on the bell, clobbered the door with her fists, and bawled for help in an echoing voice. Was that her voice? So loud?

A minute later the door opened, and Wooten peered out of the crack, musket clearly visible. "Miss Wallace!" He swung wide the door.

"Help us! Sylvie and Matthew have been shot, Eve has been kidnapped!"

Tobin was at the top of the stairs. He ran down, three steps at a time. "I heard you. I'll change immediately. Wooten, have the fastest horses brought round, then send another horse and a carriage to Greywalls. Contact the doctor and put your wife in the carriage. She'll be needed in Huntly. Miranda, you can explain to me on the way."

And then he was gone, back up the stairs. Miranda tried to warm herself. But not having had time to put on stockings, her feet were frozen, and her hands were bloodless and numb. Feeling somehow more calm now that Tobin was taking care of things, she ran up to her room and put on the necessary garments, including her spare hat and scarf and two pairs of woolen stockings.

Lady Daria entered the room, concern rooted like a magnet between her brows. "Are you all right, dearest? Wooten told me what happened."

"I'm fine." This was the last thing Miranda needed right now. But she pushed back her shoulders and forced a tight, grim smile to her mouth.

Lady Daria handed her the old hat. "I'll look after Elspeth. Have no fear."

Miranda nodded. "I know you will."

"You'd best get on then."

When Miranda raced back down to the entry, thankful that Daria knew when a situation wasn't a party, Tobin was there. "Miranda." He pulled her into his arms. "You are all right, thank God."

Wooten announced the horse was there.

"Come," Tobin said, still taking control of the situation. "Ride with me."

He helped Miranda up onto the saddle, then hoisted himself up behind her. His right arm went around her waist and held her close against him, his left hand gathering the reins. They were off, the horse galloping through his clouds of breath across the petrified moor.

Tobin's breath was warm and comforting in her ear as she turned and told him the night's events, feeling safe, finally, in the circle of his arms. Against her stomach his hand was flattened and protective, so right, the perfect span between her belly and her ribcage. Made to be there.

"*You* are safe, though," he said, after hearing the tale. "Thank God he didn't shoot you, Miranda. If something happened to you . . ." His voice trailed off.

Miranda didn't ask for clarification, for they were at the cottage and he was helping her off the horse. Hand safely in his, she ran into the house, the nausea of fear rising in her throat.

CHAPTER ❖ THIRTY

It seemed like an eternity before Mrs. Wooten arrived with Dr. Sinclair. The removal of the bullets began immediately, Sylvie still unconscious, and Matthew in much the same state.

"Better for them," the old doctor said gruffly, rather too loudly considering the circumstances. His deft fingers probed about, parting flesh and feeling muscle, seeking, finding.

Tobin wired his arm around Miranda, vowing inwardly he would never let her go again. Daria or no Daria, he would make sure she was safe by his side from now on. "We need to find that man. There's nothing more we can do here. We need to find Eve."

Miranda nodded and pulled away from his side, giving one long, last look at her brother. The other horse, ready and waiting with a sidesaddle, was next to his. It was rather disappointing to him that she should ride away from him. How perfectly she had fit into his arms, and her hair, it was soft against his cheek as it blew in the breeze, and it smelled so good. *She* smelled so good. He only wished that happier circumstances had put her where she belonged. In his arms, next to him. His hand was still tingling where it had once rested against her stomach.

"Ready?" She pulled him from his thoughts.

"Yes. Let's go."

"Matthew said he rode away from Huntly . . . east."

Tobin turned Mister Socks in that direction and started off. Miranda easily kept pace.

A bit down the road, a small public house beginning its morning preparations materialized from the morning mists. Out of the back door, dirty water flew from a pan. Tobin jumped off the horse and went to speak with the proprietor's wife, who now stood in the yard looking at them with unveiled curiosity.

"Did you see a man with a baby this morning? About two hours ago?"

She nodded. "Oh, *that* one! Aye, I saw him. Left us with tha' horse o'er there an' pulled off in a carriage tha' was waitin' fer him. Doon the road towards Aberdeen."

"Thank you." He handed her a crown and jumped back on his horse.

"Aberdeen," was all he said and they spurred their horses into action toward the depot, and boarded an early morning train.

The sun was full in the sky by the time they arrived, and the port town was bustling with activity. But Tobin saw nothing except people to question. And that is what he did.

"Did you see a man with a baby this morning?" he asked a vendor in the market, a man selling coal, firewood, peat, and kindling.

"Nay, sir. Woke up late this mornin' I'm afraid ta say. A bit too much whiskey last night. The wife was ready ta beat me o'er the—"

"Thank you." Tobin cut him off. He asked questions as they worked their way further and further down toward the docks.

The fishing boats were long gone for the day, the sea was calm. However, one boat that remained behind, sporting a broken mast, was busy being repaired. A man sat aft, mending his nets. Tobin called out to him. "Have you been here long?"

"Since afore sunrise."

Please, Lord, Tobin prayed. "I'm looking for a man with a baby. A small man. French."

"Aye, saw one o' those this morn. A wee bairn, it was."

"Did you see where they went?"

He nodded, his salty skin glistening in the sunlight. "Aye, hired a boat oot o' here no' an hoor since. One o' they Frenchies, ye say?"

"Yes."

"Aye then, that's yer man. Said somethin' aboot Paris. Offered auld Jamie a heap o' money ta get him o'er the water."

"How long before your boat is ready to set sail?" Tobin pointed to the new mast being raised.

"No' more than an hoor."

"How would you like to make *yourself* a heap o' money?" Tobin propositioned. "How would you like to take us to France as well?"

"How much is it worth ta ye?" The old man scrunched up his face.

"That baby was kidnapped, old man."

"Fair enough. We'll be sailin' in an hoor. Get yer ain vittals, will ye? I dinna have the time fer ta see ta yer comforts."

Tobin nodded and turned toward Miranda. She was so quiet. He couldn't imagine what she was feeling inside. "Let's get some food."

"I don't think I could eat."

He tucked her arm in his. "Some tea then." Yes, he was getting to know her well. Miranda Wallace never refused a cup of tea that he had ever witnessed.

"All right." She seemed content to let him lead her down the street and into an inn. "Tea would be lovely."

He knew she would say that.

"We must send a messenger to Greywalls," Miranda said later, as they sat before the fire. Tobin had eaten breakfast, and the innkeeper's wife was packing them up a parcel of food for the voyage.

"I agree."

And so a boy was dispatched toward Greywalls, where Tobin hoped Sylvie and Matthew were now firmly ensconced. It was all he could do. Now they must wait until the boat was ready to go, and hopefully, by this time tomorrow, they would be nearing Paris.

Daria tied the apron tightly around her waist and strode into the room, a woman with a purpose other than locating the perfect feather for a hat or dreaming up a new theme for a gown. She'd never before been given the opportunity to nurse sick people, and it was an incredibly rewarding experience. That preacher was quite a man, mind you. He would only leave his wife's side to relieve himself, and Daria viewed that as a marvelous way to behave toward the one you loved. This was a greater love than she had ever seen. It went beyond weddings and even companionship in one's old age. It was a consuming thing, an amazing thing. Something she had never experienced. Something she would never deny anyone if given the chance.

Elspeth had been her shadow all day, and she found she rather liked having the child there. If Daria knew anything about society, she knew that, despite Elspeth's deformity, her wit and keen sense of life's true importances would stand her in good stead. Now that Valentinia was firmly betrothed to that wispy Hamish boy, and Daria was done thwarting elopements, she would have more time to preen this child. In fact, she knew of one lad, destined to be a marquis, who was blind and hailed from a family of utter mavericks, hopeless intellectuals. He was only a few years older than Elspeth and every inch as smart as she. He hated the city, loved a good chat, and when push came to shove, was as in need of affection as Elspeth. Yes, Daria decided, Lord Hayden Walsh would do just perfectly.

All was quiet in the Wallace's room, just as Daria suspected. Sylvie had not yet fully come back to consciousness, which was a troublesome thing, and her husband was sleeping. As Daria tucked the bedclothes more firmly around his wife, the man awakened.

"How is she?" he asked. "Was the doctor by? Did I miss him?"

"He'll be round soon," Daria promised. "I sent for him an hour ago."

Matthew's face was paler than strained milk, and he winced as he sat up. "She's still unconscious."

Daria nodded. It worried her, but she didn't wish to make the man's burden any greater.

"I want you to do something for us, my lady, if you will."

"Anything you need, Reverend."

"Send for Agnes Green, Sylvie's old nurse. She lives near York on the estates of Lord Dugley."

"I know him. I'll send someone right away. In the meantime, however, you need to get more rest." Daria had never seen a more tortured-looking man in her life.

But Matthew shook his head. "Not now, my lady. I have a sermon to give in three days' time. Would you hand me my Bible?"

Daria knit her brows and did as he commanded. She suspected Matthew Wallace's commands were always attended to. "But surely someone else will do that for you?"

"The work of God must go on. Sylvie wouldn't wish for me to forsake my flock."

Daria frowned, her previous vision of this man blasted by his statement. "I think it is rather callous, if you ask me."

Matthew's eyes stormed. "I don't remember asking you, my lady."

Daria immediately regretted her outburst. And apparently, so did Matthew. He shook his head wearily. "Truth be told, my lady, I just need to try and keep my mind occupied somewhat, or I shall go mad. The earl and my sister have not returned?"

"No, but a message was delivered two hours ago. They've gone to France, to a man named Mirreault. They've gone after the baby."

Matthew paled even more.

Daria felt herself go cold. "What is it? What is wrong?"

His indigo eyes blazed. "Pray, Lady Christopher. Pray as you have never prayed before."

Goodness, but the man was positively earnest. "I haven't prayed in years, Reverend."

Matthew reached for her hand. "But God's been listening to your heart nonetheless."

"I'll try," she said, feeling discomfort throw a barbed anchor deep into her soul. "You rest now, or write your sermon, or whatever it is that helps you. I'm going to find Elspeth."

Daria knew the most important task before her now was to keep life as normal as possible for Elspeth. Of course, the child knew events had gone dreadfully wrong, but the fact was, she was more used to adversity than she was to calm, and she was handling the stressful time more beautifully than anyone else at Greywalls. Still, Daria wasn't leaving anything to chance.

By nightfall, the doctor had come and gone, saying there was nothing more he could do for Sylvie save keep the dressings clean, but quite confident she would soon come around. The shock of the blood loss would eventually wear off. Matthew would be fine, which didn't surprise Daria at all.

Daria found Elspeth in the library, tinkering at the piano. The child turned to face her. "Do ye think Uncle Tobin would teach me ta play?"

Daria shrugged. "I don't know, dearest. Some people, although they play beautifully, cannot teach." In truth, she didn't see Tobin as much of a teacher. "But do you remember his good friend, Mr. Clarkson?"

"Aye! The organist here yon do last autumn."

"Exactly. A wonderful teacher too. After we move back to London, I'm sure he'd be happy to teach music to you."

Elspeth smiled. "It was onyways so dull here at Greywalls afore ma da came home. An' then Uncle Tobin, weel, he brought music ta the hoose. An' Miss Wallace, she brought laughter, an' dis tha' no' make a bonnie mix?"

Daria sat down next to her on the old leather sofa. "Tell me about Miss Wallace. She seems like a perfectly charming woman."

"Aye, she is! An' canny too. She's fine bonnie if'n ye can see through yon port-wine stain. But do ye know"—Elspeth leaned forward—"she sets herself alongside o' me aw the time, like she sees hersel' jist as deformed."

Daria could believe it. The fact that Miss Wallace wasn't married gave testimony to the view she must have of herself. "I find her charming."

"Aye, an' ye should see her with Uncle Tobin when they are workin' together!"

This was news. "What do you mean?"

Elspeth was excited. "She's workin' on the libretto fer his opera!"

"Really!"

"Aye. An' it is fair braw too. Not aw chock full o' nonsense an' holes."

Daria could hardly believe it. The fact that some obscure governess was a keen enough writer for Tobin's libretto was astounding. She knew how picky he could be. "So you said they've been working together on it?"

"Aye. Like a daftie. She sits doon there on yon chair, an' he plays an' sings, an' she sings, not as well as he does, mind, an' the words are awful' bonnie. It's aboot the Elysian Fields an' how the braw lad rejects an eternity in paradise to bide wi' his cold porridge lass. But she's bonnie inside, an' ye'll know, that's what it's aw aboot."

Daria sat back against the couch, filling in the few blanks left to be filled. "She loves him, doesn't she?"

Elspeth slapped her hands up to her mouth, then slowly dropped them. "I've said over much."

"No." Daria sought to reassure her. "It's obvious your uncle has been off to another land, so to speak, the past few days. Does he love her?"

Elspeth shrugged. "Dinna ken. But I do know he sends fer her at aw hoors o' the day ta yon library, an' I do know tha' when she is wi' him his face is shinin' an' aw."

Daria's heart plummeted, but only for a second. And only due to the wedding plans. The truth was, she loved Tobin, but she didn't need him. She didn't feel about him the way that Reverend Wallace loved his wife. That they were to be married was truly a decision made to keep them both from a lonely old age. It was about friendship and fondness, not passion or even joy. At least from her perspective. Apparently from Tobin's too, which wasn't a great surprise.

"Yer no' mad wi' me, are ye?" Elspeth's voice pulled her back to the present.

"Of course not!" Daria hugged her tightly, feeling Elspeth's sweet shoulder blades beneath her hands. Fine shoulder blades. Perfect shoulder blades.

"An' yer no' mad wi' Uncle Tobin or Miss Wallace either?"

"Oh, no! I find it most thrilling that they have both found love. To be honest, Elspeth, I would have been nothing more than a decoration in your uncle's life, an amusement when he wasn't busy with his music. But Miss Wallace, she will be a true compatriot. And that is just what a man like Lord Youngblood has always needed. She must be a special woman."

Elspeth nodded. "Och, weel, she is tha'."

"Then I will talk to your uncle upon his return. I will tell him that his services as a suitor are no longer required!" She laughed, feeling immense relief, thinking that maybe, somewhere along the road, a love like she had witnessed between the Wallaces might someday be hers too.

Elspeth laughed with her. "Everything will be aw right, then?" she asked, still needing reassurance. "Even with Eve? She'll be comin' home ta us?"

"Yes, darling. Everything will be fine."

"An' will ye still come ta see me? I like ye fair weel, Lady Daria."

Daria hugged her. "Well, of course. You see, Elspeth, I really do believe I've made a new friend, a good friend, a friend for life."

Elspeth completed the embrace, hugging her tightly. "I love ye in the Lord, an' I love ye in ma heart," she murmured. Daria found the display of affection utterly charming.

She thought again about Lord Hayden Walsh. Yes, he would be just the ticket for this girl. She had quite forgotten about that family's propensity toward God and such. Definitely, this idea was a good one, and her mind was already full of plans. Certainly, if anyone could develop a match made in heaven for Elspeth Youngblood, it was she, Daria Christopher, matchmaker and general bluebird of happiness.

CHAPTER ❖ THIRTY-ONE

The voyage was miserable. Although the North Sea was calm, it was a bitterly cold day. And the swift breeze that hastened the journey also heightened the chill.

Tobin sat aft, on the floor of the deck. He pulled Miranda to him. "My lord," she protested, but offered no real struggle.

He lightly persisted. "We have a lot to say to each other . . . or at least, I have much to say to you, Miranda. So we might as well be as warm as possible while doing so."

She scooted closer to him, her side against his own.

"That's better." He felt a sense of peace and well-being flush through him by her contact. "I'd hate to think you couldn't understand me for the chattering of my teeth."

"It's not that I feel right about this, my lord, not with Lady Daria waiting for you back at Greywalls. But the cold has frozen my willpower."

"I wish to speak with you about Daria."

Miranda's head bowed. "What is there to say?" she mumbled from the recesses of her scarf. "She is your fiancée. Your beautiful, wonderful fiancée."

Tobin's heart spasmed in anguish. That she should have no idea what a true treasure she was, well, it made her value even more inestimable, made her more darling in his eyes. He took her chin in his fingers and lifted her face to his. That mild resistance again appeared, and soon he was staring down into two brilliantly blue, tear-filled eyes. "Daria and I will not be getting married. It was never a good idea, Miranda."

"I don't see why not," she whispered.

"Because we don't love each other."

"Of course you do. Daria—"

"—has never loved me. We only agreed to marry each other because we didn't want to be alone. Surely you can understand that?"

She nodded, trying to look down. But his fingers were firm and he would not let her. His face was inches from hers and he could feel her breath upon it. So warm and so Miranda. Oh, how he wanted to kiss her just then, to kiss her mouth, to kiss away the tears and the sorrow of years embedded in her eyes.

"I never thought I would find love," he explained. "I thought I would go through life alone, always wishing for that one, all-consuming love to come my way. And for many years I searched, but always it was the same, Miranda. Finally, I figured, that at least with Daria, I would live my life with comfortable companionship. Never did I dare to dream that I would one day find the one for whom my heart had always longed, the one who shares my dreams, my soul. But I have, Miranda. And I believe she feels the same way, although I've never asked her."

His heart was pounding. All his life he had been waiting to declare the deep love he knew he was so capable of feeling; all his life he had been wondering if it would ever come his way. "Miranda, you are that woman." Her eyes rounded. "I love you, dear woman. I love you in the way I always knew I could love, the way I've always wanted to love. The question is, do you feel the same way?"

The tears in Miranda's eyes grew. She closed her eyes and let them spill over her cheeks. Her body sagged in relief. "Yes," she said, eyes still closed. "Oh yes, my lord, I love you. I love you so much I wanted to die when I heard Lady Christopher's voice."

He pulled her close to him, quickly and tightly. And he wound his hand into her heavy hair, tipped her head back, and searched her eyes as they opened. "Have you ever been kissed, sweet Miranda?"

She shook her head.

"Before God, I desperately wish I could say the same. Nevertheless, my love, know that this is truly the first kiss of love I have ever known." And with those words hanging in the frigid air, he lowered his head, his mouth finding hers, his eyes closing as the sweet, gentle softness of her lips met with his, shy yet so willing.

This was love.

This was what he had been made to feel. This was the woman who completed him. This was the woman he would love forever.

She sighed against his mouth several moments later, and he pulled away to look at her. He felt his own eyes mist slightly as she began to cry. "I'm so happy." She nuzzled into his chest. "Oh, my lord, I've never been so happy in all my life. And I wonder when it all will end. But I cannot keep myself from loving you now, even though someday you'll become tired of this face, tired of looking upon my birthmark. I wish to heavens I had the strength."

"Miranda, you don't understand. I love you. That means every part of you."

"How can that be?" She pulled her scarf around her more tightly once again. "How can you love anything so ugly? And don't tell me it isn't ugly, my lord. Please don't tell me that."

"I don't mean to sound callous, Miranda, but I've grown used to it. I hardly see it any more. Only when you self-consciously dip your head down and to the side, trying to cover it with your hair do I say, Oh, yes, there's that birthmark. Only when you bring it up to me do I think about how difficult it is for you. Miranda, if my love didn't encompass your imperfections as well as your perfections, it wouldn't be much of a love, would it?"

Miranda shook her head.

"And you know there are plenty of imperfections you overlook in me." He lifted her chin again. "Right?"

She didn't say anything and he laughed. "See? I am right. My clothes are always rumpled, my hair is too long, I don't sleep for days on end and then I sleep for days on end, I'm really rather skinny under these layers of clothes, and I'll tell you something else." He leaned forward, whispering as though the *London Times* was around to overhear.

"What?" Miranda leaned her ear toward his mouth.

"When I feel deeply, it is too much to bear at times, and I cry. Me. A grown man."

"But I love that about you!" Miranda rushed to say.

"See? And there are all sorts of objectionable, human things I'm not even going to begin to let you know about until you're safely mine, until you're my wife and you absolutely cannot leave me." He lifted her chin again, looking at her earnestly. "I have no ring to give you here, and soon I may have no fortune, no title, not even a home. But barring all of these things, Miranda Wallace, will you be my wife?"

"Yes!" she cried without hesitation, throwing her arms around his neck. "Oh, yes, my lord."

He kissed her again, and kissed her and kissed her. The day waned, but they barely noticed the brilliant sunset. Finally, they remembered the reason for their journey and pulled apart.

"Oh, my lord," she breathed.

"And that's another thing, my love. You must stop calling me that. I am Tobin, nothing more, nothing less."

"You are my love," she said passionately, her eyes spilling over with emotion. "My only love."

"And so you are mine."

The captain of the ship interrupted them. "Ye still wantin' ta land at Calais?"

"Yes," Tobin answered. "We'll take a train to Paris from there."

"We'll be there by daybreak."

It was going to be a battle, what lay in front of them. But Tobin knew there was no one he'd rather fight alongside of than Miranda, a brave woman of fortitude and noble heart. And she belonged to him. *Praise be to God!*

⁓

Youngblood arrived at Camille's home well after supper time. He hadn't told her when he'd be back to see her, but he felt some sense of sadness when he saw her sitting alone in the kitchen with a pot of much reduced soup and cold bread. She was sketching a clumsy still life she had set up earlier. Something was happening inside Camille, as if she was beginning to shed the scales formed by the life she had led for so long, exposing the gentle pink of true womanhood beneath. Not much pink was showing yet, though, and he realized it could all go either way from here.

He apologized. "I'm sorry I didn't get here sooner."

"I already ate so do not worry yourself. Have you eaten supper?"

"Yes, but your soup smells so good I could be persuaded to eat again."

Camille smiled and set down her charcoal stick. "I believe my soup can speak for itself and indeed, it already has."

David looked in the pot as she ladled him a bowl. Cabbage and potato soup with a beef stock. The homey stew gave him comfort, reminding him of "Wifie Wooten," as Angus called her, and the many times she had come up to his room with food from the servants' dinner on those nights when, as a child, he was being punished undeservedly. He laughed out loud.

"What is funny to you?" Camille set out a spoon and a knife and placed the bowl of soup and a plate of bread and cheese between the cutlery.

"I was thinking of the Wootens, the old couple who take care of Greywalls. She was the housekeeper and he was my father's personal secretary in London when I was growing up."

"An odd match, then?"

David picked up the spoon. "In many ways, I suppose. Wooten was educated and Mrs. Wooten wasn't learned above a grammar school level. They met on the job, so to speak."

Camille's brows raised quickly. "And your parents allowed the marriage?"

"One of the few times my father was out-maneuvered. They eloped and when my parents were told, they threatened to take away the Wootens' jobs and send them out on the street without references." He dipped his spoon in the bowl and took a bite. "They expected them to beg for their jobs, but they only said, '"Go right ahead. We used to work for the Buckinghams, you know, and they've already said there is a place for us with them."'"

Camille chuckled, sat down, and sliced off a piece of Camembert. "I love them and I've never even met them." She bit into the cheese. "So what happened?"

"My parents ended up begging the Wootens to stay, and, if you can believe this from a couple who penny-pinched on everything but gowns, parties, tobacco, and alcohol, they upped their salary by half again!"

"There must have been quite a celebration below stairs that night!"

"Absolutely. And Mrs. Wooten spirited me out of my bed to be a part of it. I was only seven at the time." He spooned his soup carefully into his mouth. "It was a party like none I've been to since."

"And you've been to a lot of parties!"

He rolled his eyes. "Too many."

"How was that giant blow-bag we've come to know and hate named Claude Mirreault?" she asked, getting up to open a bottle of wine.

David shook his head, arose as well, and ladled some more soup into his bowl. "I'm not pleased with this turn of events, having to go back to the old ways."

"But surely it's not as bad as that?"

He watched the way she moved, so comfortable in her kitchen, a refined woman who could grace the table of the emperor with ease, yet navigated this humble room smoothly, her lower half swaying gently with her movements. He watched her hands, so beautiful yet strong, as they worked the cork out of the wine bottle. No woman of his class could boast such a wonderful, warm combination. Beauty plus strength plus patience. That was Camille. And she was by his side now. They were doing commonplace things together: getting soup, pouring wine, chatting. Like a man and woman meant to be together.

"Well?" Camille turned to him, taking a sip of her wine. "Are you going to continue the conversation or not? You became awfully quiet suddenly."

"If you'd like," he said, rushing on to finish lest she read his thoughts. "It's not as easy as I thought it would be, going back. Which is good in some ways, bad in others. I don't want to do the things he does, and I don't know how many times I can refuse his brandy—"

"You're refusing his *brandy*?" Camille was incredulous. "I suppose you really *do* have religion!"

They sat back down. "Believe it or not, I lost the taste for it when I was holed up in St. Ninian's Abbey. But that's the problem. Mirreault's not stupid. He's on to me, Camille. I can feel it. And I don't know why he's not exposing me sooner."

"I think you're worried more than you should be. If anyone can act a part, it's you, my lord. And remember, Mirreault doesn't have any reason *not* to believe you."

David sipped his wine thoughtfully. "Perhaps you are right, Camille."

"Of course I am. When have I ever led you astray?"

He laughed. "Plenty of times, as I recall."

She gently shoved his shoulder with her index finger, then began to roll a cigarette. "I remember it differently." She smiled, but the truth behind her words was evident. "I was just a girl from the country trying to find a life in Paris when you met me, when you introduced me to Claude Mirreault."

"I'm sorry, Camille," he whispered, reaching for the pouch of tobacco.

"Yes," she said. "You are. But I love you anyway."

~

Though the circumstances were horrid, and the weather in Paris was well below freezing, a warmth permeated Miranda, a feeling of assurance tender and good. She could never have guessed what it would feel like to be loved like this. Tobin had kept his arm around her the entire voyage, and on the train, as they thawed out somewhat, he removed her glove and lovingly stroked the back of her hand with smooth, firm movements meant to reassure. Miranda found herself in a perpetual state of inner-argument, praising God on one hand and doubting his ability to sustain this wonderful union of souls on the other.

The train pulled into Paris and they disembarked, hand in hand. "Where do we go now?" Miranda asked. She found herself staring at his beautiful face so filled with love for her. Feeling unworthy of such a blessing, she nevertheless refused to question God's goodness in answering the prayer she had hardly dared to breathe all of her life.

"To the Minister of Justice, I suppose," Tobin said, helping her through the station and out onto the street. "We'll find a cab to take us there."

One was readily available, and he helped her inside, his hand lingering on the small of her back, possessive and guiding. *I am his*, Miranda thought, still unable to believe it.

"Hopefully, he will have heard of this infamous Mirreault," Tobin suggested as the coach rolled forward. "From the history of Sylvie's family concerning that man, I feel safe in assuming the child is safe and will be held for ransom. Other than that, I have no other idea where to start. At least in an aboveboard way."

Miranda nodded. She, too, had pictured them canvasing disreputable pubs and inns, and she prayed it would be unnecessary.

The coach stopped in front of the great stone building. It was already 4 P.M., but hopefully the Minister of Justice would be there. He was. Miranda conjured up some image of a modern-day giant with hands that could crush large rocks. Perhaps he even had a scar or two and bumpy ears from untold numbers of skirmishes in his youthful days of bravery and war. Or whatever it was that Ministers of Justice used to do before they became Ministers of Justice.

They were ushered in quickly upon Tobin's giving the name Youngblood. Miranda breathed in, and walked through the tall open door. The man was positively dwarfed by the ornate room. Not a giant at all, but a small, unassuming man named Evariste Lyell. Miranda immediately took a liking to him.

He gestured to the comfortable arrangement of sofa and chairs near the windows, to the right of his desk. "If you please, sit down in comfort. Have you journeyed far?"

"Yes, we have, sir." Tobin took over, and Miranda, always a support to the strong, was glad. "We just got off the train."

"Then let us be quick about it. I'm sure you both want to get a hot bath and some dinner. In fact . . . Georges!" he called to his secretary, the man who had shown them in, "bring in a pot of hot coffee and some food."

The small man wielded such quiet authority, Miranda wouldn't have dreamed of turning him down. She nodded. Tobin accepted with ease.

"Go on, then," Lyell circled his hand. "Tell me what it is that brought you here. Does it have something to do with that brigand relative of yours, David Youngblood?"

"Indirectly, I suppose," Tobin proceeded to explain the story, Miranda supplying little details unknown to him.

Lyell nodded, his fingers steepled and steady, his eyes never leaving their faces. "A kidnapping you say?"

"Yes. Sylvie de Courcey's daughter."

"Go on."

Tobin finished up a good while later, having consumed croque monsieurs and two cups of coffee. "And so we have come to you, hoping for your help. We simply didn't know where else to go."

"It is very interesting you should come to me with this right now," he said. "I am most interested in bringing down Claude Mirreault, you see. Are you certain it is he who has kidnapped the child?"

Miranda nodded. "We can think of no other who would do so." She leaned forward and spoke softly. "We have reason to believe David Youngblood is over here as well."

"Oh, the earl of Cannock is over here most definitely." Lyell rubbed his hands together. "*Monsieur* Youngblood, *Mademoiselle* Wallace, welcome to the party."

"Were you followed?" Mirreault asked.

Didier had arrived in Versailles thirty minutes before, and after handing the screaming baby over to the cook, proceeded to collapse upon his bed. But alas, Mirreault had sent for him, and alas, here he was in the study giving an account of the speedy operation.

"No one followed me, *monsieur*. The vicar tried to. But he had been shot."

"You didn't injure anybody acutely, did you? What about the de Courcey chit? The ransom must be paid. And lifeless parents are incapable of forfeiting their francs to ransom their off-spring."

Didier decided not to mention what had happened to Sylvie Wallace. He'd had enough experience with that woman to know she was a fighter. She would live. And she would get her child back. But he, Didier Vachel, would be long gone. "Believe me, sir, you will get your ransom."

"Post the note, and you will be free to go and live your life as you've been itching to do for the past year. Unless, of course, you fancy seeing the child safely back to Scotland."

"No, thank you, *monsieur*. I'm ready to leave this all behind me now. I'm too old, you see. Too old to be in this line of work any longer." He just wanted to wake up his own man, just once would be enough, really. But he hoped he had years ahead of him to do it many times.

"I'll reward you handsomely for your effort. Seeing as it would be your last one."

Didier hesitated.

"Come now! I'll let you pick any painting you'd like down in the vault or even up here in the house. Think of it as a retirement gift. A rather large retirement gift," Mirreault wheedled. "Why not make your last job one you can be proud of?"

It made sense, in a strange way.

"So be it." Didier thought of the small Rembrandt he had always loved, the small image of Christ's face that had been down in the vault for years. "If I took the child away, the least I can do is see her properly home."

But he didn't have a good feeling about this. Taking the child back couldn't redeem her kidnapping, and a good deed at the end of a forty-year crime spree would barely tip the scales of God's justice in his favor. He should change his mind right there, but he was determined to take away as much gold as possible from Mirreault's castle. Hadn't he been the one to do most of the work? That thought was hardly a comfort.

My last job, he thought. *Finally free.*

Come quickly—Lyell.

"Most intriguing," David Youngblood said, opening the message wide and showing it to Camille.

She raised her eyebrows. "Something has happened. Evariste would not send a note around without good reason."

David felt his pulse quicken in excitement. He took her shoulders and squeezed. "We may be free of Mirreault sooner than we think!"

"*We?*" Camille responded. "You are already free, my lord. But poor Camille . . ."

He hugged her to him. "You will be free, Camille. I promise."

She pulled back, caressing his cheek with her hand. "You've made me many promises, my lord, and kept none of them. And so, I cannot believe you now."

David winced. "I keep telling you I am a new man, Camille."

"And I keep telling you to prove it."

"Just give me time."

She flicked some lint off of his shoulder, then patted it. "You'd better go. You don't want to keep the minister waiting."

Twenty minutes later he was shown without hesitation into the Minister of Justice's inner sanctum. "My lord," Lyell greeted him, bowing. "Thank you for coming on such short notice."

David shook his hand, then turned around at the sound of familiar voices behind him saying, "David!"

"Tobin! Miranda!" He rushed toward them, kissing Miranda's hand, shaking Tobin's. It was hard to look his uncle in the eye, but he did it anyway. He had no idea what these two could be doing here, and he asked them just that.

"Mirreault is up to tricks again, David," Tobin explained.

His sober tone of voice immediately set David on guard. "What are you talking about?"

"His man has kidnapped Eve. A small, dark man took her away the day before yesterday." Miranda supplied more detail.

Lyell beckoned them to come sit near his desk. The men scraped chairs across the floor, and soon they sat in a semicircle around Lyell's desk. "Do you think Didier would have brought the baby to Mirreault's chateau?" he asked Youngblood.

"Of course. Was a ransom note left?" He turned to Miranda. She shook her head.

"That will be coming shortly then."

Lyell sat back with a sigh. "I would have loved to have brought the man in on murder charges. But I suppose kidnapping will have to do. This will be easier than we thought, eh, my lord?" he said to David.

David stood, feeling grim, wary. "Let's get one thing straight: nothing is ever easy when it concerns Claude Mirreault."

"True, true. We will rely on you, on the inroads you've already made. You must get into the castle, allow some of my men inside, and produce the child. Without making Mirreault aware of what is going on. Are you up to the job?"

He thought of the forgiveness he would receive from Sylvie, of the soon-coming exile, of his someday freedom. And Camille, who deserved, more than he did, the chance to cast off the life to which he had introduced her. "I have to be."

"Good then." Lyell rose to his feet. "All our resources are at your disposal. Remember, this is our operation and we will not fail you. You won't be alone, my lord."

Lyell's words were unnecessary. David knew he wouldn't be alone. He knew that someone would be with him who was far greater, far stronger, and far wiser than any Minister of Justice or his minions could be. And though he took comfort in that fact, he had to keep himself from shaking with fear.

⁓

"She's not completely coming around yet," Matthew explained to Agnes Green, Sylvie's old nurse, governess, and friend. "Although we can wake her up enough to get her to take some liquids."

The older woman—carrying her own son Adam, just a few months older than the missing Eve—stared with consternation at Sylvie. "The doctor comes faithfully?"

"Yes. Every day, sometimes twice."

Agnes sat down next to Sylvie on the bed, caressed her hand, and smiled slightly. "You know what you're doing, don't you, child? You're just waiting to come back to us when Eve is home safe and sound." Agnes turned to look at Matthew. "I can't say I blame her. How do you feel?"

Matthew shrugged. "Exhausted. I can't sleep for worry. To think she braved so many trials, endured so much heartache so that we could be together, only to come to this. What do you really think, Agnes? Do you think she'll be all right?"

Agnes shrugged as well. "I don't know. But if I had to guess, I'd say she'll come around soon. Sylvie's like that, you know. She worries you to death, and then all of a sudden things are all right, and you've forgotten she ever made you frightened."

Matthew knew that was certainly the truth. "I'm glad you're here, Aggie."

"Have you been praying as you ought?" Agnes asked, her jowled face soft with concern.

"I've been praying as much as I am able," Matthew said, getting out of bed to exercise his wounded arm. Outside, the day was gray and dismal. It echoed the state of his heart so perfectly, so painfully, he pulled the curtains shut with a snap.

CHAPTER ◆ THIRTY-TWO

Why did it seem, on this evening of Claude Mirreault's downfall, that his chateau suddenly doubled its number of gargoyles? *Blast it, but those creatures seem especially ominous tonight,* David thought as he rode up to the castle.

He tethered his horse to a hitching post and hurried up the stone steps. Searching for the guard in the turret to his right, David looked for the sign that Lyell's men had made it to their post, had disabled Mirreault's guards.

No one there.

He looked to his left, tipped his hat.

Nothing. No hat tipped in return. No one at all.

Blast!

The mammoth door was opened. There was no going back. He reached into the saddlebag for a rolled-up newspaper. This particular prop in tonight's drama had cost Lyell a fortune in political capital.

David smiled broadly. "Didier! Has he demoted you to doorman now?"

Didier said nothing. He'd made it no secret that he had never liked Youngblood.

"Mirreault wasn't expecting me," David said.

"*Monsieur* Mirreault expects the unexpected. Come in, my lord."

"Thank you, Didier. I'm glad to see you're home safe and sound."

They were walking down the corridor toward the dining salon. "What are you talking about, my lord?"

"Come now, Didier, don't be coy with me."

He was shown back to the dining room where the money-lender was taking a late supper. Rare meat, as usual. "Sit down, my lord. Care to join me?"

Youngblood shook his head. "I've already eaten."

"Wine?"

"Not yet." He reached into his pocket and pulled out the phony newspaper. Opening to page three, he folded the paper back and into a neat rectangle. He threw it beside Mirreault's plate, the words, *Kidnapped in Scotland* at the top. "You've been holding out on me, Mirreault."

"So I've finally made the *London Times*, eh?" He tapped the paper in smug triumph.

David snatched the paper back up. "I thought we were a team."

"Oh, sit down, Youngblood, please. Such self-righteous prattle does nothing to facilitate my appetite, and as this is a particularly delicious beefsteak, you can choose to either contain yourself or leave the room until I am finished."

"Fine." David sat down, breathed in. *What had happened to the plan? Why weren't Lyell's men here yet?*

"Didier!" Mirreault bellowed and the man quickly appeared. "Look at what his lordship's got over there. Tell me, is it an accurate account?"

As Didier took the paper from David, he prayed that Miranda's recollections had been correct. Didier read out loud. "'The infant daughter of the late Count Rene de Boyce was abducted from the arms of her mother, Sylvie Wallace, in Huntly, Scotland last week. The child is believed to have been taken to England, but so far the investigation has led nowhere.'"

"They're on to us." Mirreault's great brows drew together. "Sylvie de Courcey knows it is us. She has to. She cannot be that stupid."

Didier grew uncomfortable, David noticed. Definitely a man with something to hide. And David had an idea that he had failed to tell his boss how badly Sylvie had been wounded. He decided to take the offensive. "I agree. How do they not know you have nothing to do with this, Claude? Unless, of course, there's something Didier is not telling you. From reading this account, it seems to me that Sylvie has said nothing to the authorities one way or the other. How can this be?"

Mirreault turned to Didier, set down his knife and fork. "I thought you said she wasn't hurt?"

"I never said she wasn't hurt." Didier defended himself.

David jumped on it. "But you failed to supply how grievous her wound was, didn't you, Didier? What did you do to her?"

"I shot her. In leg. I swear I didn't mean to hurt her badly, I was just trying to get the child away." His dark eyes darted back and forth, his hands rapidly folded over and over upon themselves.

"We'll talk about that later, Didier." Claude tapped Didier on the arm. "I think Lord Youngblood still cares for the wench, don't you?"

Didier, still visibly upset, said nothing.

Claude laughed out loud and turned to David. "So she broke your heart, did she, my lord?"

"Let's not go into it."

"How would you like to see her again?" Mirreault asked. "There's still more work to be done here. And obviously, Didier cannot be trusted to deal with the woman with a light hand."

David leaned forward. "I'm, as usual, all ears."

"Deliver the ransom letter to Mrs. Wallace. Or to whomever is alive to receive it. I take it she married that vicar. You might have to get it to him instead."

"I'll take care of everything. But we must settle on an agreement regarding the ransom monies. I believe long ago we decided that the new arrangement would be a fifty-fifty split." *Where was Lyell? Mirreault was confessing!*

"Bring Lord Youngblood the ransom note," Mirreault commanded Didier.

David feigned surprise. "Is the child here? In Versailles?"

Mirreault stabbed his steak with his fork. "She's here at my chateau. Downstairs, in fact."

David stood to his feet. "May I see her?"

"Didier!" Mirreault bellowed. "Bring the brat upstairs along with the note."

———

Tobin somehow knew something would go wrong. Lyell's men, as well as their own carriage, had been detained in Paris. Fire had overtaken a house along their way out of the city, and they had to pursue an alternate route. It had eaten away precious time, and they were late, arriving well after the time David was to have arrived.

Lyell opened the door before the carriage stopped. They were in the courtyard of Mirreault's chateau. Tobin and Miranda sat across from him. The minister jumped out and waved toward the castle. Waited. Nodded toward the occupants of the carriage. "It's all right. My men have properly overtaken Mirreault's guards. That was too close for my comfort." He reached into his waistcoat and pulled out a handkerchief.

Tobin got out of the vehicle, helping Miranda down. "Unfortunately David doesn't know he is adequately protected now."

Lyell waved a hand. "He can take care of himself."

Tobin put his arm around Miranda. "Are you ready, Mira? Are you sure you wish to do this?"

"Of course."

Tobin knew Miranda would always be ready for such difficult tasks. When Lyell had gently asked her to come along, to take the baby into her arms, to be a comfort to the child as soon as they had her in their custody, she hadn't hesitated in answering with a very loud, "Of course!"

And here they were now, Lyell's men in the parapets and guarding the front portal, and David inside, unaware things were going along as planned. Well, at least his nephew was famed for keeping his head clear in nasty situations.

"Nothing to do now but await Monsieur Youngblood's signal," Lyell said. "It should be a simple operation, really."

But Tobin believed his nephew. From what he had been hearing, nothing was simple when it had anything to do with Claude Mirreault. They walked forward and waited by the door.

⁓

The next five minutes were the most grueling of David's life. He tried to make chitchat, tried to act as normal as possible, tried to remember what the old David was like. He had even sipped on a glass of brandy to be convincing. Knowing Eve was coming, he went over to the curtain and flicked the left panel once, praying Lyell and his men were there now, watching for the signal. "Cold out tonight, Mirreault. I take it you'll have yourself a bed warmer!" he joked, the crude words now feeling foreign.

"Naturally!" Mirreault chuckled. "You know me when it comes to women. The only one who has ever escaped me is

Sylvie de Courcey! It amazes me that your affections for her have turned so sharply."

Youngblood turned back toward Mirreault. "It shouldn't be. You know the old expression about the fine line between love and hate."

"I've experienced it myself! Ahhh, here's Didier now."

Trying not to look too eager, David sauntered over and looked down into the swaddling blankets. Eve's little face peeped out, so unmistakably like her father's. She was struggling to sit upright and Didier, holding her as if she were a wooden board, was at a loss.

"Here," David said, trying to stifle the impatience in his voice. "She's not an infant anymore. Hold her like this." He scooped the babe up, then sat her upright, her bottom resting on his forearm. "See? She's more comfortable like this."

Mirreault laughed uproariously. "Now this is something I never thought I'd see!"

Even Didier's eyes twinkled.

"That," David said, his voice lowering, "is quite an accomplishment. Just a moment." He turned and walked through the doorway, down the corridor, and into the main hall. *Don't follow me yet*, he prayed, perspiration thick and shiny gathering on his brow, on his back. Quickly, he opened the front door and his knees buckled with relief. They were there. Miranda rushed forward and took the baby from David's arms.

A sob escaped her lips and Eve let out a wail.

Mirreault entered the hall. "What is this?"

"Get the child into the carriage," Tobin ordered Miranda, literally pushing her out the door.

Mirreault immediately pulled out a gun from his robe pocket. "Why does this not surprise me?"

Tobin stood next to his nephew, but remained silent.

"So, it's a family reunion, eh?" Mirreault laughed boldly. "Good heavens, Youngblood, I can see what you would look like had lady luck smiled upon you."

"It's over, Mirreault," David said. "We have the child back, and you will go to prison."

"How are you going to prove we had anything to do with it?" Mirreault sneered, but David could see the fear in his eyes.

"Lyell!" David called, and the Minister of Justice walked through the doorway.

"Give it up, *Monsieur* Mirreault." Lyell's voice was remarkably calm. "Your home is surrounded. And we have a room waiting for you at the Bastille."

Mirreault stood his ground. "I'll not go willingly," he declared.

"Come now, Claude," David mocked. "You know you can buy your way off eventually. Be a gentleman about it. Don't shoot your way out, buy your way out."

"What do you really know about being a gentleman?" Mirreault hissed, the man he was born to be assuming his rightful place once again. "What do you really know about any of this, *my lord*. Buy my way out indeed. You didn't really expect me to give up without a fight, did you?"

Lyell motioned his men to move forward. "Bind his hands," he ordered.

Mirreault looked around him. He was ringed by those he hated most, David knew, garrisoned by the hypocrites he believed all men to be who thought themselves good men. "Don't touch me, or I will shoot."

David laughed harshly. "Cornered at last, eh, Mirreault? How does it feel?"

Lyell was itching to move forward, his body literally bobbing back and forth. David shot him a quelling glance. "How does it feel?" he asked again. "How does it feel to be the one who is cornered?"

"You call this cornered?" Mirreault questioned loudly. "Lyell cornering me? Why, look at the man's suit! It's positively ridiculous. How could a man lacking any taste whatsoever ever corner a man like me? Didier! The book! Run!"

Didier emerged from the study at a full run, the brown book tucked tightly under his arm.

"Tobin! After that man!" David yelled. "Get that book!"

Tobin ran.

David turned back to Mirreault. "Take him, Lyell," he said. "He will not shoot." He stared at Mirreault with eyes that held no expectation. Had this man truly led him down the path to evil? Not really. David had traveled the road on his own.

Mirreault held the gun high. "I will shoot you!" he yelled, seeds of perspiration growing larger on his face.

"No, you won't." David said, and he walked forward, praying he was right, praying that the reason Mirreault had used men like himself, men like Didier, men like Yves, all of these years was because he had not the fortitude to do such deeds on his own.

His right foot stepped out. Then his left. His right hand reached forward.

He breathed in. Felt his scalp go hot.

Another step.

"I will shoot you!" Mirreault screamed again, his large eyes round.

"No." David reached for the gun.

"I will shoot you!" Mirreault yelled.

David felt his fingers curl around the cool barrel of the pistol. Mirreault's last chance had come. David felt his heart running at full speed, his own pulse hammering in his ears, shaking his body. It was a chance he was taking, but he wagered that Mirreault would have already shot if he had it in him to do so.

"I will shoot you!" Mirreault yelled, eyes burning.

The weight of the gun was transferred to David's hand.

Lyell's men stepped forward, grabbed his wrists.

They led him away, a coward finally revealed.

David ran after Didier. Tobin would need his help.

⌒

The darkness below stairs was thicker than an Irish stout. Tobin felt his way along the wall, listening for the footsteps of the man he was following. That Didier fellow.

How did I find myself in such a predicament?

Never mind. He was surely faster than the old criminal. A dim light bobbed up ahead. The man had a torch and Tobin breathed in relief. The darkness had oppressed him like a real weight. The small ray was of great comfort to him. He ran and prayed, ran and prayed.

Almost upon him now, Tobin realized. His heart was thudding madly, and he remembered how calm his life had once been, how music and art and beauty had bolstered his sense of worth, but had ill-prepared him for a moment like this. What was he going to do if the man turned on him? Tobin hadn't been in a fight since grammar school!

One thing he remembered, the best defensive strategy is to attack. And so that is what he did. Inhaling. Praying some more. Shaking his head at his own predicament, Tobin leapt through the air, tackling Didier. Into the wall they were hurled, but instead of being jammed together against hard, unmoving stone, the wall gave way, opening like a door, and Tobin fell to the floor.

Didier's torch rolled across the exposed room, shedding its meager light. And in that light money chests were balanced in tall stacks. Precious statues and artwork were lined up against the walls. It was a room Croesus himself would have envied. Didier was pinned beneath Tobin, and his eyes went round.

The ledger had been flung across the room with the force of the fall.

The small man tried to rise, and Tobin, not wanting to fight, let him.

Didier quickly went for the brown book, but Tobin was quicker. He grabbed the leather volume from off the floor, along with the torch. "Give it up, old man."

"No!" Didier cried, and in a move which startled Tobin utterly, he grabbed both the torch and the book, setting fire to one with the other. He skirted by Tobin and escaped silently down the hall. Halfway down, he dropped the flaming book, yelping in pain. Tobin followed him down the corridor, into a subterranean tunnel.

It was dark and dank, the air hardly breathable. Several minutes later he emerged into the winter night, and Didier was gone. Quickly he made his way back upstairs. All was quiet. David and Lyell talked in hushed voices near the front door. Miranda entered with the baby in her arms.

"Did you get the ledger?" David and Lyell asked.

Tobin shook his head. "Didier set it on fire. There was nothing I could do."

"Blast!" Youngblood exclaimed. "Everything was in there. Dates, people, amounts. You would have had no trouble finding witnesses to the heinousness of this man, Lyell. I'm sorry."

"Did Didier escape, then?" Lyell asked.

Tobin wiped the sweat from his face with a wrinkled handkerchief. "I'm afraid so. But I came upon something downstairs you will find most interesting." He jerked a thumb toward the staircase. "Shall we?"

"Of course," Lyell agreed. "What is it?"

"You won't believe your eyes."

~

The demise of Claude Mirreault wasn't accompanied by gunfire, shouts, or bloodshed. For such a dealer of violence, such a quiet, easy trap seemed unjust, or at the very least, unlikely. But maybe it was fitting, really. After all, Mirreault's plots were never complicated. They simply got the job done. Miranda watched as he was driven away, head bowed, saying nothing now.

"He'll get out of this," Youngblood said, shaking a weary head, curls smashed and wet. "Mark my words."

Lyell turned to Tobin. "So what do you have to show us?"

"I'll let you see for yourself," Tobin answered. "Follow me."

Miranda felt his arm go around her waist protectively as she carried the baby toward the steps. She held Eve tightly to her and slowly, painstakingly, descended the narrow spiral staircase. Both Youngblood and Lyell carried torches, following Tobin and Miranda.

Tobin stopped by an entryway and swept an arm toward the inside of the room. "Gentlemen?" he said, inviting them to enter.

"Good heavens!" Youngblood cried.

"*Juste Ciel!*" Lyell responded in kind.

Miranda stepped into the chamber, gasping at the sight of the riches. Without warning, tears began to fall, and Tobin, worried, put his hands on her shoulders. "What is it, my love? What is the matter?"

"He had all of this," she cried. "And he would have gladly destroyed my brother's life, Sylvie's, Eve's, yours, and mine, if necessary, to add to it. What could more wealth have possibly meant to him?"

David Youngblood, very pale, shook his head. "It made him the winner, Miranda."

"Against who?" Miranda asked.

"Only he could tell you," David said. "Now"—he turned his back on the vast treasure—"let us go."

Lyell hurried on ahead of them, officiously shouting for more men.

Miranda sagged against Tobin. "It's over. It's finally over."

"Lyell's men should have that pile of loot out of there in no time," Tobin said.

Youngblood laughed. "You know how it is with the government and money. Acquiring more of it is the only thing that makes them move faster than a snail's pace."

Still, Miranda felt a sense of sadness. True, Sylvie's daughter was now safe, her fortune would remain intact, and Claude Mirreault was on his way to the Bastille. But when she thought of all the havoc the man had wreaked in his lifetime . . .

Tobin jostled her a bit, trying to cheer her. "Come on, girl. It isn't every day you save the world from the grips of a madman!"

"Here, here!" Youngblood made a mock toast. "To the demise of madmen everywhere!"

Miranda looked across the treasure room at her friend, David Youngblood. She felt Eve's body, safe and warm, sleeping in her arms. And next to her was the man she loved more than she thought it was possible to love. In a strange way, Claude Mirreault was responsible for it all. A smile leapt to her lips, and she raised her own hand, pretending to hold a cup. "Here, here!" she cried.

The three of them brought their hands together in a crash, and then, fingers interlocking, they shook hands. Laughter erupted. This was truly cause for celebration!

"Blast it, but if we didn't do it!" David said.

"*You* did it," Tobin said graciously. "It took a lot of courage to put yourself in such a vulnerable position. From the time you left England you didn't know whether you were going to live or die."

"Well . . ." David smiled. "As Miranda always says, 'God is on the throne.'"

"And so he is," Miranda chimed, knowing a truer word was never spoken.

Didier watched as cart after cart, loaded with the money he had worked so hard for all of his life, rolled away from Mirreault's chateau. He beat his fists on his thighs, biting back the wails of anger that bubbled inside of him. May Hades receive them all!

Here now. Mirreault was gone. The Mirreault empire was stolen by the French government. And he, Didier, was left with nothing. A dried-up old criminal without a job to do.

What next?

The sun rose, and it wasn't the sun he had hoped would someday rise, the sun of a free man, a good man, a rich man. The gun called out to him, and he reached for it, fingers finding a home. A mind of its own, it had a mind of its own. A mind of its own.

The barrel found his mouth. A shot echoed into ears filled with blood and the sound of his own death.

CHAPTER ❖ THIRTY-THREE

A m I hearing you correctly?" Tobin blurted out in the middle of the crowded, dirty Paris railroad station three days later.

David Youngblood's announcement came as a shock to everyone. "Yes, you are, Tobin. I'm refusing the reinstatement of my inheritance. You may keep the title and all the aggravation that comes with it at least for a while."

Miranda looked quite pale. "But why?"

David shook his head wearily, and Tobin immediately understood. "It's time for me to leave, Miranda. To leave Britain, to begin a new life."

"Leave Britain?" Both Tobin and Miranda cried together.

"You can't be serious!" Tobin cried. "You're going to leave me with all . . . all of this?" He spread his arms wide.

Youngblood laughed. "I don't need any of it where I'm going!"

They returned his laughter. And then Tobin noticed Camille. She was so quiet and sad. And so beautiful. Doomed somehow.

David cleared his throat. "You must watch over Elspeth for me."

"Of course," Tobin replied. "But where are you going?"

Camille burst into tears, her hands covering her eyes. "Devil's Island! He's being sent to Devil's Island for five years!"

Tobin felt the blood leave his face. "Oh, David."

David held up a hand. "Justice will have her way, uncle. Always."

"But what shall we tell Elspeth?" Miranda asked, looking pale.

"The truth. But prepare her. I may not come home."

The truth of that statement sickened Tobin's heart. "You know we will take care of her."

"Good care." Miranda nodded.

David reached out, a strong finger tracing its way down Miranda's birthmark. "I've always known that, Miranda. As you will take good care of all the children soon coming to Grey-walls." Youngblood winked at them.

Tobin laughed. "Is it that obvious?"

"Perfectly," David said in his famous drawl, and hugged Miranda to him. "Welcome to the family. Although, I have to warn you, bearing the name Youngblood isn't always a good thing."

Miranda returned the hug, giving his shoulders a big squeeze. "You are a remarkable man, David Youngblood."

He shook his head. "No. I used to say, 'just lucky,' but now I know I am just blessed. See here"—he looked over his shoul-der—"the train is coming, and I will say good-bye."

Tobin pulled his nephew into a hard embrace. "I love you, David. You've become quite a man."

David returned the embrace. "By God's grace."

He turned to Miranda for one last hug.

"You are a good man," she breathed. "I'm proud to know you, David Youngblood. And you will come back to us. You will."

David looked down into her eyes. "As God wills, Lady Youngblood."

Miranda chuckled as the conductor called out for all to board.

"Now, then," Youngblood ordered them all for the last time, "go home. I will see you in five years."

Tobin watched as David put Camille's arm through his own, and turned in the steamy air of the train. *Surely there's a future for them*, he thought, and uttered a prayer that Camille would wait.

Miranda held Eve tightly as Tobin aided her onto the train. "Is it true," she said to him, once they were seated, "is it true that there will be new babies at Greywalls?"

Tobin smiled. "As far as I'm concerned, the sooner the better!"

"Would you truly forsake the beauty of the Elysian Fields for me?" she asked him when he pulled away. She settled the basket of lunch Camille had packed between his feet.

He sat up straight and took her hands. "The true question is, my love, would you forsake them for me?"

EPILOGUE

❖

Miranda Youngblood, Countess of Cannock, walked among the flower stalls in the piazza of Covent Garden.

Tobin handed her a lily. "I do believe the rose is vastly overrated. Look at this flower, clean lines, curves of such beauty and grace. Yet still, hardly worthy of your hand, my dear."

Miranda laughed. "Oh, Tobin. Of course it is worthy of my hand, more than worthy in fact, just downright lovely. Thank you." She leaned forward and kissed him. "You know"—she turned to him and laid a hand on his arm—"I know you find me beautiful, husband. You don't have to keep saying such things to make me believe it anymore."

"Ahh, but it is because I say such words, and mean every one of them, that you truly do believe it."

Miranda knew he was right. But sometimes, and she would never tell him this, it could be a bit embarrassing. Especially in public. For although her husband found her attractive, she realized the rest of the world did not. At times they would just gape open-mouthed at them when overhearing Tobin's loud protestations of love. A year after their wedding day, and he was even more declarative and open about his feelings than he had ever been.

It was a day to remember. The June air was calm and still cool, a fact for which Miranda, halfway through her first pregnancy, was thankful. The sun warmed their clothes. And tonight, their opera, *Fields of Gold*, would debut.

She looked ahead of her at the massive theatre, the third theatre, in fact, that stood on this spot. And it had been completed only two years previously. "I'm nervous. Are you?" she asked Tobin.

"Horribly!" he admitted, his warm smile still making her thrill.

"At least all of our friends will be there. It was good seeing John Clarkson again, wasn't it?"

"Yes. He's terribly hurt by the fact that he will not be able to debut this work as he has all my others, but I told him, 'John, your fingers may fashion the music of heaven, but your voice sounds as if it came from the pit!'"

Miranda laughed, remembering the music the organist had played for their wedding. Tobin had written every last note of it, and there hadn't been one person that day who had left feeling unhappy. That's what Tobin's music had begun doing since their return from France. It was music that uplifted the soul, encouraged men to greatness.

And now tonight, the opera would be placed before society, before critics, before anyone who bought a ticket. She felt sick to her stomach, remembering the dreams she had on occasion of being naked in the middle of the race track at Ascot, or walking through the market in Leeds wearing nary a stitch. "What if they hate it?" she asked.

"Don't you worry, dear. They'll be studying your libretto for years to come!"

"I hope so!" she said. "Still, I feel so exposed."

"If it gives you any comfort, so do I."

She could find solace in his words. Didn't they do everything together now?

"I'm terribly impressed with the soprano, Maria Rosetti." She recalled the petite woman who could sing more loudly than a small person ought.

Tobin agreed. "A lovely voice. And to think she's married to a duke!"

Miranda chuckled. "Well, it seems you're not the only man who has the good sense to marry a commoner!"

"At least I'm only a lowly earl. I've met her husband," Tobin said, his voice becoming serious. "Aaron Campbell is someone to look up to. He's made me rethink my decision to shun the House of Lords. There are a lot of wrongs that need righting these days, Mira."

They had been talking about this for months now. Should he forsake the quiet life of the country and come to London for the season each year? Tobin was loathe to do such, but Miranda found the idea exciting. "I think I agree with him," she said. "It would be a good thing."

They walked along further, stopping to peer in the vendor's booths, enjoying one another's company, as they always did.

"Are the costumes ready? The scenery?" she asked him for not the first time. Lady Daria Christopher, the self-proclaimed "designer of all things visual," had barged her way into the opera company and taken charge. The result would only have to be seen to be believed, they were sure. And yet, hadn't her outrageous outfits always been more suited for stage than everyday life?

"The Lord help the audience!" Miranda laughed.

"The Lord help us all!" agreed Tobin.

"Oh, he does," Miranda said as they entered the cool theater. "And he always will."

The darkness of the building dimmed their faces as they walked through the lobby. Inside, last-minute changes to the set were being made, hammers pounding nails, men shouting to one another. Tobin and Miranda sat at the back of the theatre and watched together, eyes shimmering in the gloom, fingers twined together.

<hr/>

A Pleasant Surprise

Having walked into Covent Garden with dread last evening, I nevertheless was intrigued with the idea of London's newest opera, *Fields of Gold*. That the musical score, written by Lord Tobin Youngblood, was lyrical and melodic, came as no surprise when one remembers his works performed regularly by John Clarkson at St. Martin's. However, the libretto, written by an unknown writer named Randy Wallace, was the surprise of the evening. This lovely story of the plain maiden Xena was played to perfection by Maria Rosetti of longtime Covent Garden fame. Xena's dearest love, a man of physical beauty named Alexander, is played by Gianni Gipelli. In this stirring opera, Alexander battles the gods for the sake of his wife. The libretto is a superb telling of love, beauty, and sacrifice. The sets and costumes lent the entire production an ethereal feel that aided the telling of the story. Hats off to all involved.

Jeremy Filburt-Downes,
The London Times, June 13, 1863

Introducing the
Shades of Eternity Series

❦

Indigo Waters: Book 1
Softcover 0-310-22368-7

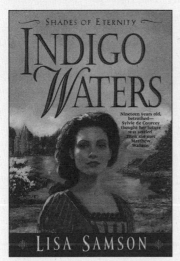

*S*he is heir to her father's wine fortune, amassed over a generation of
labor in the vineyards of Champagne,
France. But while the vast holdings of
the family estate belong to Sylvie de
Courcey, her future does not. Her
betrothal to the handsome Count Rene
de Boyce has been planned from childhood—an arrangement Sylvie knows
nothing of ... until her heart has been
given to another man.

Even as Sylvie struggles with a
wrenching choice between love and
loyalty, a deeper secret tightens its invis-
ible tendrils in a stranglehold on both
families. Rooted in the French underworld, its fruit quickly ripens into
murder and extortion.

As her world crashes to the ground around her, Sylvie discovers
faith, inner strength ... and shattering betrayal. One man alone stands
between her and the evil that closes in on every side: the man Sylvie
loves most, and cannot afford to love at all.

Set in France, England, and Scotland in the mid-1800s, *Indigo Waters*
weaves romance, suspense, unforgettable characters, and surprising
twists in a novel of unquenchable faith.

Indigo Waters is the first book in the Shades of Eternity series by
Lisa Samson. Filled with the splendor and romance of historical
Europe, these well-crafted novels trace one family's journey of faith in
the lives and loves of its members in the mid-nineteenth and early
twentieth centuries. ❦

Pick up your copy at your favorite Christian retailer.

We want to hear from you. Please send your comments about this book to us in care of the address below. Thank you.

ZondervanPublishingHouse
Grand Rapids, Michigan 49530
http://www.zondervan.com